MW01253058

Literary Lives

Founding Editor: **Richard Dutton**, Professor of English, Lancaster University

This series offers stimulating accounts of the literary careers of the most admired and influential English-language authors. Volumes follow the outline of the writers' working lives, not in the spirit of traditional biography, but aiming to trace the professional, publishing and social contexts which shaped their writing.

Published titles include:

Literary Lives
Series Standing Order ISBN 0-333-71486-5 hardcover
Series Standing Order ISBN 0-333-80334-5 paperback
(outside North America only)

You can receive future titles in this series as they are published by placing a standing order. Please contact your bookseller or, in case of difficulty, write to us at the address below with your name and address, the title of the series and one of the ISBNs quoted above.

Customer Services Department, Macmillan Distribution Ltd, Houndmills, Basingstoke, Hampshire RG21 6XS, England

Wilkie Collins

A Literary Life

Graham Law and Andrew Maunder

First published 2008 by
PALGRAVE MACMILLAN
Houndmills, Basingstoke, Hampshire RG21 6XS and
175 Fifth Avenue, New York, N.Y. 10010
Companies and representatives throughout the world

PALGRAVE MACMILLAN is the global academic imprint of the Palgrave Macmillan division of St. Martin's Press, LLC and of Palgrave Macmillan Ltd. Macmillan® is a registered trademark in the United States, United Kingdom and other countries. Palgrave is a registered trademark in the European Union and other countries.

ISBN-13: 978-1-403-94896-0   hardback
ISBN-10: 1-403-94896-8   hardback

This book is printed on paper suitable for recycling and made from fully managed and sustained forest sources. Logging, pulping and manufacturing processes are expected to conform to the environmental regulations of the country of origin.

A catalogue record for this book is available from the British Library.

Library of Congress Cataloging-in-Publication Data

Law, Graham.
    Wilkie Collins: a literary life/Graham Law and Andrew Maunder.
        p. cm. — (Literary lives)
    Includes bibliographical references and index.
    ISBN 1-403-94896-8 (alk. paper)
    1. Collins, Wilkie, 1824–1889. 2. Authors, English—19th century—Biography. I. Maunder, Andrew. II. Title.

    PR4496.L39 2008
    823'.8—dc22
    [B]   2008015890

10   9   8   7   6   5   4   3   2   1
17 16 15 14 13 12 11 10 09 08

Contents

Tables

Abbreviations

Novels

An	*Antonina* (1850; New York: Collier, 1900)
A	*Armadale* (1866); ed. Catherine Peters (Oxford: Oxford World's Classics, 1991)
B	*Basil* (1851); ed. Dorothy Goldman (Oxford: Oxford World's Classics, 1990)
BR	*The Black Robe* (1881; New York: Collier, 1900)
DS	*The Dead Secret* (1857); ed. Ira B. Nadel (Oxford: Oxford World's Classics, 1997)
EG	*The Evil Genius* (1886); ed. Graham Law (Peterborough, ON: Broadview Press, 1995)
FL	*The Fallen Leaves* (1879; Stroud: Alan Sutton, 1995)
HH	*The Haunted Hotel* (1879; New York: Collier, 1900)
HS	*Heart and Science* (1883); ed. Steve Farmer (Peterborough: ON: Broadview Press, 1996)
H&S	*Hide and Seek* (1854); ed. Catherine Peters (Oxford: Oxford World's Classics, 1993)
ISN	*I Say No* (1885; Stroud: Alan Sutton, 1995)
JD	*Jezebel's Daughter* (1880; New York: Collier, 1900)
LL	*The Law and the Lady* (1875); ed. Jenny Bourne Taylor (Oxford: Oxford World's Classics, 1992)
LC	*The Legacy of Cain* (1888; Stroud: Alan Sutton, 1993)
M&W	*Man and Wife* (1870); ed. Norman Page (Oxford: Oxford World's Classics, 1995)
M	*The Moonstone* (1868); ed. Steve Farmer (Peterborough, ON: Broadview Press, 1999)
NM	*The New Magdalen* (1873; London: Chatto & Windus, 1883)
NN	*No Name* (1862); ed. Virginia Blain (Oxford: Oxford World's Classics, 1989)
PMF	*Poor Miss Finch* (1872); ed. Catherine Peters (Oxford: Oxford World's Classics, 1995)
TD	*The Two Destinies* (1876; Stroud: Alan Sutton, 1995)
WW	*The Woman in White* (1860); ed. John Sutherland (Oxford: Oxford World's Classics, 1996)

Plays

B&W	Wilkie Collins and Charles Fechter, *Black and White: A Love Story in Three Acts* (London: Privately printed, 1869)
FD	Wilkie Collins and Charles Dickens, *The Frozen Deep* (1857); in Robert Brannan, *Under the Management of Mr Charles Dickens: His Production of "The Frozen Deep"* (Ithaca, NY: Cornell UP, 1966)
MG	*Miss Gwilt: A Drama in Five Acts, Altered from the Novel by Wilkie Collins* (London: Privately printed, 1875)
NMDS	*The New Magdalen: A Dramatic Story, in a Prologue and Three Acts* (London: Published by the author, 1873)
NT	*No Thoroughfare: A Drama in Five Acts* (London: Office of *All the Year Round*, 1868)
WWD	*The Woman in White: A Drama, in a Prologue and Four Acts* (London: Published by the author, 1871)

Secondary sources

AYR	*All the Year Round* (weekly, 1–20, June 1859–November 1868; 2nd series, 1–38, December 1868–December 1888)
B&C	William Baker and William M. Clarke, eds, *The Letters of Wilkie Collins* (2 vols; London: Macmillan, 1999)
B&G	William Baker and Andrew Gasson, eds, *Lives of Victorian Literary Figures V: Wilkie Collins* (London: Pickering & Chatto, 2007)
BGLL	William Baker, Andrew Gasson, Graham Law, and Paul Lewis, eds, *The Public Face of Wilkie Collins* (4 vols; London: Pickering & Chatto, 1999)
Clarke	William M. Clarke, *The Secret Life of Wilkie Collins* (London: Allison & Busby, 1988)
Davis	Nuel Pharr Davis, *The Life of Wilkie Collins* (Urbana, IL: University of Illinois Press, 1956)
Gasson	Andrew Gasson, *Wilkie Collins: An Illustrated Guide* (Oxford: Oxford University Press, 1998)
HW	*Household Words* (weekly, 1–19, March 1850–May 1859)
Page	Norman Page, ed., *Wilkie Collins: The Critical Heritage* (London: Routledge, 1974)
Peters	Catherine Peters, *The King of Inventors* (London: Secker & Warburg, 1991)

Pilgrim	Madeline House, Graham Storey et al., eds, *The Letters of Charles Dickens* (Pilgrim edition) (12 vols; Oxford: Clarendon Press, 1965–2002)
Robinson	Kenneth Robinson, *Wilkie Collins: A Biography* (London: Bodley Head, 1951)
Taylor	Jenny Bourne Taylor, ed., *The Cambridge Companion to Wilkie Collins* (Cambridge: Cambridge UP, 2006)
Thompson	Julian Thompson, ed., *Wilkie Collins: The Complete Shorter Fiction* (London: Robinson, 1995)
WCSJ	*Wilkie Collins Society Journal* (annual, 1–8, 1981–88; NS 1–10, 1998–2007)

Chronology of Collins's Life and Writings

	Summer	Exhibits 'The Smugglers Retreat' at Royal Academy
	Oct.	Visits France with Charles Ward
1850	26 Feb.	Charity performance of *A Court Duel!* at the Soho Theatre
	28 Feb.	*Antonina* from Bentley (first novel published)
	July–Aug.	Walking tour of Cornwall with Henry Brandling
	Aug.	Family moves to 17 Hanover Terrace, Regent's Park
1851	30 Jan.	*Rambles Beyond Railways* from Bentley
	Mar.	'The Twin Sisters' in *Bentley's Miscellany* (first contribution)
	12 Mar.	Meets Dickens for the first time at the house of John Forster
	16 May	Acts with Dickens in Bulwer Lytton's *Not So Bad as We Seem*
	27 Sept.	'A Plea for Sunday Reform' in the *Leader* (first contribution)
	21 Nov.	Called to the Bar
	23 Dec.	Christmas book *Mr Wray's Cash-Box*, from Bentley
1852	24 Apr.	'A Terribly Strange Bed' in *HW* (first contribution)
	Aug.	'Nine O'Clock' in *Bentley's Miscellany* (last contribution)
	Sept.	Stays with Dickens in Dover
	16 Nov.	*Basil* from Bentley
1853	May–June	Under the doctor, confined to Hanover Terrace
	July–Sept.	Stays with Dickens in Boulogne
	Oct.–Dec.	Tours Switzerland and Italy with Dickens and Augustus Egg
1854	6 June	*Hide and Seek* from Bentley
	July–Sept.	Stays with Dickens in Boulogne
	Dec.	'A Stolen Letter' in *The Seven Poor Travellers*, Christmas Number of *HW*
1855	11–21 Feb.	Illness during trip to Paris with Dickens
	16 June	*The Lighthouse* performed at Tavistock House
	July–Sept.	Stays with Dickens at Folkestone
	Sept.	Sails with Pigott to the Scilly Isles

	22 Dec.	'The Cruise of the Tomtit' in *HW* (first non-fiction contribution)
1856	Feb.	*After Dark* from Smith, Elder (first collection of stories)
	Feb.–Apr.	Visits Paris with Dickens
	Apr.	Takes lodgings at 22 Howland Street, off Tottenham Court Road
	June–July	Sails along the South Coast and to Cherbourg with Pigott
	June	Family moves to 2 Harley Place, Marylebone Road
	Aug.–Sept.	Visits Boulogne with Dickens
	Oct.	Joins permanent staff of *HW*
	Nov.	'Uncle George; or, The Family Secret' in the *National Magazine*
1857	3 Jan.	*The Dead Secret* begins in *HW* (first serial novel)
	6 Jan.	*The Frozen Deep* performed at Tavistock House
	24 Jan.	*The Dead Secret* begins in *Harper's Weekly* (first authorized American serialization)
	June	*The Dead Secret* from Bradbury & Evans
	21 Aug.	*The Frozen Deep* performed in Manchester
	7 Sept.	Leaves with Dickens for walking tour in Cumberland
	3–31 Oct.	'The Lazy Tour of Two Idle Apprentices' (with Dickens) in *HW*
	Dec.	*The Perils of Certain English Prisoners* (with Dickens), Christmas Number of *HW*
1858		*Le Secret* from Hachette (first French translation, of *The Dead Secret*, by E.-D. Forgues)
	Apr.	'Who is the Thief?' ('The Biter Bit') in *The Atlantic Monthly*
	June	Sailing trip to Wales
	July–Aug.	First visit to Broadstairs, Kent
	Sept.	Resigns from the Garrick Club in support of Edmund Yates
	11 Oct.	*The Red Vial* opens at the Olympic
1859	Jan.	By now living with Caroline Graves, at 124, Albany Street, Regent's Park
	Apr.	Moves to 2a New Cavendish Street, with Caroline

	30 Apr.	'Sure to be Healthy, Wealthy and Wise' in *AYR* (first contribution)
	Aug.–Sept.	Stays at Church Hill Cottage, Broadstairs
	1–14 Oct.	*The Queen of Hearts* from Hurst & Blackett
	26 Nov.	*The Woman in White* begins in *AYR* and *Harper's Weekly*
	13 Dec.	'The Ghost in the Cupboard Room' in *The Haunted House*, Christmas Number of *AYR*
1860	17 July	Charles Collins marries Kate Dickens
	15–16 Aug.	*The Woman in White* from Sampson Low and Harper & Brothers
	Sept.	Sailing trip from Newport, Wales
	3 Nov.	Unauthorized *The Woman in White* opens at the Surrey Theatre
1861		Harriet Collins now living permanently out of London
	Jan.	Leases copyrights to Sampson Low
	Apr.	Single-volume edition of *The Woman in White* from Sampson Low
1862	Jan.	Resigns from *AYR* staff
	15 Mar.	*No Name* begins in *AYR* and *Harper's Weekly*
	Aug.	Visits Whitby with Caroline Graves
	July–Oct.	Rents the Fort House, Broadstairs
	31 Dec.	*No Name* from Sampson Low
1863	Jan.	Severe attack of gout in both feet
	Apr.–June	Visits Aix-la-Chapelle and Wildbad for the waters
	Aug.–Sept.	Visits Isle of Man with Caroline and Carrie
	Oct.	Visits Italy for four months with Caroline and Carrie
	?Nov.	*My Miscellanies* from Sampson Low
1864	Apr.	Begins writing *Armadale*
	Aug.	Visits Great Yarmouth; meets Martha Rudd (?)
	Nov.	*Armadale* begins in the *Cornhill*
	Dec.	Moves to 9 Melcombe Place, Dorset Square; *Armadale* begins in *Harper's Monthly*
1865		Smith, Elder acquire WC's copyrights from Sampson Low
	27 Feb.	Visits Paris for a week
	10 Mar.	Resigns again from the Garrick Club over blackballing of W.H. Wills

1866	12 Apr.	Finally finishes writing *Armadale*
	Apr.	Visits Paris with Frederick Lehmann
	May–June	*Armadale* from Smith, Elder
	Oct.–Dec.	Visits Italy with Edward Pigott
	27 Oct.	*The Frozen Deep* opens at the Olympic
1867	Feb.	Visits Paris to work with Régnier on dramatic version of *Armadale*
	Sept.	Moves to 90 Gloucester Place, Portman Square
	Sept.–Oct.	Stays with Dickens at Gad's Hill
	9 Nov.	Sees Dickens off to America from Liverpool
	Dec.	*No Thoroughfare* (with Dickens), Christmas Number of *AYR*
	26 Dec.	*No Thoroughfare* opens at the Adelphi
1868		Martha Rudd now installed at 33 Bolsover Street (as Mrs Dawson)
	4 Jan.	*The Moonstone* begins in *AYR* and *Harper's Weekly*
	22 Feb.	Taken ill with gout in Gloucester Place
	19 Mar.	Death of Harriet Collins
	July	*The Moonstone* from Tinsley
	Aug.–Sept.	Visits Switzerland with Frederick Lehmann
	29 Oct.	Witnesses marriage of Caroline Graves and Joseph Clow
1869	29 Mar.	*Black and White* opens at the Adelphi
	4 July	First child, Marian Dawson, born
	20 Nov.	*Man and Wife* begins in *Cassell's Magazine*
	Nov.	Dispute with Belinfante Brothers in Holland
1870	12 Feb.	'A National Wrong' (with James Payn) in *Chambers's Journal*
	9 June	Death of Dickens
	27 June	*Man and Wife* from F.S. Ellis
	13 Sept.	*Man and Wife* staged by Augustin Daly in New York
1871	?Apr.	Caroline Graves returns to Gloucester Place
	14 May	Second daughter, Harriet Dawson, born
	2 Sept.	*Poor Miss Finch* begins in *Cassell's Magazine*
	9 Oct.	*The Woman in White* opens at the Olympic
	25 Dec.	*Miss or Mrs?* in the *Graphic* Christmas Number
1872	26 Jan.	*Poor Miss Finch* from Bentley
	Sept.–Oct.	Stays at Nelson Crescent, Ramsgate (for the first time?)

	Oct.	*The New Magdalen* begins in *Temple Bar* and *Harper's Weekly*
1873	Jan.	*Miss or Mrs? and Other Stories in Outline* from Bentley
	22 Feb.	*Man and Wife* opens at the Prince of Wales's
	9 Apr.	Charles Collins dies
	17 May	*The New Magdalen* from Bentley
	July	Visits Boulogne and Paris
	13 Sept.	Sails from Liverpool for reading tour of North America
	25 Sept.	Arrives in New York
	17 Oct.	Stays with Charles Fechter in Philadelphia
	22 Oct.	Breakfast banquet at Union Club, New York, given by William Seaver
	10 Nov.	Attends opening of *The New Magdalen* at the Broadway Theatre, New York
1874	7 Mar.	Leaves Boston on the *Parthia*
	18 Mar.	Arrives at Liverpool
	?Apr.	Moves Martha Rudd to Taunton Place
	Aug.	*The Frozen Deep* begins in *Temple Bar*
	26 Sept.	*The Law and the Lady* begins in the *Graphic*
	2 Nov.	*The Frozen Deep and Other Stories* from Bentley
	19 Nov.	Leases copyrights to Chatto & Windus, now his main British publishers
	25 Dec.	Son, William Charles Collins Dawson, born
1875	Feb.	*The Law and the Lady* from Chatto & Windus
	Oct.–Nov.	Travels to Brussels and Antwerp
	25 Dec.	*The Two Destinies* begins in *Harper's Bazar*
1876	Jan.	*The Two Destinies* begins in *Temple Bar*
	15 Apr.	*Miss Gwilt* opens at the Globe
	Aug.	*The Two Destinies* from Chatto & Windus
	Oct.	Visits Paris, with Caroline and Carrie (?)
	23 Dec.	'The Captain's Last Love' in the New York *Spirit of the Times* (first of 12 Christmas stories)
1877	2 July	'Mr Percy and the Prophet' in *AYR*
	29 Aug.	*The Dead Secret* opens at the Lyceum Theatre
	17 Sept.	*The Moonstone* opens at the Olympic Theatre
	Sept.–Dec.	Travels to Brussels, the Tyrol, and northern Italy
	Dec.	*My Lady's Money* in the *Illustrated London News* Christmas Number

1878	12 Mar.	Marriage of Carrie Graves and Harry Bartley
	June	*The Haunted Hotel* begins in *Belgravia*
	Nov.	*The Haunted Hotel* from Chatto & Windus
1879	1 Jan.	*The Fallen Leaves* begins in the *World*
	7 Apr.	*A Rogue's Life* from Bentley
	July	*The Fallen Leaves* from Chatto & Windus
	13 Sept.	*Jezebel's Daughter* begins newspaper syndication (Tillotson)
1880	Mar.	*Jezebel's Daughter* from Chatto & Windus
	June	'Considerations on the Copyright Question' in *International Review*
	2 Oct.	*The Black Robe* begins newspaper syndication (Leader)
1881	Apr.	*The Black Robe* from Chatto & Windus
	5 Dec.	Approaches A. P. Watt, who becomes his literary agent
1882	22 Mar.	Makes his final will
	22 July	*Heart and Science* begins newspaper syndication (A.P. Watt)
	Aug.	*Heart and Science* begins in *Belgravia*
1883	16 Apr.	*Heart and Science* from Chatto & Windus
	9 June	*Rank and Riches* opens at the Adelphi Theatre
	22 Dec.	*I Say No* begins newspaper syndication (A.P. Watt); also in *Harper's Weekly*
1884	Jan.	*I Say No* begins in *London Society*
	11 Apr.	Charles Reade dies
	Oct.	*I Say No* from Chatto & Windus
1885	June	Begins writing to Nannie Wynne
	11 Dec.	*The Evil Genius* begins newspaper syndication (Tillotson)
1886	19 Aug.	*Victims of Circumstances* begins in *Youth's Companion*
	Sept.	*The Evil Genius* from Chatto & Windus
	15 Nov.	*The Guilty River* as Arrowsmith's Christmas Annual and in Harper's Handy Series
1887	May	*Little Novels* from Chatto & Windus
	24 Dec.	'The First Officer's Confession' in *Spirit of the Times* (last contribution)
1888	17 Feb.	*The Legacy of Cain* begins newspaper syndication (Tillotson)

	23 Mar.	Moves from Gloucester Place to 82 Wimpole Street
	Nov.	*The Legacy of Cain* from Chatto & Windus
1889	19 Jan.	Shaken up in a traffic accident
	30 June	Suffers a stroke
	6 July	*Blind Love* begins in the *Illustrated London News* and other papers
	23 Sept.	Dies at Wimpole Street
	27 Sept.	Funeral at Kensal Green
1890	Jan.	*Blind Love* from Chatto & Windus
	Aug.	*The Lazy Tour of Two Idle Apprentices* from Chapman & Hall

1
Collins's Education and Reading

On 21 March 1862, approaching forty years of age and at the peak of his popularity, William Wilkie Collins sketched out his career to assist Baron Alfred-Auguste Ernouf, a French scholar about to write a critical review for a series on contemporary English novelists.[1] This 'little autobiography' included the following narrative of the author's youth:

> I was born in London, in the year 1824. I am the eldest son of the late William Collins, Member of the English Royal Academy of Arts, and famous as a painter of English life and English scenery. My godfather, after whom I was named, was Sir David Wilkie, the illustrious Scottish Painter. My mother is still alive.
>
> I was educated at a private school. At the age of thirteen, I went with my father and mother to reside for two years in Italy – where I learnt more which has been of use to me, among the pictures, the scenery, and the people, than I ever learnt at school. After my return to England, my father proposed sending me to the University of Oxford, with a view to my entering the Church. But I had no vocation for that way of life, and I preferred trying mercantile pursuits. I had already begun to write in secret, and mercantile pursuits lost all attraction for me. My father – uniformly kind and considerate to his children – tried making me a Barrister next. I went through the customary forms (with little or no serious study), and was 'called to the Bar' at Lincoln's Inn. But I have never practised my profession.
>
> An author I was to be, and an author I became in the year 1848.
>
> (B&C I, 205–8)

Contemporary sources both public and private confirm that, as far as the facts are concerned, this represents a more or less reliable account of the education of the author.[2]

After being taught at home by his mother, who had worked as a governess before her marriage, for around a year and a half from the age of eleven, Willie (as he was known until his father's death) was a day boy at Reverend James Gall's Maida Hill Academy, a preparatory school just off Edgeware Road. Later he was a boarder for two years or so at the establishment of another clergyman, Henry Cole, in Highbury Place, where his studies centred on the Classics, leaving as soon as he was seventeen. The period in between was spent travelling on the Continent *en famille*, the principal purpose being for William Collins to study at first hand the art of the Italian Renaissance. In addition to the slow journeys out through France, and back via Austria, Germany, and the Netherlands, the need to inspect the galleries, sketch the scenery, and avoid the cholera kept the Collins family on the move through much of their time in Italy itself. Only when they remained in one place for more than a few weeks (notably at Nice, in Rome, and near Naples) could a visiting tutor be recruited to teach the teenage Willie, who thus spent a good deal of his time accompanying his father or roaming alone; his mother had to give much of her attention to his nervous little brother Charley, who was still only ten when the family returned to London in 1838. Indeed, even before the Italian expedition, the Collins family had done a good deal of moving about. Partly in search of picturesque surroundings, but without leaving northwest London, they changed house six times before Willie reached the age of majority. Moreover, William Collins's most characteristic style of painting, the landscape with figures, often took him away from home, either to the estates of landed patrons or to scenic spots on the coast and in the country. On the latter occasions, he sometimes took his family with him: there was a long summer spent at Boulogne in 1829 when Charley was still a toddler, and a four-month tour of Wales in 1834 just before Willie was sent to school. Altogether then, in his youth the author received a broad and liberal education, but relatively little in the way of formal schooling.

Immediately on leaving school, Willie began to work at the office of a tea merchant in the Strand. The proprietor was Edmund Antrobus, an acquaintance of his father who later commissioned the painter to produce a group portrait of his three children. Though there is no independent confirmation that William Collins seriously considered a university and ecclesiastical career for his son at this point, later letters reveal him consulting friends in high places about the possibility of a government position, and discussing his son's future with the President of Corpus Christi College, Oxford. Judging from the quantity of uncommercial writing done at his office desk and the length of time he spent away from it, Willie must have been an unpaid apprentice supported by his father rather than a salaried employee. During the five years with Antrobus & Co., the author produced both his first signed publications: a comic fantasy in Douglas Jerrold's *Illuminated Magazine*; and his first novel, *Ioláni*, an exotic tale set in the South Pacific, which was rejected by a number of houses and remained unpublished during his life. Over the same period, Willie took at least three vacations lasting over a month: once accompanying his father on a sketching expedition to the north of Scotland, and twice back to Paris, at first with a family friend and then alone. There were to be similar lengthy continental expeditions after Collins quit the tea merchant's and entered Lincoln's Inn in May 1846, plus a lengthy walking tour of Cornwall. Since the bar examination was introduced only in 1852 and remained optional until twenty years later, all that was formally necessary for Collins to qualify as a barrister was to 'keep terms', that is, to eat the requisite number of dinners in hall over a period of years, and to pay all outstanding fees. The author was thus called to the bar in November 1851, though there is little evidence of him attending moots and lectures, or otherwise preparing to practise in law. In the meantime, though, he had already established himself as a professional author by issuing three remunerative works of varied character. These included his first published novel, *Antonina* (1850), and *Rambles beyond Railways* (1852), an illustrated travelogue based on the Cornish holiday. First of all, though, came *Memoirs of the Life of William Collins, Esq., R.A.*, the pious critical biography appearing less than two years after his father's death in early 1847, which clearly carried a symbolic value in the son's emergence as an author.

In addition to the slight disparities from the available external evidence, the 'little autobiography' that Collins sent to Baron Ernouf reveals a number of internal tensions, most notably regarding the relationship to his father. It is significant that no reference is made to the young man's thoughts of taking up his father's profession, which only seem to have been abandoned around 1849, the only year that Wilkie Collins had a picture exhibited at the Royal Academy. And beneath the pride in the father's rank and fame as a painter, there are traces of resentment and rebellion at hindrances placed in the way of the son's becoming an author. Despite the attempt to tone down the criticism ('uniformly kind and considerate to his children'), the slippage from 'proposed sending me' to 'tried making me' serves to reinforce the sub-versive sense of having 'to write in secret'. Moreover, the ambiguous nature of the father clearly extends to those values with which he is associated: seriousness, respectability, and, above all, Englishness. The point is hammered home in the triple repetition of 'English' in the opening lines, none strictly necessary. Collins's mother (née Geddes) was of North British ancestry so that it is significant that the name that the author makes uniquely his own is that of his eccentric Scottish god-father. Though the church and the law which Collins refuses may not be explicitly identified as the national institutions that they are, it is clear that a formal English education is regarded as far inferior to that encountered in the school of life on the Continent. Later in the docu-ment, in the annotation to his completed works, Collins makes it clear to his Parisian correspondent that he would have experienced a much greater degree of artistic freedom if his career had been based in France itself. These symptomatic contradictions in the author's little story of his own upbringing are indeed repeated with variations throughout his life and his writings.

The private correspondence surviving from Collins's youth character-istically reveals him writing wittily to his mother, poking affectionate fun at those in authority over him, whether his school master, his employer, or (most commonly) his father. The butts are William Collins's Tory politics, evangelical earnestness, and careful submission to social convention – plus his preference for plain English joints and puddings over Continental sauces and confections – though the son's mockery tends to be mingled with admiration for his father's determi-nation as a painter, and concern at his increasingly poor health. These complexities are retained in later letters, where we find a curious com-bination of carefree bohemianism in the life and earnest professional-ism in the work. More specifically, the author disdains conventional Christian forms of worship, especially anything approaching the Puritanical and Jesuitical extremes, but resolutely refuses any commit-ment to atheism or secularism. He is often strident in his opposition to political corruption and support of social reform, but always shies away from the fervour of the revolutionary. Wilkie Collins admires strong women who privately challenge bourgeois social and sexual boundaries, but resists any movement to allow them full legal equality or access to the public sphere. (These tensions are refracted in 'Wilkie Collins on Trousers', an anthology of memorable remarks culled from his personal correspondence.) In his private life, he steadfastly refuses marriage within his own social class, but ends up in simultaneous marriage-like partner-ships with two vulnerable women from the lower classes. In his later decades, to give a cloak of respectability to his 'morganatic' relationships and illegitimate children, he ironically reassumes his father's name in the guise of the *paterfamilias*, William Dawson, Barrister-at-Law.

Wilkie Collins on Trousers

My dear Mama | I did not write until I had tasted the cake, as I thought you would like to know that it was most *delectably luscious*. The whole parcel arrived quite safe, and I am very much pleased with the trousers, I think they are the nicest pair I ever had.

To Harriet Collins, 12 October 1839, B&C I, 7–8

I find the [Belgian] people possessed of immense physical energies – little intelligence and enormous *seats* to their breeches – The posterior portion of our Ostend waiter's trousers would have clothed a whole family of destitutes in St. Giles's.

To Harriet Collins, 31 July 1846, B&C I, 36–7

Our old locality – the market place [in Boulogne] – had a whole regiment in it today with a real live *Vivandière* ... She had on a short glazed hat, stuck very much on one side – a tight blue jacket that fitted her without a wrinkle, an ample scarlet petticoat – ample as to breadth – that came to her knees – and scarlet trousers.

To Harriet Collins, 27 July 1854, B&C I, 122–3

I have seen ... a live *'Bard'* attached to this house [in Glamorganshire] – not a venerable man with a robe and white beard but a simple-looking middle-aged farmer, in corduroy trousers and a swallow tailed blue coat, who sat down at the word of command, and sang old Welsh songs, in a shrill falsetto voice, to the strangest plaintive wild savage tunes.

To Harriet Collins, 4 June 1858, BGLL I, 161–2

I ... bless my stars that I am in Rome, and not in London, where they won't let me into the Opera unless I spend a guinea and put on a pair of black trousers first.

To Harriet Collins, 8 January 1864, B&C I, 241–3

Mrs Payn, seeing her cloth ruined, kept her temper like an angel, and smiled upon me while rivulets of Champagne were flowing over *my* dress trousers and *her* Morocco leather chair. Excellent woman!

To Frederick Lehmann, 25 October 1869, B&C II, 326–7

Your letter is addressed to me as '*Madame* Wilkie Collins'. I avow it with sincere regret but the interests of truth are sacred. The trumpet of Fame, gentlemen, has played the wrong tune in your ears. I am not the charming person whom you suppose me to be. I wear trousers; I have a vote for parliament; I possess a beard; in two dreadful words, I am – a Man.

To Belinfante Brothers, 10 November 1869, B&C II, 328–30

I can sell any work of mine I like in which I have my own copyright to an American Manager – it is a plain question of buying and selling – and my song or my play is as much that managers sole property (by common law) when he has paid me for it, as if I had sold him a horse or a pair of trousers.

To William Tindell, 19 September 1871, BGLL II, 274–5

My fixed principles have always forbidden me to become a Freemason, on the grounds that I really could *not* consent to take down my trousers and sit on a red hot gridiron, while the Perpetual Grand Master harangued me, sitting himself on a cool bottom.

To E.A. Buck, 30 December 1884, B&C II, 476–7

The little 'Dickens' Memoir interested me, it is needless to say, before I opened the pages. Last night, I just looked at them – and arrived at the conclusion that 'Frank T. Marzials' does *not* wear trousers – but petticoats.

To A.P. Watt, 29 March 1887, BGLL IV, 238

* * * * *

Before turning to the way in which these complexities manifest themselves in the writer's cultural tastes, and especially in his habits of reading, it is perhaps helpful to introduce a comparative perspective. To what extent was Wilkie Collins's upbringing, and his reactions to it as manifested in his own life choices, unusual in the mid-Victorian literary world? This question is important because it seems to us that critics who wish to claim the author as a thoroughgoing radical, in the social and cultural spheres at least, have tended to exaggerate the atypicality of his situation. The simplest way to achieve this is to briefly compare his mode of education with the experience of a number of other British novelists seeking to reach a broad social audience around the middle of the nineteenth century. Given the gendered nature of institutions of education at that time, the scope must be limited mainly to male authors, though we have allowed a couple of exceptions as a form of control. Given the limited number of successful, popularizing authors born during the 1820s, we have extended the range to a dozen years either side of Collins's year of birth. The novelists included in the survey are thus: Charles Dickens, George Reynolds, Charles Reade, Ellen Wood, James Payn, and Mary Elizabeth Braddon.[3]

- **Charles Dickens (1812–70)**   As is well known, Collins's mentor, collaborator, and close friend experienced an extremely unsettled childhood as the second of six surviving children of a naval clerk whose precarious finances led to imprisonment for debt. After an imaginative basic education at local schools in Chatham, only a family legacy released the twelve-year-old Dickens from a period of menial employment. Though he was then allowed a second spell of schooling as a day boy at the brutal Wellington House Academy, he was forced to leave at the age of fifteen to serve as an articled clerk to a solicitor. From this he soon escaped to the world of journalism and popular literature, his early serial success with *Sketches by Boz* (1833–6) and *Pickwick Papers* (1836–7) permitting him to marry Catherine Hogarth in 1836. Despite rapidly producing a large family, and celebrating domestic felicity in his Christmas books and his family miscellany *Household Words*, Dickens's own marriage collapsed spectacularly in the late 1850s when he became infatuated with Ellen Ternan, a young actress, and sought a formal separation.

- **George Reynolds (1814–79)**   Though Collins does not refer to Reynolds by name in his published works or private papers, the article 'The Unknown Public' (*Household Words*, 1858) leaves little doubt that he was familiar with the work of the most widely read novelist of the mid-century. After making his name as a Dickens imitator with *Pickwick Abroad*, Reynolds's racy 'bloods' in penny weekly numbers or in the columns of the 'penny-fiction-journals' helped to create the first mass audience for fiction. The son of a knighted senior naval officer, following an education at Ashford Grammar School in Kent, Reynolds abandoned his training at the Royal Military Institute at Sandhurst and squandered his inheritance in failed publishing ventures in Paris, returning to London with republican ideals and an intimacy with French popular fiction. A passionate hatred of the landed aristocracy, which in 1848 placed him among the leaders of the 'physical-force' wing of the

Chartist movement, is a perennial element both of his novels and political journals. Yet his political commitment was viewed with deep suspicion by more moderate socialists, who regarded his novels as morally corrupting, while Karl Marx himself saw him as a clever speculator, exploiting popular sentiment for personal profit.

• **Charles Reade (1814–84)**   Collins seems to have become friends with Reade at some point in the mid-1850s, and an intimate correspondence survives between the two over more than twenty years, with their shared passion for the drama and hatred of literary piracy being a common bond. Reade was born into an eccentric landed Oxfordshire family and educated at private boarding schools run by clergymen, before earning a scholarship to study 'Greats' (i.e. Classical literature) at Magdalen College, Oxford, from 1831. After graduating he enrolled at Lincoln's Inn. Although he duly became both a lifelong fellow of Magdalen and a Barrister-at-Law, he was to make his name not as a scholar, a clergyman, or a lawyer, but as a controversial novelist and playwright, regularly tilting against social abuses in his fiction and literary injustices through litigation. Though formal college rules enforced celibacy, for over twenty years Reade had a relationship with the actress Laura Seymour, living together with her in Knightsbridge, where Collins was a frequent visitor with his own mistress.

• **Ellen Wood (1814–87)**   Collins seems never to have come into social contact with Mrs Henry Wood, to use the married name under which her many novels were issued. However, he shared a publisher with her in the early 1870s, when he was amazed to learn from George Bentley that her books were making rather more money than his own. Ellen Price, as she was born, was the daughter of a Worcester glove manufacturer. Spinal problems in youth left her a semi-invalid so that her education took place entirely within a family that was strongly musical and devoutly Anglican. She married a wealthy banker and lived in France until around the age of forty, when her husband's financial failure forced her to pay for her own children's schooling by writing for money, most of her initial stories being accepted by Harrison Ainsworth for *Bentley's Miscellany*, and later for the *New Monthly Magazine*. Though her early sensational hits such as *East Lynne* (1861) focused on dark family secrets and adulterous liaisons, *Argosy*, the magazine she edited for nearly twenty years from 1867, and most of the fiction Wood published there and elsewhere, overtly espoused bourgeois domestic values and Conservative political ideals. Nevertheless, her own career seems to tell a rather different story about the value of a woman's initiative, enterprise, and sheer hard work.

- **James Payn (1830–98)**   Wilkie Collins first met Payn in the Dickens circle in the late 1850s, and remained on friendly terms with him for the rest of his life; in the late 1860s they were to collaborate on 'A National Wrong', an article calling for greater copyright protection for British authors in both Europe and North America. Payn became a man of considerable literary property, regularly earning more, around £3000 per annum, from his literary labours as novelist and journalist, and coming to wield considerable influence in literary London. Following the popular success of *Lost Sir Massingberd* (1864), his many works of fiction tend to rely on an entertaining mix of sensationalism and social comedy. Born in rural Berkshire, Payn seems to have disliked the country pursuits favoured by his father, a local Justice of the Peace. He was sent to preparatory school and Eton College, though he seems to have found formal education in the Classics especially distasteful. He also failed to fulfil family expectations that he would enter the army or the church. At Trinity College, Cambridge, he was a popular raconteur and became President of the Union, and at the same time got his first article accepted by Dickens for *Household Words*. Payn married happily in 1856 and had a large family, although he was also very fond of his club, the Reform, where he regularly played whist in the afternoons until incapacitated by rheumatic gout, a condition which he shared with Wilkie Collins.

- **Mary Elizabeth Braddon (1835–1915)**   Though there are no surviving letters from Collins to Braddon, the two were on visiting terms and she called to ask after him when he suffered a major stroke in the summer of 1889. Around the same time, she acknowledged Collins as the 'literary father' of her long series of popular sensation novels, beginning with *Lady Audley's Secret* (1862) which followed closely on *The Woman in White*. The daughter of a Cornish solicitor, Braddon was born in Soho and educated at a private girls' school in Kensington. In between, her father deserted the family and from the age of seventeen she took up a career as an actress to support her aging mother.[4] Finding that writing offered a more secure and remunerative career, she began to produce melodramatic tales for the penny fiction market. This brought her into contact with the Irish publisher John Maxwell. Though he was a married man with five children, she soon became his partner and bore him five children of her own. Braddon suffered a nervous breakdown following the death of her mother, and there was a major public scandal when Maxwell's wife died, but in 1874 the couple were married and continued living in an eminently respectable household in Richmond, Surrey. Thereafter, her fiction tended to balance juicy melodrama with drier social irony, so that she retained her immense popularity into the twentieth century.

Clearly there is a good deal of variation in these six little biographies of popular Victorian authors, whether in terms of social class of origin, manner and level of formal education, and choice of lifestyle in adulthood. Nevertheless it is generally clear that the conventional bourgeois model of public school followed by Oxbridge, which does seem crucial in the development of many critics, whether Matthew Arnold, Leslie Stephen, or William Morris, is far from a prerequisite for the popular novelist. On the other hand, though a degree of distance from bourgeois ideals seems a distinct plus to those seeking a mass audience, this rarely equates to a thoroughgoing commitment to social and political revolution. In each case it is the nature of the tensions, and the ways that they are resolved, that stand out and that thus require careful analysis. In this sense Collins's situation is perhaps not so unusual.

* * * * *

To trace Collins's reading preferences as they evolve over the course of his life, we need to refer to records of the library he accumulated,[5] as well as to comments scattered among published work or private papers. Still among the books he possessed when he died were copies signed in childhood of *Robin Hood*, the *Arabian Nights' Entertainments*, and Oliver Goldsmith's *Vicar of Wakefield* (1766), plus gothic romances by Anne Radcliffe inherited from his mother. There is also a school prize at the age of eleven from the Maida Hill Academy (Robert Southey's *Essays, Moral and Political* (1832)) and a birthday present at sixteen (*The Poems of Thomas Gray*). While we cannot be certain whether these latter were read with enthusiasm, there is plenty of evidence of the young author's passion for strong romantic narrative. Writing from school in Italian, Wilkie claimed that he would be inconsolable if his mother could not find his copy of *Tales for an Idler*, the first book mentioned in his surviving letters apart from the Virgil and Homer which he was forced to construe by the Rev. Cole (B&C I, 8–9). This was a miscellaneous collection of twenty tales by the 'Leading Authors of the Day', most gothic and exotic but with a handful of domestic stories by the likes of Caroline Norton, published in 1836 by Galignani, the Parisian house specializing in works in English. We must assume that it had been purchased in the French capital in its year of publication on the journey out to Italy, and had travelled around Europe with the Collins family.[6]

From his desk in the Strand, Collins wrote irreverently to his father of how he had entertained relatives at tea: 'I sat with my back to the window, and my hand in my pocket, freezing my horrified auditors by a varied recital of the most terrible portions of the Monk and Frankenstein. ... None of our country relations I am sure ever encountered in their whole lives before such a hash of diablerie, demonology, & massacre with their Souchong and bread and butter. I intend to give them another course, emphasizing, the Ancient Mariner, Jack the Giant Killer, The Mysteries of Udolpho and an enquiry into the life and actions (when they were little girls) of the witches in Macbeth' (B&C I, 13–14). Indeed, William Collins seems frequently to have expressed concern at his son's low reading and high living. In a postscript to his mother from Paris in 1845, again Wilkie responded cheekily to a message from his father: 'Give my love to the Governor and tell him that I will eat "plain food" (when I come back to England) and read Duncan's Logic and Butler's Analogy (when I have no chance of getting anything else to peruse)' (B&C I, 27–9). Although his library contained a number of devotional works signed by his mother, including a hymnbook and Jeremy Taylor's *Holy Living and Dying* (1651), these were clearly of sentimental value rather than for personal use. Though he had taken the latter with him, as promised, on his Continental tour with Dickens in 1853, he reported to his mother that 'my present course of life is not favourable to theological studies, and Jeremy is rather involved and hard to understand after a day's rolling over rough high roads in a travelling carriage' (B&C I, 98–101).

As he matured, Collins retained the taste for dramatic plots, but his interests focused increasingly on the liminal territory between romance and realism that indeed characterizes the sensation fiction in which he makes his name, where fearful and outlandish events take place in modern urban settings of the utmost respectability. The influence of the young Dickens, with his idiosyncratic mingling of the comic and the macabre, is obviously apparent in this shift. At the age of eighteen Wilkie was already familiar with *Pickwick*, and a first edition with the young man's signature remained in his library. Yet the novelist that Collins acknowledges as his master first and foremost is Sir Walter Scott, with his wildly romantic plots coupled with an antiquarian fascination with regional and historical detail. Wilkie Collins must already have been familiar with Scott's novels when he accompanied his father to Scotland in 1842, since the purpose was to prepare illustrations for a new edition of *The Pirate*; at his death his library contained nearly a hundred well-thumbed volumes by the writer, including the poetical works and miscellaneous prose, in addition to the Waverley Novels themselves. References to Scott's works are scattered throughout Collins's writings, though the praise is especially lavish in his last decade. In 1883, after his struggles to complete *Heart and Science*, he enjoyed the following rest cure: 'An armchair and a cigar – and a hundred and fiftieth reading of the glorious Walter Scott (King, Emperor, President, and God Almighty of novelists) – there is the regimen that is doing me good! All the other novel-writers I can read while I am at work myself. If I only look at the "Antiquary" or "Old Mortality", I am crushed by the sense of my own littleness, and there is no work possible for me on that day' (B&C II, 453–4). A few years later, he gave the following advice to an actor friend who wished to take up fiction: 'A last word of advice before I say good-bye. Study Walter Scott. He is beyond all comparison the greatest novelist that has ever written. Get, for instance, "The Antiquary", and read that masterpiece over and over and over again' (BGLL IV, 182–3).

Collins's passion for Scott is reflected already in the choice of subject of his first two novels, both historical romances which at the same time make a claim to documentary accuracy. Completed in January 1845 but only published in 1999, *Ioláni; or Tahíti as It Was* concerns, in the author's own words, 'savage life in Polynesia, before the discovery of the group of islands ... by civilized men'.[7] Though Collins might have also been familiar with contemporary literary treatments of his theme, notably Mary Russell Mitford's narrative poem *Christina, the Maid of the South Seas* (1811), and Byron's *The Island* (1823), his immediate sources were the narratives of travellers and missionaries. *Polynesian Researches* (3rd series, 9 vols, 1831) by William Ellis of the London Missionary Society and *Fragments of Voyages and Travel* (2nd edn, 4 vols, 1831) by the navy captain Basil Hall were both found in the author's library. Collins relies heavily on Ellis's account, but is torn between reinforcing his evangelical censure of Polynesian brutality and immorality, and relishing the escape his subject offers from the restrictions of bourgeois English mores. The most notable departure from his source is seen in the young author's treatment of gender: while Ellis describes barbarous customs such as infanticide as endemic in Polynesian culture, Collins refigures them as male oppression practised on and sometimes resisted by women.

Set in the fifth century, *Antonina; or the Fall of Rome* (1850) borrows its central theme of the cultural encounter between the extremes of Roman decadence and Gothic barbarity, as well as much of its historical detail, from Edward Gibbon's monumental *Decline and Fall of the Roman Empire* (1776–89). In literary form, though, *Antonina* is indebted to the apocalyptic imagery of Edward Bulwer Lytton's *Last Days of Pompeii* (1834) and *Old St Paul's* (1841) by Harrison Ainsworth, whose grim depiction of the 'Dance of Death' provides the model for Collins's grotesque 'Banquet of Famine' in Chapter 22. Gibbon, Lytton, and Ainsworth all indeed featured prominently in the author's library. With the novice Collins, though, the romantic treatment can be very heavy-handed. The plotting is cumbersome and thin, and frequent descriptive passages in laboriously Latinate prose are needed to stretch the narrative out to the length then required of a three-volume novel. The following evocation of the advancing army of Goths from the opening chapter is a typical example with its obsessive triadic structures:

> No brightness gleamed from their armour; no banners waved over their heads; no music sounded among their ranks. Backed by the dreary woods, which still disgorged unceasing additions to the war-like multitude already encamped; surrounded by the desolate crags which showed dim, wild, and majestic through the darkness of the mist; covered with the dusky clouds which hovered motionless over the barren mountain tops, and poured their stormy waters on the uncultivated plains – all that the appearance of the Goths had of solemnity in itself was in awful harmony with the cold and mournful aspect that the face of Nature had assumed. Silent – menacing – dark – the army looked the fit embodiment of its leader's tremendous purpose – the subjugation of Rome.
>
> *(An, 17)*

Indeed, we can only recognize hints of the preoccupations of the sensation novels that would later make the author's name when the young Collins expresses his distaste for religious fanaticism and intolerance, or lingers over moments of physical and psychological cruelty, notably the desire for vengeance of Goisvintha, the passionate sister of the Gothic chieftain, or the severity experienced by the passive Roman heroine Antonina at the hands of her puritanical father. It is significant that, just prior to publication, the author had wanted to change the title to 'The Mount of Gardens' (BGLL I, 36–7), the old Roman designation for the Pincian Hill, where the virginal Antonina is first revealed in Chapter 5, and which Wilkie and his brother had made their playground during the family's Italian adventure.

Yet the other masters that later Collins acknowledges by joining their names regularly with that of Scott are not Lytton and Ainsworth, or even his mentor Dickens. Rather they are two overseas authors known also for their coupling of realism and romance, whose complete works were also found in Collins's library. Late in his life, Collins wrote in reply to a query from an autograph hunter: 'It is not easy to tell you which is my "favourite work". I must own that I have three favourites. They are written by the three Kings of Fiction: Walter Scott. Fenimore Cooper. Balzac. And they are called: *The Antiquary. The Deerslayer. Le Pere Goriot*' (BGLL III, 420–1). Surprisingly, given that the novels were widely available in Britain from the 1830s in Bentley's series of 'Standard Novels', there are no early references in Collins's writings to the American James Fenimore Cooper, most famous for his frontier tales with the hero 'Leather-stocking'. The first mention indeed dates from an 1882 letter, though he does claim there to 'have just been reading "The Deerslayer" for the fifth time' (B&C II, 443–4). In contrast, Collins first paid tribute to the Frenchman Honoré de Balzac, author of the series 'la Comédie Humaine', as early as the 1850s. His principal comments are found in an article in *All the Year Round* where he proclaimed Balzac 'the deepest and truest observer of human nature whom France has produced since the time of Molière', lamenting that he remained almost unknown to the English.[8] Moreover, there Collins suggests (in necessarily coded language) that this ignorance may be due to the forthrightness with which Balzac deals with social, psychological, and sexual issues: 'Balzac lays himself open to grave objection (on the part of that unhappily large section of the English public which obstinately protests against the truth wherever the truth is painful) as a writer who sternly insists on presenting the dreary aspects of human life, literally, exactly, nakedly, as he finds them.' As we shall see, this was precisely the fault for which Collins himself was pilloried in reviews of his second novel, *Basil: A Story of Modern Life* (1854), which centres on a young man's rebellion against his unbending, aristocratic father, and where the influence of Balzac is most readily apparent.[9]

In the preface to that work, Collins declares his belief that 'the Novel and the Play are twin-sisters in the family of Fiction' and, in a later article in *Household Words*,[10] notes that, unlike in England, the masters of French fiction are also the masters of French drama, citing the names of

Victor Hugo, Alexandre Dumas, Frédéric Soulié, as well as Balzac. Both the plays and novels of all these writers are indeed found in Collins's library, which generally includes a fine range of works for the theatre, though it is noticeable that contemporary drama is represented rather more widely by French than English works. Later generations of French novelists are also represented in Collins's collection, though much more noticeably by writers of tales of adventure, mystery, and romance, such as Jules Verne, Émile Gaboriau, and Georges Ohnet, than by those exploring new forms of realism. *Madame Bovary* alone is there in the original French to represent Gustave Flaubert, though in an 1886 letter accepting a presentation copy from the American translator of *Salambô*, Collins strangely characterizes the author as a lesser disciple of Walter Scott. More importantly, Émile Zola and the rest of his naturalist school are noticeably absent. When asked by a friend in 1877 to recommend contemporary work, he responded: 'As to modern French novels in general, I read them by dozens on my travels – and my report of them all is briefly this: – Dull and Dirty. The "Nabob" by Daudet (of whom I once hoped better things) proved to be such realistic rubbish, that I rushed out ... to get something "to take the taste out of my mouth"' (B&C II, 409–10). The contrast with the earlier comments on Balzac is remarkable, and tells us a good deal about trends in the author's own later fiction. A similar tipping of the balance away from realism towards romance is also found in Collins's preferences in English and American fiction after the death of Dickens. Collins seems never to have read Meredith or Hardy or James, much less Moore or Gissing or Howells, instead preferring the works of a new generation of romancers such as H. Rider Haggard, R.L. Stevenson, or his young friend Hall Caine. Collins's by then rather reactionary views on realism, and its links to social reform, must be reflected in the judgement of a character in one of his late novels: 'A very remarkable work ... in the present state of light literature in England – a novel that actually tells a story. It's quite incredible, I know. Try the book. It has another extraordinary merit – it isn't written by a woman.' (*BR*, 328)

* * * * *

To conclude this survey of Collins's reading habits, it may be helpful again to introduce a comparative perspective. Here it is convenient to contrast the library accumulated over a lifetime by Wilkie Collins (together with his partner/housekeeper Caroline Graves, though her contribution to the collection seems to have been negligible) and that of G.H. Lewes and George Eliot (1819–80) (Mary Ann Evans). The comparison is possible because, though comprehensive information is undoubtedly lacking in each case, both have been reconstructed in a good deal of detail, and analysed according to common principles, by the bibliographer William Baker.[11] The comparison is significant because Lewes (1817–78) and Collins have a number of things in common apart from the generation to which they belonged and their unconventional sexual partnerships. Like Collins, Lewes compensated for a lack of formal schooling through experience on the Continent; they thus shared from youth a passion for French culture generally, and its theatre in particular. In adulthood, their circles overlapped and the two occasionally met and corresponded. In the early 1850s, for example, they engaged in a public debate concerning paranormal phenomena in the columns of the *Leader*, a radical weekly review of which Lewes was a founding proprietor and editor, while Collins was a regular contributor. Collins presented private experiments in which he had personally participated as reliable evidence of the validity of clairvoyance, though Lewes, then a convinced positivist, remained entirely sceptical. Indeed, in most other respects also they were poles apart. Lewes seems to have been illegitimate, was abandoned by his father as an infant, and had to fend for himself from an early age. Though Lewes produced several works of fiction and drama as a young man – Collins owned a copy of his first novel, *Ranthorpe* (1847), and at the theatre in late 1851 enjoyed his *Game of Speculation*, an adaptation of a Balzac comedy – he made his name and his living as a scholarly journalist of considerable intellect with equal expertise in literature and science. Most importantly he chose as a life partner one of the most intellectually gifted women of the period, carefully fostering her career as a novelist and in the process enriching his own understanding of the complex relationship between mind and body. These contrasts are starkly reflected in the personal libraries of Lewes and Collins.

Though it is relevant that Lewes and Eliot probably possessed well over four times the six hundred or so titles recorded in Collins's collection, this is not merely a question of scale, since there are similar differences regarding period, language, subject, and genre. Lewes and Eliot owned many volumes of antiquarian interest, dating from as early as the first half of the sixteenth century, whereas the vast majority of Collins's books were published in the nineteenth century. Less than half of the Lewes–Eliot collection was in English, with significant holdings in Latin and Italian, and not far short of a quarter in both French and German; Lewes learned the latter with the assistance of George

Eliot and went on to become a distinguished student of Goethe. Only around one-fifth of Collins's collection was in languages other than English, almost all in French, with the remainder generally association copies or translations of his own work. As we have seen, while boarding at Highbury Place Collins wrote letters home in Italian (to keep in practice but perhaps also to avoid censorship by Henry Cole) and, approaching fifty, he suggested jokingly to Charles Reade that they 'correspond for the future in that language' (BGLL II, 287–8). In reality, as an adult he seems to have read little in Italian. Though Lewes and Eliot also had major collections of philosophy, theology, history, and literature, the majority of their volumes in fact concerned science, medicine, and allied areas. In contrast, considering Collins's fascination with exploring unusual psychological and physical states, it is surprising how few of his books concern the study of mind and body. The graphic arts are also rather under-represented, given his family background, and in fact the large majority of Collins's titles belong to the field of literature, the lion's share of fiction, but also including many theatrical works, with a relatively small collection of poetry, and little of that lyrical.[12] A large proportion of the remainder consists of works of history, biography, criminology, and travel. Most of Collins's books are narrative or dramatic in form, with a strong preponderance of contemporary popular works, while the Lewes–Eliot literary collection includes many volumes of critical and textual scholarship, both ancient and modern. While their letters are full of impassioned discussions of the seminal thinkers of the day (J.S. Mill or Thomas Carlyle, Charles Darwin or Herbert Spencer, Auguste Comte or Karl Marx, John Henry Newman or T.H. Huxley, Matthew Arnold or William Morris), we look in vain for similar themes in Collins's own correspondence.

The general purpose of this exercise is not to belittle Collins – the intellectual depth and range of Lewes and Eliot was in every way extraordinary – but rather to show clearly that his commitment to popular literature was impassioned and thoroughgoing, but that he had few pretensions to being a serious scholar. A similar lesson is learnt from the author's access to serial publications, which should not be forgotten in any survey of reading in the Victorian period. From Collins's collected correspondence, we gather that, though he is a *Times* subscriber, he also regularly takes the old weekly theatrical paper, the *Era,* and the new popular halfpenny evening *Echo.* He browses monthly literary magazines such as *Bentley's Miscellany,* the *Cornhill,* and *Temple Bar,* where his own work appears, and glances at weekly literary papers such as the *Athenaeum* and *Saturday Review*, where his own work is likely to be noticed. But he consistently avoids the heavy quarterly reviews, whether the Whig *Edinburgh*, the Tory *Quarterly*, or the Radical *Westminster*, as well as more modern formats such as the secular *Fortnightly* or the religious *Contemporary*. He thus advises his mother in 1863: 'Whatever the critics may say, readers are certainly grateful for a story that interests them. So don't mind what the Quarterly Review, or any Review says. Or rather, do as I do – don't waste your time in reading them' (B&C I, 226–7). There is thus little reason to believe that the author was being self-deprecatory when, recalling his literary tastes as a boy in an after-dinner speech on his arrival in New York, he confessed: 'At that time of my life, as at this time of my life, I was an insatiable reader of that order of books for which heavy people have invented the name of "light literature".'

2
Collins's Circles

After Dickens, whose need for boisterous company after literary labour could border on the manic, Wilkie Collins was by nature one of the most convivial of Victorian novelists. With the resounding success of *A Woman in White* in 1860, his flamboyant presence was much in demand at social gatherings. Following a bout of illness in the mid-1860s, he replied to a renewed dinner invitation from Lady Goldsmid: 'If I am alive, it is needless to say how gladly I shall take my place at your table. If I am *not* alive, be so good as to look towards the conservatory, when the butler comes round for the first time with the Champagne. You will perceive a Luminous Appearance – with an empty glass in one hand ...' (B&C I, 247). On his death, William Holman Hunt, one of his oldest surviving friends, still remembered him thus: 'No one could be more jolly than he as the lord of the feast in his own house ... The talk became rollicking and the most sedate joined in the hilarity; laughter long and loud crossed from opposite ends of the room and all went home brimful of good stories.'[1]

The present chapter, however, is only incidentally concerned with charting Collins's career as a reveller, and rather aims to describe the main social sets in which the author mixed as a young man, suggesting the impact that they had on his development as a writer. This influence was by no means always a short-term one, and indeed many of the intimate friendships the author formed in youth lasted him into old age. Two groups are important here: the young figure painters knocking on the doors of the Royal Academy from the mid-1840s, and the young literary journalists gathering outside the office of *Household Words* from the early 1850s. Neither group was uniform or united in any simple sense. The artists included not only the leaders of the rebel Pre-Raphaelite Brotherhood, fellow students of Wilkie's brother, but also members of the slightly older and more subservient generation of practitioners met through the author's father. The writers Dickens gathered around him included both the most dedicated of professionals and the fastest of bohemians, with the opposites occasionally combined in the same figure. These configurations indeed seem to symbolize tensions in Wilkie Collins's own social and aesthetic commitments. Apart from the author's affiliation to both, there was also a degree of overlap and interchange between the two groups. The most characteristic artistic genres of the high Victorian period were dramatic in form, with figure painting in particular attracted to biblical, historical, and literary subjects. At the same time, the line between literature and the press was wafer thin, the journalist frequently also donning the hat of novelist, critic, or poet. The theatre was also an institution that combined visual spectacle, stirring narrative, and social conviviality, so it was perhaps inevitable that the two groups tended to come closest to combining in their passion for amateur theatricals.

* * * * *

'Although I do not follow my father's profession ... I live very much in the society of artists' (B&C I, 31), Wilkie Collins wrote at the age of twenty-five. This was in a letter concerning the recently published *Memoirs* of his father, to the New England novelist, R.H. Dana, who had supplied information about his own brother-in-law, the painter William Allston. Allston had been a close friend of William Collins, acting as godfather to his second son Charles Allston Collins (1828–73). In 1843, the year that Allston himself had died, the fifteen-year-old Charley had been accepted as a pupil at the Royal Academy schools, much to the delight of his father but perhaps also in part due to his influence. There Charley joined company with the prodigious John Everett Millais (1829–96), who had become the Royal Academy's youngest ever student in 1840 and had already won a medal for drawing, and the following year was joined by William Holman Hunt (1827–1910) and Dante Gabriel Rossetti (1828–82), who both had to struggle even to gain admission. In the autumn of 1848, to their almost immediate notoriety but lasting fame, these three young art students were to form their 'Pre-Raphaelite Brotherhood'. Their programme seemed above all to derive from the influential art critic John Ruskin's injunction to 'be humble and earnest in following the steps of Nature, and tracing the finger of God'.[2] Always prone to proselytize, Rossetti must have been the ringleader, since the other nominal members brought in to bring the number up to the magical seven were primarily his contacts. Although Charley Collins had modified his own technique as a painter along the approved lines and became fascinated with Rossetti's pious elder sister Maria, he was never formally included in the Brotherhood. This was clearly a double disappointment to a young man already lacking in self-esteem and of nervous disposition, who always invited the protectiveness of his more ebullient elder brother.

In the autumn of 1848, around eighteen months after William Collins's death, Harriet Collins and her two sons moved to a smaller house in Blandford Square, Marylebone, which soon became a haunt for younger members of the Royal Academy. According to Catherine Peters, liberated from her husband's anxious care, Harriet's personality 'underwent a startling transformation', so that the house offered 'an easygoing atmosphere – smoking was allowed and meals were always informal' (Peters, 81–2). Along with lesser-known students such as Henry Brandling, who was to tour Cornwall with Wilkie Collins and provide the illustrations to his *Rambles beyond Railways*, first Millais and then Hunt joined the gatherings. Rossetti, however, who did not exhibit at the Academy and soon ceased to attend its schools, was never part of the set. Indeed, Wilkie Collins does not refer to Rossetti in his private papers and, in common with many contemporary commentators, seems to have filled the vacant place in the triumvirate with his own younger brother. Yet the gatherings at the Collins's house also included a generation of painters rather older than Wilkie, notably Edward Ward (1814–79), Augustus Egg (1816–63), and William Frith (1819–90). These three friends had been the core of the 'Clique', a group specializing in historical subjects formed back in the late 1830s; all had recently been elected Associates of the Royal Academy. The Collinses had first come across Ned Ward studying art in Rome in 1837 in the course of their grand tour, and the two families soon became intimately linked. By the mid-1840s Ned's father was the family's bank manager at Coutts & Co. in the Strand, while his elder brother Charles, also employed at the bank, had married Wilkie's favourite cousin Jane and become his preferred travelling company on his Continental jaunts. It was presumably Ned Ward who introduced his fellows in the Clique to William Collins and his family, for both Egg and Frith seem to have known Wilkie as a teenager.

In theory, the Brotherhood should have been sworn enemies of the Clique, so it is interesting to see the opposed forces at the mid-century joining gaily in riotous amateur productions of Goldsmith's *Good Natur'd Man* and Sheridan's *The Rivals* at the 'Theatre Royal, Back Drawing Room' in 38 Blandford Square, with Wilkie Collins as grand circus master. These youthful frolics were the source of many of the author's most lasting friendships. But both Egg and Ward died before their time, and Millais was perhaps always closer to Charley, so it was Holman Hunt, who, despite his religious fervour and frequent visits to the Holy Land in search of Biblical subjects, tended to be by the author's side at the most solemn moments in his later life. He represented the author when Wilkie was too sick to attend his own mother's funeral in March 1868; he chalked a final portrait of Charley on his death bed from cancer of the stomach in April 1873; and he was one of the mourners at Collins's own funeral at Kensal Green in September 1889. When Hunt brought Wilkie the news of Augustus Egg's untimely death in March 1863, the author is reported to have broken down with the words: 'And so I shall never any more shake that dear hand and look into that beloved face! And Holman, all we can resolve is to be closer together as more precious one to the other in having had his affection.'[3]

Given the public furore raised by the Pre-Raphaelite rebellion in the late 1840s and his own links with its members, it is worth considering the nature of the controversy and the position that Wilkie Collins adopted towards it in his own writings – both public and private. Here, we need first to recognize that Hunt and Rossetti, in particular, did not always see eye-to-eye on the future of English painting, so that the Pre-Raphaelite project itself tended to move in contrary directions. Following Ruskin's advice – to reject the idealization and universal-ization underlying neo-classical models of beauty and steadfastly learn the lessons of natural history – implied an advanced, modernizing process. Yet the compositional style, rhetoric, and above all the name chosen by the Pre-Raphaelites seemed to suggest a rejection of scientific progress and a return to mediaeval simplicities. In the anxious state of early Victorian Protestantism, these progressive and regressive tendencies could look very much like the counter threats of secularization and Romanization, so that the Brothers were often attacked on both counts. There had been grumblings in the Academy and negative reviews in the journals as soon as it was revealed what the 'mystic monogram' PRB stood for,[4] but it was a bad-tempered article in *Household Words* during the 1850 Academy Exhibition that opened the floodgates of public antagonism towards the young rebels. Under the title 'Old Lamps for New Ones', the reformist Dickens began by mocking the PRB for its regressive tendencies. These were linked explicitly to despised factions both political and religious, in particular, Benjamin Disraeli's 'Young England' Movement, with its distrust of capitalism and idealization of mediaeval social relations, and John Henry Newman's Tractarian Movement, with its love of religious ritual and symbolism that led straight back towards Rome. Yet, in a lengthy and virulent attack on Millais's 'Christ in the House of His Parents', the only painting specifically referred to in the article, Dickens also took aim at the modern vices of secularism and naturalism, describing the figure of the mother of Jesus, for example, as 'a kneeling woman, so horrible in her ugliness, that ... she would stand out from the rest of the company as a Monster, in the vilest cabaret in France, or the lowest ginshop in England'. And in his eagerness to hint that the perversity of the painters might even extend to sexual matters, Dickens permitted himself an unusually broad *double entendre*, suggesting that, if permitted to take hold in the Royal Academy, the 'absurd principle' of realism 'might place Her Gracious Majesty in a very painful position, one of these fine Private View Days'.[5] The storm of protest continued throughout the summer of the Great Exhibition, when London was thronged with foreigners, and questions of national tradition and national progress were especially compelling. In May 1851, *The Times* thus launched a tirade against 'that strange disorder of the mind or the eyes which continues to rage with unabated absurdity among a class of juvenile artists who style themselves P.R.B.', abusing Millais, Hunt, and Collins in equal measure. The intemperance of the attack prompted Ruskin himself to write a pair of letters to the editor defending the young artists' 'fidelity to a certain order of truth',[6] before summarizing his opinions in a pamphlet. But even Ruskin's support was not unreserved. While insisting that the artists' argument was not so much with the Renaissance Masters themselves as with the narrow teachings of the Academy schools, he recognized 'Romanist and Tractarian tendencies' in the PRB's appeal to the early Italian masters.[7] At the same time, he acknowledged their 'morbid tendencies', in particular regretting that both Hunt and Millais had selected models of a type 'far inferior to that of average humanity'.[8]

There is no doubt that Wilkie Collins was aware of these clashes and their significance. In the January 1849 letter to R.H. Dana already cited, Collins had commented in some detail on the two published volumes of Ruskin's *Modern Painters*, criticizing the 'violent paradoxes' of the first, but overall praising the author's 'deep sympathy with the highest purposes of Art – poetical observation of Nature'. And in offering a Christmas book to his publisher in late 1851, he proposed that 'the three illustrations should be done by three young gentlemen who have lately been making an immense stir in the world of Art, and earned the distinction of being attacked by the Times (*any* notice *there* is a distinction) – and defended in a special pamphlet by Ruskin – the redoubtable *Pre-Raphael-Brotherhood*!! One of these "Brothers" happens to be *my* brother as well – the other two Millais and Hunt are intimate friends' (B&C I, 72–3). When Millais's frontispiece (in the event the only illustration) came in for a jibe from the *Athenaeum* reviewer that it was 'less affected and angular than might from such a source have been expected',[9] Collins made a promise (apparently unfulfilled) to his friend Edmund Yates, editor of the *Leader*, that he would borrow the artist's diary and 'do something amusing ... about the Pre-Raphael painting School in the country' (B&C I, 78–80). Yet in his public utterances Collins is rather more wary in his support of the rebels. Two key texts here are his own review of the 1851 Academy Exhibition, and his 1854 novel *Hide and Seek*, which is set principally in the painter's studio.

Collins's most explicit judgements appear in the anonymous Academy review for *Bentley's Miscellany*, where he touches on the landscapes and portraits only at the end, but devotes the lion's share of what is a substantial article to the figure painters. There, it is true, the greatest space is given over to 'the "new," or "Pre-Raphael" style',[10] represented by Millais, Hunt, and Charley Collins, who are praised in turn for their 'refinement', 'brilliancy', and 'dramatic power'.[11] Yet an even more fulsome welcome is given to the historical subjects of Ward, Egg, and Frith, for their 'purity and truth',[12] while the harshest criticism is reserved for William Dyce and Ford Madox Brown, those more experienced artists most sympathetic to the Pre-Raphaelite aesthetic, whose works betray 'absence of any attention to harmony'.[13] And a similar judgement also extends to the young rebels, who as a group are criticized for a lack of judgement in selection of subjects and models, so that in Millais's 'Woodman's Daughter', for example, the painter is blamed for not choosing 'a child with some of the bloom, the freshness, the roundness of childhood, instead of the sharp-featured little workhouse-drudge whom we see on his canvas'.[14] Remarks like these are especially troubling when we recall the author's stout defence of the harsh demands of Balzacian realism in the preface to *Basil*, on which he must then have already been at work.

Collins's complex responses to Pre-Raphaelitism are also reflected more obliquely in *Hide and Seek* (1854), the novel that followed *Basil*. Both novels share a focus on a young man's rebellion against an overbearing, puritanical father, but in most other respects they create very different imaginative worlds. This time the hero's character is marked by an irreverent ebullience that finds its outlet in drunken revelry rather than in Basil's emotional and sexual intensity. The hero of *Basil* had rejected a career in the law to marry the daughter of a linen-draper; that of *Hide and Seek* runs away from the office of a tea merchant to apprentice himself to an affably eccentric painter, whose studio must be based on that of William Collins in the author's childhood. As Aoife Leahy has recently demonstrated, the novel is thus filled with 'mischievous and covert' references to the Pre-Raphaelite controversy,[15] which probably escaped common readers but must have been easily decoded by the author's artistic friends. The painter is driven to adopt the orphan heroine because of her striking resemblance to a Raphael 'Madonna', the pet name by which she is generally known. Her ideal beauty presents no temptation to the hero, and fortunately so since she turns out to be his half-sister. The artist's pedagogical principles are a parody of those used in the Academy schools; he tells the hero, who wishes immediately to draw from nature, 'you must purify your taste by copying the glorious works of Greek sculpture – in short, you must form yourself on the Antique' (*HS*, 128). But if these comic hints allow *au fait* readers to recognize authorial sympathy with the Pre-Raphaelite rebels, the form of the novel tells a very different story. Far from being a further Balzacian exercise in social and psychological realism, *Hide and Seek* leads towards a celebration of comic and sentimental domesticity that recalls the early works of Dickens.

These conflicts and equivocations concerning the Pre-Raphaelite project run deep in Collins's character as an author and must reflect the complex network of personal attachments and obligations enveloping him as a young man. There was still the felt need not to break faith with the more sentimental painterly project of his father, which he had described with surprising sympathy in the *Memoirs*. More directly, Collins obviously felt an obligation to maintain a balance between his loyalty to his younger brother's brotherhood and to his three more senior painter friends. We should note here, however, that, if not Ned Ward himself, both Frith and Egg were perhaps already being drawn subtly towards the concerns of the PRB, the sympathy soon manifesting itself directly in their turning from historical to contemporary subjects, such as the former's gay crowd scenes, 'Ramsgate Sands' (1854) or 'Derby Day' (1858), and the latter's sombre triptych 'Past and Present' (1862). And, of course, we must recognize that it was precisely at this time that Collins came under the powerful personal influence of Charles Dickens, whose animosity to the Pre-Raphaelites was not merely a passing fancy, and to whom *Hide and Seek* was dedicated as a 'token of admiration and affection' (*HS*, 3). It is to the group of young journalists gathered around Dickens that we must now turn.

* * * * *

In his 1849 letter to R.H. Dana, in celebrating the present time as 'a great age for authors', Collins had mentioned in passing that 'Dickens told a friend of mine, that he had made *four thousand guineas* by his last year's Christmas book'. The friend must have been Augustus Egg, who had joined Dickens's amateur theatrical company in the summer of 1847 in a production of *The Merchant of Venice* for the benefit of Leigh Hunt. In March 1851, Egg recommended Collins as a likely new recruit for Bulwer Lytton's *Not So Bad as We Seem*, to be performed in aid of the recently founded Guild of Literature and Art (see Chapter 7). Egg was not the only Academy artist in the Dickens circle: the Irish popular historical and portrait painter Daniel Maclise (1807–70) was an intimate friend. He had recently illustrated several of Dickens's Christmas books and painted the well-known 'Nickleby' portrait of the glamorous, youthful young author back in 1839. At that time Dickens had also known Wilkie's godfather, David Wilkie, well and commissioned a picture from William Collins.

The young Collins was naturally delighted to take on the part of valet to Dickens in the starring role in Bulwer's comedy, and the two thus met for the first time on 12 March 1851 at a reading of the play in the house of the journalist and critic John Forster, one of Dickens's closest friends and confidants. Dickens's first letter to Wilkie, an amicable response to a late request for a seat for Charles Ward at the final rehearsal, nevertheless hints unmistakably that the 'faithful and attached valet' should not get ideas above his station (Pilgrim VI, 385). At first only a couple of performances were planned, but soon there were additional nights, other pieces on the bill, and a series of provincial tours lasting until the autumn of 1852, by which time master and servant had become intimate friends. The irreverent, ebullient young author quickly replaced Maclise as Dickens's favourite companion for his 'nightly wanderings into strange places' around London (Pilgrim VI, 82–3).[16] The same is true of Boz's periodic jaunts on the Continent without his family, beginning with the Italian expedition at the end of 1853, when Augustus Egg was also of the company. For Collins, the relationship must have retained a good deal of hero-worship; the first of his few surviving letters to Dickens is signed off, 'as usual and always my excellent manager's attached and obedient servant' (BGLL I, 50–1). For Dickens, whose marriage was clearly already troubled, these escapades obviously served as a psychological and probably sexual release.

Yet we should recognize that these slumming expeditions often served other, more professional purposes, so that the Dickens–Collins relationship at this time might also be represented as that of master and apprentice in the field of investigative journalism. As we shall see in more detail in Chapter 4, Collins quickly picked up from Dickens his idiosyncratic style of reportage, highly personalized and anecdotal, with many of the qualities of first-person literary narrative. Collins had been the youngest member among the cast of *Not So Bad as We Seem*, where he rubbed shoulders with not only painters and playwrights, but also a group of veteran journalists, including such household names as Charles Knight, Douglas Jerrold, and Mark Lemon, as well as John Forster himself. When Collins began to write for Dickens's *Household Words* in the spring of 1852, though, he was joining a group of junior contributors all to some extent in the position of disciples.

In *Dickens's 'Young Men'* (1997), his seminal study of this set, Peter Edwards unfortunately begins from the assumption that 'Wilkie Collins, who rapidly acquired an independent reputation, was never one of them'.[17] However, a great deal can be learned from tracing Collins's early connections not only with George Augustus Sala (1828–95) and Edmund Yates (1831–94), on whom Edwards concentrates, but also with the likes of James Payn, whose intimacy with the author was outlined in the previous chapter, or John Hollingshead (1827–94), who described Collins as his 'friend and brother worker on *Household Words*'.[18] Though Collins was certainly the first to make his name as a novelist, the rest were not slow to cross the thin line between journalism and literature; and while Collins was the only one to be taken on to Dickens's editorial staff, this was not until he had served a five-year apprenticeship as occasional contributor. It is true that Collins was the first one to breach the rule of anonymity in Dickens's family journals, beginning in 1857 with his first full-length serial novel, *The Dead Secret*, which was widely advertised as his own work. Yet Collins shared the frustration that all articles not only appeared unsigned, but also were subject without notice to extensive revision by the editor, so that their contributions were often taken to be either written by Dickens himself or in slavish imitation of him. It was clear that these young apprentices appreciated the opportunity to learn from such an accomplished craftsman, but all were doubtful whether this fully compensated for Dickens's 'putting a bushel over the lights of his staff ... keeping them in that obscurity which inevitably meant indigence, while he was attaining, and properly attaining, every year greater fame and greater fortune', as Sala later put it with only a touch of exaggeration.[19]

Collins probably first met these young journalists in the course of the 1850s at Dickens's 'Noctes', the suppers that he threw regularly for his literary staff in the office in Wellington Street off the Strand, or at the nearby Albion Tavern, which Hollingshead described as 'the homely dining-place of Charles Dickens, Wilkie Collins, and half the blend of literature and journalism in the 'fifties and 'sixties'.[20] Throughout that decade at least all, including Collins himself, were in some sense bohemians, that is, rebels against bourgeois social conventions. However, the term can cover two rather different lifestyles, represented respectively by Sala and Yates. Both came from theatrical families well known to the young Dickens, but Yates was never more than an occasional visitor to Bohemia while Sala took up residence full-time. Sala seems to have been illegitimate, was brought up between Brighton and Paris, and began to look after himself in the mid-1840s by, among other activities, writing penny fiction for the *Family Herald* and illustrating penny dreadfuls for publisher Edward Lloyd. In the 1850s, he seems to have drunk and gambled his way through his journalistic income, and only found stability at the end of the decade when he began to live with a semi-literate servant girl. Near the end of his life, Sala claimed that, while contributing to *Household Words*, he worked on average less than four hours a week. He described the set he then belonged to rather romantically as

> not miserably nor desperately poor, but philosophically, joyously, and to some extent it would seem voluntarily so. ... the principal reason for our indigence ... was that most of us were about the idlest young dogs that squandered away their time on the pavements of Paris or London. *We would not work.*[21]

Perhaps rather more accurately, he was described as 'often drunk, always in debt, sometimes in prison and ... totally disreputable' by his sometime colleague Hain Friswell who was sued to the tune of £500 for his candour.[22]

In contrast, Yates's parents were so successful in their theatrical careers that they sought a more respectable profession for their son; after a classical education at Highgate School, at sixteen he was placed as a clerk in the post office, where he remained in employment until 1872. In the meantime he also engaged in Herculean literary labours as playwright, poet, novelist, editor, and journalist, including his forty or so pieces for Dickens's family miscellanies. In 1853, he married a daughter of the wealthy Wilkinson family of sword-makers, and by the end of the decade already had a large family. Though he became intimate with Sala in the middle of the decade, and clearly spent a fair amount of time with him in drunken revelry, his lifestyle remained closer to that of the bourgeois professional than the out-and-out bohemian. In 1857 he wrote a description of Wilkie Collins's work ethic that might have been applied with equal justice to himself: 'No barrister or physician ever worked harder at his profession, or devoted more time, or thought, or trouble to it, was prouder of it, or pursued it with more zeal or earnestness than Mr Collins has done with regard to literature.'[23] In his private life, of course, Collins stayed a good deal closer to Sala's model, and it was indeed his uncanny ability to combine the pleasures of the bohemian with the painstaking work of the bourgeois professional that most endeared him to Dickens. When George Sala contributed the first of his many dramatic sketches of London life, 'The Key of the Street', to *Household Words* in autumn 1851, Dickens commented to his subeditor, W.H. Wills: 'There is nobody about us whom we can use, in his way, more advantageously than this young man.'[24] Over the next five years or so Sala indeed wrote almost 150 articles for the paper, more than any other contributor not on the office staff. However, around the middle of the decade, Dickens began to realize that Sala was 'living very queerly',[25] and the opportunity to join the staff was offered not to him but to Dickens's faithful valet, Collins, who could provide a similar service and rather more reliably. This in the sense both of keeping to deadlines, and of skirting around subjects likely to give offence to the middle-class family audience.

Until late in life Collins was to remain in personal contact not only with Sala and Yates, but also with Hollingshead and others among 'Dickens's young men', collaborating with or supporting them on a variety of projects, whether journalistic, theatrical, or literary. Of those three, Collins seems to have been least close to Sala, though this may be simply because so few letters written to him have survived. However, they worked together on two of the best of the special Christmas narratives for Dickens's miscellanies: 'The Seven Poor Travellers' (*Household Words*, 1854), where Sala offered 'a delightful sketch of two French children' (B&C I, 129–30), and 'The Haunted House' (*All the Year Round*, 1859), where Dickens disguised him in the frame narrative as 'Alfred Starling, an uncommonly agreeable young fellow of eight-and-twenty ... who pretends to be "fast" (another word for loose, as I understand the term)'.[26] In 1856 Dickens had sent Sala to Russia to report on the closing stages of the Crimean War, and he was thereafter to find his most effective journalistic role as travelling correspondent and leader writer for the *Daily Telegraph*, then still a populist liberal organ. In early 1871, Sala penned a *Telegraph* editorial supporting Collins's attack in *Man and Wife* on the contemporary cult of athleticism (see Chapter 8), and the latter reported himself 'delighted to find you using that great influence and circulation to set the muscular manner before the public eye in the proper light' (BGLL II, 238–9). At the end of the same decade, another letter shows them plotting together for their rights as authors, both annoyed that Douglas Jerrold's son, Blanchard, who had also been counted among Dickens's young men in the 50s, had failed to promote the cause of international copyright as he had promised (see BGLL III, 195 and 252).

As early as the mid-1850s Collins had helped Yates to place poems in the radical weekly *The Leader*, then owned by his friend Edmund Yates (to whom we shall return in Chapter 4), and later he was to provide valuable support when Yates got into trouble in his better-known role as the pioneer of 'personal' or 'society' journalism. He developed this persona (now known less elegantly as the gossip columnist) as the 'Lounger at the Clubs' in the *Illustrated Times* from 1855, as the 'Literary Talk' columnist in *Town Talk* in 1858, and, most importantly, from 1874, as founding owner and editor of the *World*, which quickly became the premier society weekly. Collins joined Dickens in strongly supporting Yates against Thackeray in the 1858 affair at the Garrick Club, of which all four were then members (Pilgrim VII, 588 and 599–601). Nevertheless, Yates was eventually expelled for ungentlemanly conduct, that is, refusing to apologize after publishing a distinctly unflattering sketch of the author of *Vanity Fair* in the columns of *Town Talk*. Many years later, in 1884, Collins was prominent among those who rallied round Yates when he was sentenced to four months imprisonment for publishing a criminal libel on the Earl of Lonsdale in the columns of the *World* (BGLL IV, 26–7 and 86). Yates was to return the favour on numerous occasions, publishing a number of adulatory articles in his various periodicals; and on Collins's death in 1889, Yates was to write openly of his 'warm and pleasant intimacy' with 'dear good staunch Wilkie'.[27]

John Hollingshead's upbringing was petty bourgeois rather than bohemian, and he started out in life in unsuccessful commercial activities, later claiming that he had learned his literary style on the streets, 'from costermongers and skittle-sharps'.[28] Though he had already been working with Yates and Sala on the *Train*, his first contribution to *Household Words* was 'Poor Tom – A City Weed', in October 1857, a sympathetic sketch of proletarian life in the metropolis. Over the next five years, Hollingshead contributed nearly a hundred articles to Dickens's miscellanies, many of the rest also concerning 'Underground London', the title chosen in 1862 for one of his many collections of reprinted pieces, though a number that also reflected his passion for the popular theatre. Collins first met Hollingshead at an office dinner in January 1858, and the two were among the party organized by Dickens to visit an allegedly haunted house in Cheshunt in preparation for the first *All the Year Round* Christmas number. In the following decade, Hollingshead suggested a couple of joint projects, neither of which came to fruition. At the beginning of 1863, Collins received an invitation to act as conductor of a new literary monthly, but, despite the fact that Hollingshead would have the task of subeditor ('*Valuable* as I know your co-operation would be to me'), was compelled to decline due to ill health and existing commitments (BGLL I, 288–9).[29] Shortly afterwards Hollingshead turned to theatrical management and in late 1868 took over a new playhouse built next door to the *All the Year Round* office, the Gaiety Theatre, which quickly became famous for both musical shows and social dramas by the likes of Tom Robertson and Dion Boucicault. Collins, who had bemoaned the sufferings of theatre audiences on more than one occasion in *Household Words*, attended a couple of early shows and found it 'the most comfortable elegant, and beautifully-decorated Theatre I have ever seen' (BGLL II, 127). Like Sala, whose *Wat Tyler M.P.* opened at the Gaiety at Christmas 1869, Collins also responded positively to a commission from Hollingshead and initially planned to write *Man and Wife* as a drama for the Gaiety, but eventually decided to compose the novel first, so that when the play eventually appeared in early 1873 it was played by the Bancrofts at the Prince of Wales Theatre (see Chapter 7). However, around the same time, Collins was to provide solid support to Hollingshead in his unsuccessful legal battle to protect novelists against unauthorized dramatic adaptations, and this brought him again into personal contact with William Moy Thomas (1828–1910), another of the young contributors to *Household Words* in its early days. Thomas was then secretary of the Association to Protect the Rights of Authors and a member on the Royal Commission on Copyright, so that through these connections Collins was drawn more formally into the growing movement to defend literary property.

These ongoing literary relations with the young journalistic set forming around Dickens in the 1850s thus both point towards and help to explain the extraordinarily wide variety of literary projects in which Wilkie Collins became engaged in the course of his career. The most common thread in the pattern of his relations with Sala, Yates, Hollingshead, and the rest, however, must be the persistence of a shared concern for the rights and wrongs of authors. This can be traced once again, both directly and indirectly, to their early contact with

Dickens: directly, because, ever since his first visit to America in the early 1840s, Boz had been loud in his complaints against the exploitation of literary labour; and indirectly, because contributing to *Household Words* had been their first experience of losing control over their own writings.

* * * * *

Before turning in the following chapter to the nature of the literary market place when Collins commenced his literary career, it is worth considering a final point. Though this chapter has perhaps given the impression that Collins's social world around the 1850s was entirely male, this was clearly not the case. Both Jane Carpenter (his cousin) and Nina Chambers (the niece of Dickens's trusted subeditor at *Household Words*, W.H. Wills) were very close to Wilkie before they were married, at which point their respective husbands, Charley Ward and Fred Lehmann, also became Wilkie's friends. Yet it is true that the artistic circles in which he moved, whether painterly or literary, were dominated almost entirely by men. It was not, of course, that there were no women painters and writers, but rather that they did not have the same freedom of access to the public sphere. Wilkie's maternal aunt Margaret Carpenter, Jane's mother, was a successful portrait painter; but as a woman, though she exhibited at the Royal Academy virtually every year for half a century, she was never eligible to become a member. It was the same with Henrietta Ward, the much younger wife of Ned Ward whose elopement Wilkie Collins had helped to plan, and who became in her own right a distinguished historical painter. Though her husband both designed the costumes and played the misanthrope Croaker, she not could take part at all in the production of *Good Natur'd Man* at Blandford Square, since she gave birth to their first child on the night of the performance. In a similar way, there were a number of regular female contributors to *Household Words*, but none of them came near the Office, which functioned very much as a gentleman's club. Notable here are Elizabeth Gaskell (1810–65) and Adelaide Anne Procter (1825–64), both of whom were fellow contributors with Collins, Sala, and Dickens himself, to 'The Haunted House' in 1859. Yet neither could serve on the 'Committee of Concoction', as it was dubbed in jest,[30] or ever be invited to the 'Noctes'. As a married woman, of course, Gaskell could not even own literary property in her own name. These legal and social disabilities faced by women artists in the mid-nineteenth century were challenged by only a small minority, so that they were removed only with painful slowness.

In this respect, Collins was certainly no John Stuart Mill. There is no evidence of him expressing sympathy or support for the likes of Carpenter and Gaskell in the face of such disadvantages. Though Collins began early in his life to feel an unusual degree of sympathy for sexually vulnerable woman, whether among the lower classes or on the bohemian margins of society, he was never to offer much in the way of solidarity with women of his own class attempting to establish a foothold in the bourgeois world of professional work.

3
Collins and the Earlier Victorian Literary Marketplace

At the beginning of Wilkie Collins's career as an author, the British publishing industry was still only beginning to move towards mass production. Though the first half of the nineteenth century witnessed remarkable advances in printing techniques and a rapid increase in literacy, for the most part books remained luxury items readily affordable only to the wealthy. In other words, publishing shifted rather more slowly and unevenly from petty-commodity to commodity production than other key sectors such as energy, transport, textiles, or food. One major cause was the range of onerous imposts on publication (most notably, on advertising, on newspapers, and on paper for printing itself), which remained in force into the second half of the nineteenth century. This was well after most other such restrictions on trade had been removed: even the notorious 'corn laws', imposing a tariff on imported wheat, had been repealed in 1846. While the 'taxes on knowledge', as they were dubbed by their many opponents, had been originally intended by the authorities principally as a way of stifling political dissent, they continued to serve as a significant source of public revenue. Another important reason can be found in the staunch conservatism of the book trade itself, as symbolized by the reactionary practices of the Booksellers' Association dominated by traditional firms such as Longmans and Murrays, whose interests lay in maintaining high fixed prices and preventing competitive underselling. Thus, though the tax burden weighed rather more heavily on periodical publications, the market for new books was much slower to change, and 'print-capitalism' (in Benedict Anderson's phrase)[1] emerged first with various kinds of serial publication. Three overlapping forms are important here: number books, that is, single texts issued in parts as fascicles, which could be bound into volumes on completion; periodicals with miscellaneous contents, including both magazines and newspapers; and series of reprinted books, in standard formats at lower prices. By constantly encouraging consumers to come back for more, a mechanism still very familiar to us today from serial dramas such as *Doctor Who* or narrative chronicles such as *Harry Potter*, these modes of publication helped create commodity texts with significant surplus value. Beginning with the market for books themselves, whether original or reprinted, and then turning to part and periodical publication, the present chapter aims to describe this general material context in some detail, at the same time locating within it Collins's specific engagement with the gradual transformation of print culture.

* * * * *

When Collins began to establish himself as a novelist in the 1850s, the major metropolitan circulating libraries already exercised a virtually hegemonic control over new works of British fiction in volume. In a comical letter to Charles Ward from a village outside London in 1850, Collins complained not only of 'an unnecessarily large supply of fresh air', but also of 'a d-d absence of cabs, omnibuses, circulating libraries, public houses, newspaper offices, pastry cooks shops, and other articles of civilisation' (B&C I, 60). The library vogue had begun as early as the mid-eighteenth century, but the custom of borrowing reading matter, rather than purchasing it for private use, was greatly stimulated by a steep inflation in the price of books in the first quarter of the nineteenth century, reflecting economic instability during and following the Napoleonic Wars. However, it was not until after the mid-century, when prevailing economic conditions encouraged a shift to the mass production of copyright works, that the library system came to be dominated by Charles Edward Mudie. Setting up shop in 1842, Mudie moved to extensive new premises in New Oxford Street in 1852, by which time he was already offering a speedy and efficient lending service not only to metropolitan readers but to those in the provinces and colonies also. As the adjective suggests, 'Mudie's Select Library' was particular both about the social standing of its clientele and the 'moral' status of the works it approved for rental. The basic annual subscription was a guinea, which allowed only a single volume to be borrowed at a time, but the most popular was the two-guinea subscription which permitted the taking out of four volumes simultaneously, and was thus geared to the form of the multi-volume novel.[2]

In such a way the market for new novels long remained dominated by the form of publication in which Walter Scott's 'Waverley' novels had appeared in the 1820s – the three-volume set sold at the prohibitive retail price of a guinea and a half, or 'three-decker' as it was known after the massive battleships of Nelson's time. This format had become so entrenched by the time that Wilkie Collins was a young man that, in his letters, he could describe two irate French stage-coach drivers as 'swearing three-volumes-post octavo' (B&C I, 22–4), or the disappointments in getting up amateur theatricals as sufficient to 'fill a three volume novel' (BGLL I, 31). For much of the nineteenth century, then, print-runs of first editions typically numbered in the hundreds rather than the thousands, of which the bulk would go to the metropolitan circulating libraries. While only the wealthiest individuals were in a position to purchase such editions, Mudie's subscribers could gain access to large quantities of new books each year for little more than the cost of a single set. This monopolistic system guaranteed a small but stable return to conservative publishers at a time of rapid change, and a living to marginal literary talents. But it also severely limited the potential readership and rewards of writers seeking a popular audience, and restricted political or aesthetic experiment in fiction through the fear of what the Victorians called 'Grundyism' – the dead hand of social propriety and sexual prudery.[3] As the century progressed, there was an increasingly loud chorus of protests from progressive authors and enterprising publishers against Mudie's stranglehold on the ideological content and material form of the novel – something we discuss in Chapter 10 – but the circulating library system retained grip until close to the end of Victoria's reign.

Mudie's long-held sway over the market for new books in general, and new novels in particular, is by now something of a cliché. What tends to receive less emphasis, though, is that one consequence of the steadfast conservatism of the book trade in original work was the enterprise and versatility found in the subsequent reprint market. In contrast to the immobility of the price of the three-decker, the cost of reprinted works declined steadily during the Victorian period. Such reissues, both of books still in copyright from the original or another publisher, and those already out of copyright, tended to be packaged and marketed as a series of works by an individual author or in a branded 'library'. Unlike the first multi-volume edition, they tended to conclude with a catalogue of 'announcements' advertising the publisher's wares in the same or other series. Though inexpensive novels out of copyright had begun to appear rather earlier from firms such as Whittingham's, the then partners Henry Colburn and Richard Bentley were probably the first established publishers to begin reissuing their own successful three-decker novels, in single volumes at six shillings in a 'Standard Novels' series from 1831.

By the mid-century this practice had become the norm. The new firm of Routledge was the most successful in buying up residual fiction copyrights, including the historical novels of Bulwer Lytton and Harrison Ainsworth, and exploiting them in cheap editions, notably in the long-running shilling Railway Library founded in 1848. The success of this venture in turn encouraged more venerable publishers to develop cheaper reprint formats. Thus, from the later 1850s there appeared numerous series of two-shilling 'yellowback' reprints, bound in boards covered in glazed coloured paper bearing a striking illustrated cover, conspicuously on sale up and down the country at the chain of railway bookstalls owned by W.H. Smith. (Smith also operated a nationwide circulating library, second only to that of Mudie.) As the century wore on, the period between initial publication as a three-decker and reprinting in a single volume steadily shrank, while the range of reprint formats available gradually expanded, so that eventually towards the end of the century, with the flimsy sixpenny paperback in double columns, successful novels became cheaply available to a mass audience in volume form only a year or so after initial publication.

When Wilkie Collins began to write, of course, this trend was still at an early stage. As the son of an Academy painter largely dependent for a respectable income on the good will of wealthy patrons, Collins's initial ideas of the nature of authorship, as well as his early engagements with publishers, tended to be rather backward-looking. His first, rejected novel *Ioláni* was submitted by his father at the beginning of 1845 to Longmans, the oldest and most conservative of the London houses with a very limited list of fiction, who would only consider publishing entirely at the author's expense.[4] Though the manuscript of the next book *Memoirs of the Life of William Collins* was initially offered to Murray's,[5] the book was eventually published on commission by Longmans, with the author responsible for soliciting two hundred subscriptions out of the five hundred copies sold, and only thus managing to recoup the initial outlay on paper, printing, and binding. Thus, among the author's surviving early correspondence, there remain many obsequious letters to his father's former colleagues and patrons, including Sir Robert Peel to whom the work was dedicated (BGLL I, 21–8). Yet, as revealed in the *Memoirs of the Life of William Collins*, which listed not only the initial buyers and sale prices of all his father's paintings but also the published engravings taken from them, Collins must already have been aware that even the fine artist could both reach a wider audience and benefit financially from techniques of mechanical reproduction. Indeed, one of Wilkie's first publications must have been the letterpress to accompany an engraving of William Collins's 'Rustic Hospitality' in 1844 (BGLL I, 12–13), while in 1850 he was astounded that Landseer could earn £3000 'for the mere right of making a print' of his latest success at the Royal Academy, 'Duke of Wellington Re-visiting the Field of Waterloo' (B&C I, 61–3).

When Collins resumed writing fiction, he turned first to the house of Richard Bentley, who had parted acrimoniously from Henry Colburn in 1832, but retained the reputation as the foremost publisher of fiction for the circulating libraries. Bentley purchased outright the copyright of each of Collins's first three full-length novels, which appeared as three-deckers. These were *Antonina* (1850), the historical romance started in 1846 but laid aside until he had performed his literary duty to his father's memory, plus *Basil* (1852) and *Hide and Seek* (1854). Moreover, in 1851–2 he wrote a series of short pieces for the monthly *Bentley's Miscellany*, as well as a Cornish travelogue (*Rambles beyond Railways*) and a Dickensian Christmas book (*Mr Wray's Cash-Box*), both published as slim single volumes. Despite its rather turgid prose, *Antonina* received a number of encouraging reviews and sold surprisingly well as a three-decker, the first edition of around 500 being cleared in three months. Collins had received a respectable £200 for this first novel, and, on Dickens's advice, was now in a position to issue an 'ultimatum' demanding £350 for *Basil* (BGLL I, 78–9). At this time there was a good deal of social contact between Collins and Richard Bentley or his son George, who held a regular literary 'Conversazione' on Wednesday evenings (BGLL I, 70–1). Collins also tried to support the New Burlington Street publisher in a series of battles against high prices and restrictive practices. In 1852, he was on the side of Bentley, John Chapman, and other upstart liberal houses, against venerable conservatives such as Longman and Murray in a legal battle over control of the Booksellers' Association (BGLL I, 71–2). Here, the conservative cartel was forced to disband when the court ruled in favour of the free-traders. Ironically, however, the ruling served principally to assist Mudie to begin to negotiate large discounts on the price of new books which smaller libraries, private clubs, or individual purchasers could not hope to obtain.

The following year Collins supported Bentley's plan to attack 'the present extravagantly absurd prices charged for works of fiction', by lowering the price of new three-deckers such as *Hide and Seek*, Collins's third novel then still in progress, to half a guinea for the complete set rather than merely a single volume (BGLL I, 87–8). Unfortunately, in this case Collins's publisher was attacking from a position of financial weakness rather than strength, and the plan came to nothing. Soon, with 'the depressing effect of the Russian [Crimean] war upon the sale of books', the publisher's finances were so unstable that he was forced to sell off many of his assets to avoid bankruptcy.[6] No second edition of *Basil* was called for, and the offer for *Hide and Seek* fell to £150, with sales proving even more disappointing. There was no move to issue any of Collins's novels as single volumes in the 'Standard Authors' series, and instead Richard Bentley tried unsuccessfully to sell back his copyrights to the author (BGLL I, 104–5). Bentley then auctioned off *Basil* to the highest bidder and the novel appeared briefly as a yellowback in 'Blackwood's London Library' in 1856. This was the first cheap reprint of a Collins novel, though of course it resulted in no direct financial gain to the author.

Largely for these reasons – but also perhaps under the personal influence of Dickens, who, ever since a series of contractual quarrels with Richard Bentley in the late 1830s, had harboured a grudge against 'the Burlington Street brigand' (Pilgrim I, 618–9) – Collins eventually parted company with the house. He then auctioned more limited rights in his next four works (two collections of short tales as well as two full-length novels) to the highest bidder, which thus appeared from different publishers without conspicuous benefit to the author – at least until *The Woman in White* was sold to Sampson Low in 1860. The same publisher was then successful in the bidding for the reissue in single volumes of Collins's backlist, which thus appeared in a uniform cloth-bound edition from 1861, and as a series of yellowbacks from 1864. It is thus safe to conclude that, whatever the author's personal intentions, there is little evidence of Collins's fiction reaching a wide audience until his work began to be serialized in Dickens's weekly miscellanies.

* * * * *

We have already suggested that one consequence of the conservatism of the Victorian trade in new works of fiction in volume form was the increasingly lively market for subsequent reprints. Another was the even more remarkable development of various modes of prior publication in serial form. The primary motivation stimulating serial publication was economic: publishers could thus spread the cost of production, and readers the cost of purchase, painlessly over the period of issue. In addition, both parts and periodicals were distributed through widely dispersed channels, including hawkers, general stores, and the postal service, thus offering the reader an immediacy of access to written information that traditional booksellers could not hope to match. Throughout the nineteenth century, literary material, works of reference, and historical, scientific, and devotional texts were amongst the wares distributed by the 'number trade', that is, works in parts sold door-to-door. Over the same period periodical production grew exponentially: the aggregate number of newspaper stamps issued per year during the first half of the century increased almost 500 per cent from around 16 to 80 million, the number of British newspaper titles listed in Mitchell's *Newspaper Press Directory* rose from 551 to 2468 between 1846 and 1901, while the number of magazines published jumped from 537 to 2446 over the period 1864–1901, both commensurate increases in percentage terms.[7] Moreover, the communities of readers served by these journals were characterized by social class, geographical region, gender, and generation, as well as according to affiliation to trade or profession, and religious denomination or political party, and their needs were consequently varied and complex.

Yet, to the disappointment of many contemporary commentators, the serial publications which reached the widest audience were those which offered light entertainment in the form of instalment fiction. The presence of the novel in parts became so pervasive that the motivation could be no longer simply a matter of economy. As Linda Hughes and Michael Lund conclude in *The Victorian Serial* (1991), 'something in the culture of the period made it especially receptive to the serial': 'Serialization was aligned with fundamental middle-class values: a belief in historical progress; acceptance of biological evolution; and commitment to the ideal of marriage and family extending over time.'[8] By the second half of the century, a large majority of 'original' novels published as books had thus appeared previously in monthly or weekly instalments, as independent numbers, in magazines, or in the columns of newspapers. Around the beginning of Charles Dickens's career as a writer in the mid-1830s there were already clear signs of such a transformation in serial publication, and indeed the young Dickens himself contributed not a little to the revolution.

Dickens worked for the press before he became a novelist, edited half-a-dozen journals during his career as a writer, and typically chose to divide his time equally between journalistic and literary endeavour. Further, the two novels which helped to make 'Boz' a household name for the early Victorians, *The Pickwick Papers* (1836–7) and *Oliver Twist* (1837–9), were both first issued in illustrated monthly instalments.[9] The former appeared in twenty independent shilling parts of thirty-two pages in coloured wrappers, while the latter was serialized a couple of chapters at a time in twenty-four consecutive numbers of *Bentley's Miscellany*, a new magazine selling at half-a crown. Neither publishing format was then entirely original, but both quickly became key vehicles for literary material aimed at a broad middle-class audience measured in the tens of thousands, and Dickens's intervention was decisive. Reprinting valued works serially in parts was already common by the mid-eighteenth century,[10] but the runaway success of *Pickwick* started a fashion for original fiction in this medium that lasted for twenty years and more. Captain Marryat, Albert Smith, and Charles Lever were among the authors who were quick to jump on the bandwagon set rolling by Dickens, though Thackeray and Trollope were perhaps the only major authors who remained there with him. The twenty monthly parts in distinctive duck-green wrappers remained Dickens's own favourite mode of initial publication until the end of his career, though by then, as John Sutherland acknowledges, the format was fast becoming 'as antediluvian as the powdered wig or the buckled shoe'.[11]

If magazine serialization was thus rarely Dickens's preference, his decision to take on the editorship of Bentley's new magazine and run his second novel through its pages nevertheless had a significant impact. Fiction had been a feature in a variety of periodicals since the mid-eighteenth century,[12] and monthly miscellanies had carried new novels in instalments before *Oliver Twist*, notably *Blackwood's* (1818) and *Fraser's* (1830). But these were both weighty, pricey Tory organs noted also for their critical reviewing, whereas *Bentley's* took a liberal line following the Reform Act, was less expensive, and aimed above all to entertain. Almost immediately it attracted a large readership and served as model for similar enterprises, notably Colburn's reformed *New Monthly* (new series, 1837) and *Ainsworth's Magazine* (1842). In the longer term, it can be seen as setting a precedent for the creation of 'house magazines' by the publishers of novels for the circulating libraries in order to showcase their most popular authors, a process which culminated in the *Cornhill Magazine* from Smith, Elder in 1860.

This transformation in serial publishing for the middle classes was thus already well established at the beginning of Collins's literary career. However, during the first decade or so, he was not in a position to take advantage of either option for the monthly serialization of his novels. By then, the fashion for publication in parts was no longer new, and was only a safe investment for established novelists at the peak of the popularity, and it had never been a method much favoured by the firm of Bentley, which much preferred to distribute its publications in the multi-volume format geared to the circulating libraries. Moreover, the heavy reliance of *Antonina* on description at the expense of dialogue and action, the stark realism and modernity of *Basil*, and the lack of tonal and scenic variety in both, would have discouraged any publisher from issuing them in a serial format that rewarded movement and suspense. Collins's relationship with the house gained him early access to the pages of *Bentley's Miscellany*, but the bulk of his contributions were non-fiction and his only stories to appear there were short comic or melodramatic tales, such as 'Perugino Potts' or 'Nine O'Clock' (in February and August 1852, respectively). It is true that *Hide and Seek*, a novel dedicated to Dickens and indeed indebted to him for its combination of mystery and comedy, would have lent itself well to serialization in a monthly magazine. But in early 1851, just when Collins began to contribute to the *Miscellany*, Bentley's deteriorating financial position had forced him to forego lengthy serial fiction in its pages, and by the end of 1854 he was happy to sell the magazine outright to Harrison Ainsworth.

* * * * *

By the mid-century the lessons of mass production had been absorbed by those authors and publishers seeking to reach a newly literate urban proletarian readership measuring in the hundreds of thousands, bringing in what Louis James has called 'the era of mass popular fiction'.[13] Before the mid-century, the traditional rural popular literary genres of the ballad and chapbook had been superseded by the urban form of the 'penny blood', which appeared either in independent penny weekly parts or in the columns of penny weekly papers. Typical titles were *Ada the Betrayed* (1841–2) and *Varney the Vampire* (1845–7), both by James Rymer. These can be seen as cheaper, miniaturized versions of the bourgeois monthly formats, just as the narratives themselves often parodied and plagiarized the genres then favoured by the middle classes, whether historical romance, criminal melodrama, or picaresque comedy. Edward Lloyd of Salisbury Square, on the wrong side of Fleet Street, was the most enterprising part publisher, and George Reynolds the most notorious of the penny novelists, with his *Mysteries of London* running in parts for over ten years from 1845, sales of which were rumoured to have approached half-a-million. Though the *Family Herald* (1843–1940) and *London Journal* (1845–1912) were the best-selling titles with a regular readership of a quarter of a million or more, Lloyd and Reynolds also issued their own weekly miscellanies. These were all *Bentley's* in little, featuring a variety of instructive and entertainment matter in addition to generous helpings of serial and complete fiction.

These developments in the proletarian literary marketplace dismayed many middle-class commentators, especially those committed to popular education and self-improvement. The 1850s thus witnessed new efforts to create or reshape cheap weekly family-oriented publications to reclaim popular fiction for the forces of enlightenment, whether evangelical or utilitarian. Notable here were not only papers from religious organizations, such as the Religious Tract Society's *Leisure Hour* (1852), but those from commercial publishers such as *Cassell's Family Paper* (1853) or *Chambers' Journal* (new series, 1854). More significantly for our purposes, we should perhaps include among such publications Dickens's own new periodical venture of March 1850, the twopenny weekly *Household Words*. In a flyer advertising its opening number, Dickens claimed that the new journal was 'designed for the instruction and entertainment of all readers' (cited in Gasson, 49). In fact, *Household Words* sold only around 40,000 copies a week, though perhaps double that for the special Christmas numbers. However, as was suggested in a review of *Great Expectations* in *The Times*, the weekly serial story had hitherto been 'connected with publications of the lowest class – small penny and halfpenny serials that found in the multitude some compensation for the degradation of their readers', where 'lust was the *alpha* and murder the *omega*', but Dickens had succeeded in demonstrating that the medium itself was 'not incompatible with a very high order of fiction'.[14]

Collins's response to these developments in the mass market is reflected in a fascinating article for *Household Words* in 1858 entitled 'The Unknown Public'. There, he recognizes at the outset that the bulk of the contemporary reading public is composed of readers of what he calls the 'penny-novel-journals', whereas 'the subscribers to this journal, the customers at publishing houses, the members of book-clubs and circulating libraries, and the purchasers and borrowers of newspapers and reviews' represent only a small minority.[15] He arrives at the optimistic conclusion that, in the not far distant future, 'the readers who rank by millions will be the readers who give the widest reputations, who return the richest rewards, and who will, therefore, command the service of the best writers of their time'.[16]

Yet the article as a whole reveals a curious social embarrassment at the immediate prospect of an audience of common readers. The dominant tone is comic, and the laughter is directed not only at the serial stories in miscellanies such as the *London Journal* and the *Reynolds's Miscellany*, which are dismissed swiftly for their dullness and sameness, but also at 'the social position, the habits, the tastes, and the average intelligence of the Unknown Public', as inferred from the columns devoted to 'Answers to Correspondents'.[17] Here, by way of illustration, the narrator rather superciliously offers a lengthy catalogue of correspondents 'utterly impervious to the senses of ridicule or shame', beginning:

> A reader of a penny-novel-journal who wants a recipe for gingerbread. A reader who complains of fullness in his throat. Several readers who want cures for gray hair, for warts, for sores on the head, for nervousness, and for worms. Two readers who have trifled with Woman's Affections, and who want to know if Woman can sue them for breach of promise of marriage. A reader who wants to know what the sacred initials I. H. S. mean, and how to get rid of small-pox marks.
>
> Another reader who desires to be informed what an esquire is. Another who cannot tell how to pronounce picturesque and acquiescence. Another who requires to be told that chiaroscuro is a term used by painters. Three readers who want to know how to soften ivory, how to get a divorce, and how to make black varnish. A reader who is not certain what the word poems means; not certain that 'Mazeppa' was written by Lord Byron; not certain whether there are such things in the world as printed and published Lives of Napoleon Bonaparte.

The article thus assumes a yawning social divide between the readers of the penny miscellanies and the 'known reading public', that is, the subscribers to Dickens's twopenny miscellany – 'We see the books they like on their tables. We meet them out at dinner, and hear them talk of their favorite authors.'

Yet by this time papers such as the *Family Herald* had already begun to target a lower-middle-class domestic audience that must have overlapped to some extent with that of *Household Words*, if there were any truth in its claim regarding 'the instruction and entertainment of all readers'. In fact, in the year before Collins's piece appeared, the editorship of the *London Journal* was taken over briefly by Mark Lemon, founder of *Punch* and Collins's fellow actor in Dickens's amateur theatricals. And around this time other sensation writers were prepared to take the risk of appearing in the cheapest weekly miscellanies. As noted in 'The Unknown Public' itself, Charles Reade's *The Double Marriage* was first published in serial form under the title 'White Lies' in the *London Journal* as early as 1857, while by 1863 Braddon's *Lady Audley's Secret* and *Henry Dunbar* (under the title 'The Outcasts') had also appeared there. Given the attitudes reflected in 'The Unknown Public', it is unsurprising that Collins himself felt no immediate temptation to encounter such a broad social audience, though letters at the beginning of the

1870s show that he was then more than willing to consider distributing his backlist fiction cheaply through the weekly numbers trade or in penny journals in order to reach the widest audience and reap the greatest rewards (BGLL II, 169–70).

Collins's apprenticeship in writing fiction in instalments was in fact sponsored entirely by Dickens in *Household Words*. Collins's first effort was in April 1852 in the form of the much anthologized short tale 'A Terribly Strange Bed'. However, his contributions soon began to include longer stories issued in several parts, from 'Gabriel's Marriage' (16–23 April 1853), a melodrama set during the French Revolution, to the comic pseudo-autobiography, 'A Rogue's Life' (1–28 March 1856). It is significant that most of the periodical pieces Collins produced in the 1850s, both fiction and non-fiction, are in the voice of a dramatized first-person narrator. And even those tales originally told in the third person, such as 'Gabriel's Marriage', acquired a similar dramatic quality when they were incorporated within the elaborate frame narrative that Collins constructed when he gathered his shorter fiction into the volumes *After Dark* (1856, from Smith, Elder) and *The Queen of Hearts* (1859, from Hurst & Blackett). Here, the author was clearly influenced by the regular experience of collaborating with Dickens on collections of tales for the *Household Words* Christmas issues, beginning in 1854 with 'The Seven Poor Travellers', the first to have a unifying framework that was both structural and thematic.

However, it was not until later in the decade that Collins had the chance to run a full-length novel in the columns of *Household Words*. Dickens himself doubted the value of a long serial by Collins to the journal – 'I feel perfectly convinced that it is not one quarter so useful to us as detached papers, or short stories in four parts'[18] – but he was forced to concede in order to persuade Collins to join the permanent staff of the journal. *The Dead Secret*, the author's fourth novel, thus ran in twenty-three weekly instalments from the beginning of January until mid-June 1857, when it was reissued complete in two volumes from Dickens's publishers, Bradbury and Evans. Ironically, though Dickens himself seemed satisfied with the resulting narrative, some contemporary reviewers regarded it as a poor imitation of the Boz style.[19] More generally it was viewed as one of Collins's weaker efforts, with the action, characterization, and writing criticized alike as rather thin. The main reason was probably that the author had underestimated the difficulties of serial composition, and in particular the constraint of having published the beginning of a story when the end was not yet in sight. Caught up in the excitement of working with Dickens both on 'The Wreck of the Golden

Mary', the 1856 *Household Words* Christmas number, and on the play 'The Frozen Deep' (performed by Dickens's amateur company from 6 January 1857), Collins was never more than a few weeks ahead of the printers. The plot hangs on a hidden letter containing the guilty secret of an illegitimate child, Rosamund Treverton, which is only revealed a generation later when the she has grown up and married a man who has been deprived of his sight; the central character, the mother, is a vulnerable female servant, Sarah Leeson, oppressed by guilt and prone to mental instability; in minor roles the cast includes eccentrics such as the misanthrope, the hypochondriac, and the cheerful uncle with a mania for Mozart. All these are traits familiar from Collins's later successful works but in *The Dead Secret* they are accompanied by a major structural flaw. This is not so much that the author reveals the secret too early and the reader is forced to rely on expectation more than suspense, but rather that, as Catherine Peters suggests, 'the facts of the plot are revealed, but the dramatization of them is withheld until the end, when they are brought to life in second-hand narration' (Peters, 17).

* * * * *

From 1857, however, all of the author's full-length novels were to appear first in instalments. More than Dickens, who always preferred the open spaces of the expansive monthly number, it was Collins who was to gain a reputation as the master of the mechanics of the weekly serial: the striking opening to increase the chance of a serial's 'taking' with subscribers, the episodic integrity of the compact instalment, the manipulation of mystery and suspense, and the frequent 'climax and curtain' endings required to make readers come back for more. But, as we have seen in this chapter, the author's previous engagements with the literary market offered little to prepare for the extraordinary success of *The Woman in White*, where Collins melded a complex, enigmatic plot with first-hand narration. Running as a serial in Dickens's new family weekly *All the Year Round* from November 1859, it aroused wide interest with its eerily enigmatic opening and deft manipulation of suspense, causing queues on publication day and quickly raising the circulation into six figures. When the triple-decker appeared from Sampson Low in August 1860, it went through an unprecedented eight editions before Christmas. We shall return to this moment in Chapter 5.

4
Collins as Journalist

While it is known that Wilkie Collins published something over a hundred non-fiction articles in a variety of periodicals throughout his career, the precise number remains decidedly uncertain. Though the relevant volume of the current edition of the *Cambridge Bibliography of English Literature* came out as recently as 1999, the Collins entry still has quite a few gaps and question marks. Something similar is in fact true of many other major Victorian novelists. The main reason is that anonymity remained the norm in the Victorian press until well after the mid-century, and authors sometimes explicitly requested that their contributions be included unsigned. After a disagreement on the religious line taken by the *Leader*, for example, Collins requested that 'my name may never be appended to any future articles I may write' (B&C I, 83–6), while, as we saw in Chapter 2, Dickens tried to keep strictly to the rule of anonymity in both *Household Words* and *All the Year Round*. The office book detailing payments to *Household Words* contributors has fortunately survived, but that for *All the Year Round* has been lost, and it is uncertain whether one was ever kept for the *Leader*. Altogether Collins reprinted less than thirty of his journalistic pieces, almost all in *My Miscellanies* (1863), with the lion's share from *Household Words*, while his private papers often do not shed any light on the obscurities. The result is that there is no definitive listing of Collins's contributions to two of the three periodicals in which his journalism most frequently appeared, and there are likely to be more unrecognized early pieces in other journals.

A secondary reason for the confusion over Collins's journalism is that, with the emergence of a more personal, anecdotal style of journalism, it is not always easy to make a clear-cut distinction between non-fictional and fictional pieces. This blurring of boundaries can be seen equally in Collins's fantasy on the coming of the railways, 'The Last Stage

Coachman' (1843), his first identified publication, and the trio of tales of justice miscarried entitled 'Victims of Circumstances' (1886–7), as well as in many of the pieces in Dickens's magazines in the 1850s and 1860s. A further complication here is that there remains some uncertainty about what exactly Collins contributed to collaborative narratives such as Dickens's special Christmas numbers of *Household Words* and *All the Year Round*. Thus, though most of Collins's tales were reprinted by the author sooner or later in volume form, when Julian Thompson tried to assemble his *Complete Shorter Fiction* in 1995, it was by no means easy to decide what should be included.

While, as shown in Table 4.1, the present chapter helps to solve one or two specific bibliographical puzzles, its main aim is to provide a broad overview of Collins's miscellaneous contributions to periodicals. The discussion will cover both the particular print contexts in which they appeared, and their general influence on Collins's development as a novelist. We include not only the discursive, journalistic articles, but also the short works of narrative fiction, plus the broad grey zone in between. In order to bring Collins's career as a writer of tales into sharper focus, we will give over some space in the later part of the chapter to a comparison with that of Elizabeth Gaskell. The emphasis will thus be mainly but not exclusively on the earlier part of Collins's writing life.

Table 4.1 Journal articles by Wilkie Collins not listed in the *Cambridge Bibliography of English Literature* (3rd edn, 1999)

Leader*

'The New Dragon of Wantley: A Social Revelation' (Portfolio), 20 December 1851, 1213–4.

Review of 'Le Prophète' (The Arts), 10 June 1854, 547.

Review of 'Le Bijou Perdu' (The Arts), 10 June 1854, 547–8.

Review of 'Grisi in Lucrezia Borgia' (The Arts), 17 June 1854, 572.

Review of 'Sunshine through the Clouds' (The Arts), 17 June 1854, 572–3.

Review of 'A Batch of New Books' (Literature), 24 June 1854, 593–4.

Review of 'The German Exhibition' (The Arts), 24 June 1854, 596.

Brief untitled notice of 'operatic matters' (The Arts), 1 July 1854, 619.

Untitled paragraph on 'dearth of literary enterprise' abroad (Literature Summary), 15 July 1854, 665.

Untitled paragraphs on the drama in Paris and Munch (Literature Summary), 22 July 1854, 687–8.

'Miscellenea' (Literature), 20 January 1855, 65–7.

Review of 'The Easter Pieces' (The Arts), 14 April 1855, 357.

Review of 'A Batch of Books' (Literature), 28 April 1855, 403.

Review of 'The Royal Academy Exhibition' (The Arts), 4 pts, 5–26 May 1855, 428–9, 452, 475–6, 500.

Review of 'Haymarket Theatre' (The Arts), 12 May 1855, 453.

Chambers's Journal[†]

'A National Wrong' (with James Payn), 12 February 1870, 107–10.

Youth's Companion[‡]

'The Hidden Cash' ('Victims of Circumstances' III), 21 April 1887, 178.

Attributions:

[*]See Wilkie Collins, *The New Dragon of Wantley*, ed. Graham Law (London: Wilkie Collins Society, 2007). This list includes only those items for which there is some form of documentary evidence of authorship and is thus highly unlikely to be comprehensive.

[†]See James Payn & Wilkie Collins, *A National Wrong*, ed. Andrew Gasson, Graham Law, & Paul Lewis (London: Wilkie Collins Society, 2004).

[‡]See Wilkie Collins, *The Victims of Circumstances*, ed. Graham Law (London: Wilkie Collins Society, 2002).

* * * * *

Collins began to publish regularly in periodicals around 1851–2, during which period he became a frequent contributor not only to *Bentley's Miscellany* (1837–68), but also to the *Leader* (1850–60) and *Household Words* (1850–9). Though it ran over a parallel period to Dickens's first miscellany, the *Leader* was in fact the odd one out, and in more than one sense. While *Bentley's Miscellany* was an illustrated monthly and *Household Words* a twopenny-plain weekly, both had the format of a magazine with miscellaneous contents, including a good deal of fiction, but excluding news. The *Leader*, on the other hand, was a weekly news-paper and thus had to pay the stamp tax up until 1855, when it was abolished: it gave most of its space to the 'News of the Week' together with commentary on it by both editors and readers, in the 'Public Affairs' and 'Open Council' columns. There were normally substantial review sections on 'Literature' and 'The Arts', plus an occasional 'Portfolio' of poetry and literary essays, but not much in the way of fiction. Exceptions here were Harriet Martineau's series of utilitarian fables, 'Sketches from Life' (1850–1), J.A. Froude's children's tale, 'Cat's

Pilgrimage' (June–July 1851), and perhaps a comic or melodramatic tale in the Christmas issue. Moreover, with Thornton Hunt and G.H. Lewes as its leading lights, the *Leader* was a radical organ, committed to socialism, secularism, and rationalism. Priced at sixpence, the paper was obviously beyond the economic reach of most proletarian readers, but there was a regular column expressing solidarity with 'Organizations of the People'. *Bentley's Miscellany* and *Household Words*, on the other hand, were never more extreme than liberal reformist. In fact, Bentley's financial difficulties in the early 1850s meant that, in order to avoid alienating potential conservative readers, his house magazine exhibited even more political soft-pedal than usual. And, while Dickens was perhaps at his most socially committed in the 1850s, as John Hollingshead put it, 'he was swayed by every breath of feeling and sentiment. He was a Liberal by impulse, and what the "DRYASDUST" school [Carlyle's derisive term for utilitarian] would have called a "wobbler"'.[1] Arguably, much the same could be said of Collins himself.

In all likelihood, Collins never contributed to the political departments of the *Leader*, and all his early contributions were in the 'Portfolio'. Even his first essay, 'A Plea for Sunday Reform', was hardly as sympathetic to a secular viewpoint as the title suggests; its principal demand was for enlightened entertainment for the poor on the Sabbath, in the form of open public galleries in the afternoon and free sacred concerts in the evening, with the aim of cultivating 'tastes and faculties which God has given to man to exercise; and which are, therefore, fit tastes for God's day'.[2] Soon afterwards, as mentioned in Chapter 1, Collins produced 'Magnetic Evenings at Home', the series of sensational accounts of the powers of mesmerism, based on experiments witnessed at a private house in Somerset at New Year, 1852. G.H. Lewes, who commissioned the articles, responded with marked scepticism. One of Collins's main points in favour of the mesmerist was the inegalitarian assumption that the experiments had been conducted by 'a gentleman of honour and integrity, whose position placed him above the slightest imputation of acting from a motive of personal advantage'.[3] Under the influence of the French positivist Auguste Comte, Lewes admitted that hypnotism could induce coma, but rejected the validity of clairvoyance. He was less interested, though, in the risk of charlatanism on the part of the mesmerizer than in the psychological suggestibility of the medium, concluding that 'the fallacy of clairvoyance is ... the interpretation of a *dreaming* power as a *seeing* power'.[4] While both authors claimed an objective stance in the face of these phenomena, they were clearly separated by a gulf both temperamental and philosophical. These tensions came to a head in February 1852 in correspondence with its editor, Edward Pigott, where Collins objected strongly to 'certain doctrines of *"Leader" religion'*, as evidenced by contributions by Thornton Hunt and others which he judged to be blasphemous. He concluded with a resounding personal credo: 'I am neither a Protestant, a Catholic – or a Dissenter – I do not desire to discuss this or that particular creed; but I believe Jesus Christ to be the son of God' (B&C I, 83–6).[5] Although Collins remained on friendly terms with Pigott – the two were soon to become keen sailing companions – for a period of around two years he seems to have submitted nothing at all to the *Leader*.

What happened next confirms that there were ideological tensions not only between Collins and the paper, but also between Pigott and his fellow editors. In mid-1854, the *Leader* office was shaken by rumours, soon to be confirmed, that Hunt had long been the sexual partner of Lewes's wife, Agnes, had had more than one child by her with the husband's sanction, and that Lewes himself was now cohabiting with Marian Evans, subeditor of the *Westminster Review*, and the young woman who would soon become famous as the novelist 'George Eliot'. Despite his own unconventional liaison formed only a few years later, Collins was indignant with Lewes in particular, advising Pigott to extricate himself as soon as possible from such 'a dangerous and degrading connection' (BGLL I, 106–7). When Lewes and Evans escaped from the scandal to Germany, Pigott, who came from a wealthy Somerset family and had had financial control of the paper since late 1851, was left not only to deal with the fallout but also to find a replacement for his most active reviewer. (To make matters worse, Pigott's older brother Henry had recently shown symptoms of severe mental illness, eventually leading to his death in a lunatic asylum in January 1858.) Collins immediately stepped in, mainly out of sympathy for Pigott, but perhaps also with the aim of boosting his own earnings after receipts from *Hide and Seek* had fallen below expectations. He began to act as a regular reviewer for the paper, covering in fairly equal measure not only literature and the theatre, but also the visual arts. As we saw in Chapter 2, this was a task which he had already performed at *Bentley's Miscellany* for a few months back in the summer of 1851. In late 1854 when Pigott was away in Paris on business, Collins even seems temporarily to have taken on editorial responsibility, just as he was to do with *All the Year Round* in late 1867, while Dickens was on his reading tour of America. At the *Leader*, the role of reviewer lasted something over a year, with a gap in the late summer of 1854 when Collins was staying with Dickens at Folkestone, and ending only after Lewes returned from the Continent and resumed reviewing duties. This year or so of journeyman work at the *Leader* – once more covering the Royal Academy Exhibition in a series of weekly reports, and frequently 'doing' a batch of books, or two or three theatrical performances – clearly stood the author in good stead when he joined the editorial staff of *Household Words* in the autumn of 1856.

* * * * *

By the mid-1850s, Collins's offerings to Dickens's weekly miscellany had already shifted from short tales to non-fiction. Collins wrote around fifty such pieces before he resigned from the *All the Year Round* editorial staff at the beginning of 1862; thereafter he contributed only a handful, the last probably being 'The Dead Lock in Italy'. This was a report on the progress towards Italian unification, sent back from Rome in November 1866 during the course of a Continental tour with Edward Pigott. Only a minority of these journal contributions, however, take the conventional form or the discursive essay of review, criticism, biography, or history. Examples here might be 'Portrait of an Author, Painted by his Publisher' (reviewing Edmond Werdet's *Portrait Intime de Balzac*), 'To Think or be Thought For' (a critique of British art criticism), 'Douglas Jerrold' (an affectionate sketch based on the biography by his son Blanchard), and 'The Poisoned Meal' (the record of a criminal case illustrating the 'corruptions of society in France before the Revolution'),[6] all reprinted in *My Miscellanies*. Yet even here there is a discernable tendency towards personalization and/or dramatization of the theme. More typically, the criminal or historical incidents that Collins classifies in *My Miscellanies* as 'Cases Worth Looking At' or 'Nooks and Corners of History' unashamedly take the shape of tales of mystery and sensation. Themes previously treated conventionally, such as the notice of an exhibition or the record of a journey, reappear in parodic form as humorous personal anecdotes, as in 'The Royal Academy in Bed' or 'My Black Mirror'. Even serious literary subjects, such as the emergence of a mass audience (in 'The Unknown Public'), or the debased state of English drama (in 'Dramatic Grub Street'), are dealt with ironically in the first person, or through an imaginary dialogue, while the political report on 'The Dead Lock in Italy' takes the form of a letter from an Englishman visiting Rome, to an Italian exile in London. Most typical, however, are the dramatic comic monologues that Collins creates to draw 'Sketches of Character', evoke 'Fragments of Personal Experience', or air 'Social Grievances'. Representative cases would be 'Pray Employ Major Namby' (a cry from the heart of a single lady beseiged by a noisy military neighbour), 'Laid Up in Lodgings' (an autobiographical account of encounters with female servants in Paris and London), and 'A Petition to the Novel Writers' (an elderly gentleman's complaint against the man-hating heroines of contemporary fiction), all again selected to reappear in *My Miscellanies*. In other words, the bulk of Collins's articles in Dickens's miscellanies belongs to that broad grey zone between journalism and fiction. Though the form of the comic monologue clearly owes a good deal to the Inimitable Boz, Collins had made his first experiments here in 'The New Dragon of Wantley' (*Leader*, 20 December 1851) or the more familiar 'Passage in the Life of Perugino Potts' (*Bentley's Miscellany*, February 1852). The former is a recently identified anecdote narrated by an eccentric amateur naturalist in a rural parish, where the inhabitants have been terrorized by his escaped reptile. What is interesting here is that the butt of the humour is less the mediaeval fears of the villagers than the modernizing obsession of the narrator, so that the story comes close to parodying the radical earnestness of the *Leader*, in its call 'for an immediate supply of Missionaries of the Brotherhood of Common Sense to convert Stoke Muddleton'.[7]

The key point concerning Collins's non-fiction contributions to Dickens's weekly miscellanies is that there is little evidence of tensions with the dominant editorial line. The only Collins piece to be rejected by Boz seems to have been the melodramatic tale 'Mad Monkton' in 1853, because its theme of hereditary insanity had the potential to offend 'those numerous families in which there is such a taint'; at the same time, Dickens let Collins know that there were 'many things, both in the inventive and descriptive way, that he could do for us if he would like to work in our direction' (to W.H. Wills, Pilgrim VII, 23). As discussed in Chapter 3, though *Household Words* claimed to serve 'All Classes of Readers', the circulation suggests that few were in fact purchased in working-class districts. Certainly the audience imagined throughout Collins's articles seems consistent with the 'known reading public' described in 'The Unknown Public'. Where overt sympathy with working-class characters is expressed in the dramatic monologues, it tends to be directed towards the type of vulnerable young female servant encountered in 'Laid Up in Lodgings'; much shorter shrift is given to older specimens such as the monthly nurse 'Mrs Bullwinkle', whose omnivorous appetite threatens to bankrupt her long-suffering employer. The social grievances which obsess Collins's comic monologists are also a far cry from the reforms demanded by the Chartists. Here, a typical example is 'Strike!', a piece from February 1858 never reprinted by the author. Speaking for and to 'Englishmen of the middle classes', the narrator complains that, while they have fought hard for 'the promotion of religious and political reforms', they put up too easily with social grievances.[8] Beginning with an anecdote about how the residents of a small English town combined to defeat the exorbitance of a monopolistic fishmonger, he demands similar actions to have communication cords installed in trains, to improve the comfort of both the London omnibus and the London theatre, and to reduce the costs of private education. Given the frequency with which these calls are repeated in Dickens's papers, by both Collins and others, it is clear that the irony works with rather than against the speaker.

Overall, we must conclude that the degree of investment in the genre of the comic monologue in Collins's articles for *Household Words* and *All the Year Round* tends to work against intense participation in projects of social reform. This is especially noticeable in comparison with the tone of Collins's journalism in later decades. While it is true that the author contributed relatively few articles to periodicals after the mid-1860s, and a number of those take the amicable form of personal reminiscences, there are also several extremely aggressive pieces on the rights of authors, where the humour is much more dark and bitter. Most notable here are 'A National Wrong' (with James Payn in *Chambers's Journal*, 12 February 1870) and 'Considerations on the Copyright Question' (in the New York *International Review*, June 1880), a pair of attacks on the 'piracy' of American publishers in the absence of relevant international copyright agreements.

* * * * *

In writing of Collins short fiction we prefer to avoid using the term 'short story', because, in Britain at least, the phrase did not come into common use until late in the nineteenth century, when it was associated with the aesthetics of early modernism, with its preference for realism, irony, and compression. Around this time, there appeared a number of articles claiming convincingly that the form had originated in America, where short narratives of local colour had long been popular.[9] Yet there was clearly no shortage of British shorter fiction earlier in the Victorian period, especially in general periodicals aimed at a family audience, where such narratives often functioned as fillers between the runs of full-length serial novels, though they were occasionally given pride of place in their own right. There the term 'tale' was still generally used for self-contained narratives which often recalled the oral traditions of pre-industrial society, with their distinctly gothic flavour and regular recourse to the first and second person. Tales of the supernatural told around the fireside on long dark nights are perhaps naturally associated with the mid-winter period. But there are also cultural and economic reasons for the powerful association between Victorian tales and Christmas as a domestic institution. John Plunkett's work on Queen Victoria as the first 'Media Monarch' shows how important the press then was in melding the concepts of the bourgeois family and the nation state,[10] while Simon Eliot's bibliometric research on nineteenth-century publishing trends makes it clear how and why the Christmas period emerges as the climax of the publishing year in the early Victorian decades.[11] Eliot summarizes:

> The creation of the Christmas card, the introduction of the Christmas tree and the other traditions associated with Germany (partly through the influence of the Prince Consort), the sequence of Dickens's Christmas stories ... all had their rise in the 1830s and 1840s. As these innovations coincided almost exactly with the emergence of the October-December season as the largest book-issuing period, it would be most improbable if these were not ... causally connected.[12]

Dickens's massive contribution both to the invention of the family Christmas and to the emergence of mass-circulation journals was thus determined not just by his talent and personality, but also by the fact that his literary and editorial projects so neatly encapsulated the spirit of the times.

Regardless of where precisely we draw the line between non-fiction and fiction, it remains true that during his career Collins contributed over fifty tales to periodicals, of which the majority also appeared during the 1850s and 1860s in Dickens's family miscellanies, *Household Words* and *All the Year Round*, both in ordinary issues and in the special Christmas numbers. Following his reading tour of America in the winter of 1873–4, however, Collins also began to provide an annual series of tales for the Christmas holiday issue of the popular New York sporting weekly, *The Spirit of the Times*. This series formed the core of his last collection of shorter fiction, *Little Novels* (1887). It is also true that the majority of Collins's shorter works of fiction were published first at the festive season and have more than a hint of gothic. The first clear-cut example, though, was 'The Twin Sisters', which appeared in *Bentley's Miscellany* in March 1851, but remained among the dozen or more tales that were never reprinted during the author's lifetime. Though this

apprentice effort is in many ways untypical – it has a contemporary setting and is written in the third-person – it does announce one of
Collins's most consistent gothic themes, that of the *doppelgänger* or
double, represented here by the wrong identical twin to whom the hero
at first proposes. As Catherine Peters notes, Collins prefigures Robert
Louis Stevenson in his use of 'the double in investigations of the
shadow-self: the underside of a personality which compensates for inadequacies in the external persona, or, suppressed or denied full expression, takes revenge in unexpected ways' (Peters, 92).

   Yet, even after Collins began to offer his tales to Dickens in the 1850s
and write for the special Christmas numbers of the magazine, there
were a number of stories that did not appear in *Household Words*. One,
as we have seen, was the rejected 'Mad Monkton'; another was 'The
Siege of the Black Cottage', first issued in February 1857 in New York in
Harper's New Monthly Magazine. This is the short, dramatic story of the
bravery of a poor stone-mason's daughter, narrated by the woman herself. The main events take place when the eighteen-year-old Bessie is left
alone at night in an isolated cottage, and acts with unexpected courage
and ingenuity to protect a large sum of money, left in her care by a
wealthy neighbour, from a violent gang of ruffians. But there is also a
frame narrative, where the adult Bessie, now married to a rich gentle-
men-farmer, explains to a young visitor how her social advancement
came about as an indirect reward for her energetic performance under
siege. The tale's underlying theme is thus a questioning of the conventionally assigned class and gender roles of the mid-Victorian period.

   It is significant but not surprising that this story has often been mistakenly attributed to Elizabeth Gaskell, by both nineteenth-century
indexers and twentieth-century scholars.[13] Collins and Gaskell's careers
as writers of tales run in parallel fashion to a remarkable extent. Both
made early appearances in monthly journals edited by others (Gaskell
in *Howitt's Journal* and Collins in *Bentley's Miscellany*, most notably),
defected later to more prestigious and remunerative venues such as
Smith, Elder's *Cornhill*, but in between remained very faithful to
Dickens's cheap weekly miscellanies. In Gaskell's case this phase
spanned from 'Lizzie Leigh' (*HW*, 30 March 1850, the first number) to
'Crowley Castle' (*AYR*, Christmas 1863); in Collins's from 'A Terribly
Strange Bed' (*HW*, 24 April 1852) to a share in *No Thoroughfare* (*AYR*,
Christmas 1867). Within these periods, among the most telling were the
tales appearing in the extra Christmas numbers. In total, there were
seventeen such issues, published continuously from 1851 to 1867.
Gaskell appeared in five, though in the initial two cases, *A Round of*

Stories by the Christmas Fire (*HW*, 1852) and *Another Round of Stories* ... (*HW*, 1853), as the titles suggest, there was no frame narrative or unifying concept other than that of Yuletide itself. Collins appeared in a total of nine, all with strong conceptual frameworks, including eight consecutively from 1854–61, and in two cases – *The Perils of Certain English Prisoners* (*HW*, 1857), and *No Thoroughfare* – the work was co-authored by Dickens and Collins alone. The processes involved have been analysed in detail by Lillian Nayder in *Unequal Partners* (2002), her study of collaborations between the two authors. But it can also be argued that Gaskell and Collins were themselves literary collaborators, since both contributed to not only 'A House to Let' (1858) but also 'The Haunted House' (1859) – respectively the last Christmas number of *Household Words*, and the first of *All the Year Round*. Moreover, during the 1850s at least, even those works of shorter fiction by Gaskell and Collins that were *not* subject to Dickens's control as editor reveal his influence to a remarkable extent. Though neither was to repeat the experiment, both Gaskell's *The Moorland Cottage* (1850) and Collins's *Mr Wray's Cash-Box* (1852) are apprentice Christmas books, which follow the format popularized by the master Boz in his series beginning with *A Christmas Carol* back in 1842. Again, in the later 1850s, when both authors began to gather their shorter tales from periodicals into collections for book publication, the model was clearly the Dickens Christmas number with its elaborate narrative framework. In 1859, Gaskell's *Round the Sofa* employed the device of a weekly *soirée* at the residence of a doctor in Edinburgh's Old Town to recontextualize six of her previously published tales. Issued in the same year, Collins's second collection, *The Queen of Hearts*, makes use of the Sheherazade-like conceit of an elderly lawyer and his two brothers spinning stories to detain his beautiful young ward, so that his absent son will have time to return from the Crimean War to claim her heart. Included there among the ten reprinted tales was the one from *Harper's Monthly*, now under the title 'Brother Owen's Story of the Black Cottage', though the original frame of Bessie's address to the young visitor had been stripped away.

However, when we look more closely at the parallel outputs of shorter fiction from the pens of Gaskell and Collins, it is clear that there are significant differences of literary form alongside the similarities of publishing format. The most striking disparities concern the degree of tension with the models laid down by Dickens, the general point being that Gaskell typically displays a good deal more resistance than Collins. Let us look again at our examples. Regarding the early Christmas books, Collins's *Mr Wray's Cash-Box*, with its urban setting, gothic cast of eccentrics, wry humour, and sentimental ending, is far more in keeping with the Dickensian Yuletide spirit than Gaskell's *The Moorland Cottage*, where the *dénouement*, with its symbolic drowning and resuscitation of the heroine, seems more in the Easter vein. In the case of the collections of tales, Gaskell's narrative framework in *Round the Sofa* is far more perfunctory, accounting for only 3 per cent of the total word count as opposed to 18 per cent in the case of Collins's *The Queen of Hearts*. In correspondence with a friend, Gaskell wrote off her own flimsy construction: 'You will be seeing a book of mine advertized; but don't be diddled about it; it is only a REpublication of H W Stories; I have a rascally publisher this time ... & he is trying to pass it off as new.'[14] In contrast, Collins was outraged when the *Athenaeum* reviewer dismissed his collection as merely a reprint from *Household Words*, stoutly defending the new narrative framework: 'If the critic in question will be so obliging as to open the book, he may make acquaintance with three stories ... which he has not met with before in Household Words, or in any other English periodical whatever; and he will, moreover, find the whole collection of stories connected by an entirely new thread of interest ...' (BGLL I, 181).

Perhaps the most telling cases, though, are found in those special Christmas narratives to which both Gaskell and Collins contributed. Here the varying levels of resistance are obviously related to the fact that, as a woman, Gaskell was excluded from any editorial role in Dickens's journals, whereas Collins was a paid member of staff at the period in question. In 'A House to Let', Collins's 'Trotter's Report', with its focus on the restoration of the lost boy, not only reinforces Dickens's theme of the gift of the Christ child, but is also committed to the narrative frame (constructed together by the two men) to such an extent that it cannot stand independently as a short tale: in his introduction to *The Complete Shorter Fiction* Julian Thompson notes that 'Trotle's Report' belongs to a group of contributions to Christmas numbers 'not ... sufficiently self-contained to merit reprinting here' (Thompson, xiii). In contrast, Gaskell's contribution, 'The Manchester Marriage', one of her most anthologized tales, remains almost entirely independent of the frame and again more strongly evokes the spirit of Easter, with its *dénouement* in the sacrificial death of the first husband, Frank Wilson, and the consequent redemption of the second, the Manchester man Openshaw. Moreover, the sympathetic treatment of Openshaw can be interpreted as a second response to Dickens's intemperate assault on 'dryasdust' Manchester values in the person of Gradgrind in *Hard Times*, which Gaskell's *North and South* had succeeded as a serial in the columns of *Household Words*. A similar argument could perhaps be made about 'Blow Up with the Brig!' and 'The Crooked Branch', the contributions by Collins and Gaskell respectively to 'The Haunted House'. In this case, however, we will focus instead on the editor's reaction, as reflected in the frame narrative itself, which in this case was constructed single-handedly by Dickens. There, as noted in Chapter 2 with regard to George Sala, each of the fictional house guests to tell a story is given a persona that parodies the personality of the real contributing author, and thus reveals his or her identity to those in the know – with the marked exception of Gaskell herself. Feminist versifier Adelaide Anne Procter, for example, becomes 'Belinda Bates, ... [who] has a fine genius for poetry, ... and "goes in" for Woman's mission ...', while the stocky sailing fanatic Collins, becomes 'one "Nat Beaver", ... with a thick-set wooden face and figure, and ... a world of watery experience'. Gaskell, in contrast, appears in the guise of Dickens's lawyer Frederick Ouvry: 'Mr Undery, my friend and solicitor: who came down, in an amateur capacity, ... and who plays whist better than the whole Law List ...'. In thus symbolically excluding her from the group around the Christmas fire, Dickens must have been signalling his awareness of and annoyance at Gaskell's efforts to resist his narrative schemes.

Seen in this context, the confusion over the authorship of 'The Siege of the Black Cottage' becomes more comprehensible and enlightening. Though they tended to negotiate them in different ways, Gaskell and Collins clearly shared many of the same constraints as writers – and especially as writers of shorter fiction – whether from the prevailing print culture of the mid-Victorian era in general or specifically due to their dependence on Dickens.

* * * * *

Finally, two more general conclusions. First, that Collins's extensive work as a journalist from the early 1850s clearly provided a good training ground in the innovative mix of story-telling techniques – first-hand narration, private correspondence, the personal diary, public documents, and the rest – that the author was to exploit so successfully on a grand scale in *The Woman in White* and the other major sensation novels of the 1860s. As we have seen, many of these devices were explored not only in the shorter works of fiction, and the frame-narratives in which they were later enclosed, but also in his even more varied output of personalized and dramatized journal articles. Second, that Collins's sense of the social mission of the writer clearly did not appear quite so suddenly and unexpectedly as has sometimes been suggested.

Looking closely at the author's earlier journalistic productions, it is clear that Collins was not averse to taking up causes in his writings of the 1850s and 1860s. But there it was channelled to a large extent away from the novels themselves, whereas, in the later decades, when he ceased to contribute articles so regularly to periodicals, his social concerns seemed to have followed the course of least resistance and flowed naturally into the later fiction. We will return to this topic in more detail in Chapter 8.

5
Collins and London

London is the main setting for several of Collins's novels, and in this chapter we will examine three of the most striking. These texts – *Basil* (1852), *Hide and Seek* (1854), and *The Woman in White* (1860) – can also be taken as representative of Collins's novelistic work in the first decade of his career, demonstrating his early attempts to push the boundaries of what was deemed 'proper' to mid-Victorian readers and reviewers. Both *Basil* and *Hide and Seek* can loosely be classified as *bildungsromans* (novels of personal development), but they are also mystery novels involving the uncovering of family secrets. *The Woman in White* is what we would today recognize as a detective story or thriller, but like *Basil* it uses some of the tropes of the novel of horror to expose the darker side of 1850s England. The 'great world of London' (*DS*, 220) in which each of these novels is principally set was also where Collins lived and worked for most of his life. Born in New Cavendish Street, Marylebone, and dying less than quarter of a mile away at 82 Wimpole Street, he rarely resided more than a few steps from the south-west corner of Regent's Park. London was, he always felt, his natural habitat, a place where, in 'the mighty vitality of the great city' (*B*, 49), his writing career could best develop.

All the same, the author's novels typically give us double-edged view of the capital. Collins's London may not have the idiosyncratic detail and atmosphere of Dickens's, but the city is nonetheless present as a distinct environment full of meaning. In particular, London is a stronghold of English civilization but also a place that is vulnerable to attack and a site of personal danger. Some later novels – notably *Armadale* and *The Moonstone* – convey this in lurid ways, starting off in the strange and alien worlds of the West Indies or India, but going on to depict how these events have inexorable consequences in the supposedly impregnable centre of the modern world. Showing the terrifying eruption of spectres of monstrosity, Collins uses many of the conventions of what we have come to recognize as gothic writing. However, Collins's texts differ from late eighteenth-century manifestations of the gothic novel, in which horrible crimes and sinister plots are kept at a safe distance by their exotic location. Collins's fictions, which critics have sometimes labelled 'urban gothic' but which are more commonly called 'sensation novels', describe the intrusion of the monstrous much closer to home. They thus reveal what Henry James famously termed 'those most mysterious of mysteries, the mysteries which are at our own doors ... the terrors of the cheerful country house and the busy London lodgings ... infinitely the more terrible'.[1] When the mysterious woman in white taps Walter Hartright on the shoulder on the moonlit Finchley Road, he describes how 'every drop of blood in my body was brought to a stop' (*WW*, 20). Walter's initial reaction is one of blind terror, followed by puzzlement at discovering that this young girl is not a streetwalker but is being chased through the city's respectable streets by the keepers of a private lunatic asylum. It is not sixteenth-century Italy but nineteenth-century London that is the site of this persecution. Walter's bemused attitude is significant, for as Count Fosco later points out, while the Englishman is 'quickest ... at finding out faults that are his neighbours', he is 'the slowest ... at finding out the faults that are his own'. Walter thinks Fosco is the monstrous 'barbarian' at the gate but the Count's point is that he is only the catalyst that allows latent monstrosity to emerge: the monster is already there, lurking within the civilized English character itself (*WW*, 238).

Collins's own dreams of metropolitan life were well satisfied. He knew almost everyone worth knowing in the capital's glittering worlds of art, literature, and the theatre. As we have seen, in his youth he mixed with up-and-coming painters from the Royal Academy, and his early professional life was spent among the influential set congregating at the offices of *Household Words*, in Wellington Street, off the Strand. He was thus part of Dickens's glamorous Tavistock House group and took part in their famed amateur theatricals, performing before the Queen on 16 May 1851. He attended social events at the houses of millionaire Sir Francis Goldsmid or Angela Burdett Coutts, rumoured to be the richest woman in Britain. As an adult he lived in a succession of comfortable homes, replete with servants, in respectable West End locations: with his mother principally at Blandford Square, Hanover Terrace, and Harley Place, and on his own account at New Cavendish Street, Harley Street, Melcombe Place, Gloucester Place, and finally Wimpole Street.

It was a fine life, with plenty of champagne and caviar. But London was also the natural habitat for a man with a secret life. 'I can feel safe from discovery nowhere but in London', announces a character in *The Dead Secret* and Collins seems to have agreed (*DS*, 220). This second life inevitably led him to less salubrious addresses, such as Howland Street, off Tottenham Court Road, where he took lodgings with Caroline Graves, 'the (female) skeleton' in his closet, as Dickens dubbed her (Pilgrim IX, 388–90), or Bolsover Street, where he installed Martha Rudd as 'Mrs Dawson', and where she gave birth to his two daughters.

Of course, Collins's wanderings in the metropolis made him aware of far lower depths: later in life he noted that London was 'the city of social contrasts' with 'the mansion and the hovel ... neighbours in situation' (*ISN*, 51). Indeed, few people could shut their eyes to the fact that under the trappings of civilization there existed 'a world of shadows', camouflaging a crude barbarism (*TD*, 116). Events such as the 1849 trial and public execution of Frederick and Maria Manning for the murder of their lodger, the transportation in 1857 of Frederick Redpath for embezzling funds from the new underground railway, the trial of nurse Catherine Wilson in 1862, which revealed her as a mass poisoner, or the imprisonment in 1868 of 'Madame' Rachel Leverson, whose New Bond Street beauty parlour was exposed as a front for fraud, abortion, and blackmail, put on display the underside of upright prosperous Britain celebrated at the Great Exhibition of 1851.[2] Some suggested that modern urban living was making the population progressively susceptible to both disease and a tainted moral environment, which made itself felt in the population's inability to resist the lure of sensuality or crime. This new 'condition of England', 'progress and decline ... strangely mixed' as John Ruskin put it,[3] prompted questions in the daily and periodical press about what appeared to be a swelling social and moral decadence.[4] 'We seem to be going back to the morality of the last century', complained one *Times* correspondent: 'Illicit connexion is no longer called adultery, but a "temporary engagement" ... robbery is called "defalcation."'[5] Moreover, as a writer for the *Lancet* pointed out in 1861, it was not only the working classes who were afflicted by these morbid conditions. 'Are not', he asked, 'the aristocracy and the care-worn citizens of the city, anxious, eager, depressed, with soul and body intent on business and breathing all day long pestilential exhalations, subject to them too?'[6]

Collins's novels thus convey some of the strains generated by contradictions at work at the 'heart of empire': a widespread sense that progress was ushering in a modernity which conflicted with long-held cultural values – stability, integrity, patriotism, moral uprightness. While his own background was, he admitted, that of a son of a '"high Tory" and sincerely religious man' (B&C II, 541), Collins liked to declare himself a radical in spirit at least, with no time for 'wretched English claptrap'.[7] He was also prone to announcing himself a spokesman against hypocrisy and smugness, particularly as represented by 'the great middle class of our British population' (*HS*, 28). He regularly mocks his countrymen and their insularity via characters such as the steward Betteredge in *The Moonstone*:

> ... here was our quiet English house suddenly invaded by a devilish Indian Diamond – bringing after it a conspiracy of living rogues, set loose on us by the vengeance of a dead man ... Whoever heard the like of it – in the nineteenth century, mind; in an age of progress, and in a country which rejoices in the blessings of the British constitution?
>
> (*M*, 88)

Collins's texts thus tap into a growing 1850s sense of cultural malaise and, like gothic novels more generally, they do so in a way designed to shock. As the *Athenaeum* noted in 1866, he is part-satirist in that his work is invariably shot through with attempts to 'lay bare the "blotches and blains"' which polite society likes to keep hidden (cited in Page, 147).

Collins is interested, too, in the relationship between the past and the present and with the implications of the past for 'civilized' Europeans, including the possibility that modern nations could regress as well as progress. His work thus contains traces of the popular degenerationalist anthropology starting to emerge in the 1850s. Moreover, fears about the bestial heritage of humanity, atavism, criminality, and insanity are all underlined by an often-nightmarish vision of the capital city, which represents a civilization threatened by the encroachment of the primitive forces of the uncivilized world and the repressed unconscious looming up out of the darkness – 'its evil ripening ... impenetrably veiled', as Basil terms it (*B*, 178). As David Glover points out: 'London was the symbolic in ... Victorian and Edwardian imaginaries where boundaries threatened to dissolve.'[8] Collins draws attention to his characters' positions within a changing social structure in a changing city; he follows not only those who succeed but those who fail and are consumed by modern life. In *Basil*, the eponymous hero's ruin is charted within a Darwinian frame of reference, with its focus on the brutal side of mercantile culture embodying not only the 'vampyres that suck the life of London' (*B*, 48), but also a more modern kind of urban savagery present in the new suburbs. This is then extended in *The Woman in White* – a text with more than its share of 'primeval' men and 'wild' 'primitives'. Collins thus uses familiar London landmarks – the Zoological Gardens, Hyde Park, Oxford Street, Chancery Lane, and Regent's Park – not only to create a sense of 'place', but also to suggest the kinds of civilized values under attack.

* * * * *

Until recently, *Basil* had received little critical attention. There are, nevertheless, good reasons for studying the novel, not least for the way in which it rehearses the main concerns of Collins's later and better-known work. Notable are the challenges to identity, sanity, and selfhood posed by unscrupulous relatives and scheming acquaintances, the disjunction between appearance and reality, particularly in middle-class homes, plus the suggestion that violence is not confined to the rough London streets but forms part of the fabric of suburbia. As Catherine Peters notes, the novel shows 'the shadow side of the commonplace', making the sites and silences of the half-built London suburbs seem eerie and sinister (Peters, 118). In this respect *Basil* can be seen as an early example of the sensation novel – that scandalous sub-genre of realist fiction beginning to flood the market in the mid-nineteenth century, its popularity in part the result of a titillating treatment of the 'counterworld' of Victorian life.[9] This is a narrative form which Collins is sometimes (mistakenly) credited with inventing single-handedly. Yet two novels published in 1855, Noell Radecliffe's aptly titled *The Secret History of a Household* and Caroline Clive's story *Paul Ferroll* of an outwardly respectable man who has murdered his wife, both created a bigger stir than *Basil*. And all three had been preceded by Sophia Crawford's bigamy novel of 1851, *A Double Marriage*, its topicality cemented with a key scene set in the Great Exhibition, or, of course, Edward Bulwer Lytton's *Lucretia*, loosely based on the career of the forger and poisoner Thomas Wainwright, which had scandalized readers as early as 1846.

Subtitled 'A Story of Modern Life', whilst, *Basil* was indeed the first Collins novel with a contemporary setting and a realistic approach: before publication Richard Bentley had insisted that the narrative be toned down – cleaned up is perhaps a more accurate description – in a number of places (BGLL I, 80). On the hand, the publisher did arrange for his house magazine, *Bentley's Miscellany*, to review the new work provocatively alongside Thackeray's recent historical romance *Henry Esmond*:

> We have put these two books 'over-against' each other ... because they have no kind of family resemblance. ... There is the same difference between them as between a picture by Hogarth and a picture by Fuseli. ... 'Basil' – although a story of to-day, although all its accidental environments are of the most ordinary character, although the scene is laid in a scarce-finished suburban square (say Brompton or Camden Town), although some of the personages are nothing more romantic than London linen-drapers ... is a story remarkable for nothing so much as its intensity – for the powerful excitement it must provoke in every breast ... It is a story of love and hatred ... The *intense* everywhere predominates. It is of the Godwin school of fiction. A single grand idea runs through the whole. There is a striking unity of purpose and action in it ... The fatality of the Greek tragedians broods over the drama. There is a Nemesis not to be escaped. The hero of the tale sees a pretty girl in an omnibus; and he – goes to his doom.[10]

Although it could be cited as an example of a publisher's 'puff', as a summary of the contents of Collins's novel, this notice is pretty shrewd. The review opens with an acknowledgment of the novel's modernity ('a story of to-day') and a suggestion that Collins is the true recorder of contemporary life, just as Thackeray is the chronicler of 'olde-England'. The references to Fuseli suggest the book's disturbing tone, but put together with references to Greek tragedy ('fatality ... Nemesis') imply that this is a sophisticated book for educated grown-ups. The reference to the Romantic free-thinker William Godwin is designed to prompt remembrance of *Caleb Williams*, Godwin's pioneering detective novel of 1794, but also suggests that this new work carries a similar challenge to contemporary thinking – philosophically as well as morally. *Basil* certainly tells of tragic flaws, of sexual obsession, of revenge, of murder, of the past returning to haunt the present. Other dominant themes in the novel include the problems of inter-class relations, the isolation of individuals, the difficulty of 'knowing' the other, the destructive power of sexual attraction, the prevalence of marital cruelty – what Collins describes as 'those ghastly heart-tragedies ... which are acted and re-acted, scene by scene, and year by year, in the secret theatre of home' (*B*, 75–7).

In a letter of dedication addressed to Edward Ward, Collins also states tantalizingly that the story was founded on 'a fact within my knowledge', and that the course of the story was guided 'by my own experience, or by experience related to me by others ...' (*B*, xxxix). Some biographers have suggested that the basis for this 'experience' may have been Collins's own private life, or that of his worrying younger brother Charles – rumoured to have got himself entangled with a working-class woman. Irrespective of this, the novel's eponymous hero is a recognizable literary type – obvious forerunners are the naïve heroes of Walter Scott, such as Edward Waverley in *Waverley* (1814), or Dickens's David Copperfield (1850), another young man who puts pen to paper in order to try and make sense of a disturbing past and to assert some sense of personal identity. Basil first appears to the reader as a dutiful, earnest, and good-hearted young man but one whose upbringing has left him restless and directionless, save for a vague wish to break free from his domineering father. He has little to do with his days until he sees Margaret on the omnibus, and is drawn by a combination of sexual attraction and social rebellion to engineer marriage with her. Basil's written account of his fleecing at the hands of Mannion and the Sherwins is an attempt to put his failures 'to some warning use' – despite the pain their writing out causes him. The resulting story is so shocking and troubles him so much that he 'dare not read the lines which my own hand has traced' (*B*, 340).

Basil thus reflects Collins's complex interest – half fascination, half disgust – in his upper-class hero as a social subject forced to deal with the changing social make-up of London. For all Collins's bohemianism and democratic principles, there is considerable space given over to questions of gentlemanly conduct and class position. Basil claims to be angry against his father because he cannot make the marriage to Margaret public. He walks the smog-filled streets with 'bitter thoughts against his inexorable family pride, which imposed on me the concealment and secrecy, under the oppression of which I had already suffered so much' (*B*, 91). In fact he finds the slimy Mr Sherwin equally distasteful and cannot imagine what his father would say about Mrs Sherwin. As a tradesman, Sherwin is not part of Basil's 'set' and he is presented as the antithesis of 'good breeding'. The offence to Basil's delicate sensibilities caused by Sherwin's interest in buying and selling things – including his own daughter – is a reminder that he represents the inversion of the gentlemanly masculine ideal who to the upper-class Englishmen is also 'other'. At the same time these exchanges signal that our perception of the family is in some degree a product of Basil's conventional, even naïve, perceptual lens, through which Sherwin (a man of 'low character' who has clearly not received the benefits of a public school education) is focalized. We see the position from which Basil, as the seemingly reliable narrator of the story, is writing. He expresses not only an emotional feeling but also a social and ideological attitude, one which provides much of the momentum of the narrative.

The novel's recreations of modern social tensions are heightened by Collins's use of a number of melodramatic or gothic gestures. At times, the conflict between hero and villain is given almost mythic status, with Basil standing in for a particular kind of chivalric, sensitive Englishman,[11] whose vividly imagined adversary Mannion – a reworking of Dickens's villainous clerk Carker from *Dombey and Son* (1848), who elopes with his employer's wife – sucks his lifeblood in vampiric fashion. This supernatural dimension to the novel is encouraged by the way in which Mannion and Margaret, the faithless wife, are both ascribed monstrous aspects: 'fiend souls made visible in fiend shapes' (*B*, 173–4). When Basil is invited to Mannion's lodgings, a storm rages outside and the hero notes a 'flash [that] came and seemed to pass right over his face. It gave such a hideously livid hue, such a spectral look of ghastliness and distortion to his features that he absolutely seemed to be glaring and grinning on me like a fiend' (*B*, 130). Later Mannion re-appears like Frankenstein's monster – his face disfigured – to taunt Basil, the manufacturer of his monstrosity: 'Do you know the work of your own hands, now you see it?' (*B*, 303). Compared with other delineators of mid-Victorian life such as Anthony Trollope, Collins can be highly theatrical. Mannion's rapacious designs on both the father's wealth and the daughter's body suggest that his origins lie not just in the supernatural but in melodrama, and his behaviour provokes the appropriately heightened language. Yet at the same time we are encouraged to contemplate in Mannion an example of the modern well-read and self-made man, who, thanks to his father's hanging, finds himself excluded from society.[12] As a professional man, his personality is also built up by his association with some of the qualities considered typically masculine in Collins's day – logical thinking, energy, calmness – which allow him to carry out his scheme so effectively.

The relationship between character and environment, which is a central part of Collins's writings generally, is another striking presence in this early novel. Repeatedly Collins chooses to set his fiction around the clash between one of his protagonists (usually a young man) and a remote, unfamiliar location, an encounter which is both physical and psychological. What he offers his readers is not just the unknown but a new experience or new way of looking at something which may already have been familiar. As we have seen, *The Woman in White* has such an encounter as its starting point. Likewise *Basil* is essentially structured on the disjunction between the surface of the 'dreary' suburban villas north of Regent's Park, 'a lonely ... colony of half-finished streets ... wretched patches of waste-land half built over' (*B*, 31–2, 158), occupied by the Sherwins – supposedly the places of domestic peace of popular Ruskinian mythology – and the dark underside, which plunges Basil into chaos. When the door opens 'with a report like a pistol', his first meeting with the Sherwin family in their 'oppressively new' house becomes a sinister moment (*B*, 61). Collins allows his readers to detect the evil, if unnamed, presences which Basil experiences only as 'strange unutterable sensations'. Foremost amongst the untoward goings on is the way in which Mrs Sherwin is persecuted in her own home, the very space supposed to be both a woman's sanctuary and her stronghold. As we discover in Mannion's letter to Basil, she is subject to 'a life of the direst mental suffering' (*B*, 238), and, thanks to her husband, exists under the 'the instinct of terror' in her own home (*B*, 249). 'My life', she tells Basil, 'has been all fear ... fear of my husband, and even of my daughter' (*B*, 217–18). As is apparent in his later novels, Collins can be quite explicit in his analysis of the intricate and darker shadings that make up the power dynamics of such relationships. In showing Mrs Sherwin's evident terror of her husband (as indeed that of Laura Fairlie in *The Woman in White*), Collins here anticipates the revelations made by Frances Power Cobbe in her infamous 1878 article 'Wife Torture in England', that men's lack of respect for women, fostered by women's degraded status both within the family and beyond – especially when existing alongside female submission – contributes to the burden of violence borne by women both inside and outside the home.[13]

The sense of disturbance in *Basil* – that suburban London is 'a site of fraudulent familial, fiscal and sexual speculation', as Tamara Wagner puts it[14] – is also apparent in the way in which the other female characters are represented, particularly Margaret Sherwin. As a young, beautiful female character in a story about a young man ensnared into a dastardly plot, the function of Margaret seems fairly predictable; by captivating Basil as soon as he claps eyes on her but betraying him with Mannion, this calculating, self-obsessed *femme fatale* allows Collins to associate the figure of 'woman' with death, destruction, and moral emptiness. She is a life-denying rather than life-giving force: 'The great motive power which really directed her was

Deceit', Mannion tells Basil (*B*, 239). Or again: 'If she had loved you for yourself, loved you for anything besides her own sensual interests, her vulgar ambition, her reckless vanity, every effort I could have made against you would have been defeated from the first' (*B*, 245).

In this sense *Basil* can seem conventional in its analysis of male–female relations. We are encouraged to view Basil's sister Clara as the epitome of womanly goodness, the 'angel' of popular mythology, while Margaret, grasping, cruel, and shallow, is her counterpoint – the manipulative 'whore':

> She was at the window – it was thrown wide open. A bird-cage hung rather high up, against the shutter panel. She was standing opposite to it, making a plaything for the poor captive canary of a piece of sugar, which she rapidly offered and drew back again, now at one bar of the cage, and now at another. The bird hopped and fluttered up and down in his prison after the sugar, chirping as if he enjoyed playing *his* part of the game with his mistress.
>
> (*B*, 37)

In this passage it is tempting to see Collins who, in many of his novels draws on different popular genres, using the association of young women and caged birds made available by narrative painting. Collins clearly wants his readers to be able to visualize the action. Yet there is a strong symbolic and ideological content in Collins's fiction which is very much to the fore in passages like this. The scene clearly looks forward to Basil's relationship with Margaret; Basil is like the 'poor captive canary', trapped in a cage and who behaves 'as if he enjoyed playing *his* part of the game'. Again he does not comprehend what he sees and, like the canary, does not realize that he is being manipulated. Later he is witness to a more disturbing scene when the canary is killed by the cat and Margaret tries to kill the cat: 'Near the fire-place with the poker she had just dropped on the floor by her side, stood Margaret. Never had I seen her look so beautiful as she now appeared, in the fury of passion which possessed her' (*B*, 133–4). Part of the terror inspired by Margaret's wielding of the (phallic) poker stems from a sense that this reflects a more symbolic destruction of 'home', that special sanctified place, a refuge from the threats of the external world and that which occupies a key role in Victorian domestic ideology. In this home wives and daughters supposedly occupy 'privileged' spaces, as helpmeets and nurturers of the family, and above all as moral guides. In *Basil*, as in other sensation novels, the actions of characters are often disruptive of this entire social fabric – intentionally or unintentionally – and the idea of the home as a place of peace is seen to be illusory. The breakdown in familial and social relations which culminates in Mannion's seduction of Margaret in the seedy hotel – 'I listened; and through the thin partition I heard voices – *her* voice, and *his* voice. *I heard and I knew* my degradation in all its infamy, knew my wrongs in all their nameless horror' – proved impossible for many contemporary reviewers to stomach (*B*, 160). This was one of the scenes that prompted accusations from the *Westminster Review* (amongst others) that the book was 'gross' (Page, 53). The text underlines the fact that the domestic space, the home, which has been established as the bedrock of the social order (the foundation of an ideal, ordered society) is being destroyed – from within as well as from outside. In Margaret – mercenary, amoral, and aggressively sexual, a woman with 'the bad instincts of an animal', as Mannion puts it (*B*, 239) – Collins presents what for many Victorians would have been a chilling picture.

* * * * *

The picture of London offered in *Basil* is profoundly pessimistic – the capital is morally and spiritually dead – and something of this mood is still apparent in Collins's next novel *Hide and Seek*. There Collins continues his attack on the spread of suburbia and the desecration of the surrounding countryside at the hands of profiteers. His central family, the Thorpes, live in 'a dismal uniformity of line and substance' aptly called Baregrove Square and Collins is at pains to convey the stultifying tedium of this existence (*HS*, 10). Again like *Basil*, *Hide and Seek* is a story of two Londons – one public and one private. In its minute descriptions of the debased and dismal conditions experienced by those living in the modern city it invites comparison not only with Gaskell and Dickens in their depictions of slum life, but also with the kind of fiction dealing with middle-class London life starting to appear from such writers as Anthony Trollope and Ellen (Mrs Henry) Wood. *Hide and Seek* also has ingredients of the sensation novel in that it is a novel with a secret, although the mystery of Mary (Madonna) Grice's parentage is not *that* mysterious. Collins's decision to make his heroine deaf and dumb was, however, unusual and represents an early example of his interest in characters with some form of disability. (Later cases include Oscar Duborg in *Poor Miss Finch* (1872) and Miserrimus Dexter in *The Law and the Lady* (1875).) The novel is also in part *bildungsroman*, describing the journey towards maturity of twenty-one-year-old Zachary Thorpe, who, like Basil, is a restless individual in search of a pseudo-parent to replace his own sternly religious father. Here, the novel's sympathies are with Zachary, prompting an ironic examination of the ways in which the respectable middle-classes bring up their young. Valentine Blyth, Mary's own foster father, a mediocre artist, is one contender for the role of substitute-father, but Zachary starts to see the mysterious loner Matt Marksman – a man with a scalped head and experience of the American 'Wild West' – as a more exciting prospect. Matt is an outsider who, while in London, inhabits a different and darker part of the city: one of dingy lodging houses, dirt, and alcoholism. Matt's own quest is to find his unmarried sister, who left home some years before on discovering she was pregnant. Matt recognizes Madonna as his own niece, and swears revenge on the lover who deserted his sister and caused her death. This is revealed to be Zachary's father, making Zachary and Madonna brother and sister. The writing is at a much lower pitch than *Basil* but its message is not dissimilar: living in a conventional family can be a repressive, joyless affair and even outwardly respectable people have dark secrets.

On the other hand, the author was right to claim that in *Hide and Seek* he was 'piping quite a new tune' which would 'make the readers of *Antonina* and *Basil* prick up their ears, and at least allow that I have given them some fresh variations which they did not expect from me' (BGLL I, 88). As we saw in Chapter 2, this time the hero's character is marked by an irreverent ebullience that finds its outlet in drunken revelry rather than in Basil's emotional and sexual intensity. Reverting to the comic spirit that he had explored in his 1851 Christmas book *Mr Wray's Cash-Box*, Collins dedicated the novel to Dickens 'as a token of admiration and affection'. Although Dickens, in returning the compliment, claimed patronizingly that he did not 'recognise much imitation' of himself (Pilgrim II, 570), other commentators were quick to notice the new influence. W.M. Rossetti in the *Morning Post* saw the novel as combining 'the narrative and descriptive felicity' of Dickens with 'the satirical humour' of Thackeray.[15] Geraldine Jewsbury, the *Athenaeum's* notoriously stringent reviewer, observed:

> In *Antonina* and *Basil* Mr Collins showed himself possessed of gifts of genius; but in those works his strength was like the strength of fever and his knowledge of human nature resembled a demonstration in morbid anatomy. Over both those works there hung a close, stifling, unwholesome odour ... In his present work, *Hide and Seek*, he has ceased walking the moral hospital to which he has hitherto

confined his excursions. Here we have health and strength together …
a work which everyone should read.

(cited in Page, 56–7)

But not all saw the Dickensian influence as so benign. The most per-
ceptive response to Collins's early work appeared in a lengthy review
article by the French critic and translator Émile Forgues in the *Revue des
deux mondes* in November 1855. This was an overwhelmingly positive
evaluation which saw in Collins the one English writer who could legit-
imately be viewed as the literary heir to the uncompromising French
realist, Honoré de Balzac: 'We believe in his future … we recognise in
him the major qualities of the novelist, above all, skill in the art of narrative and delicacy of observation' (cited and translated in Page, 63–5).
Yet the highest praise was reserved for *Basil*, while *Hide and Seek* was
seen in parts as 'feeble' and 'hackneyed'. Thus Forgues warned Collins
against being 'captivated, and too readily contented, by an ingenious
notion'. What also seemed likely to stunt Collins's artistic development,
Forgues suggested, was that he lacked nerve. Like all British authors, he
was liable to tone down the more daring elements of his work when
faced both with the comic-sentimental model of Dickens and the prud-
ishness of the circulating libraries.

* * * * *

The Woman in White is a much more frightening and frightened text
than *Hide and Seek*, both in its revelation of the disruptive forces at
work in the 'stir and turmoil of a London street' (*WW*, 420), and in its
suggestion of what needs to be done to control such forces.[16] It is often
regarded as the most sophisticated sensation novel produced by Collins –
or indeed anyone else in the Victorian period – marking his transition
into multiple-narrative, a mode of storytelling to which he would
return at different points in his career, notably in *Armadale* (1866) and
The Moonstone (1868). As we saw at the end of Chapter 3, in both serial
and volume form *The Woman in White* sold much better than anything
Collins had done to date, and generated a good deal of critical attention.
In *Blackwood's* Margaret Oliphant noted how Collins 'startles and thrills
his readers; everything is legitimate, natural and possible … The reader's
nerves are affected like the hero's … He, too, is chilled by a confused
and unexplainable alarm' (Page, 113, 119). Novels dealing with 'some
carefully prepared enigma' (Page, 109) had a lengthy history, and for
some reviewers the excitement surrounding the novel's much-vaunted

'newness' was overdone. Collins had simply 'overlaid', as *The Observer* put it, 'the epistolary form' (Page, 88) with a version of the domestic gothic, a sub-genre stretching back to Mary Shelley's *Frankenstein* (1818) and Thomas De Quincy's *Confessions of an English Opium Eater* (1822). And precedents could even be found for presenting the evidence through multiple-narration i.e. for an enigmatic story written 'by more than one pen, as the story of an offence against the laws is told in Court by more than one witness' (*WW*, 1). These include Dickens, who in 1852 had published *Bleak House* with its alternating narrators, or Dinah Mulock Craik in her 1859 murder story *A Life for a Life*, also narrated via diaries and letters.

But just as important influences can be found in Collins's non-fictional reading. The author's letters and notes for the novel reflect his long-term interests in psychology and mental illness, and in crime and the law, as well as in the *doppelgänger* tradition involving doubling and the uncanny. He was familiar with the scandalous cases reported daily from the Divorce courts and kept press cuttings of criminal trials.[17] In 1858, the country had been gripped at attempts by the novelist Edward Bulwer Lytton, M.P., to have his exasperatingly sane wife Rosina put in a private asylum.[18] In 1859 and 1860 a parliamentary 'Select Committee' published its findings into the operation of lunatic asylums, reflecting public fears that innocent people were being locked up in them by relatives who wanted them out of the way. In 1856 Collins had bought a copy of Maurice Méjan's *Recueil des Causes Célèbres*, containing an account of the Marquise de Drouhalt's long legal battle for her rightful inheritance after unscrupulous relatives had her imprisoned in an asylum. The emphasis on mesmerism, harking back to the investigative articles written by Collins on this subject for the *Leader* in the spring of 1852, is another technique used to give the novel a contemporary resonance, while concomitantly acknowledging its debt to an older, less obviously scientific, sinister tradition. B.A. Morel's pioneering discussions of degeneracy are also hinted at in *The Woman in White* as a way of explaining the deterioration of the effete Fairlie family.[19] It can also be productive to look the way in which Collins makes use of writers as different as the feminist Mary Wollstonecraft, and Sarah Stickney Ellis, famous for her conduct books for women, both hovering over the text. Thus *The Woman in White* is indebted to a whole range of nineteenth-century cultural forms – painting and drama as well as fiction and non-fiction.

It is possible, though, to begin a discussion of Collins's most famous novel by comparing it with the neglected first novel we have been discussing, *Basil*, and in particular by thinking about the differences between the depictions of the male protagonists. Just as the tragedy of the earlier text follows on from Basil's (feminine) lassitude and inertia, his belief that the 'mountain-path of Action' is not his proper 'path' (*B*, 342), so a key moment in *The Woman in White* comes when that novel's hero, on experiencing similar feelings, is instructed by the novel's tougher heroine, Marian Halcombe, to 'crush' his emotion, not to 'shrink under it like a woman' but to 'trample it under foot like a man' (*WW*, 71). In this sense Walter, the drawing master, a kind of male governess, is the natural successor to Basil – a nervous, sensitive type, who is sexually humiliated because he is set on the pursuit of a woman he cannot have. Walter, we are told, learns to have 'faith in [his] manhood' (*WW*, 71); he provokes pity, admiration, and exasperation in more-or-less equal measures, but he is also part of the focus of the text's interest in questions of gender and sexuality. Collins's depiction of Walter's progress and recovery follows a definite pattern, from over-sensitivity due to an implied feminine weakness, quashing this via overseas adventures '[i]n the stern school of extremity and danger' (*WW*, 415), to his re-appearance in the guise of a nineteenth-century 'action hero', capable of that 'inevitable suppression' of feelings which marked the mid-Victorian manly man: 'no tears soothed my aching eyes' he remarks (*WW*, 415, 416). In his new role as amateur detective, who patrols the capital, Walter takes up the position not only of upholder of the moral law, but bloodthirsty avenger as well: 'Those two men shall answer for their crimes to ME, though the justice that sits at tribunals is powerless to pursue them. I have given my life to that purpose; and alone as I stand, if God spares me, I will accomplish it' (*WW*, 410).

Oddly placed as an outsider, in *The Woman in White* Collins is able to flag up an uneasy sense of deficit in both 1850s England and in his characters' behaviour within it. So, as has been suggested, one way of reading *The Woman in White* is to say that, like a conduct book, the text teaches young men and women how to behave. It famously announces itself as 'the story of what a Woman's patience can endure and what a Man's resolution can achieve' (*WW*, 1). In the middle-class Walter Hartright it models proper masculine behaviour, in aristocratic Percival Glyde, improper and unmanly conduct. Many of the novel's initial reviewers saw the story in this light, and it is a theme taken up by D.A. Miller who shows how Collins's representation of Walter, in particular, can be situated within much wider 'cultural' fears of the 1860s. These concern the need to patrol and maintain the health of the empire via its men; the way in which 'gender slippage' was encouraging the emergence of 'the woman in the man', and 'female contagion' was becoming a matter of increasing 'panic' for those interested in domestic – and national – stability.[20] Influentially, Miller draws together three different 'ideological valences' of the 1850s: the investigation of illicit sexuality, the establishment of domestic order, and Collins's own stance as a guardian of morality.

It is within these contexts that we should read *The Woman in White*'s own apparently obsessive flagging of manly behaviour, most obviously embodied in Walter, who returns from the expedition to Honduras 'a changed man ... my will had learnt to be strong, my heart to be resolute ...' (*WW*, 415). In 1860, fears about the dangers to society caused by an unrestrained (alien) sexuality were acute and Collins's middle-class characters – Walter Hartright, Vincent Gilmore, and Professor Pesca – can be seen as 'investigators' and 'inquisitors' whose 'self-mastery' over their own 'feminine strain'[21] and surveillance of those potentially unruly men, Percival Glyde and Count Fosco, is a necessary aspect of modern industrial society. The novel therefore stresses vigilance. More recently, Richard Nemesvari has drawn further links between the novel and wider cultural discourses.[22] He, too, argues that Collins's nightmarish account of the 'infiltration' (*WW*, 96) by Count Fosco – a man who looks like 'a fat St. Cecilia masquerading in male attire' (*WW*, 230) – together with his strange hold over Sir Percival, reads like a case study in 'homosexual panic'. At the same time, in the presentation of the languidly effeminate Frederick Fairlie ('a bundle of nerves', *WW*, 348), we see something of the anti-social practices and enervating consequences of homosexuality, as detailed by nineteenth-century sexology and medical guides. Whether the 'intimate' (*WW*, 243) relationship between the foreign-educated Sir Percival and his 'bosom friend', Count Fosco (*WW*, 243), would have suggested homosexuality to Collins's contemporary readers is difficult to ascertain; partly this is because, as Nemesvari notes, the novel's investigators, led by Walter, are too delicate to make inquiries. What *is* certain is that by allowing himself to become enslaved to Count Fosco, Sir Percival neglects his wife; his energies are dissipated through pleasure rather than being devoted to the uses for which they were designed (i.e. reproduction and paternity). The scenes in which Fosco treats Glyde as a kind of lapdog are instances of this, as well as being an example of the troubling way in which the novel blurs traditional gender roles. Other instances, according to Nemesvari, are Glyde's unexplained nervousness, and his obsession with cutting walking sticks which he uses for beating down tall plants, 'compulsive behavior, combining as it does the castrative acts of "cutting and lopping" with the creation of a series of new phallic objects, each of which proves to be ultimately unsatisfactory [and] represents sexual insecurity'.[23] The novel suggests that such unmanly relations between men are loathsome, dangerous, and un-English, depriving the men involved of valuable reserves of energy which could have been used as they were intended, i.e. in the service of work and empire. This is in contrast to Walter who becomes 'the embodiment of the bourgeois compulsory heterosexuality that the novel is so anxious to create and support'.[24]

The Woman in White, then, can be read as a text contributing to the constitution of middle-class subjectivity by promoting (via the techniques of terror) the need to incessantly monitor the self and others. Sir Percival is finally punished by being burnt alive in a church, a spectacularly melodramatic conflagration, which reads like divine intervention – 'the Visitation of God' as Walter puts it complacently, exposing in a striking way his own ruthlessness (*WW*, 532). Walter claims (perhaps unconvincingly) that he is powerless to save Sir Percival and can only watch this semi-public execution: 'Before I could move, before I could draw my breath after that discovery, I was horror struck by a heavy thump against the door, from the inside. I heard the key worked violently in the lock – I heard a man's voice, behinds the door, raised to a dreadful shrillness, screaming for help' (*WW*, 526–7). It is only with tough action taken outside the law, with Walter, Pesca, and Marian working together in a tribal re-inscription of self-controlled (masculine) energy, that British society can return to more normative relations of social exchange. To follow the logic of this argument to its conclusion, the cathartic cremation of Sir Percival and the subsequent stabbing of Count Fosco at the hands of the Carbonari – which, as Walter puts it, is part of his 'day of reckoning' – are acts of public service designed to cleanse the nation (*WW*, 640).

As well as 'preaching to the nerves',[25] *The Woman in White* also concerns the conflict between the old and the new, between the effete landowning classes long in decline, and the emerging power of the professional bourgeoisie.[26] Collins asks us to accept the aspirational lower middle-class drawing master, Walter, as a suitable figure to whom to entrust the administration of the story and the deeds of derring-do related within it. Walter is the new 'modern citizen' as described by Ronald Thomas in 'Detection in the Victorian Novel', charged with overthrowing the corrupt aristocratic villains who embody 'Rank and Power' (*WW*, 422).[27] Of course, among the sinister things that strikes a resisting reader of the text is the way in which at the novel's end Walter has taken over where Sir Percival left off, holding sway at Limmeridge House.

Clearly, as a work of fiction, *The Woman in White* need not be assumed only to have a pedagogical function relating to male or female behaviour; it has also been considered, for example, as a vehicle of the inscription of anxieties about competing 'master' races, about identities and borders more generally, a reading which does not exclude or repress *The Woman in White*'s gendered possibilities but merely shows how in this, as in any multivalent text, a number of different impulses operate simultaneously and overlap. At the time of the novel's composition in 1859 these anxieties were made more acute in the context of normative conceptions of identity by other malevolent British-based 'undesirables' who seemed to be encroaching on London – Italian revolutionaries, French spies, alcoholics, socialists, spiritualists, Jews, homosexuals. In *The Woman in White*, the 'perplexingly contradictory' Count Fosco, an androgynous, 'immensely fat' voluptuary with 'peculiarities', moving noiselessly in exotic clothes and constantly sucking sweets, has been seen to stand for all of these, a nightmare figure for an anxiety-ridden readership (*WW*, 220).

While the association of the Count with foreign influence is relevant to contemporary associations of, for example, homosexuality with alien cultures, it also gains a good deal of impetus from the sense that the Count, with his peculiar combination of cosmopolitanism and debased primitivism, with 'his remarkable likeness, on a large scale, of the Great Napoleon' (*WW*, 221), is a contaminating monstrous 'European Other', an alien aristocrat transported to democratic England, where he invests himself with the advantages of his wife's money and a quasi-feudal power over the people he mesmerizes. The Count's mobility thus becomes both a repressive imposition of upper-class values and an exemplary narrative of what Lillian Nayder describes as 'reverse colonization', a 'fear that the British are in a state of moral and racial decline, and hence vulnerable to attack'.[28] Collins's own dislike of the British sense of superiority has been taken as providing the soil from which this idea sprang. But it can also be related to contemporary anxieties about racial superiority and Britain's status as a superpower. In the early 1860s, correspondents to *The Lancet* diagnosed England as 'a literal breeding ground of decay';[29] economic and technological success were being bought at the cost of 'mental alienation' and sexual immodesty.[30] The devastating effects of the Crimean War, the first major war of Victoria's reign, were followed in 1857 by the massacres of British women and children in the so-called Indian Mutiny, events which, as

Maureen Moran notes, 'drove home the fragility of Imperial rule'.[31] London in the 1850s was also swarming with exiled Italian revolutionaries seeking an independent Italy from Austria, their presence encouraging a sense of 'political intrigue and violence' (Peters, 215). In 1859 there were fears, too, that France was gearing up for an invasion of Britain.

Collins's fiction is designed partly for a metropolitan audience encouraged to believe in British superiority over 'less-civilized' nations. But it was also written on the cusp of a change between the unlimited expansionist ethos of Britain's imperialism, paraded and celebrated in the Great Exhibition of 1851 (the year in which much of the story is set), and fears that Britain was losing her power as quickly as she had gained it and was being overrun. As Walter Hartright observes, Fosco's invasion of Blackwater Park is followed by the rapid advance of this horrid alien colonizing germ on the centre of empire, London. Seeing Fosco leave his respectable-looking house in St John's Wood (the scene of abduction and imprisonment), Walter's sense of the Count's proprietorial attitude as trolls down the London streets is acute: 'he sauntered along ... humming to himself, looking up from time to time at the houses and gardens on either side of him with superb, smiling patronage. If a stranger had been told that the whole neighborhood belonged to him, that stranger would not have been surprised to hear it' (*WW*, 580–2). Later, the sight of the Count leading the applause at Covent Garden opera house – one of London's centres of culture – 'serenely satisfied with himself' causes Walter to appreciate the danger: 'He looked about him ... "Yes! Yes! These barbarous English people are learning something from ME. Here, there and everywhere, I – Fosco – am an Influence that is felt, a Man who sits supreme!" If ever face spoke, his face spoke then, and that was its language' (*WW*, 583–4).

This all-encompassing fear of the 'Other', and especially of a foreign, aristocratic predator with designs on 'John Englishman' as the Count nicknames the typical subject of Queen Victoria (*WW*, 237), is one reason for the text's obsession with surveillance – the possibility of identifying and overseeing, but also the possibility of being deceived by someone's appearance which may only be the semblance of reality. Collins's own interest in the difficulties of finding out what people are 'like' makes itself felt throughout his fiction from *Antonina* to *Blind Love*. In *The Woman in White*, a novel preoccupied on all kinds of physical and psychological levels with doubling, betrayal, 'pretending', and 'dreaming', it is the escapee Anne Catherick's striking resemblance to Laura that proves central to Fosco and Glyde's dastardly plans, so that

Anne is dressed in Laura's clothes in order to fake Laura's death. Elsewhere it is the convincing turn of the 'lurking reptile', Mrs Catherick, as a 'respectable' churchgoer that enables her to live a new life as a 'lady' in 'a black silk gown', aided by her innate cunning and her skill in blackmail (*WW*, 499, 494).

Dallas Liddle has noted how one of the things which made novels such as *The Woman in White* thrilling and frightening was the way they 'implied that both personal and class identity in contemporary Britain were fluid and unstable rather than secure, and thus potentially subject to manipulation, misrepresentation, and outright theft'.[32] As part of his sinister scheme for 'conquest' (*WW*, 239–40), the wig-wearing Count Fosco, as other critics have noted, is also interested in role play, a skill which helps him obtain a 'grotesque impenetrability'.[33] As Marian notes, he is kind to his pets, appears 'as nervously sensitive as the weakest of us', and has an evident taste for pastries, akin, as Fosco tells her to 'the innocent taste of women and children. I love to share it with them, it is another bond, dear ladies, between you and me' (*WW*, 243). Marian also notes that at times it is 'almost impossible to detect, by his accent, that he is not a countryman of our own' (*WW*, 221). In preparing for his visit to England, the Count, 'cunning as the devil himself' (*WW*, 331), studies its inhabitants in detail and through them, he tells Walter, has come to understand the English and the 'moral clap-traps' which ensure that 'English society ... is as often the accomplice, as it is the enemy of crime' (*WW*, 238). Understanding the English and their customs gives him the power to pass through the country, to colonize their women, or even worse, their men, invasively through 'filthy' and 'un-English' sexual practices, turning them into clones of himself. He is recognized as 'a man who could tame anything', and thanks to his charisma and a 'luminous' knowledge of mesmerism, has the power to do so (*WW*, 219). The Count is a threatening presence because, although elderly, obese, and effeminate, he is also a chameleon, a fantasy stereotype of enhanced masculinity who confronts the native Englishman with his own sexual inadequacy and with the even more horrendous possibility that a generation of women is looking elsewhere for sexual or social satisfaction. While Collins suggests that the patriot (masculine) is a stronghold of British values and a powerful antidote to the slimy charm of the Count, the weak-willed, leisured English men Percival Glyde and Frederick Fairlie are liable to go over to the other side; they may even be, like Marian, an enemy of the Count, but unable to resist his blandishments. This is the reason, it is often suggested, that, in the logic of the text, women require surveillance because they are by nature unruly and disloyal, subject to continuous internal rebellion fermented by their reproductive systems. Marian announces of her own experience of being drawn to Fosco: '[h]is voice trembled along every nerve in my body, and turned me hot and cold alternately' (*WW*, 261–2). So it is that the narrative moves inexorably towards Fosco's removal and assassination, and the subsequent imposition of sentimental discourse over the passive Laura and energetic Marian in the novel's final pages – an event marking the 'resolute' re-claiming of London and the determined re-shaping of women into English national subjects whose role is to 'be' not to 'do'.

* * * * *

The Woman in White is thus a text that brings together several strains of the author's work. Whether writing a short tale, a novella, or a full-length novel, Collins claimed to be '[d]irecting my characters and my story ... towards the light of Reality wherever I could find it' (*B*, xl). Yet he sought to do this in a way that would allow him to respond to the demands and opportunities of the marketplace, including the public interest in shocking crime and 'deviant' human behaviour. He used the forms of the gothic and the sensational to unsettle readers' sense of life as they knew it by questioning ideas of 'reality' whereby respectability seemed knowable and recognizable, and by shining the spotlight on the horrific and the freakish in modern London life and consciousness. In this way Collins flags the discrepancy between Britain's 'greatness', its wealth and apparent strength, and the counterfoils of crime, immorality, and disease at the same time as he anticipates the existential images used by the later generation of modernist writers. As Walter, Marian, and Laura take refuge in the 'house-forest of London' they feel 'as completely isolated in our place of concealment, as if the house we lived in had been a desert island, and the great network of streets and the thousands of our fellow creatures all round us the waters of an illimitable sea' (*WW*, 420, 442). The reader is forced to think about the alienating tendencies of urban life and the vulnerability of those who live there – especially in the horrible face of primitive, unpredictable disordered forces – and in *Basil* and *The Woman in White* Collins exploits these ideas to the full. He also, of course, suggests that these forces can be overcome if modern men stir themselves into action. However, as we shall see in the next chapter, the task of finding appropriate models for modern women proves more problematic.

6
Collins and Women

The previous chapter looked at the ways in which Collins's novels draw attention to the sinister possibilities within the fabric of middle-class life in London, and their impact on the lives of characters both male and female. Here we will consider further how Collins's texts engage with the roles of women and their assigned place in society. Contemporary reviewers of Collins's fiction often saw his novels as dealing at least in part with the 'Woman Question', or what Queen Victoria termed the 'mad wicked folly of "Women's Rights"'.[1] In 1856, Dickens was lavish in his praise of Collins's 'The Diary of Anne Rodway', in which a poor London needlewoman investigates a murder, noting 'the admirable personation of the girl's identity and point of view' (Pilgrim VIII, 161–3). Back in 1850, a reviewer for the *Edinburgh Review* said something similar about *Antonina*, presenting it as a story of 'conflict between the old and the new ... [between] a pure-minded Roman girl, and a voluptuous senator'.[2] Collins was, *Lippincott's Magazine* noted in 1868, one of a handful of male novelists possessing 'the power of delineating a heroine who shall be neither a dressed-up doll nor an impossible angel. Rosamund in *The Dead Secret*, Magdalen Vanstone in *No Name*, Marion Halcombe in *The Woman in White*, and Rachel Verinder [in *The Moonstone*] ... bear witness to the truth of this assertion' (cited in Page, 180). Collins indeed deals with the position of women in almost all his works: the choices women make, the pressures on them to act in a certain way, their departures from conventional standards of behaviour, their sexuality, and their relations with men. In this chapter, however, we will focus on three novels of the 1860s generally reckoned part of Collins's 'major phase': *No Name* (1862), *Armadale* (1866), and the acclaimed detective novel, *The Moonstone* (1868).

From what we know of Collins he would seem an unlikely figure to urge a more sympathetic understanding of woman's role in society – at least on the surface. According to many contemporary accounts, he enjoyed a hedonistic bachelor lifestyle, a good deal of which revolved around the male-dominated world of London's club-land. He could be contradictory in his views of women's roles, ambitions, and responsibilities – at times radical, at others reactionary. In 'Bold Words by a Bachelor', for example, written shortly before the passing of the Matrimonial Causes Act of 1857, he described as 'senseless', the 'prejudice which leads some people ... to the practical confession ... that they would rather see murder committed under their own eyes, than approve of any project for obtaining a law of divorce which shall be equal in its operation on husbands and wives of all ranks'.[3] Elsewhere, however, he was wont to complain of women encroaching on men's sphere. 'Ladies of the present century', he announced with fogeyish irritation in an 1858 article, 'have burst into every department of literature, have carried off the accumulated raw material from under men's noses, and have manufactured it to an enormous and unheard of extent ... I am told that out of every twelve novels or poems that are written, nine at least are by ladies.'[4] Like the writers of Victorian conduct and literature, Collins the novelist also often appears to urge his women readers to identify themselves with their domestic responsibilities. In *Basil*, the approving comment about Clara's abilities 'in disciplining her own feelings into subserviency' (*B*, 90) seems to come straight out of one of the books of advice to young women written by Sarah Strickney Ellis which were so popular as Christmas gifts in the 1840s and 1850s. Collins's novels also tend to conclude with the apparent endorsement of conventional (gender-based) standards of behaviour: the idealization of home, and the sanctity of marriage, both of which play a crucial role in the institutional definition of women.

Some critics have suggested that this ambivalence – between Collins's sympathetic awareness of the restrictions imposed upon women's lives in the mid-nineteenth century and the conservatism of some of his responses – has its origins in his relations with the women in his own family and social circle. The lively but domineering Harriet Collins, who can be seen as what Jane Gallop terms 'a phallic mother' whose influence was impossible to shake off,[5] has lain behind some interpretations, as have the details of Collins's domestic arrangements as an adult. Collins benefited more than most from the sexual double standards of his day, which discreetly licensed the free reign of men's sexual drives outside marriage; he was both a sympathizer with and exploiter of lone women.

His early letters reveal an unusual interest in the serving maids encountered both at home and on his travels. Before meeting Caroline Graves sometime in the early 1850s, there seem to have been assorted prostitutes and actresses picked up with (or without) Dickens. Later there was the servant girl Martha Rudd, twenty-one years his junior, and housed from 1868 as 'Mrs Dawson' in a cottage round the corner from the house Collins shared with Caroline. Both women came from relatively humble backgrounds. Caroline, though she had a tendency to inflate her social status, claiming as her father a gentleman of the name of Courtney, was in fact the daughter of a carpenter called Compton and had kept a tobacconist's shop after her husband's death in 1852. Martha was the daughter of a shepherd; whether Collins first encountered her as a servant at a Norfolk inn or on his mother's domestic staff remains a matter of conjecture (see Chapter 11). Martha is a more shadowy presence than Caroline and few of Collins's friends seem to have met her. In contrast, Caroline, rather better educated and more obviously 'lady-like', was more visible and often acted as hostess when Collins entertained male friends to dinner. By the standards of mid-Victorian polite society, both women were effectively 'fallen', thanks to their relationship with Collins. At the same time, if their positions were undoubtedly insecure, they were clearly preferable to eking out a grim living as a servant or shop assistant. Collins, by all accounts, was loyal and generous to both; at the end they were joint beneficiaries in his will. Nonetheless, as far as his own complicated domestic arrangements were concerned, Collins was able to have his cake and eat it too.

Other women friends have caught biographers' attentions: Frances Dickinson, a novelist trapped in an abusive marriage (whose life it has been suggested was one of the influences behind the stories 'A New Mind' (1859) and *The Evil Genius*);[6] Nina Lehmann, a brilliant pianist whose status as a married woman prevented her from performing publicly; Catherine Dickens, forced out of the family home by her husband in 1858 because of his infatuation with the young actress Ellen Ternan; and Catherine's daughter, Katey, married unhappily to the querulous Charles Collins in 1860. Potentially more troubling to biographers is the mock-romantic relationship which Collins established towards the end of his life with the eleven-year-old Anne Wynne. In the course of regular home visits and correspondence over four years, they constructed an elaborate role-play in which the aging author and little Nannie acted the parts of man and wife (B&C II, 493–513). Although Collins had avoided marriage throughout his life, he was thus prepared to act out a fantasy version with a pre-pubescent girl. Taken collectively and speculatively

the details of Collins's close relationships with these and other independent women – the actresses Ada Cavendish, Laura Seymour, Kate
Field, and Mary Anderson, for example – may suggest one reason why
different ideas of the family, domesticity, and of women's roles form
such an important part of Collins's novels. They may indeed represent
social documentary, wish-fulfilment, or even a kind of therapeutic writing out of a complex private life.

But recognizing biographical aspects of Collins's writing should not
mean that we dehistoricize it or ignore other contexts. His portrayal of
women doubtless had personal resonances, but it also drew on contemporary conventions. The middle and later decades of the nineteenth
century saw great changes in women's lives, the implications of which
have been the subject of important scholarship by (amongst others)
Mary Poovey, Nancy Armstrong, and Lyn Pykett.[7] The emergence of the
'The Woman Question' in the 1860s – including debates about female
emancipation and freedom of choice, about a woman's rights to education and professional training and to earn and keep her own income
and property, her right to be recognized as an independent legal entity
and a British subject, her right to petition for custody of her own
children – was seen by some as a threat to the stability of Victorian
patriarchal culture. As Lynda Nead has noted, the 'separate spheres'
ideology, which provided the foundation stone of the Victorian social
structure, 'was part of a wider formation of class identity, nation and
empire. ... International leadership and the domination of foreign com-
petition were believed to depend directly on the existence of a stable
domestic base and social stability'.[8] But by the 1860s there was a feeling –
encouraged by sensation fiction – that modern woman was, as Lyn
Pykett puts it, 'in flight from motherhood, family responsibility and
domestic existence'.[9] The response of many to what the journalist Eliza
Lynn Linton scathingly described as 'hybrid', 'unnatural', and 'unloving
women', with their 'restless discontent with all their work',[10] was to seek
anxiously to re-contain them in a domestic framework.

Students of mid-Victorian fiction do not have to read too widely to
realize just how much novelists of the time were preoccupied with the
issue of 'woman': the 'monstrous' woman, the 'prostitute', the emanci-
pated woman who commits the cardinal sin of 'unsexing' herself by questioning the sacraments of marriage and motherhood altogether. Collins's
fiction engages with many of these character types and plot models, as
indeed with other discourses of the 1860s – medical, social, racial – about
womanhood and femininity which formed part of a wider uncertainty
about modern identity. It is striking, for example, how in texts such as

Basil, Hide and Seek, and *The Woman in White* Collins seems to adopt a conservative male-gendered stance with the result that his interest in women in society is one that we have no difficulty in labelling 'patriarchal'. In *The Woman in White*, for example, both Laura Fairlie and Marian Halcombe end up making do with less, but in settling for less they are, we are told, entirely contented. Yet, while the markers of an ideal conventional femininity form an important touchstone, they are also called into question. The novel underlines clearly the ambivalence of the fundamental mid-Victorian middle-class feminine ideals of the 'good' wife and mother. Laura Fairlie is exactly the passive, 'angelic', childlike, open-hearted, and innocent woman of the mid-Victorian domestic ideal. Yet it is the fact that she adheres so completely to this cultural ideal that makes her unfit for survival in the modern world. So, while Collins does not explicitly offer a proto-feminist critique of his society in the way that, for example, outspoken women writers of the 1850s and 1860s such as Caroline Norton or Frances Power Cobbe do, it is difficult to read his work without noticing his unusual interest in the obstacles women face. Often overshadowed by Collins's other novels of the 1860s, *No Name* provides a useful starting point for investigating his ambivalent treatment of gender and female subjectivity.

* * * * *

Like *The Woman in White*, before its appearance in three volumes *No Name* ran in weekly instalments in *All the Year Round*, from mid-March 1862 to mid-January 1863. It thus formed part of a lengthy series of sensational works by male authors appearing in Dickens's new miscellany: it was preceded by the editor's *Great Expectations* and Bulwer Lytton's *A Strange Story*, and soon followed by Charles Reade's *Hard Cash*. Around this time Reade had also complained disdainfully that the circulating libraries would 'only take in ladies' novels', that is, novels by and about women.[11] One of the few serials by a woman in the early volumes of the magazine was Elizabeth Gaskell's melodramatic novella, *A Dark Night's Work*, which immediately succeeded *No Name*. In contrast, the contemporary novels by Collins's main female competitors in the sensation market appeared first in magazines whose fiction sections were dominated by women authors. Mary Braddon's 'horsey' novel of female rebellion, *Aurora Floyd*, ran in the bohemian monthly *Temple Bar*, while Ellen Wood's staunchly moral murder mystery *Mrs Halliburton's Troubles* appeared in the evangelical family weekly *Quiver*, both more or less concurrently with *No Name*. In opening every issue with a lengthy episode from a work of fiction, as well as in refraining from sounding a domestic note in its title, *All the Year Round* established for itself a significantly different periodical identity from that of *Household Words*. Nevertheless, as Deborah Wynne points out, *All the Year Round* was still concerned to 'to steer a safe course between conservatism and unacceptable excess'.[12] Something similar can be said of *No Name* in its engagement with the 'Woman Question'.

As so often in Collins's novels, the central concern in *No Name* is 'the plotting of individuals' attempts to sustain, or acquire social respectability', as Christopher GoGwilt puts it.[13] The novel opens with the destruction of the idyllic world of Norah and Magdalen Vanstone, as the sudden deaths of both their parents and the subsequent discovery of their illegitimacy lead to the loss of their inheritance and name alike. Norah, the conventional sister, accepts her situation and resigns herself to life in servitude as a governess. Magdalen, on the other hand, is 'not made for the ordinary jog-trot of a woman's life' (*NN*, 147). Shunned by her 'respectable' fiancé and his family because of the 'stain' upon her life, she falsifies her identity and chooses a subversive, subterranean existence as actress and fraud. Reading the first volume, Edward Pigott told Collins that 'the female interest' was 'the strongest he ever met with' (B&C I, 255). There was obvious topicality in the representation of two such contrasting women: Norah, all fortitude, resignation and suffering, against Magdalene's independence, determination, and unscrupulousness.

The novel's central interest remains Magdalen's embattled psychology; a young woman equipped with an 'elastic ever changing face' making her lonely journey towards revenge, and prepared to break almost every social and moral rule in order to succeed. With no position to lose, 'young, handsome, clever and unscrupulous', Magdalen embarks on a campaign of 'attack' (*NN*, 248). Using a succession of disguises, together with 'the legitimate weapons of her sex' and the help of a con man (self-described 'moral agriculturalist', Captain Wragg), she succeeds in marrying her repulsive, effeminate cousin, Noel Vanstone (*NN*, 248). The novel presents marriage as a form of legalized prostitution which Magdalen, despite her sense of 'horror' (*NN*, 437), rationalizes by reckoning that Noel will soon die and that she will thus recover her late father's estate. Her successive steps towards this goal are repeatedly figured as triumphs – at least until the sudden reversal triggered by her nervous collapse. While Collins does depict the unruly heroine with a degree of distaste, he also positions her so that we feel sympathy for her, particularly in light of the entrenched male attitudes she is up against. The ambiguities in the character of Magdalen have to do with the fact that a very complex – or perhaps confused – representation is taking place through her. This affects how we as readers perceive her. Collins's heroine negotiates and reacts against a set of ideologies that are simultaneously constructs and very real for her; her movements are curtailed by them. It is in this sense that the novel can be read as a powerful attack on the subject positions available to Victorian women. On the other hand, as the story progresses we also get a sense that, here as in other novels, Collins himself cannot think beyond the restraints of a patriarchal culture and the stereotypical representations this involves; he comments for example on Magdalen's snake-like movements and her 'shameful painted face' (*NN*, 272). He also decides to present Magdalen's story as an inherently moral tale, claiming that the novel depicts 'the battlefield of mortal conflict', an internal struggle for his heroine's soul between 'forces of Good' and 'the roused forces of Evil within herself' (*NN* 146, 147).

One of the most discussed incidents in the novel is the scene in which, as her wedding day approaches, Magdalen buys a bottle of laudanum and contemplates suicide while looking out over the harbour. The result is another example of Collins's powerfully visualized scenes. Setting and psychology coalesce, interweaving the past, present, and future:

> … The bottle was so small, that it lay easily in the palm of her hand. She let it remain there for a little while, and stood looking at it.
>
> 'DEATH!' she said. 'In this drop of brown drink – DEATH!'
>
> As the words passed her lips, an agony of unutterable horror seized on her in an instant. She crossed the room unsteadily with a maddening confusion on her head, with a suffocating anguish at her heart. She caught at the table to support herself. The faint clink of the bottle, as it fell harmlessly from her loosened grasp, and rolled against some porcelain object on the table, struck through her brain like the stroke of a knife. The sound of her own voice, sunk to a whisper – her voice uttering that one word, Death – rushed in her ears like the rushing of a wind. She dragged herself to the bedside, and rested her head against it, sitting on the floor. 'Oh, my life! my life!' she thought; 'what is my life worth, that I cling to it like this?'
>
> (*NN*, 497–8)

Collins positions us as readers so that we become voyeuristic spectators of Magdalen's misery. Her contemplation of suicide, an act which, as

Barbara Gates claims, many God-fearing Victorians 'feared far more than they did murder',[14] is another sign of her being beyond the pale. Unable to make up her mind, Magdalen decides to trust to 'chance'. Looking out the window she will take the overdose if an odd number of boats sail past in the following thirty minutes. When an even number passes by, she feels that Providence is with her after all.

Collins's position on the 'Woman Question' in *No Name* can be seen more clearly if we consider his representations of the feminine alongside those of rival sensation novelists. When Magdalen is described as floating in disguise between social classes, the reader of *No Name* may be reminded of two other proto-feminist bestsellers of the early 1860s: Ellen Wood's *East Lynne* (1861) and Mary Braddon's *Lady Audley's Secret* (1862). In all three texts there is a similar emphasis on performance as the central part of women's identity, as well as a focus on the female outsider or 'castaway' who eventually cracks under the demands of her role. Magdalene's willingness to sell herself as a commodity, her recognition of herself as a sexual object is a further link to these other 'fallen' women. Unlike them, though, she is redeemed and survives. Collins himself affected to despise the professional success of Ellen Wood, but the objections made by contemporary critics to *No Name* were very similar to those levelled at Wood's *East Lynne*. That is, that there was something irresponsible and even unnatural about turning an illegitimate criminal woman into a legitimate sympathetic heroine, and about the spectacle of women actively soliciting danger and the physical and mental self-assertion it involved. As is evident in the critical vocabularies used by reviewers – in particular the liberal use of epithets such as 'vulgar', 'coarse', and 'unpleasant' – many critics struggled to reconcile the heroines given them with their preconceived image of 'woman'. In *Blackwood's Magazine*, for example, Margaret Oliphant (who had made the same point about Ellen Wood's adulterous heroine, Isabel Vane) objected to the unrealistic outcome of Magdalene's 'career of vulgar and aimless trickery and wickedness ... from all the pollutions of which he [Collins] intends us to believe that she emerges, at the cheap cost of a fever, as pure, as high minded, and as spotless as the most dazzling white of heroines' (cited in Page, 143). As Oliphant noted, there is something very convenient about the final chapters which depict Magdalen's breakdown. Hers is the kind of conveniently vague-but-life-threatening illness which Victorian novelists found so useful. And while Magdalen herself may become incoherent, her own story is actually very tidy. She emerges from her illness reborn, with a restored identity created by her realization of the possibilities inherent in being a good wife.

Yet while *No Name* is escapist, it also propagates a number of ideological messages at a time when, as Jeffrey Weeks argues, 'socialization'
was a 'determining notion' and marriage still its 'social cement'.[15]
Alongside its condemnation of the marriage laws which disadvantage
women and their children, and the limited choices available to unmarried women, *No Name* is a text designed to remind its female readers
of their social responsibilities, of the joys and privileges of domesticity
and of the fact that being a wife is woman's primary duty as a citizen.
Simplicity, self-abnegation, passivity – these are the touchstones of
Magdalen's new 'feminine' nature, learned from her adventures and
from the tutelage of her fiancé, Captain Kirke, rather than the insensate
love of pleasure which characterizes her at the beginning of the novel.
So while *No Name* can be read initially as a forward-thinking mediation
on female subjectivity and selfhood, as in *The Woman in White*, this
narrative is eventually replaced by a more conventional re-establishment
of woman's 'proper' sphere.

* * * * *

In August 1861, well before *No Name* had even begun its serial run in *All
the Year Round*, Collins had been able to obtain an agreement with
George Smith for his next novel *Armadale*. The sum involved was as
much as £5000 for both book rights and serialization in the *Cornhill
Magazine*. Collins was triumphant: 'No living novelist (except Dickens)
has had such an offer as this for *one* book' (B&C I, 200), he claimed with
pardonable exaggeration.[16] This was to be the first, and indeed the only
appearance of a Collins serial in a monthly miscellany of top rank with
high-quality illustrations. A key to the magazine's success had always
been the domestic serials by the likes of Anthony Trollope, Elizabeth
Gaskell, and George Eliot, which helped attract readers who knew that
they were unlikely to encounter anything offensive. Together with
magazine's emphasis on eclectic but non-controversial family reading –
fiction and non-fiction – this had brought it widespread acclaim. By
November 1864, though, when *Armadale* eventually began its run, the
Cornhill had already past its heyday. With the break between Smith
and his editor Thackeray in 1862 the magazine had lost much of its
original lustre, as well as over half of its initial 100,000 readers.
Moreover, in its steady concern with adultery, illegitimacy, poisoning,
blackmail, insanity, and homosexuality, *Armadale* seems aimed at a
rather different magazine. 'Did you get the Cornhill?' Collins asked his
mother shortly before the novel ended its run, 'Was there ever such a

dull Magazine? I wonder anybody reads it' (B&C II, 273–4). Certainly the novel which, Collins admitted, made even 'my own flesh creep' (B&C I, 250) sits rather oddly against the *Cornhill*'s focus on the bourgeois family reader.

The first instalment, for example, appeared alongside Gaskell's domestic story *Wives and Daughters*, as well as articles on 'Middle-Class Education in England', Scottish farm labourers, General Gordon's imperialist exploits in China, and an article on polygamy discussing the large surplus of unmarried women. Taken together these articles uphold British middle-class standards of behaviour, in particular the construction of the separate spheres ideology around which so much of society's ideas about men and women had been founded. *Armadale*, however, can be read as probing mid-nineteenth century conceptions of manhood and womanhood. Unlike other writings in the *Cornhill* the picture of middle- and upper-class life offered in Collin's novel is dark and depressing: Britain is morally bankrupt. It is against the backdrop of the monstrous egotism and stunted intelligence of the novel's middle-class men that the voracious, fiendish energy of Lydia Gwilt makes its presence felt. A poisoner who shares Magdalene Vanstone's talent for impersonation, Lydia might exhibit beauty and charm but she is also intelligent, logical, resourceful, and ambitious. Posing like Mary Braddon's Lady Audley as an experienced governess, she appears the epitome of the trustworthy and ultra-respectable veiled Victorian woman: 'Perfectly modest in her manner, possessed to perfection of the graceful refinements of a lady ...' (*A*, 373). However, Collins's glamorous descriptions of Gwilt – her 'magnetic influence', 'allurements that feast the eye', and 'sexual sorcery in her smile', all hint at the danger that lies beneath (*A*, 373).

At first glance, the narrative that Lydia Gwilt creates for herself seems to be a mundane if unpleasant story of 'self-help' – to ironize Samuel Smiles's famous rallying call – in which she exploits her beauty to gain respectable social standing. However, as the novel progresses, it becomes apparent that Lydia's power lies in her manipulation of the very qualities that embody the feminine ideal. As Lyn Pykett puts it, 'the novel exploits the fear that the self-sacrificing passionless gentility which constitutes the feminine idea is merely a form of acting or impersonation which masks female passion or self-interest'.[17] Lydia, described very deliberately as being un-English, is characterized by her 'extraordinary independence' and drive (*A*, 617). Almost until the end she is without remorse. In *Basil*, Margaret Sherwin may die miserably, but she has already redeemed herself through a purifying rite of typhus fever after begging Basil's pardon. In *No Name* Magdalene is even more stricken with guilt until she entrusts her body and soul into the hands of Captain Kirke. In *Armadale* Lydia is apparently less troubled by the implications of her long career of wrongdoing and has a strong instinct for self-preservation: 'Nobody ever yet injured me ... without sooner or later bitterly regretting it', she announces (*A*, 362).

Comparison of Lydia Gwilt with earlier female characters reminds us that Collins tended to do three main things when he focused on women. First, to make a spectacle of femininity, whether of the passive, victimized variety (Clara Hallward in *Basil*, Laura Fairlie in *The Woman in White*) or in the form of the *femme fatale* (Margaret in *Basil*, Magdalene Vanstone in *No Name*, or Lydia Gwilt in *Armadale*); second, to hint at how firmly entrenched were the legal, economic, and social conventions under which women lived; third, to suggest that women might have other desires beyond acting as man's 'helpmate'. There was also the disturbing suggestion that, as Lynda Hart points out, '[t]he trajectory of "normal" femininity and that of fallen womanhood were not two parallel lines incapable of meeting; on the contrary a slippery slope lay between the two states'.[18] In *Armadale*, Lydia, treated with 'unexampled barbarity' (*A* 519) by her abusive first husband, is not against the idea of marriage or motherhood itself but she is unwilling – or cannot afford – to commit herself exclusively to any of her future partners. Whereas in *No Name* Magdalene's adventures take place within a cultural framework centred round family and home that she both understands and ultimately seeks to return to, Lydia is not so easily controlled. Manipulating both Allan Armadale and Ozias Midwinter, she leaves a trail of destruction in her wake. Collins's depiction of Lydia's rise and fall follows a definite pattern, from servitude – as a blackmailing lady's maid – to gradual attempts at independence – as a Brussels bar-room pianist, and an accomplice to a female card-sharp – to respectability, via marriage to the abusive Mr Waldron. But this is a relationship which is likened to that of master and slave, until Lydia, having embarked on an affair with a Cuban army officer, uses poison to free herself. She then faces blackmail from the private detective James Blackwood before her homicidal proclivities emerge again and she practices a dual existence – as 'pattern wife' and scheming killer. At the very end of the novel, Collins tries to temper the radicalism of his characterization through a gesture of self-sacrifice. Lydia kills herself with the poisoned gas intended for her husband. As she does so she pens a note to Midwinter, instructing him to 'forget [her] ... in the love of a better woman': 'I might perhaps have been that better woman myself, if I had not lived a miserable life before you met with me. ... The one atonement I can make for all the wrong I have done you is the atonement of my death. ... Even my wickedness has one merit – it has not prospered. I have never been a happy woman' (*A*, 653).

Despite this admission of 'gwilt', *Armadale* did not enjoy a good press when it first appeared. In 1866 the novel was condemned for the same reasons that recent critics have embraced it, namely its focus on the mind of a woman who kills, and its insinuations about the moral basis of Empire. George Smith, who confessed himself 'pleased' with the first instalment (BGLL I, 332), grew more alarmed as the serial progressed and the *Cornhill*'s sales figures declined.[19] The novel did not sell well in volume form: out of a print run of 1286, only 1118 were sold and of these Mudie took 500 at only half the nominal price. By the time he issued a single-volume edition in November 1866, it was clear to Smith that his investment had not paid off. Collins, however, was proud of the new book: 'My own idea is that I have never written such a good end to a book, as I have written this time. At any rate, I never was so excited, myself, while finishing a story as I was this time. Miss Gwilt's death quite upset me' (BGLL II, 33). Yet this pleasure was undermined by the reviews. There were critical encomia for its boldness, its plots, and audacious narrative techniques, in the *Reader* for example,[20] but the book's 'difficult' terrain also offended many readers. 'Characters are wrought with strange insight', admitted the *Evening Standard*, but 'the self revelation of the innermost mind of a woman who has been forger, murderess, thief, leaves every feeling revolted'.[21] Many contemporary critics regarded *Armadale* as a retrograde step in the history of fiction, 'an unhappy invention' as the Bishop of St David's put it, 'creating an insatiable demand which must be met by less and less wholesome food'.[22] The novel was also denounced in a widely quoted article in the *Westminster Review*, which accused it of having 'all the interest, and also the literary power of a police report' (Page, 159). Other critics drew attention to the way in which Collins seemed to blur the distinctions between right and wrong. The *Spectator* accused Collins of trying to elicit the reader's sympathy for 'a vulgarized Becky Sharp ... a woman fouler than the refuse of the streets, who has lived to the ripe age of thirty-five, and through the horrors of forgery, murder, theft, bigamy, gaol and attempted suicide, without any trace being left on her beauty' (Page, 149–50). 'What artist', Henry Chorley asked in the *Athenaeum*, 'would choose vermin as his subjects' (Page, 147).

The critical reviews of *Armadale* are significant because they suggest some of the restrictions under which Collins and his peers wrote. The power of the novel *per se* to corrupt and seduce impressionable readers with 'subtle poison'[23] was a recurrent topic of concern in the 1850s and 1860s. Sue Lonoff has provided useful discussions of these fears and Collin's impatience with what he described as 'readers in particular' (i.e. critics) and 'the narrow limits within which they are supposed to restrict the development of modern fiction – if they can ...'.[24] So too has Kate Flint, in *The Woman Reader 1837–1914*, where she locates these anxieties in the context of mid-Victorian assumptions about gender. As Flint notes, women were believed to have a physiological suscepti- bility to the effects of novels. The sensation novel in particular, 'took advantage ... of an assumed innate faculty which might under certain circumstances be regarded as one of women's strengths, but which should not be exploited at the expense of her simultaneously held rational capabilities, and, above all, at the cost of the necessary exercise of self-control'.[25] The idea that sensation fiction furnished middle-class homes and their female occupants with examples of bad practice was part of the message of the *Westminster Review*'s article (cited above) and was also present in a review by the *London Quarterly Review* in which it was suggested of *Armadale* that 'the tendency of the multiplication of these tales is to create a class of criminals, if they do not already exist' (Page, 156–7). According to mid-Victorian theory, sensation novels were perceived to be initiating the next generation of wives and mothers into a set of values unconstrained by hegemonic institutions such as the family or the church. Certainly it is true that in such works as *No Name* and *Armadale* – novels which talk of 'the misery of being a woman' (*A*, 432) – Collins offers challenging representations of women's lives. It has also been suggested that these could also be used to quite subver- sive effect, allowing readers to envisage their own lives differently. In this sense these novels might be said to have offered women the kind of 'escapist fantasy' described by Alison Light in her study of romance fiction, where 'heroines are able to take up what would usually be seen as the masculine reins of power and sexual autonomy'.[26]

* * * * *

Initially entitled 'The Serpent's Eye', *The Moonstone* was serialized in *All the Year Round* from early January to early August 1868. It proved to be Collins's last contribution to the magazine while Dickens was alive. Though, in an echo of the excitement generated by *The Woman in White*, crowds again besieged the magazine's offices in Wellington Street for the closing episodes, Dickens himself seems to have lost patience with Collins's reversion to the mode of multiple narration. 'The construction is wearisome beyond endurance, and there is a vein of obstinate conceit in it that makes enemies of readers', he confided to W.H. Wills at the end of the run (Pilgrim XII, 158–9). Collins himself described the finished novel as

> ... the best book I have written. I believe in it myself to have a much stronger element of 'popularity' in it than anything I have written since 'The Woman in White'. *That* book Mr Mudie, and the Librarians took in *driblets* – just as the public *forced* them. And *this* book let us hope, will be another example of that sort of *legitimate* sale which springs from genuine demand.
>
> (B&C II, 309)

His success, he decided, lay in giving the public what it wanted. With *The Moonstone* he seems to have done just this, and the novel has often been acclaimed as Collins's most sophisticated and accomplished work.

The novel is gripping and insightful, logical and confusing, tautly plotted but also multi-layered. Thematically it covers a wide range of topics and strands of 1860s debate, each of which has been the focus of recent criticism: empire, science (including mesmerism, hysteria, somnambulism, trances: theories of the unconscious and dreams), freemasonry, drug-taking, gender, ecology, the criminal body, the role of the literary critic, and the process of reading. Few, meanwhile, would disagree with Ronald Thomas's assertion that the novel is 'a watershed moment' in the history of the detective genre, the 'prototypical English detective novel'.[27] Its narrative techniques (eleven narrators and thirteen narratives) helped in establishing a tight structure; its setting (the remote country house which is a kind of microcosm of England), its suspects (all inmates), the evidence (all circumstantial), its detectives (all eccentric, invasive, disruptive), and its interest in the developing science of forensic investigation and the search for clues, helped establish conventions for detective fiction that are still around today.

Carefully crafted and technically confident, *The Moonstone* has been seen as the highpoint of Collins's achievement. As his letters reveal, he poured all of his intellectual and physical energies into its writing. He drew on a number of literary traditions including the epistolary novel, the satirical novel, and the colonial adventure story. It is also heavily allegorical and, as Steve Farmer notes, 'offers the light entertainment of mystery or romance at the same time it promotes a dark and stinging social commentary'.[28] We are made aware, for example, of the arrogance of English colonialists – their presumption that they can ignore the demonic, alien history of the diamond which they have plundered. The English now find themselves under siege. As Franklin Blake tells Betteredge: 'When I came here from London with that horrible Diamond … I don't believe there was a happier household in England than this. Look at the household now! Scattered, disunited – the very air of the place poisoned with mystery and suspicion' (*M*, 244). To take this idea a step further, we might also argue that this story, which ends littered with corpses, is about a 'past' which can never be forgotten. To quote Eric Sundquist, 'remembrance' is often literally that 'one remembers what has been dismembered, reconstructs what has been shattered and atones for what has been ruined or murdered'.[29] The narrative of *The Moonstone* is an act of recalling and paying the costs of Britain's settlement, colonization, and exploitation of India.

In postcolonial terms, *The Moonstone* seems to be an Indian Mutiny novel, in which the fantasy of an ordered society is shown to be just that – a fantasy. However, this is not the only way of approaching the novel. Critics interested in issues of gender might also say that what makes this story interesting is the use it makes of the links between colonial and patriarchal oppression. Lillian Nayder sees the novel as 'combining a critique of empire and British domination with one of male privilege and enforced powerless among women'.[30] The sense of disturbance in *The Moonstone* is intensified by the very bleak vision of family life which is presented; the home is a space of safety but also of danger, whose boundaries are shifting and unstable; behind the smooth façade of family, it is suggested, jealously and passion fester and threaten even the most comfortable of domestic situations. Contextually *The Moonstone* exploits the horror provoked by a real-life scandal – the infamous 'Road' murder of 1860. In this much-discussed case a sixteen-year-old girl, Constance Kent, was accused of slitting the throat of her four-year-old brother and shoving him down the family privy; part of the police case rested on the mystery of a bloodstained night-gown. There was public outrage at the interrogation of a young middle-class girl, but this went hand in hand with a prurient curiosity about the domestic details of the family. Kent confessed in 1865, stood trial and only escaped hanging by having her death sentence commuted to life imprisonment by Queen Victoria.

If we examine the novel closely it is not difficult to appreciate why recent critics have made much of the links between *The Moonstone* and the Road murder. As Elizabeth Rose Gruner has noted, Collins's novel is self-consciously constructed as a novel of secrets and, like the Road murder, deals with the same 'impulse to secrecy ... to cover up the family's complicity in crime', during a period in which (to quote Elaine Showalter) 'secrecy was basic to the lives of *all* respectable women'.[31] Like *The Woman in White* and *No Name*, *The Moonstone* is partly about the choices open to women, what they want (or think they want) and the kind of behaviour they exhibit while trying to get it. Rachel Verinder, described as 'dashing' and 'stiff-necked' (*M*, 108–9), whose name recalls the long-suffering Rachel in the Bible, is the character in this story that stands out most as a representative of assertive modern womanhood. However, there are a number of other female types in the novel: Miss Clack, an evangelical hypocrite and hanger-on, whose name is presumably meant to remind us of noisy chatter, and whose sexual repression and desire for the masterful blonde preacher Godfrey Abelwhite, are revealed through her own narrative of events; Rosanna Spearman, a lonely maidservant, disfigured by having one shoulder bigger than the other, who, tormented by repressed desire for Franklin Blake, drowns herself in the Shivering Sands, a deceptively quiet stretch of wasteland that all of a sudden will 'move and shudder', sucking people down to their deaths in its 'fathomless depths' (*M*, 305); Lady Verinder, Rachel's mother, who accepts her domestic role, conscious of her superiority – social and otherwise – over others; Mrs Abelwhite, 'a large silent, fair-complexioned woman ... never known to do anything for herself ... accepting everybody's help, and adopting everybody's opinions' (*M*, 307). It is Rachel's relationship with these women – or lack of it – which provides the basis for most of the text's debates, and one important point of contrast between Rachel and her cousin, Miss Clack, lies in their ideas about women's prescribed behaviour. Rachel is 'reckless and defiant' and lacking 'all lady-like restraint in her language and manner' (*M*, 308, 265); Drusilla Clack is a snobbish Victorian prig who casts herself as the sole 'Christian Englishwoman' of her acquaintance (*M*, 308). She has no doubt about what women ought to do and condemns 'the most awful backslidings of modern times' (*M*, 292). However, her views on the importance of social complaisance clearly belong to a morally questionable scheme of 'training and principles' (*M*, 293), a position which in Rachel's eyes seems destructive to women's happiness as well as hypercritical. In contrast, Rachel, 'secret, and self-willed; odd and wild, and unlike other girls of her age', belongs to a more modern outlook (*M*, 283).

The notion that *The Moonstone* should be read as a female-centred text has been given further impetus by the novel's emphasis on sexual frustration and sexual conflict. Much has been made of the unconscious and uncanny elements in the novel (embodied in the Shivering Sands). Additionally, the idea that the stone of the title – a diamond ('as large as a plover's egg') may, 'like all gems, may be linked with women and sexuality' has caused the novel to be seen as both a Freudian and a feminist text.[32] As one reading of the novel has it, the removal of the diamond by Franklin Blake suggests the 'symbolic defloration'[33] first of a country (India) and later of a woman (Rachel Verinder). In turn, it is not very difficult to see that Rachel's own secret, which provides the basis for the most important personal conflict in the novel, is that her love for Blake is also sexual as well as spiritual. That she desires Blake might thus be read as a mark of subversion in the sense that (1) he is undesirable as a suitor, and (2) it is the feminine woman who is doing the desiring. The entire novel is suffused with images which suggest ways in which Rachel's self-containment masks not just knowledge of the crime, but an inward struggle to resolve complex choices of sexuality, morality, and way of life, and the masochistic self-repression in the name of duty which is often assumed to be typically Victorian. This sub-plot is reminiscent of a conduct book, but it can also be read as a response to contemporary anxieties about womanhood. Faced with 'The Girl of the Period' (the title of Eliza Lynn Linton's controversial 1868 articles in the *Saturday Review*), Collins gives his readers an unconventional woman, labelled 'odd' (*M*, 217), but he also shows that she is not the 'masculine' man-hater but, more complexly, a woman who struggles to keep her feelings in line with older conventional models of feminine feeling. The heroine cannot voice what she knows and feels.

In its exposé of the corruption at the heart of the English home, *The Moonstone* can seem another pessimistic text. Its positive values lie partly in the loyalty exhibited by the novel's heroine; they lie in selfless outsiders like Ezra Jennings and finally in the hint that in 1848 – a year of bloody revolution in Europe – Britain may suffer the same fate. Limping Lucy's violent condemnation of Franklin Blake, whom she holds responsible for Rosanna Spearman's suicide, finishes with the words: 'Ha, Mr Betteredge, the day is not far off when the poor will rise against the rich. I pray Heaven they may begin with *him*' (*M*, 248). This suggestion of a harsher political dimension to the novel gains force when we realize that, as Martin Priestman has noted, the expected 'happy ending [i.e. the engagement of Rachel and Franklin Blake] … depends on the sacrifice or self-sacrifice of numerous less fortunate female victims of social deprivation or persecution', whose voices are buried or silenced.[34] As a working-class woman lacking the commodity of beauty, Rosanna Spearman is virtually invisible to her superiors; Franklin Blake is callously indifferent to her death and her voice can only be heard second-hand, after her death via the letter she leaves behind.

* * * * *

Although it is not as obviously focused on the role of women as *No Name* and *Armadale*, *The Moonstone*, like the earlier novels, invites inspection by anyone interested in the issues surrounding the topic of 'male feminist voices'.[35] Collins's attempts to survey the choices and restrictions on women once again lead him to numerous representations of and reflections on patriarchy, while his own performance leads him to adopt many narratorial disguises. But in trying to locate Collins's writing about women within some of the contexts in which they were produced and read, the situation remains complex. His novels validate female intelligence and initiative, and suggest that female fulfilment and a sense of self is desirable. In *No Name*, for example, Magdalene Vanstone is represented losing her moral bearings but also as trapped in that part of the nineteenth century which is still ruled by rigid patriarchal assumptions and she retains the readers' sympathies almost throughout. Yet the fate of all the heroines discussed in this chapter also suggests that women can only really be safe and fulfilled within a conventional family unit as loving wives and mothers.

Another way of approaching this element of Collins's writing is to note, as Toril Moi does in *Sexual Textual Politics*, that women in fiction act as spaces onto which men project their own fears and anxieties about female sexuality: 'Behind every angel lurks the monster, the observed of the male idealization of women is the male fear of femininity. The monster woman is the woman who refuses to be selfless, acts on her own initiative ... a woman who rejects the submissive role patriarchy has reserved for her.'[36] What this also means, of course, is that 'beneath the ample heaps of contempt ... foisted on women by men' feminist critics have been able to uncover 'signs of feared female potentials and struggles'. This is what Michael Ryan, in a useful summary, describes as the horrible 'counter-possibility – that women might be more powerful than men'.[37] The genres for which Collins is most famous – sensation, supernatural, gothic – are often taken as fertile sites for this kind of representation. However, what we as readers might also consider is the ways in which images of women in Collins's texts, and the plots of female destiny foisted on female characters, such as Margaret Sherwin in *Basil*, Magdalen Vanstone in *No Name*, or Lydia Gwilt in *Armadale*, may offer glimpses of the way mid-Victorian male power is maintained through representation and stereotype, at the same time as they also suggest the insecurities underlying this operation. Unruly, excessive female figures tend to be chastened – either by marriage or violent death. Thus exactly how we are meant to read the rebellious women who re-appear throughout Collins's work remains a point of debate. Do we cheer when they are vanquished? Or do these monstrously energetic women represent fantasies of escape from gender roles?

7
Collins and the Theatre

Throughout his life Collins was obsessed by the drama. His first recorded visit to a theatre was in Paris in 1844, when he saw the great French actress Rachel (B&C I, 25). As recorded in Chapter 2, in his early twenties he and a group of friends put on plays at the family home in Blandford Square, and it was his love of such amateur theatricals that first brought him into contact with Dickens. In 1850, he extended his theatrical ambitions, adapting a French play and performing it under the title *A Court Duel* as part of a charity benefit at the Royal Soho Theatre in Dean Street. In 1854–5 Collins's regular work as reviewer for the *Leader* gave him access to a wide range of theatrical performances, and this experience also makes itself felt in a number of articles for *Household Words*, beginning with 'Dramatic Grub Street' in 1858.[1] Most famously, his early novel *Basil* is prefaced by the much-quoted declaration that the novel and the drama are 'twin-sisters in the family of fiction' (*B*, xli), while he later told a French critic, 'if I know anything of my own faculty, it is a dramatic one' (B&C I, 208). There is thus a period from the late 1860s to the late 1870s when rather more of Collins's energies go into the play than the novel. In a letter to his publisher, he even threatened to abandon fiction altogether (BGLL II, 417), while he confided to the actor Wybert Reeve that he harboured the dream of becoming 'a theatrical manager'.[2]

Collin's passion for the theatre took hold at a pivotal moment. In the early years of Queen Victoria's reign, the drama was regarded as a second-rate artistic form. The respectable middle class had largely abandoned it, while playwrights and actors – as Collins notes in 'Dramatic Grub Street' – did not have the same *cachet* as poets or composers. However, by the end of the 1840s, the theatre was starting to shake off its 'low' and populist image as the haunt of rowdy young men, pickpockets, and prostitutes. Several leading actors, including William Charles Macready, Charles Kean, and Samuel Phelps, made strenuous efforts to try and revitalize theatrical culture, while Queen Victoria herself became 'a leading patron of the drama'.[3] During the 1850s a number of London theatres were refurbished as managers sought to create a more glamorous ambience. The Olympic and Adelphi Theatres in the West End – the two venues in which most of the plays Collins wrote were performed – were typical in this respect.[4] The insides of both were shaped like an 'elongated horseshoe',[5] with pit seats that curved round and a wide stage separated from the audience by a decorated proscenium arch (a 'frame' at the Olympic) and an 'act drop' (i.e. curtain). Though there was seating for 890 at the Olympic and 1500 at the Adelphi, both theatres had excellent sightlines. The stages were wide and had trap doors built into the floor; any part of the stage could be removed so that a chasm could be represented and the Adelphi was famous for its 'sinking stage'. There was also space behind and underneath the stage for the specially designed machinery used for special effects: overhead wires for ghosts, water scenes in huge tanks with lakes and moving ships, and treadmills for real horses. A notable feature of the Olympic – a theatre which boasted a 'highly fashionable audience' as part of its attractions[6] – was its gas lighting which could be raised or dimmed as the mood required and the lavishly decorated auditorium, with gold pillars and delicate arabesque ornaments decorating the boxes. This new emphasis on social respectability did not necessarily mean that the plays presented changed overnight, but play-going started becoming more acceptable to the middle-class audience some of whom, thanks to improved transport links from the suburbs, started to return to the theatre.

Collins was obviously aware of this change in atmosphere and the potential it offered for re-energizing theatrical culture. In *Household Worlds*, he had written scathingly of 'the systematic neglect of the theatre' and its 'needful reform', of 'the shameful dearth of stage literature' and the difficulties for serious dramatists in getting their plays adequately represented on stage.[7] His own melodrama, *The Lighthouse*, he felt impossible to cast: 'The principal part really requires a first-rate serious actor – and where is he to be found, Anno Domini 1855, in this great and prosperous Kingdom of England' (B&C I, 142). But still the theatre drew him in with a sense of its potential. 'Of one thing I am certain', he wrote in 1858, '… there is no want of a large and a ready audience for original English plays possessing genuine dramatic merit, and appealing, as forcibly as our best novels do, to the tastes, the interests, and the sympathies of our own time.'[8] However, he decided to shun the West-End theatre's reliance on 'gorgeous' historical dramas, complete with pretty costumes and lavish backdrops.[9] Melodrama, he decided, was the genre most sympathetic to his own style.

In opting to write melodrama, Collins was choosing to exploit what was a long established and enormously popular dramatic form. In the middle of the nineteenth century a series of spectacular smash hits – amongst them Dion Boucicault's *The Corsican Brothers* (1852) and *The Colleen Bawn* (1860), and Tom Taylor's *The Ticket of Leave Man* (1863) – had helped invigorate this kind of drama in which, as Henry Arthur Jones recalled in 'The Theatre and the Mob' (1895), success was dependent on 'the most prodigious excitement, the most appalling catastrophes, the most harrowing situations'.[10] Writers such as J.B. Buckstone, Douglas Jerrold, George Dibdin Pitt, and C.H. Hazelwood were recognized, alongside Boucicault and Taylor, as the main melodramatists, and they had to compete with what Collins termed 'the rank and file of hack writers',[11] who made a living selling plays to working-class theatres.[12]

Summarizing the characteristics of melodrama, David Mayer notes the form's emphasis on suffering and pain and its depiction of 'a world which may be explained in comparatively simple terms of good and evil'.[13] Invariably the main emphasis is on an exciting plot, constructed around ordinary men or women coping with highly pressurized situations: dastardly criminal schemes, missing relatives, false imprisonment, forgery, murder. The characters are likely to include a virile hero forced to endure a range of physical trials, a beautiful, 'swooning' heroine of unstained virtue contrasted with an aggressive and vindictive 'wicked' woman, and a predatory (upper-class) villain to be resisted at all costs. Yet while melodrama was exciting it also served an ideological function. Writers aimed to satisfy their audiences' desires for escapism, providing thrills and physical danger, both in the modern urban world and in far-flung places, but they also offered psychological reassurance and a familiar narrative coda as the hero and his solid English values emerge triumphant. As Mayer points out, these thrilling dramas also served to 'critique matters of daily concern … which were otherwise disturbing to discuss', addressing issues of urban poverty, class, alcoholism, illegitimacy, social ostracism, and empire.[14] In 1852, Queen Victoria was roundly condemned for her excited visits to Charles Kean's production of the 'creepy'[15] melodrama *The Corsican Brothers* (Collins also went at least twice) – a play which the *Theatrical Journal* labelled a 'silly wild impossible farrago' and 'vulgar Victorian trash', symptomatic of the degradation of the stage.[16] By way of a riposte, Kean and his supporters believed that 'the government could not find a more powerful engine for the direction of the public mind than the theatre ... both in a social and political point of view', via which audiences 'might be guide[ed] into a wholesome channel'.[17]

Unfortunately, Collins recorded few thoughts on his own dramatic efforts. 'An audience cannot be excited without being thrilled. It cannot be thrilled without being made to feel', was his cryptic observation in a tribute to the actor Charles Fechter.[18] When, in 1859, a fan asked him for advice about playwriting, Collins told her to 'study the laws of dramatic construction by reading the best *modern* English and French plays, and by taking every opportunity of seeing them represented on the stage' (BGLL I, 173). It is tempting to see him in his own melodramas merely trying to exploit a popular genre in another bid for financial success. Nonetheless it was clearly a literary form in which he felt comfortable and confident, and which on occasions brought him the critical and pecuniary recognition he craved. Thus in 1871 the *Daily Telegraph* made the following comments on Collins's own stage adaptation of *The Woman in White* at the Olympic Theatre:

> When one of our very first novelists – and a novelist who possesses in a higher degree than any of his brethren, the brilliant dramatic power in which stage writers are singularly deficient – takes to writing for the stage, the stage is sincerely to be congratulated. ... It was very fairly subject of regret to hear lavish praise heaped upon the Sardous, the Augiers, and the Dumas of another country ... when we had in our midst an author who in power and dramatic mechanism can surely take his stand very fairly beside them ... the Stage should claim Mr Collins.[19]

Working with the staple ingredients of 'extraordinary events' and 'strong and deep emotions' (*B*, xli), Collins went on to become, as Edward Dutton Cook suggested in 1876, a fully fledged playwright, 'a dramatist not less than a novelist',[20] mixing different settings and themes, working with the sensational, the gothic, the psychological, the historical, and the topical. He indulged his taste for landscapes full of wild scenery and charismatic criminals, showing examples of ostentatiously heroic behaviour, while painting nightmarish scenarios where the struggle for survival ends in death for at least one of the protagonists. In this chapter we will focus on the production of five of these plays: the Dickens vehicle *The Lighthouse* (1855), the criminal drama *The Red Vial* (1858), the co-authored sensation dramas *The Frozen Deep* (1856) and *No Thoroughfare* (1867), and the plantation drama *Black and White* (1869). We will also consider Collins's efforts to adapt his own novels, an important part of his activities in the 1870s and 1880s.

For the most part, critics have tended to ignore these works viewing them as second-rate or embarrassing; if these texts have any interest, the argument goes, it is as quaint examples of hackwork produced for 'the people' by a man who wanted cash and was careless about what he wrote. As plays they clearly *are* written with an eye to what Collins thought would sell, and some were written for 'star' actors with lots of opportunities for barnstorming. But the plays are also interesting in their own right: they demonstrate attempts to master different theatrical techniques; they demonstrate concern with social isolation, offer scope for reader-identification, and feed anxieties prompted by 'real-life' events; they are sometimes didactic but often offer reassurance. They demonstrate too how Collins writes within and out of the ideological values of his age, continuing, for example, his interest in 'masculine' and 'feminine' behaviour. What is also particularly striking about the works for the stage is that they are all played out in very specifically described locations, an obvious testament to Collins's interests in the interplay between character and environment and in the clash of cultures.

* * * * *

As with so many things in Collins's early life, it was Dickens who helped lay the ground for what followed. By the 1850s, Dickens was full of projects for charitable theatricals which would support the newly established Guild of Literature and Art, and in which he – as director, producer and, of course, star – would lead a crack-team of amateurs picked from his bohemian set. As we saw in Chapter 2, the first recorded meeting between Dickens and Collins came in March 1851, when Dickens invited the young apprentice author to take the part of the valet, Smart, in Edward Bulwer Lytton's *Not So Bad as We Seem*, a comedy set in Grub Street in the previous century. Collin's talents as an actor in no way matched those of Dickens but his enjoyment of the experience comes across very strongly in his letters. After a series of performances in London, the first on 16 May in the Duke of Devonshire's library in Mayfair before Queen Victoria herself, Dickens took his troop on tour. Bath, Manchester, and Liverpool were among the cities visited. Collins, still impressionable enough to be dazzled by Dickens's celebrity, was suitably astonished at the company's reception: 'Our triumph in Manchester was worth all our other triumphs put together', he told his mother:

> Two thousand, seven hundred people composed our audience – and such an audience! They never missed a single 'point' in the play and applauded incessantly. *My* part, you will be glad to hear, was played without a single mistake – and played so as to produce some very warm congratulations from my Manager and indeed from the whole company. The dress and wig made me (everybody said) look about *sixteen* …
>
> (B&C I, 181)

Collins's acting in fact received mixed responses – Janet Wills described him as 'a most unloving and unlovable actor', whose performance only his mother could find engaging (cited in Peters, 12) – but he clearly loved the attention and applause. More importantly, it was this association with Dickens that allowed the 'practical acquaintance with the stage' which Collins believed so valuable (BGLL II, 172–3). As the friendship between the two men deepened, and more Guild plays were put on – September 1852 saw productions of Charles Matthews's farce *Used Up* and J.R. Planché's *Charles XII* – Collins started to become more prominent in the amateur theatre company. He also began to write plays, and so it was at Tavistock House on 19 June 1855 that *The Lighthouse* received its first performance. Based in part on the *Household Words* short story 'Gabriel's Marriage' (1853), the play, a 'regular old-style Melo Drama', as Dickens described it (Pilgrim VII, 624–5), proved a surprising hit. Its plot centres on three men cut off from the outside world for a month within a lighthouse. The eldest is an old man, Aaron Gurnock (played by Dickens), who is haunted by his complicity in a murder many years previously. As the effects of starvation take hold, he begins to hallucinate and the ghost of the murdered woman stands at his bedside telling him to speak, and he reveals to his son what has happened.

The dramatic preoccupations underlying the first production of *The Lighthouse* are unusually well documented because London University professor Henry Morley kept a diary recording his visits. Morley's pronouncements testify to the care taken over the performance and the seriousness with which Dickens regarded the venture:

> An exquisite picture … of Eddystone as it stood on those days, from the pencil of Mr Stanfield, was the drop scene and the actors

were exhibited throughout as shut up in a little room within the lighthouse. ... Similar exigencies appear also to have been consulted in the manner of developing the play; the crime, the wreck, and all the events upon which hangs the passion of the story, not being produced upon the scene but breaking out from the narration of the actors. None of the leading incidents are shown actually, but their workings on the minds of the three lighthouse men who are the chief performers ...[21]

The plot is far-fetched and the play has dated, but at the heart of it is the interest in psychological structures that would become central in Collins's work. Morley was struck by the emphasis on the central character's 'horrible sense of blood-guiltiness'. *The Lighthouse's* success, he believed, was owing to the 'serious' attention bestowed on Gurnock, 'an enfeebled body and a stricken soul, in solemn awe of the spirit world, emotions shifting with the changes of his bodily condition', all of which was helped by Dickens's graphically simulated scenes of terror.[22] The play was not naturalistic in the twentieth-century sense. Dickens – an actor like his idol William Macready in the so-called Romantic tradition – focused on a strong representation of the passions and emotions and gave a performance which would be seen as exaggerated today. But his playing quickly became legendary, and proved a hard act to follow. When the play transferred to the Olympic Theatre in August 1857 the part was taken by Frederick Robson, a highly regarded actor. Robson, however, was criticized for not placing sufficient emphasis on the tortured side of the character's mind, though this did not stop the success of the production, which garnered 'a perfect hurricane of applause' (BGLL I, 149). But it was perhaps an early indication of how the presence of Dickens, as both frustrated actor and indefatigable master of ceremonies, was difficult to escape.

The 'immense success' of *The Lighthouse* at the Olympic boosted Collin's sense of his playwriting ability: 'I have engaged to do them another', he told his mother exultantly (BGLL I, 151). But the result was the ambitious melodrama *The Red Vial*, which proved a far less congenial experience for both author and audience when it received its première at the Olympic on 11 October 1858. It was never printed but the plot, or a version of it, was reused by Collins for the 1880 novel *Jezebel's Daughter* (see Chapter 10). The inspiration for *The Red Vial* is not recorded, though its general framework of intrigue and retribution would have been familiar enough to Victorian playgoers. As in *The Lighthouse*, there is an eerily claustrophobic setting and the past returns to haunt the present. Madame Bergmann (played by Fanny Stirling), the widow of a toxicologist, steals money from her employer Isaac Rodenberg, whose partner she wants her daughter to marry. Fearful that her theft will be found out she pours poison from a red vial into a drink intended for Rodenburg. However, she is observed by the half-witted servant Hans Grimm (played by Robson) who administers a draft that in fact functions as an antidote but brings on the appearance of death. The climactic scenes thus take place in the Frankfurt 'dead-house', where bodies are bought before burial in order to test whether life is truly extinct. There the supposed corpse comes back to life, to the delight of the half-wit and the horror of the would-be murderess, who becomes the accidental victim of her own poisonous preparations.

With some exaggeration Edmund Yates recalled *The Red Vial* as a 'dead failure'.[23] *The Times* opined that while 'great pains' had been taken 'to give something of an elevated character' to the drama, 'the subject was obviously repugnant to the audience'. It had been left to Robson and his actors to grapple – not altogether successfully – with the moral complexities of presenting a play about a devoted mother who is also a cold-blooded poisoner. The reviewer expressed sympathy for Mrs Stirling who had tried to give some dignity to the 'manifestly repulsive' part by playing it as a Victorian Lady Macbeth.[24] Part of the problem was that the play seemed a let-down after the success of *The Lighthouse*. Audiences expected something exceptional from the promising young playwright, not a grim potboiler unrelieved by any kind of humour – such at least was the opinion of Henry Morley. He felt that the difficulties lay not so much in the play's subject matter as in its unrelieved grimness: 'Mr. Collins has experimented in a drama without one break in the chain of crime and terror, and the audience therefore makes breaks for itself at very inconvenient places. ... It needs the highest and truest exaltation of the lineage of the drama to keep an audience in an English playhouse in a state of unbroken solemnity for two hours at a stretch ...'.[25] The author – as he was wont to do – blamed the critics and the audience for not having the wit to appreciate it.

* * * * *

In the early 1860s Collins's success as a novelist had largely distracted him from theatrical pursuits. But, following the lukewarm response to *Armadale*, in the autumn of 1866 he decided to revisit *The Frozen Deep*, co-written with Dickens and the most successful of the Tavistock House plays. The play had originally been unveiled to audiences in January 1857 when Dickens had played the role of the obsessive, vengeful anti-hero, Richard Wardour, a man flawed by emotional instability and a violent temperament. As a depiction of English heroism and self-sacrifice, *The Frozen Deep* had been nothing if not topical, mining two familiar Victorian seams: the interest in second sight and altered states of consciousness and the fascination with exploration of uncharted regions such as the Arctic Circle. As Collins began drafting the script in the summer of 1856, the fate of the missing polar explorer Sir John Franklin had become the talk of London. Franklin's expedition had set off from England in May 1845 in search for the Northwest Passage, and was last sighted two months later. Amongst those joining in the search was John Rae in 1849. From Eskimos in possession of objects belonging to sailors on the expedition, he learned that the ships had become caught up in the ice and the crews had tried to walk to safety across the hundreds of miles of frozen peninsula. Forty bodies had been discovered, alongside cooking pots filled with human flesh. Based on this information Rae returned to Britain to report that the Franklin expedition had met a fate 'as terrible as the imagination can conceive',[26] and there was a public outcry over the thought that civilized Englishmen could eat one another. Dickens, too, was outraged at the very suggestion and ran a series of articles in *Household Words* (1854–7) defending Franklin.

It is thus likely that *The Frozen Deep* was partly intended to convince audiences of Franklin's heroism and even to encourage another rescue expedition (see Pilgrim VII, 453–6). Yet the play itself is not concerned overtly with Franklin or indeed cannibalism. The opening action takes place in a country house in Devon, and details the anxieties of four young women each of whom has a relation or lover on a polar expedition. Clara Burnham is particularly fearful – not only has her fiancé gone, but so too has a ruthless neighbour whose suit she has rejected, and who has vowed to kill the man who has robbed him of her if their paths should ever cross. Her fears are heightened by the prophecies of an old Scottish nurse who claims second sight and who tells of a bloody vision from across the seas. The scene then shifts to the Arctic, where the lost heroes are found stuck in a hut, cut off from civilization and with little chance of being rescued. The decision is taken to send out an exploring party to find a way through the barrier of ice. They cast lots and Clara Burnham's fiancé Frank Aldersley (played by Collins) joins the expedition. Just before the party sets out, an accident allows Wardour, the rejected lover who now knows that Aldersley is his rival, to join the group. In Act III several of the Arctic party who have now been rescued are preparing to return home, but Frank Aldersley and Wardour are still missing. The ladies who have come out from England in search of the missing men shelter in a cave. Suddenly a wild and ragged figure rushes in. This turns out to be Wardour who has escaped from the ice floes, but has become half mad in the process. He is preparing to leave when he is recognized by Clara. He is thus charged with the murder of Aldersley: 'Look at this conscience-stricken wretch! Confess, unhappy ruin of a man! Tell us how it was done' (*FD*, 157) Wardour, however, staggers out, returning with Aldersley in his arms. Although he has been tempted to kill Aldersley or desert him on the ice, his innate nobility has prevented this and he has carried his weaker rival back to Clara. Having accomplished this, Wardour collapses and dies at Clara's feet.

In some ways *The Frozen Deep* conforms to the recognizably melo-dramatic pattern of two lovers separated but threatened by the same villain. In keeping with the genre, the language is often highly wrought, like the hero's dying speech: 'You will remember me kindly for Frank's sake? Poor Frank! Why does he hide his face? Is he crying? Nearer Clara – I want to look my last look at *you*. My sister, Clara! – Kiss me, sister, kiss me before I die!' (*FD*, 160). But where the play gains its complexity is via the character of Wardour itself. The hero-villain is built up from a position of weakness in Acts I and II – littered with references to his obses-sive, unmanageable behaviour – to a display of superhuman strength and depth of passion beyond the grasp of the other more prosaic characters:

> I took him away alone – away with me over the waste of snow – he on one side, and the tempter on the other, and I between them, marching, marching, till the night fell ... If you can't kill him, leave him when he sleeps – the tempter whispered me – leave him when he sleeps! I set him his place to sleep in apart; but he crept between the Devil and me, and nestled his head on my breast and slept *here*.
>
> (*FD*, 158–9)

Dickens had introduced a panoply of special effects and scenic devices to convey the themes of the play. The Arctic backdrop mirrored the 'ice bound' condition of Wardour's own mind, 'a disordered state of strong passions which have temporarily overpowered or "frozen" the noble sentiments', as Brannan puts it.[27] Wardour's overcoming of his 'mad' jealousy and his self-sacrificing behaviour was a way of reassuring the audience that men – Englishmen at any rate – are essentially good. The play is liberating but ultimately safe; things are put right in the end. It is notable that Collins has the anarchic Wardour die in the final scene.

Despite his heroic gesture Wardour has already demonstrated – in a manner that looks back to Mannion in *Basil* and forward to Sydney Carton in Dickens's *A Tale of Two Cities* – that he can find no contentment in civilized society.

Dickens's commitment to the play was apparent, not least from his decision to tour it in Manchester with a semi-professional cast (including a young actress Ellen Ternan, for whom he would separate from his wife, Catherine). Dickens's letters celebrate the play's triumphant reception there. In September 1857, he told Angela Burdett Coutts that he had been 'very excited by the crying of two thousand people over the grave of Richard Wardour' (Pilgrim II, 876–7). Later he wrote of the sense of power derived from having 'a couple of thousand people all rigid and frozen together, in the palm of one's hand – as at Manchester'.[28] The apparent power of the play to move audiences was widely acknowledged: John Oxenford in *The Times* praised the 'web of emotion' in the final act.[29] When Queen Victoria commanded a performance at Buckingham Palace in July 1856 she recorded in her diary 'an admirable melodrama ... most interesting, intensely dramatic and most touching and moving at the end'.[30]

When Collins and Dickens considered reviving the play for the professional theatre in 1866, it must have seemed that there were more triumphs to be had. Both authors' names now had sufficient pull to attract the interest of a theatre manager. In fact when the play opened – with a good deal of fanfare – at the Olympic on 17 October, it met with a disappointing response. Some newspapers even reported the play being booed and hissed by the Olympic's audience. The radical *London Review* called most of the characters 'mere sketches' and the costumes 'unnatural and ridiculous'. It suggested the only reason the play had succeeded in 1857 was the celebrity connections: 'There is flunkeyism in supposing that because the play was successful when performed by Mr Charles Dickens and his friends ... because it was commanded by her Majesty – a fact weakly mentioned in a mixture of large type and italics on the playbill – it will equally suit an audience out of kid gloves, and accustomed to expect a large amount of amusement and excitement for a shilling.'[31] This suggests not only that the moment for a patriotic defence of Franklin's heroic expedition had passed – well before 1866 it was clear that Rae's account was substantially true[32] – but also that Collins had yet to find a form of melodrama that would convincingly appeal to a popular audience in a public theatre.

* * * * *

Collins was not put off, however, and throughout 1866–7 he toiled at two more plays which would signal his arrival as a successful dramatist. The first was a dramatization of *Armadale*, originally carried out in order to protect his dramatic copyright and later revised and staged as *Miss Gwilt* (Globe Theatre, 15 April 1876). The second was *No Thoroughfare* whose popularity and profitability was apparent in its season at the Adelphi: it initially ran for 150 consecutive performances from 26 December 1867, while Dickens supervised a concurrent New York production. Collins reported to his mother: 'The play goes on wonderfully. Every night the Theatre is crammed. This speculation on the public taste is paying, and promises long to pay me, from fifty to fifty-five pounds a week' (BGLL II, 105). By any reckoning this was a good amount. Meanwhile the publication of *No Thoroughfare* as a story in the Christmas number of *All the Year Round* in 1867 resulted in record sales of 200,000. But *No Thoroughfare* is a significant work in another way: it is the last of what we might call Collins's apprenticeship pieces for Dickens, the final time the two men worked in collaboration. Cynics said that the play was lazily put together. First there was the section set in a foundling hospital which was obviously written by Dickens, and then there was the larger section set in Switzerland written by Collins. In the *World*, Edward Dutton Cook suggested that '[w]ith a little unpicking of the stitches tacking the two tales together, they would entirely fall apart, and stand confessed as two novelettes, each complete in itself ...'. Where mentor and mentee had once worked well together, Cook now observed 'an incompatibility of temper between the works' and the two sections seemed 'strange bedfellows'.[33] Dickens, though he claimed joint authorship confessed himself 'reduced to the confines of despair by its length' (for which he blamed Collins). Initially the play's six acts ensured that performances ran four hours.[34]

Ungracious though Dickens's remarks may seem, Collins was certainly starting to take the lion's share of the organization in theatrical matters. It was Collins, rather than Dickens, who steered the London production with the play's director and leading man, Anglo-French actor Charles Fechter (1822–79), who played the villain Obenreizer, and the Adelphi actor-manager Ben Webster (1798–1882), who played Joey Ladle. Although temperamental, Fechter was capable of forming theatrical taste. His naturalistic, meditative portrayal of Hamlet had earned him plaudits, and his management of the Princess's Theatre had helped that house to a period of financial stability and artistic respectability. Webster was a comic actor who had created his own following with *One Touch of Nature* (1859) and *The Dead Heart* (1859, a loose adaptation of

A Tale of Two Cities). Collins was flattered that these celebrated men of the theatre wanted to be involved. Altogether, *No Thoroughfare* is a striking example of the successful fare of the London theatre of the 1860s, and a sign that Collins had at last hit upon a mode of melodrama that would attract a popular audience. The ambitious use of spectacle in the play is one of its most striking features and an indication how stagecraft had developed in the decade since *The Red Vial*. In 1860–1, the Adelphi had premiered Boucicault's smash-hit plays *The Colleen Bawn* with its famous diving scene and *The Octoroon* replete with an exploding steamboat. Following Dickens's advice to climax their own story with a stunning fight on the Alps, Collins tried to draw out the 'horrors and dangers' inherent in such a setting, and to 'get a very Avalanche of power out of it and thunder it down' on the audience's heads (Pilgrim XI, 413).

In *No Thoroughfare*, the Swiss villain, Obenreizer, is displaced in the affections of his ward, Marguerite, by George Vendale, the play's English hero. Since Vendale is a double threat because he seems likely to discover an embezzlement of company funds, Obenreizer determines to kill him. Journeying to Milan to 'help' in Vendale's investigation of the fraud, Obenreizer drugs his companion at an inn in the Alps. The following morning, a blizzard rages. Obenreizer leads a drowsy Vendale over the Simplon Pass where he intends to leave him to die of exposure. 'The journey of your life ends here', he announces. Vendale, who has not suspected Obenreizer, is stunned. The villain's social mask is dropped and his true intentions revealed:

> OBEN: I am the thief and the forger. In a minute more, I shall take the proof from your dead body!
>
> VEN (*confusedly; feeling the influence of the laudanum*) You villain! What have I done to you?
>
> OBEN: Done? George Vendale! You shall hear what you have done. I love Marguerite! I sacrificed my honour, I took the money which was not mine, to buy luxuries for *her*! *I* love Marguerite – and you are the man who has come between us! ... You carry my ruin at this moment in the pocket of your coat! You disgrace me in her eyes, if you live to see her again. You die!
>
> (*NT*, 65–6)

However, Vendale manages to escape from Obenreizer's clutches and heroically throws himself over the precipice in order to expose the villain and save the heroine from him. Obenreizer's removal and the discovery of secret papers revealing Vendale's middle-class legitimacy is the means by which harmony is restored.

In this sense, like many Victorian melodramas and novels, one of the goals of *No Thoroughfare* is to (re)establish the rightful ownership of a particular piece of property and establish the moral rights of hero over villain. In *No Thoroughfare*, the hero's reward is both the business *and* the girl. Having thoroughly undermined the ideas of inherited wealth and position in the representation of Walter Wilding (a product of the foundling hospital) at the beginning of the play, Collins triumphantly reinserts them at the end, with Vendale as the owner of a successful wine-importing business, the husband of Marguerite, and thus the potential progenitor of a new middle-class dynasty. What is striking about the play is that although the plot encourages us to believe that Vendale's rise is a natural one – as natural as his growth into a specimen of English perfection – his role in the play is fairly passive. It is the heroine, Marguerite, together with the villain, Obenreizer, who demonstrate deeds of daring. In Act III Marguerite pleads with Vendale not to travel with her guardian to Milan. Vendale's servant, Joey Ladle, who also has suspicions of Obenreizer proposes to Marguerite that they follow them.

> JOEY: Have you got courage to do a desperate thing?
>
> MAR: Try me! I'm no fine lady. I'm one of the people, Joey, like *you*!
>
> (*NT*, 54)

Yet having displayed admirable pluck and enterprise in her pursuit of Obenreizer and rescue of Vendale, Marguerite is then stripped of these qualities. Once she is engaged to Vendale she presents herself as a woman fully submissive to middle-class authority, and the end of the play celebrates the fact that after her marriage Marguerite's position will be much more clearly secured.

Nonetheless, audiences were invited to see that there are some un-answered questions about the version of genteel femininity which now surrounds Marguerite and about the cultural frame of reference that sustains it. This also comes across in Collins's representation of Obenreizer. In 1867 so persuasive was Fechter's performance of a man in the grip of an obsession that it became impossible to pigeonhole him as a cardboard villain. Instead, he became, as the *Weekly Theatrical Reporter* noted, a 'sympathetic' character, whose explicit mockery of English repression struck a chord with the audience, just as Count Fosco had done.[35]

'Can your sound English sense understand a man who sacrifices everything to one dominant idea? I dare say not. You are so well brought up in
England; you are so prosperous and so rich!' (*NT*, 23). Collins allows him
so much space on stage in which to articulate his grievances and question
English manners and mores, that Obenreizer is liable to appear an
increasingly intriguing figure. His suicide by poison at the end of the
play – part of the expulsion of the villain that melodrama demanded –
struck a tragic as well as a cathartic note.

No Thoroughfare's mixture of familiar and unfamiliar ingredients,
together with the Adelphi's high production values, meant that the production was reckoned exciting. The combination of the lavish scenery
and the fine performances of Fechter and Carlotta Leclerq (Marguerite)
were judged to bring the play to life. Altogether it was a happy and fruit-
ful experience for Collins. His new friendships with Fechter and Leclerq
were to act as catalysts for the ideas in his next play, *Black and White*
(1869). Convinced that with *No Thoroughfare* he had found a successful
formula for sensational melodrama, Collins took the germ of a plot suggested by Fechter and planned on reaping a similar financial harvest.

* * * * *

Black and White opened at the Adelphi on 29 March 1869. The play
seemed guaranteed a lively audience, and it did well enough, running
for around sixty nights. Collins later claimed that the play was received
with 'tumultuous applause',[36] although reviewers at the time were more
circumspect. The *World* told its readers that the new play was 'not a
work of high order, but it is certainly a commendable specimen of its
class'.[37] The play was reckoned less spectacular than *No Thoroughfare*,
but potentially more interesting with its concern with disguise and role
play, confusions over racial identity, and disputes over property.
Comparisons were made with other slave plantation works, notably
Harriet Beecher Stowe's *Uncle Tom's Cabin* and Boucicault's *The Octoroon*.
In *Black and White* a sense of local colour – or what Collins presumed
was local colour – was created via the introduction of slaves with
(imagined) Caribbean dialect and manners. At the same time, the play
revels in the intensity of feelings of passion, jealousy, and hatred among
the inhabitants, with an emphasis on jokes and music, duelling and
riots, all neatly wrapped up in an eleventh-hour resolution, with the
hero vindicated and the villain brought to ruin. All these elements
conspire in a lurid way to make *Black and White* almost a parodic
version of Collins's other dramatic works.

The setting is Trinidad in 1830 just prior to the abolition of slavery. The heiress Emily Milburn falls in love with Count Maurice de Layrac and accepts his proposal, despite the fact that Stephen Westcraft, another plantation owner, already considers Emily engaged to him. The rejection thus triggers plans for revenge by the brutish and clinically manipulative Westcraft. Meanwhile de Layrac is summoned to the deathbed of a quadroon, Ruth, who reveals she is his mother and warns him to leave as there is a man on the island with a grudge to settle. As her son he is technically a slave: 'Son! on the day when you set foot again on the soil of this island, the laws of free England deserted you' (*B&W*, 24). Both Emily and Westcraft (who has climbed up onto the roof of the hut) overhear these revelations. Knowing de Layrac to be of mixed race, Emily now feels 'revulsion' towards him: 'Oh the shame of it! ... a lady is degraded if a slave's hand touches her. A slave's lips have touched mine!' (*B&W*, 27–8). Her lover in turn offers to release her: 'The slave blood runs in my veins – the slave nature can bear anything' (*B&W*, 29). Westcraft meanwhile uses the information to get revenge. He publicly proclaims de Layrac a slave and buys up the estate to which he belongs, thus becoming his master. To counter this, Emily plans to buy de Layrac for herself – almost as if he is her plaything. Matters are resolved when a servant breaks into the estate and discovers old documents granting de Layrac's mother her freedom. He is not a slave after all and the play ends with Emily defying convention to marry de Layrac: 'My friends may dread the scandal mongers of the island. I despise them! ... I am an orphan like you; I have no ties to keep me here. ... Will you take me away with you, to-morrow, as your wife?' (*B&W*, 49–50). Meanwhile, Westcraft faces his nemesis through financial ruin brought on by taking control of an estate he can ill afford. The British government will shortly abolish colonial slavery altogether and the island's way of life will change forever.

On the face of it *Black and White* bears out one of the frequent complaints made of Collins's plays by his contemporaries, namely, that his work was unduly crowded. The *Theatrical and Musical Review* was one of several papers to comment on 'the breathless rapidity with which the most conflicting events succeed one another'.[38] But the charge that *Black and White* is merely a piece of theatrical escapism is undercut when the play is viewed as an examination of the origins of Britain's colonial power. Ruth's seduction – or rape – at the hands of her white master deliberately reminds the reader of the repression involved in Britain's control of her colonies. It can also be seen to anticipate questions about the 'white man's burden' (in Kipling's famous phrase), an issue starting to emerge as a source of some anxiety in 1860s Britain. This is one of the intriguing readings suggested by Audrey Fisch in her essay 'Collins, Race and Slavery', where she also argues that *Black and White* not only 'reflects mid-Victorian England's ideological investment in the moral and national rightness of the decision to abolish colonial slavery', but also offers a warning about the potential for 'colonial alienation and/or rebellion'.[39]

As has been seen, part of the interest of Collins's texts more generally is the way in which they seem revolutionary and reactionary at the same time, exposing the contradictions embedded within the ideologies of gender and race of their day. In the relationship between its hero and heroine *Black and White* – like the novella *Miss or Mrs?* (1871) – appears to support inter-racial marriage, as well as advocating what nowadays would be called a 'multi-racial' society.[40] In contrast the deathbed reconciliation between Ruth and de Layrac is presented by Collins without irony as a supremely moving event. Its sentimental and homiletic paeans to motherhood, the tragic predicament of mother and son, and the scene's emphasis on social ruin, victimization, and lingering death was intended as powerful 'weeping' melodrama, of the kind later immortalized in stage versions of Ellen Wood's *East Lynne* with its famous tag line, 'dead, dead, dead, and he never knew me, never called me mother!'[41] – and thus likely to offer significant resonance for Victorian audiences. In fact, in 1869 reviewers were less affected than Collins had hoped by this celebration of the natural bond between mother and son and laughed at the 'ludicrous' sight of the villain, Westcraft, perched improbably and invisibly on the roof of the hut.[42] The *Athenaeum* declared: 'Something of absurdity attaches to the character of the Count ... So great is his love for the mother he has seen for five minutes that he forgets she had sold him to strangers, and proudly avows himself her child.'[43] But the play's ideological message shifts again, as within this scene Collins also plays out for his audience some of the period's troubled questions about race and gender relations. He suggests, for example, that having a black mother – or black ancestors – is not anything to be ashamed of. Elsewhere, the notion that Emily has been 'bolder than a woman should be' (*B&W*, 50) is also deliberately controversial on Collins's part, at the same time that it points to his and his audience's confusion about the boundaries of female conduct and behaviour. In suggesting the doubleness of de Layrac and the reaction of Emily (self-disgust mixed with sexual longing), Collins confirms not only his own but also his culture's expectations of women, only to show them as fractured. The confusions symbolized by the violent destruction of de Layrac's identity and the changed status of his body (from that of master to a servant/object), together with the vigorous pushing of sexual desire underground were those of the mid-Victorians more generally. The complicated schema of Emily's relations with de Layrac is used as means of criticizing the ways in which racial, social, and sexual identities are created and deployed, but also to tease and titillate the audience.

* * * * *

Though *Black and White* was successful on stage, it never won the popularity of *No Thoroughfare* and was never revived. This may have been due in part to the untimeliness of the theme in 1869, only a few years after American Civil War came to an end, ushering in the era of emancipation promised in Lincoln's proclamation of 1 January 1863. As Collins acknowledged, 'our subject was slavery; and even the long-suffering English public had had enough of it'.[44] Collins's partnership with Fechter also ended and the actor emigrated immediately afterwards to America, where he was dogged by scandal, alcoholism, and bankruptcy. Instead Collins began to put his theatrical energies into creating stage adaptations of his own novels. The main works in question were: *Armadale* (published in 1866; later revised and performed at the Globe Theatre as *Miss Gwilt* in 1876); *No Name* (adapted first by W.B. Bernard on Collins's behalf in 1863, then by Collins in 1870 and produced at the Fifth Avenue Theatre, New York, in 1871); *Man and Wife* (published as a book in 1870, and premiered as a play at the Prince of Wales Theatre, 1873); *The Woman in White* (Olympic Theatre, 1871); *The New Magdalen* (written at the same time as the novel, and produced at the Olympic Theatre, 1873); and *The Moonstone* (Olympic Theatre, 1877). *No Name* was not the only dramatization to appear across the Atlantic, so that, during his North American reading tour, his hostess in Boston was able to describe him as 'a kind of superior Boucicault' on account of his facility in adapting his works for stage performance (Clarke, 174).

Dramatizing novels for the stage was a major part of the Victorian theatre industry. The tradition had begun at the beginning of the nineteenth century with the novels of Samuel Richardson, Walter Scott, and Mary Shelley, followed in the 1830s by versions of Harrison Ainsworth and Dickens. The fashion continued to flourish and by the time Collins was starting to become successful, the appetite for stage adaptations appeared voracious. In 1860, *The Times* in a review of the Surrey Theatre's unauthorized version of *The Woman in White* observed how

> ... once a tale becomes generally popular, a desire to see it as a dramatic form immediately spreads like an epidemic. ... Whether a story be fitted for stage purposes or not people do not even inquire, nor even care. They only want to see the personages they have read about clothed in a visible form and turn from the book to the stage as a child turns from letter-press to pictures.[45]

Such notions of gullible audiences of limited intelligence, which, as we saw in Chapter 6, contributed to fears about the corrupting effects of sensation novels in the 1860s, also played a key role in debates about stage adaptations. This was true to the extent that many observers came to view adaptation as symptomatic of a widespread degeneration of theatrical taste which pandered to the lowest common denominator. Adaptation was also perceived as a form of physical assault or burglary, as bad as any of the crimes portrayed in *The Woman in White* or *Armadale*. Collins himself regarded the adaptors as 'thieves' (B&C II, 363). Others agreed, calling these 'literary cracksmen' the 'curse of the stage', making their dishonest living by serving up 'scrapings' from 'Charley Dickens' and 'extracts from the Newgate calendar', according to the *Theatrical Journal* in 1857.[46] The paper went on to complain that 'the adaptor of novels ... and the pilferer are truly the real cause of the present depression of our drama. These shabby-genteel Grub-sheets ... flourish and fill their pockets, while all good and true hands fail'.[47]

Although adaptation was identified by critics as a corrupt and lazy theatrical form, theatre managements and actors quickly realized that popular novels were worth exploiting. Not only *The Woman in White* and *Man and Wife*, but also less-obvious contenders such as *Poor Miss Finch* or short stories like 'A Fatal Fortune' promised guaranteed profits. They were there for the taking because the law offered little or no protection. A series of legal actions initiated by Charles Reade in the early 1860s served mainly to confirm that 'representing the incidents of a published novel in a dramatic form upon the stage, although done publicly and for profit, is no infringement of copyright'.[48] Collins's sense of grievance concerning this issue was always intense. Near the end of his life he summed up the situation in a single curt sentence to a fellow novelist: 'the stupid copyright law of England allows any scoundrel possessing a pot of paste and a pair of scissors to steal our novels for stage purposes' (BGLL IV, 299). The only recourse was to organize 'copyright performances'. The novelist would hastily write a dramatic version of the work, and then bring together a group of actors to read it through; other friends would watch as 'witnesses', in this way making the performance the basis for a claim to copyright. Collins was attuned to these defensive strategies and his letters are full of references to reactions when his novels were 're-fitted' for the stage – either by himself or others.[49] Partly he wanted to protect what he considered his own property, but he also felt that he was the only person who understood his work sufficiently well to be able to do it. To an unusually courteous request for permission to dramatize *Poor Miss Finch*, he replied: 'as the writer of the novel, I venture to claim the sole right of dramatising it' (BGLL II, 330–1).

In practice, however, things were a little more complicated. A cynic might say that Collins's adaptations of his novels were simply money-spinners, allowing him to regurgitate old material for extra profit, while the complexities of the novels are distorted by being squeezed into the straightjacket of stage melodrama.[50] Yet he was also an adaptor, who, unusually for his time, was very conscious that he could not simply transfer dialogue from page to stage verbatim. He described his own stage version *Man and Wife* as an 'entirely new Dramatic Story' (BGLL II, 136), and in all the dramatizations there are quite striking differences between novel and play. Examples include Franklin Blake's theft of the diamond in full view of the audience in Act I of *The Moonstone* (1877), while at the end of Collins's own version of *The Woman in White* Count Fosco is stabbed silently on stage by two members of the Brotherhood, twisting the audience's sympathies at the end of the play. Watching the same adaptation, the *Era* wrote how 'the prodigious effect of the [new] scene where Count Fosco first unfolded to Sir Percival his infamous design, its innocent victim lying meanwhile unconscious before their eyes, must be seen to be believed.[51] A similar effect is achieved in *No Thoroughfare*. The avalanche which kills Obenreizer in the serial story is replaced on stage by (self-administered) poison, giving the villain a more ambiguous status. In *Miss Gwilt*, Lydia is presented less as a scheming murderess than as a fallen woman who would reform if only given the chance – 'rather sinned against than sinning', as *The Times* put it.[52] Dr Downward, on the other hand, is a much more visible and controlling presence. In this adaptation Collins also makes very striking use of 'pictures' and 'tableaux', part and parcel of the staging patterns of melodrama. Midwinter's declaration 'I stay!' as he realizes the true identity of the new governess and stands transfixed, is the curtain line of Act I of *Miss Gwilt*; Act III ends with the thud as Lydia Gwilt collapses, having heard a gunshot from the yacht which then sails past the window; Act IV culminates in Dr Downward escorting Miss Gwilt to the asylum: 'Forgive me – and forget me!' cries Lydia Gwilt as she takes her poison, 'Farewell forever!' (*MG*, 102). The final curtain closes with a tableau asserting the bond which exists between men, as Allan '*bends over*' the injured Midwinter and '*takes his hand*' (*MG*, 102).

Collins's adaptations do not then destroy the texts but re-visualize them – and ask the audience to do the same. But Collins also wanted to challenge – if not shock – his audience. When *Man and Wife* opened at the fashionable Haymarket Theatre on 23 February 1873 under the management of Squire and Marie Bancroft, Collins claimed to have aimed deliberately for 'strong drama ... making the flesh of "drawing-room audiences" creep' (BGLL II, 136). Though the play ran for 136 nights, critics protested that *Man and Wife*'s subject matter was 'fundamentally repellent' and too 'painful' for theatrical performance.[53] *Man and Wife* was quickly followed by *The New Magdalen*, which had a similar effect when it opened at the Olympic Theatre on 29 May 1873. Collins persisted with his habit of sitting in on rehearsals, giving strict instructions as to how the play was to be performed and cast (BGLL II, 395). In this instance he was at pains to ensure that his lead actress, Ada Cavendish, made the 'fallen' woman, Mercy Merrick, a far more attractive character than the 'pure' woman, Grace Roseberry, whose identity she has stolen. As the *Athenaeum* noted, so successfully was this managed that Grace, pleasant enough at the beginning of the play, had become an absolute 'fiend' by the end. In contrast, Mercy Merrick appeared almost saintly. This was deemed irresponsible:

It is all very well to preach that a penitent woman may be reclaimed ... it is a more serious thing to hold before the young the idea that absolute purity and highest grace are the result rather of a fall into the gutter and a subsequent ablution than a course of consistent rectitude.[54]

The New Magdalen was one of several contemporary plays dealing with questions of sexual behaviour. In the *Athenaeum* Collins's play was reviewed alongside *Les Idées de Madame Aubray* by Alexandre Dumas *fils* at the Princess's Theatre, another story of the *demi-monde*. Both plays argued for forgiveness for 'fallen' women, but Collins was judged rather bolder. His customary nervousness on opening night evaporated, when he took a curtain call and was cheered to the echo. He wrote to a theatrical friend: 'The reception of my *New Magdalen* was prodigious.

I was forced to appear halfway through the piece, as well as at the end. The acting took every one by surprise, and the second night's enthusiasm quite equalled the first. ... We have really hit the mark' (BGLL II, 406).

* * * * *

Despite this new-found confidence, Collins reached the peak of his dramatic success with *The New Magdalen*. While he went on writing plays up almost until his death, he was less committed. He continued to enjoy extensive social contacts in the theatre and became fascinated by a number of popular performers, notably the American actress Mary Anderson. However, the less than dynamic production of *The Moonstone* (Olympic, 1877) suggested to observers that Collins's creative energy was running low. Collins tried to reassure the New York impresario Augustin Daly that he had plenty of '*original* plays in my mind (*not* adaptations from my novels) – and I want to appeal to the American public' (BGLL IV, 402). But his last original drama proved to be the ill-fated play *Rank and Riches*. Despite the lavish staging, this had the distinction of being laughed off when it premiered at the Adelphi Theatre in June 1883. The *Dramatic Notes's* critic described it as 'having not a single redeeming feature', expressing himself mystified how 'a man of reputation could come to sign his name to such rubbish and how a manager possessing the slightest experience could be found to give it a trial'.[55] Near the end of his career Collins made a final, forlorn attempt to compose narrative and dramatic versions of a single plot with *The Evil Genius* in 1886, but, though the still incomplete play underwent a ritual 'copyright performance', it was never professionally produced.

At the beginning of this chapter, we quoted Collin's belief that his own faculty was 'a dramatic one'. The extent of this 'faculty' remains a matter of some dispute, but most critics have echoed Edmund Yates in seeing his dramatic efforts as more 'dramatic sketches' than fully-formed plays. 'As a dramatist', Yates added, 'Wilkie Collins cannot be considered to have been successful.'[56] Yet it is also possible to detect a more adventurous spirit and coherent purpose in Collins's plays – particularly the later adaptations.[57] There we sense a conflict between the practical demands of writing for a 'stock' company and a desire to push the boundaries of what could be said and done. Taken together, *The New Magdalen* and *Man and Wife* can be seen as indicative of a significant shift in the direction of Collins's playwriting. Specifically, they represent an edging away from sensational melodrama towards the framework of the so-called well-made play and the problem play, forms which would come to dominate the British and French stages in the 1880s and 1890s. The well-made play involved a 'tight logic of plot, the subordination of character to situation' and 'a secret known only to some of the characters and usually shared with the audience, one character trying to keep it hidden or another trying to uncover it. Initial exposition is normally followed by ups and downs in the characters' fortunes and leads via the mechanical creation of suspense to the inevitable resolution in a *scène à faire*'.[58] Collins read the works of the leading practitioners of the form, Eugene Scribe (1791–1861) and Victorien Sardou (1831–1908), and shared with them the commitment to an entertainment and exciting, larger-than-life plot. As it developed during the course of the nineteenth century, the 'well-made' play took over some of the functions of melodrama in tackling social issues, and taking on an additional label: 'the problem play'. The problem to be resolved by the end of the play was often related to questions of male–female relations – marriage, divorce, prostitution, the sexual double standard, women's rights – as well as issues surrounding business ethics and alcoholism. The social problem was usually voiced through different characters on stage including the figure of the *rasionneur*, a right-thinking character – Patrick Lundie in *Man and Wife*, for example – who guides the audience's response. Later in the century, with the growing influence of Henrik Ibsen, A.W. Pinero and Oscar Wilde were acclaimed as masters of this kind of drama. Without making any great claims for Collins as a radical or experimental playwright, it is possible to see the adaptations of his didactic novels in the early 1870s as forerunners of this style.

8
Collins as Missionary

What brought good Wilkie's genius nigh perdition?
Some demon whispered – 'Wilkie! have a mission.'
(Algernon Swinburne, *Fortnightly Review*,
November 1889)

Novelists with a mission were hardly a rarity in the Victorian period. From the 1830s, journals of popular education had begun to employ short and serial fiction as a vehicle for messages either evangelical or utilitarian, and as the century wore on a similar medium was exploited by an increasingly wide range of crusading bodies – all the way from the temperance league to the suffragettes. Even writers of 'bloods' in penny weekly numbers for a working-class audience typically spiced their melodramatic tales with condemnations of aristocratic vice and praise for honest labour, the most notorious example being the republican George Reynolds who also ran a radical weekly paper. Major writers were themselves by no means immune to the attractions of didacticism, often combining the roles of novelist and journalist in rather similar fashion. From the mid-1840s, those willing to employ works of fiction to advocate their varying solutions to the pressing problem of the 'Condition of England' after four decades of rapid industrialization included Disraeli (in the trilogy beginning with *Coningsby*, 1844), Gaskell (with *Mary Barton*, 1848, and *North and South*, 1855), Charles Kingsley (in *Alton Locke*, 1850, and *Yeast*, 1851), plus of course Dickens himself (in *Hard Times*, 1854). In the mid-1860s, George Eliot with *Felix Holt* (1866) and Anthony Trollope in *Phineas Finn* (1869) were among the novelists to intervene in the debate around the second reform bill of 1867, which extended the franchise to many working men. It was in fact around this time, following the publication of *Man and Wife* in 1870, with its frontal attack on the cultivation of athleticism in English education and its strident protests against the anomalies and injustices of British marriage law, that Collins began to acquire a controversial reputation as a novelist with a purpose. In a sense, however, Collins had always been a writer with missionary tendencies. As we saw in Chapter 4, his work as a journalist throughout the 1850s on both Pigott's radical *Leader* and Dickens's liberal *Household Words* encouraged him regularly to write as a social critic, though there his reformist zeal was typically restrained by the comic form of the dramatic monologue. And, as we have seen elsewhere, in early novels such as *Antonina, Basil, The Woman in White*, and *No Name*, in particular, Collins is keen to draw attention to the legal disabilities and social vulnerabilities of young women, but in these cases the point is typically made by implication only, through the outrageous situations permitted and indeed encouraged by the genres of gothic and sensation. From the early 1870s, however, his various social protests are incorporated much more explicitly and aggressively into his works of fiction.

The most popular explanation of this sea change has been the increasing literary influence of Charles Reade following the death of Dickens, Collins's first and greatest mentor. Reade's work indeed provides the most important precedent for the combination of sensational form and social purpose. As we saw in Chapter 1, Reade had long cultivated a controversial public profile, writing frequently to the press to protest at literary wrongs and engaging frequently in litigation to defend his literary rights. Moreover, from *It is Never Too Late to Mend* in 1856, with its vivid depiction of solitary confinement and other horrors of the contemporary prison regime, Reade evolved a distinctive system of documentary composition for a lengthy literary form that he called the 'Matter-of-Fact Romance'. Large quantities of press clippings, government statistics, and personal memos were collected together in notebooks devoted to specific abuses, which were then incorporated (often *verbatim*) into emotionally charged melodramatic plots designed to shock the reader into an active response. Reade's method reached its apogee with *Hard Cash* (1863) and *Put Yourself in His Place* (1870), which, respectively, denounced abuses in private lunatic asylums and terrorist outrages on the part of trade unions. While Collins was never quite so systematic or so flagrant, he clearly learned a good deal from Reade's missionary methods. But it is perhaps too easy to read a symbolic meaning into the fact that Dickens died suddenly in the month that *Man and Wife* was published in book form, and that, at the funeral on 14 June 1870, as they stood side by side over the open grave, Reade laid his head on Collins's shoulder and wept (Peters, 319–20). In fact, Collins and Reade had already been good friends for at least a decade, often exchanging encouraging criticism of each other's work-in-progress whether fictional or dramatic, and there is little sign in the extant correspondence of any new phase in the relationship after Dickens's demise.

Underlying Collins's shift towards the fiction of social purpose, there in fact seems to be not a single cause but a complex of literary and social factors. One was Collins's growing annoyance with the mid-Victorian publishing regime (see Chapters 3 and 10), which encouraged the unwarranted intrusion of conservative literary middlemen – publishers and editors as well as reviewers – into what Collins rather naively assumed to be a direct, intimate relation with his reading public. This frustration was often vented not only in aggressive prefaces to his works, but also in provocative narratorial statements within the fiction itself. In this sense it is no accident that the beginning of Collins's missionary phases coincides with his increasing commitment to theatrical activities, where he also dreams of establishing more immediate contact with a popular audience. A related factor here is Collins's tendency to move away from the multiple-narrative technique perfected in *The Woman in White* towards a more conventional story-telling style in the third person, which permits *ex cathedra* authorial pronouncements. A characteristic example is found in the Prologue to *Man and Wife*, where a description of Irish marriage law by one of the characters is glossed by the narrator, 'that law still stands – to the disgrace of the English Legislature and the English Nation' (*M&W*, 27). But the most obvious factor was his gradual withdrawal from journalistic activity during the 1860s, following his resignation from the editorial team of *All the Year Round*, so that he then tended to channel his interest in the social topics of the day directly into current literary work. In his dedicatory preface to *Jezebel's Daughter*, he thus claimed 'the same liberty' in the treatment of adult subjects as 'a writer in a newspaper', and likened the role of novelist to that of 'a clergyman in a pulpit' (*JD*, 6).

Whatever the causes underlying Collins's adoption of the stance of the novelist with a purpose, there is no doubt that the move has had a bad press. In his obituary assessment cited at the head of this chapter, Swinburne was by no means uniformly critical of Collins's later fiction, recognizing that 'nothing can be more fatuous than to brand all didactic or missionary fiction as an illegitimate or inferior form of art' and offering praise to *Man and Wife* in particular (Page, 262). However, his witty parody of Alexander Pope's couplet obviously struck a chord.

Well before that, contemporary reviewers had tended to be amused rather than impressed by the author's social missions, often finding them difficult to take seriously in combination with Collins's continued preference for frauds, murders, and the other paraphernalia of sensational narrative. The author's hectoring prefatory remarks, in particular, with their references to painstaking research, documentary accuracy, and social relevance, tended to raise critical hackles; with *Jezebel's Daughter*, for example, the *Spectator* reviewer sneered, 'Is Mr Collins ... a moral reformer, or is he merely an ingenious story teller? ... It would seem ... that Mr Collins is inclined to take himself quite seriously ...' (Page, 208).

In this chapter we will thus look at some of the most striking examples of these later novels and the ways in which they engage with the social concerns of the time. With some regret we shall leave aside those narratives where the missionary impulse seems only of secondary importance: *Poor Miss Finch* (1872), which challenges prejudices based on physical disability and physical characteristics like skin colour; *The Law and the Lady* (1875), which attacks the intermediate Scottish verdict of 'Not Proven' in a detective story recalling the notorious Madeleine Smith poisoning case of 1857, and featuring a determined and resourceful female sleuth; *The Two Destinies* (1876), with its extraordinary defence of telepathic communication, and its dedication to Charles Reade as an 'old friend and brother in the art'; the anti-Jesuit novel *The Black Robe* (1881); and *The Legacy of Cain* (1889), where the deterministic nature of contemporary theories of heredity is explored and exploded. Instead we shall concentrate on *Man and Wife* (1870), *The New Magdalen* (1873), *Heart and Science* (1883), and *The Evil Genius* (1886), where the didactic urge is most explicit. (Other 'novels with a purpose' are discussed in some detail in the following chapters, notably *The Fallen Leaves* (1879) in Chapter 9, and *Jezebel's Daughter* (1880) in Chapter 10.)

* * * * *

Man and Wife, the novel which signalled Collins's emergence as a novelist of social protest, was serialized in *Cassell's Magazine* from 20 November 1869 and appeared in three volumes in June 1870, published on a commission basis by the antiquarian bookseller F.S. Ellis. Rather earlier, Collins's correspondence shows him consulting with both his solicitors, Bentham and Tindell, concerning marriage under the Irish and Scottish legal systems (B&C II, 313; BGLL II, 139–40) and on matters of physical education and athletic culture with the journalist

Joseph Parkinson (B&C II, 323–5; BGLL II, 153–4). With the novel well under way, in the autumn Collins told his American publishers that he was attempting 'to strike an entirely new vein' (BGLL II, 155–6). He provided more detail in a long letter to his old friend Fred Lehmann, then on a business trip to the United States:

> I sit here all day, attacking English Institutions – battering down the marriage laws of Scotland and Ireland, and reviling athletic sports – in short writing an *un*popular book, which may possibly make a hit, from the mere oddity of a modern writer running full tilt against the popular sentiment, instead of clinging to it.
>
> (B&C II, 326–7)

The legal anomalies and injustices in question concern the impediments to 'mixed marriages' between Catholics and Protestants under Irish law, and the countenancing of 'irregular marriages' under Scottish law.[1] Public attention was drawn simultaneously to these legal defects through the celebrated 'Yelverton Case' running through the courts from 1858. When the case finally reached the House of Lords in 1864, judgement was given by a single vote in favour of the Irish Protestant Captain Charles Yelverton, who was thus declared innocent of bigamy, and against the English Catholic Theresa Longworth, who had claimed that she was legally united with Yelverton under both an irregular Scottish ceremony and an Irish rite conducted by a Roman priest. The vexed questions arising from this case were among those considered by the Royal Commission on the Laws of Marriage reporting in 1868, and largely dealt within the Marriage Causes and Marriage Law Amendment Act (33 & 34 Vict. c. 110), passed after the publication of *Man and Wife*.[2] The author's attack on the cult of athleticism was not aimed at the 'muscular Christianity' advocated a decade earlier by Charles Kingsley and Thomas Hughes – in Chapter 5 we saw how the idea of 'manliness' was given a positive interpretation in *The Woman in White* – but rather at more recent campaigns to enforce physical education in state schools.[3]

While writing the novel, the author also provided detailed feedback on the serial instalments of Charles Reade's current protest novel, *Put Yourself in His Place*, and it seems likely that Collins received similar comments in return (B&C II, 333–5). This may be one of the factors encouraging the author to take such an aggressive line with his publishers during the production of *Man and Wife*. On negotiating the contract with Cassell's, aware of the firm's evangelical affiliations and the family readership of its house magazine, Collins had insisted on a clause restraining the editors from making any substantive alterations to his manuscript (BGLL II, 147). When Collins was asked to remove an expletive from the sixth weekly part, he reported himself 'ready to make what concessions I can to your ideas of what is due to your constituency, at the outset of our literary connection', but warned that this was not to be taken as a precedent: 'It is quite possible that your peculiar constituency may take exception to things to come in my story ... which are connected with a much higher and larger moral point of view than they are capable of taking themselves. In these cases, I am afraid you will find me deaf to all remonstrances ...' (BGLL II, 152). Only a few weeks later, Cassell's informed the author that a translation of his novel was to appear in a Dutch magazine without authorization from or payment to the author, and he promptly requested their assistance in publicizing what he saw as an act of piracy. He thus engaged in a provocative exchange of letters with the Dutch publishers, and had them published prominently in the *Echo*, the popular London evening paper owned by Cassell's, along with a lengthy editorial on 'Mr Collins and his Rights'.[4] When the Dutch publishers conceded, Collins wrote triumphantly to Reade, 'if you and I could get our brethren ... to agree together – we should have international copy right all over the world' (B&C II, 333).

With the birth of Marian Dawson in July 1869, the first of his three children by Martha Rudd, Collins was anxious to increase the return on his literary capital, and had begun to investigate the possibility of reprinting his backlist novels in a cheap serial format; but the negotiations came to nothing and he was left scrambling to find a volume publisher for his latest offering, rejecting a poor offer from Tinsley, and being himself turned down by Cassell's. The publishing arrangements with F.S. Ellis for the three-decker edition of *Man and Wife* were thus in themselves a sign of the author's uncertainty regarding his position in the literary marketplace. Ellis had little experience of fiction publishing or the circulating libraries, and the author became dissatisfied with both the printing and advertising arrangements. Shortly after publication, Collins wrote to his solicitor to complain: 'Mr Ellis is damaging the chances of the book by keeping its publication as profound a secret as he can. ... How are the people to know that the book is ready? ... He is losing the whole advantage of my name and position with novel-readers, by the manner in which he is neglecting the advertising, at the very time when the book stands in the utmost need of it' (B&C II, 343). In the event, Collins's worries seem to have been unfounded; the circulation of *Cassell's Magazine* rose to 70,000 while *Man and Wife* was running, and Ellis's first edition of 1000 copies sold out in within a fortnight and a second had to be rushed out.

Given the revival of interest in 'The Woman Question' in the period and the increasingly loud calls for a Married Woman's Property Act which would allow wives some protection for their own estate or income, there was evident topicality in the discussion of disabilities suffered by women on account of opaque marriage legislation. This is most notable in the depictions of the entrapped wives Anne Silvester and the mute servant Hester Dethridge, who despite class difference is Anne's *doppelgänger*. But it is also apparent in the no-holds-barred portrait of Geoffrey Delamayn, a brutish athlete, an 'idol' of 'popular worship' (*M&W*, 77), on whose systematic abuse of women society turns a blind eye. Geoffrey, described as 'an animal' and a sexual sadist, is a perverted version of Kingsley's 'muscular sportsman', a type admired by many but loathed by the notoriously sedentary Collins. As Julian Hawthorne recalled, the author 'had ever slumped at his desk and breathed only indoor air. ... Though the England of his prime had been a cricketing athletic, outdoor England, Wilkie was soft, plump and pale' (Peters, 341). In the novel, Collins's mouthpiece Sir Patrick Lundie announces: 'I don't like the model young Briton. I don't see the sense of crowing over him as a superb national production because he is big and strong and drinks beer with impunity, and takes a cold shower bath all the year round. There is far too much glorification in England, just now, of the mere physical qualities which an Englishman shares with the savage and the brute.' (*M&W*, 68). The novel's central interest is Anne's Silvester's struggle to survive the brutal treatment at the hands of Geoffrey who, thanks to the vagaries of the Scottish marriage laws, finds himself legally bound to the woman he had only wanted to seduce. The novel's climax was, even by Collins's standards, unusually lurid. There we see Hester – a woman symbolically and literally battered silent, who has murdered her own husband because the law allows her no legitimate means of escape – rescuing her spiritual sister, Anne, and attempting to strangle Geoffrey herself – in the same moment that, weakened by over-training, he suffers a fatal stroke.

Despite the popular success of *Man and Wife* both in narrative form and on the stage, many reviewers objected both to its didactic tone and to its social message. Most notably, the *Saturday Review* suggested that the story unfolds in a slow and 'artificial' manner, co-incidences are rife and 'the characters play hide and seek in a manner unknown in real life – not from want of sense, but obviously with the view of prolonging our suspense – and ... it requires a clear head to remember the varying relations of the characters throughout the entanglements in which they are involved'; more significantly, the paper took a derisory attitude to the novel's declared social purposes: 'If one moral is generally too much, two morals are surely unjustifiable. Mr Collins might be content with assaulting running and boat-racing without breaking a lance at the same moment against all our marriage laws' (cited in Page, 182–3). Reviewing the novel for *Blackwood's Magazine*, Margaret Oliphant complained that Collins's characters acted 'contrary to the commonest laws not only of conventional morality but of ordinary reason' [i.e. no one would believe that an intelligent and virtuous woman like Anne Silvester would allow herself to be seduced by Geoffrey Delamayn], and that the novel's message fell flat because Collins's 'strength, which lies in plot and complication of incident, does not lend itself successfully to polemics' (cited in Page, 188). But when the reviewer for *Putman's Monthly Magazine* described Geoffrey and Anne as comprehensible purely in the context of the fashion for 'characters ... standing for ideas',[5] he was also suggesting links between Collins's aims and those of Dickens, whose later 'Condition of England' novels, *Bleak House* (1852) and *Our Mutual Friend* (1865), share *Man and Wife*'s angry tone. As a study in amorality and 'the savage element in humanity' (*M&W*, 79), Geoffrey Delamayn also carries echoes of Tito Melema in George Eliot's *Romola* (1863) and the bullying Sir Hugh Clavering in Anthony Trollope's *The Claverings* (1867). Collins's novel can also be read usefully alongside Oliphant's *The Ladies Lindores* (1873), for both works present the home in Gothic terms as a place of torture and imprisonment, ruled over by loutish, tyrannical husbands, whose deaths come as a source of relief. More generally, then, *Man and Wife* can be related to an increasing concern in the fiction of the 1870s with female powerlessness in marriage.

* * * * *

As the title indicates, *The New Magdalen* is the story of a 'fallen woman', whose efforts to escape from her past are constantly thwarted by the prejudices of 'respectable' society. The novel opens powerfully with the meeting of two young English women, a lady traveller in distress and a volunteer nurse, on a battlefield during the Franco-Prussian war. They narrate their respective hard-luck stories: Grace tells how she has been orphaned abroad and is returning home with a letter of introduction to a wealthy family friend; Mercy tells of her foster-father's incestuous desire as she reaches adolescence, her rape while drugged and subsequent descent into prostitution as a means of survival, and her efforts towards rehabilitation via penitential work for the Red Cross. When Grace – small-minded and contemptuous of the other's predicament – is hit by a German shell a new prospect opens up for Mercy: '*She might be Grace Roseberry if she dared!* ... A new identity, which she might own anywhere! a new name, which was beyond reproach! a new past life into which all the world might search and be welcome' (*NM*, 37–8). At first her plan to regain respectability seems to succeed, but Grace makes an unexpected and vengeful return, and Mercy's fiancé breaks off their engagement. She confesses her path of deception to Julian Gray, a high-minded clergyman who has fallen in love with her. They eventually marry but are rejected by society, and the novel ends as they abandon England to make a fresh start in the New World.

The novel is thus another text questioning the behavioural norms for women dictated by society. It also takes up a complex of themes familiar to readers of the earlier fiction: good and bad breeding; social imposture and social exclusion; English hypocrisy and complacency, and the prevalence of the double standard; the family sphere as a place of danger as well as safety, society's more systematic abuse of women, and the catastrophic effects of losing respectability. The novel's closing chapters sound a more general alarm concerning moral degeneration and national decline, in the voice of the preacher-protagonist:

> How often ... have I thundered with all my heart and soul against the wicked extravagance of dress among women – against their filthy false hair and their nauseous powders and paints! How often ... have I denounced the mercenary and material spirit of the age – the habitual corruptions and dishonesties of commerce, in high places and in low! What good have I done? I have delighted the very people whom it was my object to rebuke.
>
> (*NM*, 395)

Initially, Mercy appears as one of Collins's female fantasy figures – a 'degraded and designing woman' (*NM*, 385), who declares, 'I deny that I have done wrong. Society has used me cruelly; I owe nothing to Society. I have a right to take any advantage of it if I can' (*NM*, 223). Thus there are echoes of Magdalen Vanstone in *No Name* and Lydia Gwilt in *Armadale*, as well as of Walter Hartright in his encounter with Mrs Catherick in *The Woman in White*. But the hard-hitting tone of the representation wavers in the portrayal of the relationship between

Mercy and Julian Gray. (In this respect, as indeed more generally in its narrative structure and social message, *The New Magdalen* bears a good deal of similarity to George Reynolds's early melodramatic tale of a modern Magdalen, *Rosa Lambert; or, the Memoirs of an Unfortunate Woman*, which appeared in penny numbers during 1853–4.)[6] In the second half of his novel, Collins offers social critique watered down with crude religious allegory, so much so that Swinburne was to find the work 'feeble, false and silly in its sentimental cleverness' (Page, 261). To other readers also, Gray seems too Christ-like, Mercy too self-abasing, Horace too much the Pharisee, and Grace too vengeful and 'viperish' (*NM*, 228).

The New Magdalen is a novel which in its situations, structure, and settings was deliberately designed for dramatic adaptation, very successfully as it turned out. As shown in Chapter 7, Collins's own stage version of the novel was played to popular acclaim in May 1873, at the same time as the book version was published, and there were revivals throughout the Victorian period, followed by a number of silent film versions before the First World War. The serial also did well. In May 1873, the *Penny Illustrated Magazine* reported that *Temple Bar* had become 'the most sought after monthly of 1873', thanks to Collins's story. This was despite – or perhaps because of – the 'nauseus episode' detailing in 'repulsive detail' Mercy's fall from grace; on this subject Collins was counselled to note the proper 'delicacy' of Dickens's (more conventional) treatment of the theme of the fallen woman in his presentation of Little Emily in *David Copperfield*.[7] Overall, however, the novel did little to consolidate Collins's reputation and English sales were, he noted, 'thoroughly discouraging – the New Magdalen in book form, barely realising £300 ...'. Collins blamed the failure on the stranglehold of Charles Mudie and the circulating libraries on the distribution of new books (BGLL II, 401).

* * * * *

Appearing almost a decade after *The New Magdalen, Heart and Science: A Story of the Present Time* shares the earlier novel's sense of moral outrage and didactic tone. It also exhibits indebtedness to earlier character types: there is an idealistic young professional (Dr Ovid Vere); a beautiful, persecuted, and orphaned heiress (Carmina Craywell); a scheming, psychopathic, older woman (Mrs Gallilee); a sinister doctor (Nathan Benjulia); and a topical target: cruelty to animals in scientific experiments. Set in London and treating the medical and moral issues surrounding the vivisection debate of the 1870s and 1880s, under the stewardship of RSPCA, the Victoria Street Society for the Protection of Animals, and the London Anti-Vivisection Society, and with prominent agitators such as Frances Power Cobbe, Robert Browning, and Lewis Carroll, *Heart and Science* had an evident mission. 'I am striking a blow in this new story at the wretches who are called vivisectors', Collins told Wybert Reeve in August 1882 (BGLL III, 363). Collins claimed to have researched his topic thoroughly, or at least as thoroughly as Charles Reade would have done, by reading press reports and by following the trial in 1881 of Dr David Ferrier, who was acquitted of participating in cerebral dissection of a living monkey without a license. Collins had sold the story in advance simultaneously to the metropolitan monthly *Belgravia* and a syndicate of weekly newspapers, and was forced to produce the manuscript quite quickly; just after completing the story at the end of 1882 he described himself as 'mercilessly excited ... writing week after week without a day's interval of rest' (B&C II, 453). Reporting on the serial's reception, and smarting after the abject failure of his play *Rank and Riches*, he observed:

> The success of the book here has been extraordinary. 'Benjulia' has matched 'Fosco'. While the dramatic critics declare that I have written vilest rubbish – the literary critics congratulate me on the production of a masterpiece!
>
> (B&C II, 460)

Reviewers, while admiring Collins's stamina in continuing to produce fiction at such regular intervals, in fact expressed a number of reservations. '[T]he chief drawback of the book, one which it shares with most of its class, is that except the ill-conducted and ill-fated Benjulia there is scarcely anybody in whom it is possible to take much interest', said the *Pall Mall Budget*.[8] Praise from the *Fortnightly Review* was qualified by the reflection that 'the serious novel of vivisection, fair-minded and properly informed ... founded faithfully upon life, instead of extracted from the depths of the author's moral consciousness, still remains to be written'.[9]

Collins's 'moral consciousness' certainly looms large. There is the suspicious attitude towards what we would now call psychiatrists – 'experts' in the diseases of the human mind and their supposed cures. A kind of 'a living skeleton', 'hideously' tall and thin, Dr Benjulia has 'a mania' for scientific experiments (*H&S*, 95), but his is the touch of death rather than life. His moral attenuation means that he is prepared to allow not only helpless animals but also young women to face death in the furtherance of medical knowledge. (One of the messages that the novel sends out is the analogous situation of the helpless laboratory animals and those other underdogs, Victorian women.) Also present in the novel are shock and sensation – the realization that the strange and the sinister can be encountered even in a familiar environment like the middle-class home. Once again a key presence is the figure of what Barbara Creed has called the 'monstrous feminine', a figure which can (like many of Collins criminals – male or female) be situated in relation to what Julia Kristeva has famously termed 'abjection', namely, that which does 'not respect borders, positions, rules', that which 'disturbs identity, system, order' and which threatens life.[10] In *Heart and Science* the malevolent, abusive mother Mrs Gallilee is a woman whose narcissistic pursuit of her scientific hobby has 'deliberately starved her imagination, and emptied her heart of any tenderness of feeling which it might once have possessed' (*H&S*, 67). Mrs Gallilee's strangeness, her vanities, her emotional anaesthesia, her alienation from her family, and her ruthlessness exhibit themselves throughout in her spiteful treatment of Carmina, though her true self is only fully revealed when she is removed to a lunatic asylum where she can give full rein to her mania. Suspicion of the crimes committed in the name of science seems to have strengthened Collins's tendency to endorse the traditional values of domesticity and woman's 'proper' but passive role as guardians of the home, curbing – in this novel at least – his tendency to submit those values to sceptical inquiry.

* * * * *

The Evil Genius: A Domestic Story centres on a seemingly ideal bourgeois marriage which breaks down when the husband (Herbert) becomes infatuated with the vulnerable young woman (Sydney) recruited as a governess for his daughter (Kitty). As discussed in Chapter 10, the novel avoids sensationalism and tends towards comedy. After their separation, the wife (Catherine) is persuaded to petition for divorce to secure custody of Kitty. The affair between Herbert and Sydney does not last; the prospective second marriage of Catherine to a philanthropist (Bennydeck) comes to nothing; and the novel ends with Kitty contriving the reconciliation and remarriage of her divorced parents. Though not inclined to rate Collins's work very highly, the *Saturday Review* found 'real pathos in the figures of the two women who sacrifice themselves ... for a man immeasurably inferior to both of them'.[11] Originally given the ironical title 'Home! Sweet Home!' (BGLL IV, 117–8), the novel's social purpose principally concerns the operation of family law. Debate and legislation in this area in the second half of the nineteenth century centred on two conflicts: that between marriage as a religious and a social union, and thus between the jurisdiction of the ecclesiastical and civil courts; and that between patriarchal and liberal notions of the status of the wife and children within the family. There are three key pieces of English legislation here.[12]

The Matrimonial Causes Act of 1857 created a new civil Divorce Court with jurisdiction over both judicial separation (transferred from the ecclesiastical courts) and judicial divorce (replacing divorce by private Act of Parliament). This simultaneously took the regulation of the breakdown of marriage out of the hands of the church, and slightly increased the chances for women and members of the upper middle class to petition for divorce. But the grounds for divorce retained the concepts of matrimonial offence and the guilty party, and with them the patriarchal discrimination between definitions of adultery for the husband and the wife. The high cost and social stigma of a successful petition meant that instances increased only from 141 in 1861 to 477 in 1901 (from 0.04 to 0.08 per thousand unions), though those by women now consistently accounted for just over 40 per cent of the total.[13] The Married Women's Property Act of 1882 introduced a distinct status in law for married women, breaching the common-law concept of coverture, that is, that on marriage a husband acquired ownership or control of his wife's property and assumed the accompanying legal rights and responsibilities. The Guardianship of Infants Act of 1886 questioned the common-law presumption of the paramountcy of the father's claims in matters of child custody, and asserted the equal importance of the mother's wishes and the child's welfare. These issues are represented in or inform Collins's narrative, but there they are complicated by the question of Scottish family law. In the area of divorce the key differences were that, in Scotland, judicial divorce had been available since the sixteenth century, that desertion was also a ground for petition, and, crucially, that there was a single definition of adultery which applied to both husband and wife.

Catherine is thus persuaded by her lawyer that a petition for judicial divorce is the only way to guarantee sole custody of her daughter Kitty. A *de facto* separation or a private separation agreement would both, in common law, leave custody of Kitty to Herbert. But since Catherine and Herbert were married under Scottish law, she can petition for divorce on the sole grounds of his adultery with Sydney, and expect custody of Kitty as the innocent party. However, the scenes showing the court judgement and public reaction to it illustrate respectively the centrality of the concept of wrongdoing in decisions on divorce and the subsequent exclusion of even the innocent party from polite society. At the same time, the novel sometimes exhibits a surprising degree of sympathy with the notion of divorce as contrary to the teachings of Christ. This view underlay the stance taken by those such as William Gladstone and Bishop Wilberforce who felt bound by Christian conscience to oppose the 1857 bill clause by clause as it passed through Parliament. In the novel it is the view taken initially by Catherine and absolutely by Bennydeck. Nevertheless there is little doubt that Collins's concern is predominantly secular and psychological. His overall inclination is clearly to support the move away from the patriarchal concept of matrimony as a strategy for the preservation of property and the male line, and towards the liberal view of the marriage union as an equal partnership. The issue of the day was that of child custody, and the drift of the narrative is to offer imperative psychological evidence in support of the wishes of the mother and, most notably, the welfare of the child.[14] In the process, however, and under the pressure of the demands of comic closure, Collins gets himself into the curious position of seeming to support the double standard on adultery of English law against the single standard of Scottish law. In the novel's concluding chapters, the author's mouthpiece comes to the following conclusion:

> ... where the husband's fault is sexual frailty, I say the English law which refuses Divorce on that ground alone is right, and the Scotch law which grants it is wrong. Religion, which rightly condemns sins, pardons it on the condition of true penitence. Why is a wife not to pardon it for the same reason? Why are the lives of a father, a mother, and a child to be wrecked, when those lives may be saved by the exercise of the first of Christian virtues – forgiveness of injuries? In such a case as this I regret that Divorce exists; and I rejoice when husband and wife and child are one flesh again, re-united by the law of nature which is the law of God.
>
> (*EG*, 347)[15]

It is difficult to understand how closing off Catherine's option of petitioning for divorce, with the consequence that custody of Kitty would have passed to Herbert, would have made forgiveness and reconciliation more likely – and this a question which the psychological emphasis of the narrative will not allow us to ignore. The reason given here in support of the double standard is the sexual frailty of the male rather than the need to ensure legitimate succession, but the conservative implications are reinforced by the powerful resurgence of the religious rhetoric.

* * * * *

As indeed with Charles Reade, Collins's treatment of social problems in the later novels can sometimes be both iron-handed and feather-brained. There are also occasions when he seems merely to be riding the latest hobby-horse – that is, picking up an issue of the day and exploiting it as raw material for his latest fictional project but dropping it soon after the novel achieves satisfactory sales. This appears to be true both of the topic of athleticism in *Man and Wife* and vivisection in *Heart and Science,* where in neither case is there any evidence of the author's continuing concern with the issue once the book is written. When George Sala wrote a leader in the *Daily Telegraph* supporting Collins's mockery of moral muscularity in *Man and Wife,* and attacking W.H. Dixon's campaign at the Metropolitan School Board to enforce physical drilling in all establishments, Collins was copious in his thanks, but thereafter seems to have concerned himself not at all with matters of public education (BGLL II, 238–9). Although, when *Heart and Science* was published in volume form in April 1883, both in his preface and in a personal letter, Collins had cordially acknowledged Francis Power Cobbe's loan of books and other materials while he was preparing his case against animal experiments, when he was invited in 1887 to hear her speak at the annual meeting of what had by then become the Victoria Street and International Society for the Total Abolition of Vivisection, he seems to have pleaded a fictional previous engagement (BGLL III, 402, and IV, 237–8). On the other hand, in Collins's campaigns against laws directly and indirectly enforcing the social disabilities of women in the private sphere at least, there is undoubtedly a good deal of long-term commitment and a manifest consistency with the preoccupations of the novels written before the author was saddled with the title of a social activist. Perhaps indeed even the appeals against the athlete and the vivisector can be metaphorically linked to the same cause, as oppression of and violence against weaker creatures, whether younger boys in public schools or dumb animals. Perhaps Wilkie's genius and his social missions are not quite so alien from each other as Swinburne's couplet has led us to think.

9
Collins Overseas

The flourishing of Collins's career as a writer coincided with a series of momentous political conflicts which, though they often took place a long way from home, created considerable domestic alarm when reported in the London press: the republican revolutions and nationalist rebellions that shook Europe in and after 1848, the periodic outbreaks of imperial tension both external and internal, represented respectively by the Crimean War of 1854–5 and the Indian Mutiny of 1857–8, or the long Civil War beginning in 1861 that nearly tore apart the United States, to mention only the most newsworthy. This chapter focuses on the English author's personal engagement with this wider world, not only directly via foreign travel and correspondence but also in a more dispersed way through his fictional deployment of alien settings and characters, and through his responses to the international publication and reception of his work.

As mentioned in Chapter 1, Collins was an enthusiastic traveller. He was proud of his immunity to seasickness, and, as shown in Table 9.1, in addition to the transatlantic voyages permitting his North American reading tour of 1873–4, he seems to have made the crossing to continental Europe around twenty-five times in all. Though Paris was his most common destination, he made the lengthy journey to Italy on five separate occasions, including the trip with his parents as a teenager, and on three others made it as far south as Switzerland or the Black Forest. On his youthful visits to the Continent, Collins looked not only to broaden his cultural horizons but also to escape from the restrictions imposed by bourgeois English society to a world of bohemian license and adventure. In middle age he more often sought professional advancement as a writer, rest after literary labour, or recuperation from bouts of ill health, while his deteriorating physical condition seems to

Table 9.1 Overseas travel by Wilkie Collins

Age	Period	Main destinations	Travel companions	Notes
5	Summer 1829	FRANCE (Boulogne)	father, mother & brother	
12–14	Sept. 1836–Aug. 1838	FRANCE (Paris/Nice) ITALY (Genoa/Pisa/ Florence/Rome/ Naples/Ischia/Venice)	father, mother & brother	
20	Aug.–Sept. 1844	FRANCE (Paris)	Charles Ward	
21	Sept.–Oct. 1845	FRANCE (Paris)	alone	
22	July–Aug. 1846	BELGIUM (Antwerp/Brussels)	Charles Ward	
23	Aug. 1847	FRANCE (Normandy/Paris)	Charles Ward	
25	Sept. 1849	FRANCE (Paris/Tours/Orleans)	Charles Ward	
29	Aug. 1853	FRANCE (Boulogne)	alone	visiting Dickens
29	Oct.–Dec. 1853	FRANCE (Paris/Strasbourg) SWITZERLAND (Lausanne) ITALY (Genoa/Milan/Naples/ Rome/Florence/Venice)	Charles Dickens, Augustus Egg	
30	July–Sept. 1854	FRANCE (Boulogne)	alone	visiting Dickens
31	Mid-Feb. 1855	FRANCE (Paris)	Charles Dickens	
31	6–7 Aug. 1855	FRANCE (Boulogne)	Dickens party	overnight stay
32	Mar.–Apr. 1856	FRANCE (Paris)	alone	meets Dickens
32	June–July 1856	FRANCE (Cherbourg)	Edward Pigott	sailing trip

32	Aug.–Sept. 1856	FRANCE (Boulogne)	alone	visiting Dickens
39	Apr.–June 1863	GERMANY (Aachen/Wildbad)	German courier only	taking the waters
39–40	Oct. 1863–Mar. 1864	FRANCE (Paris/Marseilles) ITALY (Rome/Naples/Florence)	Caroline & Harriet Graves	for health reasons
41	Feb.–Mar. 1865	FRANCE (Paris)	Fred Lehmann	for about a week
42	Apr. 1866	FRANCE (Paris)	Fred Lehmann	for about a week
42	Oct.–Dec. 1866	FRANCE (Paris) ITALY (Milan/Bologna/Rome)	Edward Pigott	collaborating with Régnier in Paris
43	Feb.–Mar. 1867	FRANCE (Paris)	alone	with Régnier
45	Aug.–Sept. 1868	SWITZERLAND (St Moritz) GERMANY (Baden-Baden)	Fred Lehmann	for health reasons
49	July 1873	FRANCE (Boulogne/Paris)	alone (?)	
49–50	Sept. 1873–Mar. 1874	USA (New York/Boston/ Chicago) CANADA (Toronto/Montreal)	alone (with Frank Ward as occasional secretary)	reading tour
51	Mar. 1875	FRANCE (Paris)	alone (?)	for about a week
51	Oct.–Nov. 1875	BELGIUM (Brussels/Antwerp) HOLLAND (The Hague)	Caroline Graves (?)	for about a month
52	Sept.–Oct. 1876	FRANCE (Paris) SWITZERLAND (?)	H.P. Bartley (to Paris), Caroline & Harriet	for about a month
53	Sept.–Dec. 1877	BELGIUM (Brussels) GERMANY (Bavaria) ITALY (northern)	Caroline Graves	

have discouraged any further foreign travel after the end of 1877. Up until his mother's death in the spring of 1868, his letters back home to family and friends typically leave us a fairly detailed picture of his activities and experiences abroad; thereafter, there are a number of significant gaps where it is difficult even to be certain where he went or who his travelling companions were. On the other hand, the author's later decades saw an increasing number of intimate correspondences with friends overseas. These notably included François Régnier, leading actor of the Comédie Française, whose efforts to create dramatic versions of Collins's novels for the Paris theatre were interrupted by the Franco-Prussian War of 1870–1, and the New York journalist Colonel William Seaver, who had earned his title in the Civil War and was later to cross swords with the English author concerning the long-standing Anglo-American copyright conflict.

As shown in Table 9.2, Collins had begun to reach an audience overseas remarkably early in his career. Visiting the German spas in the spring of 1863, he had written proudly to his mother: 'As for your eldest son, he is as well known here as in London. ... German readers, French readers, American readers, – all vying in civilities and attention' (B&C I, 219–20). Harper and Brothers, whose editorial staff Seaver joined during the Reconstruction, had become Collins's official American publishers as early as 1850, paying for advance proofs from *Antonina* onwards in the face of unauthorized editions. By the end of the following decade Collins had begun to arrange for colonial editions of his work to appear in Australia as well as Canada, and was soon able to boast of his latest novel that 'Dutch, German, and Russian translations are all in progress – and now I am told that there is likely to be a "market" for me in Sweden, Poland, and (I think) Denmark ...' (BGLL II, 378). By the 1880s there were even to be versions in languages as exotic as Bengali and Japanese.[1] However, the most influential translations, if not quite the earliest, had appeared in Paris, the twin centre with London of an increasingly global fiction distribution network.[2] In early 1856 the short story 'Mad Monkton' had appeared as 'La recherche du mort' in *La revue britannique*, shortly after Emile Forgues's enthusiastic critical survey of the English author's early writings in *La revue des deux mondes*, while the same scholar's translation of *The Dead Secret* (*Le secret*, 1858) began an unbroken sequence of French editions of Collins's major novels.

The choice of 'Mad Monkton', with its macabre climax among the ruins of a Neapolitan convent, as a representative work to introduce Collins to a French audience is perhaps symptomatic. Here, as in a

Table 9.2 First overseas publication in major countries of volumes by Wilkie Collins

	Country	Date	Work	Place: Publisher	Earlier serial publication
In English	USA	1850	*Antonina*	New York: Harper	
	Germany	1856	*After Dark*	Leipzig: Tauchnitz	
	Canada	1870	*Man and Wife*	Toronto: Hunter, Rose	
	Australia	1883	*Heart and Science*	Melbourne: Robertson	*The Moonstone* in (Brisbane) *Queenslander*, July–Dec. 1868
In translation	Germany	1850	*Antonina*	Leipzig: Kollmann	
	Russia	1857	*The Dead Secret*	St Petersburg: Glazunov	
	France	1858	*The Dead Secret*	Paris: Hachette	
	Holland	1858	*The Dead Secret*	Amsterdam: van Kampen	
	Italy	1870	*The Moonstone*	Milan: Treves	

number of the other early shorter tales – notably 'A Terribly Strange Bed', which takes place in a Parisian gambling-house, and 'The Yellow Mask', centring on an artist's studio in pre-modern Pisa – there is an obvious association between continental settings and events with a strong whiff of gothic. Though, as we saw in Chapter 1, Collins's highly flavoured but frequently rejected first novel, *Ioláni*, was set in the exotic island of Tahiti, in later works the foreign settings chosen are generally those with which the author was personally familiar from his travels. All the same, these locations more typically serve as venues for heavy melodrama than social realism. This is equally true in *Antonina* of the Pincian Hill in Rome, over which little Willie and Charley Collins had roamed in the 1830s (see Chapter 1), and in *The Haunted Hotel* with its later scenes set in Venice, where the author again seems to have ended up on his final Continental trip in late 1877. The countercurrents of sentiment and irony in the author's treatment of continental settings – often distant in time as well as space – can indeed function to draw attention to uncertainties in Collins's sense of himself as a modern Englishman. Collins's encounters with American subjects reflect a different, though related, pattern of tensions. There the author seems torn between admiration of the values of cordiality and sincerity seen as characteristic of simple settler communities in the New World, and disgust at what he perceives as the rapacious self-interest increasingly dominating American commerce. To maintain this difficult balance, society in the Old World has to be represented by turns as hypocritically sophisticated and honourably impartial. The subsequent two sections will thus concentrate respectively on the complexities underlying Collins's engagement with Italian and American themes.

* * * * *

Collins first returned to Italy as an adult in company with Augustus Egg and Charles Dickens in late 1853. Well before then, the drive for national unification from the north by King Charles Albert of Sardinia had been repressed by the Austrians, the French army had restored papal authority in Rome, and the republican revolutionaries Mazzini and Garibaldi were again in exile. Dickens's letters home focus a good deal on the personal inadequacies and eccentricities of his travelling companions,[3] while Collins's correspondence is concerned almost exclusively with foreign scenes, events, and characters. A major reason is that his series of long letters home – not only to his mother (from Lausanne, Milan and Venice), but also to Charles Ward (from Genoa), to Edward Pigott (from Naples), to his brother (from Rome), and to John Millais (from Florence)[4] – were written with more than half an eye on subsequent publication. Back in London, Collins offered to adapt the series for *Bentley's Miscellany*, where, among the 'quaint odds and ends of travelling observation', he intended to include '*un*conventional opinions on the subject of Art' and expose 'the Papist ceremonies and superstitions'. Unfortunately the offer seems to have been turned down, presumably because a similar series of travel articles had only recently appeared in the magazine.[5] In the original letters there is surprisingly little evidence of animus against the Vatican,[6] and indeed we generally find little of overtly political import. It is only in the account of the border crossing from Switzerland that there is much sense of imperial oppression or Italian patriotism, the later symbolized by a blind fiddler on the ferry across Lake Maggiore whose passionate rendering of his 'national songs' brings the author close to tears (B&C I, 101–5).

Elsewhere, the personal note is generally reserved for nostalgic reminiscences, as when the author revisits 'all the favourite haunts on the Pincian Hill, that we used to run about as little boys', in the letter to Charley Collins from Rome (B&C I, 112–6). This sense of returning to the past even acquires gothic overtones in exotic Venice, with its 'turbaned Turks and petticoated Greeks', where, despite arriving in modern style via the new railway, Collins soon finds himself back 'on the dark water in a boat of the middle ages, rowing along streets of water that have not altered for the last four hundred years' (B&C I, 117–9).

While the *risorgimento* was still incomplete – between Victor Emmanuel's assumption of the title of King of Italy in February 1861 and the liberation of Rome in September 1870 – Collins returned to Italy on two different occasions. In the company of Caroline Graves and her twelve-year-old daughter Harriet – their first trip abroad together – Collins headed for Rome and Naples in the autumn of 1863 to avoid the harsh English winter, only returning in the spring of 1864. Since taking the waters in Germany had done little to improve his own gouty condition, and both his travelling companions also suffered a good deal on the Italian journey, it is hardly surprising that the author's letters home focus a good deal on physical discomforts and the weather that gives rise to them. The main political message, though, is *plus ça change*: 'Political convulsions may do what they please – Bourbons may be tumbled down and Victor Emmanuels may be set up – Naples keeps its old cheerful dirty devil-may-care face in spite of them' (B&C I, 235–8).

The second trip was to Rome in the autumn of 1866 in the company of Edward Pigott, by then 'the chief writer on foreign politics in *The Daily News*' (BGLL I, 273). This was a rather more brisk affair: they reached Milan in just ten days and were only away from London altogether for under eight weeks. Apart from a couple of apologetic letters to the convalescent Nina Lehmann for failing to visit her in Pau, little correspondence survives from this trip. However, Collins did send back a journalistic piece for *All the Year Round*, 'The Dead Lock in Italy' published on 8 December 1866. Subtitled 'A Letter from an Englishman in Rome, to an Italian in London' – the latter an imagined political exile akin to Professor Pesca in *The Woman in White* – it offered, in the familiar Collins manner, a personalized account of the nation's prospects at this crucial political juncture, shortly after the province of Venetia had been ceded to Italy and just before the French garrison was bound by treaty to leave Rome. Recalling previous trips to the city four, eleven, and twenty-eight years previously, the autobiographical Englishman notes that, despite the superficial signs of modernization, nothing

much has changed deep down. Though he declares himself unequivo-
cally 'on the liberal side' and passionately declares his wish to see 'this
nation great, prosperous and free, from one end of the peninsula to the
other', his forecast is pessimistic. He offers more than one reason why
the Pope's political power will not vanish with the French troops, but
the fundamental cause is seen to be 'the inbred national defects of the
Italian character', which explain not only the fascination of
Catholicism for the mass of the people but also why the trains didn't
run on time on the author's journey towards Rome. Yet, alongside this
distinctly English sense of moral superiority, at times it is possible to
detect regret that the land of childhood mystery might be subject to the
enlightening forces of political modernization.

* * * * *

These conflicting currents underlying the author's engagement with
the Italian question are equally apparent in Collins's novels, where the
sensational mode functions at the same time to expose ideological
cruces through its realistic use of social settings and to obscure them
under the cloak of melodrama. In *The Woman in White*, for example,
though we have two major Italian characters who are revealed in the
closing scenes to be exiled members of the same Italian secret
'Brotherhood', the narrative does not attempt to engage in any concerted
way with the political complexities of Italian nationalism. Rather both
partake of a freakishness that is inseparable from their national identity,
so that the extremely corpulent Count Fosco and almost dwarfish
Professor Pesca stand together at the end of the novel as mysteries that
must remain unsolved. However, these tensions are even more remarkable in *The Haunted Hotel: A Mystery of Modern Venice*, where, as suggested
by the double oxymoron of the title, contemporary Italy provides the
principal location for the most blatantly gothic of Collins's mature works
of fiction. The narrative concerns a thoroughly up-to-date insurance
fraud that precipitates the brutal murder of an English aristocrat in a
mouldering palace associated with the excesses of the Venetian
Inquisition. After it is transformed into an international hotel with all
the latest conveniences, in the modernized death chamber the victim's
relatives undergo a gruesome series of supernatural occurrences for
which the narrator explicitly refuses to offer any rational explanation.

Written in mid-1878, the novella clearly recycles experiences from the
author's fifth and final visit to Italy the previous autumn. This time
Collins went with Caroline Graves only, leaving his stepdaughter,

Harrriet, at Gloucester Place to deal with correspondence, and journeyed for around two months via Brussels, Munich, and the Tyrol to northern Italy, coming home by way of Paris. His travels within Italy are by no means clear. Apologizing to the publisher Bernard Tauchnitz for failing to call on him in Leipzig on the return journey, he described them as 'of so erratic a nature ... that it was impossible for my letters to follow me' (BGLL III, 175). However, though we have no knowledge of the accommodation they occupied, it is probable that the pair made it as far as Venice: the phrasing of the personal correspondence is echoed by *The Haunted Hotel* in those passages describing the peregrinations of the victim's relations as they converge on the Adriatic resort. For example: Collins writes from Brussels that he is 'on [his] way to South Germany and the Tyrol' (BGLL III, 173), and, once back in London, that he has 'just returned from a three months tour in the Tyrol and in north Italy' (BGLL III, 178), while in *The Haunted Hotel* the hero Henry Westwick (the victim's brother) announces that the victim's nephew and his bride 'are going to Germany and the Tyrol, on their way to Italy. I propose that we allow them a month to themselves, and that we arrange to meet them afterwards in the North of Italy – say at Venice' (*HH*, 131).

A further autobiographical link is provided by the novella's involvement with the drama. Another of the victim's brothers, Francis, is a theatrical entrepreneur who takes the opportunity to visit Milan and Florence in search of a beautiful Italian ballerina for 'a new form of theatrical attraction for the coming winter season' (*HH*, 136), and even convinces the murderess to shape her lurid confessions in the form of a melodrama for the London stage. As we have seen in Chapter 7, Collins invested a great deal of time and energy in trying to advance his own reputation as a playwright, adapting his narratives for theatrical performance regularly if not with uniform success. During this period Collins tended to blame the failures on his unwillingness to deflect attention from his serious social themes by pandering to popular taste – whether in the form of melodramatic excess or leggy dancing girls.[7] More specifically, just prior to the final Italian journey he was preoccupied with completing an adaptation of *The Moonstone* to open in London at the Olympic, with performances also projected in the United States and Italy. This proved no great success, though the Italian dramatic version of *The New Magdalen* had recently been very well received.[8]

Virtually no hint concerning Collins's assessment of the political condition of the fully united Kingdom of Italy is found either in his correspondence or in *The Haunted House* itself. In late 1870, when the final withdrawal of the French garrison during the Franco-Prussian War allowed the Italian army to take the papal states and Rome with little resistance, Collins had been far more concerned with the fate of Paris and his friend François Régnier, who he feared might be among those besieged in the city.[9] No letters back home from Italy appear to have survived from his final visit, and in the period in between the only references to the country concern the publication or performance of the author's works there. For no obvious reason, *The Haunted Hotel* is set back in the autumn of 1860 and the spring of 1861, the period when the south was taken and Victor Emmanuel crowned King of Italy, but Venetia remained in the hands of the Hapsburgs: the only faint echo of this history is that, among the many black marks against her, the murderess is rumoured to be 'a spy in the interests of Austria' (*HH*, 24). Elsewhere in the narrative, to bear an Italian name seems sufficient to position a character on the sinister side.

The perpetrators of the insurance fraud are the Countess Narona, with a 'ghastly complexion' (*HH*, 10) and 'wild black eyes', gifted with second sight (*HH*, 20), and the enigmatic Baron Rivar (it is never quite clear whether he is her brother, her lover, or both), an 'inveterate gambler' with an unhealthy fascination for 'experiments in chemistry' (*HH*, 50). As though bewitched, Lord Mountbarry breaks his engagement to the long-suffering English heroine Agnes Lockwood and marries the Italian countess, insuring his life in her favour for a large amount. Once hidden away in Venice, the Lord is poisoned in Borgia fashion by the Baron, who dissolves the body in acid and hides the head in a secret compartment above the death chamber. The third and most harrowing of the haunting scenes that take place there is experienced by Agnes herself. Her struggle to find sleep in what is by then Room 13A of the Palace Hotel is described with a fine psychological detail that recalls a similar scene in the early short story 'A Terribly Strange Bed'. But what descends slowly from the ceiling towards Agnes is not a murderous contraption operated by human agency but the decomposing head of her former fiancé, which at the last moment turns to fix a glassy stare on his murderous wife who is sitting by the bedside. Though the narrative ends with the fittingly painful deaths of both Baron and Countess, and with the happy union of Henry and Agnes, who wisely pass their honeymoon not on a Continental tour but 'in the retirement of a cottage on the banks of the Thames' (*HH*, 261), there is no attempt to explain away the supernatural events.

It seems clear that Collins's fiction is more likely to lose the fine balance between realism and melodrama characteristic of sensation fiction and be pulled towards gothic excess when continental settings and characters become dominant. The author's treatment of Italian themes, by turns nostalgic and critical, thus serves to highlight ambiguities in Collins's sense of his own identity as both modern and English.

* * * * *

Whether measured by distance or time, the most extended journey undertaken by Collins throughout his literary career was the long-anticipated North American reading tour of 1873–4. Despite his original intention to make it all the way across the Continent to visit relatives in San Francisco, a growing aversion to railroad sleeping cars ensured that, in the event, he got no further west than Chicago. Nevertheless, there was still a good deal of coming and going back east. He arrived in New York, where he was lionized by his American publishers, Harper and Brothers, and left from Boston, where Sebastian Schlesinger, a business associate of his friend Fred Lehmann, offered not only generous hospitality but also easy access to New England literary society. Collins travelled more than once between the two cities, especially enjoying the scenery of upstate New York, where he was a frequent guest at the country retreat of the Bigelows, diplomats whom he had met in London through John Forster. In addition, he made trips down to Philadelphia and Washington and up over the border as far as Montreal and Toronto, where he met his Canadian publishers Robert Hunter and George Rose. The author seems to have earned rather less than expected from the tour; the frequency of his performances was limited by his poor physical condition and the size of his audiences was affected by the severe economic downturn, while Collins felt that he had been 'mismanaged and cheated' by the agents initially handling his bookings (BGLL III, 3–4). Yet, despite the problems and disappointments, in the same letter home he described the American people as a whole as 'the most enthusiastic, the most cordial, and the most sincere' that he had ever encountered. Indeed, a similar note is struck with some frequency in the author's personal correspondence, not only during the trip but also before and after. As early as 1858, in a letter to the editor of the recently founded Boston *Atlantic Monthly*, the author had expressed 'a real interest of the strongest kind in wishing to see America', describing such a trip as 'the completion of an Englishman's education' (BGLL I, 166–8). On leaving America he repeatedly expressed the hope that the visit would not be his last, a sentiment that recurs even into the 1880s in letters to intimate American friends such as Schlesinger, Jane Bigelow, or William Seaver.

Though American themes can be traced in a number of the novels written after the author's tour, the most consistent engagement with Collins's experience across the Atlantic is found in *The Fallen Leaves*

(1879), where the main narrative opens on board a steamship bound from New York to Liverpool. There the qualities of enthusiasm, cordiality, and sincerity are again celebrated, not only in the young English hero Amelius Goldenheart, whose character has been formed in a primitive Midwestern community run on Christian Socialist principles, but also via his friend and mentor, the gaunt New Englander Rufus Dingwell. With the latter's frankness seen as 'one of the indisputable virtues of his nation' (*FL*, 54), he quickly becomes the moral touchstone of the novel. If the naivety of both Amelius and Rufus occasionally gives rise to comic misunderstanding once they are in Europe, more generally their simple candour is contrasted favourably with the stiffness and hypocrisy shown to be typical of polite society in England. (The novel thus forms an interesting contrast with *Daisy Miller*, Henry James's story of the American innocent abroad, published in the same year.) The key social problem identified in *The Fallen Leaves* – the yawning metropolitan gulf between a West End where wealth is conspicuous but vice remains hidden and an East End where both poverty and prostitution are rife – is one which only colonial outsiders such as Amelius and Rufus seem capable of bridging imaginatively. Similarly, as in *The New Magdalen* (see Chapter 8), the only salvation offered to the outcast women identified in the title seems to be the possibility of a fresh start in the New World. Though the narrative culminates in the marriage of Amelius not to the spoilt heiress Regina but to 'Simple Sally', the lost child that he rescues from the streets, the celebrations are muted and the ending inconclusive. Taken aback by the harsh criticism the novel received from British reviewers, Collins never produced the planned sequel treating the vicissitudes of their married life. But, in response to one of many requests from American readers in particular, he suggested that the companion story might end tragically due to 'the outer influence of the world which surrounds the husband and wife – the world whose unchristian prejudices they have set at defiance' (B&C III, 429). It seems likely then that, in the sequel, Collins intended the couple to remain in darkest England rather than to head for pastures new on the other side of the Atlantic.

Yet the overwhelmingly positive representation of American qualities and values in *The Fallen Leaves* does not tell the whole story. As articulated elsewhere in both his public and private writings, Collins's response could be rather more complex, while his interactions with the American business community became increasingly embittered. Even during the North American tour, he tended to recoil from the brash commercialism of the latest urban developments. Out of sorts after the long westward journey, he confided to Jane Bigelow back at Highland Falls: 'I am not sorry to leave Chicago. The dull sameness of the great blocks of iron and brick overwhelms me. The whole city seems to be saying "See how rich I am after the fire, and what a tremendous business I do!"' (B&C III, 8–9). Comments such as these suggest that the author's admiration for what he saw as core American values reflected an idealized vision of a more simple colonial community, which turned a blind eye to the economic ambitions of a metropolitan nation state ready to challenge European dominance. Collins's reactions a decade earlier to the outbreak of the American Civil War tend to confirm this reading.

The most explicit expression of Collins's sympathies for the Southern cause is found in a letter to Fred Lehmann, when the latter was about to set off on a lengthy business trip to New York and Boston in the summer of 1862. This was the period when a series of major setbacks in the Virginian Peninsular Campaign for the Union army under General George B. McClellan had forced the President to launch a massive new recruitment initiative. Collins's response was scathing:

> The one chance for that miserable country on the other side of the Atlantic is, that these two blatant impostors Lincoln and McClellan will fail to get the 300,000 new men they ask for. If I thought it would be the least use, I would go down on both my knees, and pray with all my might for the total failure of the new enlistment scheme.
> (B&C I, 209–10)

This seems to represent a consistently held attitude, at least in the early stages of the Civil War. In a fragment from a letter to an unidentified friend that probably dates from late 1861 – when the *Trent* Affair (the seizure by the captain of a Union warship of Europe-bound Confederate commissioners while on board a British mail steamer) almost lead to military conflict between the North and Great Britain – the author writes of the 'Yankees': 'I have never believed in the peaceable telegrams from those ruffians across the Atlantic – and I find, in today's *Times*, that the signs of the future are darkening. Sooner or later, war is certain with them ...' (BGLL II, 23–4). In another fragment to an unknown American correspondent on the 'hideous struggle', probably dating from the following year, Collins concludes roundly: 'Better your one Republic should be in two than that the cause of Freedom should suffer in American hands' (BGLL I, 286).

In Britain, of course, such a marked lack of sympathy with the Union cause was not limited to Wilkie Collins.[10] The English press both

metropolitan and provincial was becoming increasingly liberal in political complexion and typically supported the North, while radical populist papers were virulent in their condemnation of the slave economy
of the Confederates States. Yet venerable Tory organs such as the
Quarterly Review were not afraid to speak out against 'the peculiar vices
of democracy' and in sympathy with the economic plight of the gentlemen landowners of the South,[11] while *The Times* itself tended to see
the root cause of the conflict in the protectionist policies being pursued
by the Northern states in rapacious pursuit of their own commercial
interests. With the Liberal Party in power throughout the Civil War, official British policy remained the studied neutrality that had been insisted
on at the time of the *Trent* Affair.[12] But in the summer of 1862
Palmerston's government was leaning towards recognizing the
Confederacy after its military successes, and even turned a blind eye
towards the building in British shipyards of ironclads for the South's rebel
navy, notably the *Alabama*, which would wreck havoc on Union merchant shipping for almost two years. On 7 October Chancellor Gladstone
created a sensation when, despite his personal abhorrence of slavery, he
confidently anticipated 'the success of the Southern States so far as
regards their separation from the North', declaring that the Confederates
'... have made an army; they are making, it appears, a navy; and they
have made what is more than either – they have made a nation'.[13]

   Collins's evident antipathy to the Northern cause thus does not imply
any degree of support for the slave system itself. In fact, as Lillian
Nayder has shown, Collins's characteristic empathy with the down-
trodden made him unusually sensitive to imperialist abuse of subject
races.[14] Typically, in a New Year 1874 letter to Frederick Lehmann,
Collins remarks that he prefers Negro attendants. Rather, we can assume
that his political sympathies during the Civil War tended to follow the
editorial line pursued by *The Times*, to which, as we have seen, he was
a faithful subscriber. This indeed was the line taken by his friend and
mentor Dickens,[15] as reflected in a famous paragraph to his Swiss correspondent William de Cerjat:

> I take the facts of the American quarrel to stand thus. Slavery has in
> reality nothing on earth to do with it, in any kind of association with
> any generous or chivalrous sentiment on the part of the North. But
> the North having gradually got to itself the making of laws and the
> settlement of the Tariffs, and having taxed the South most abom-
> inably for its own advantage, began to see, as the country grew, that
> unless it advocated the laying down of a geographical line beyond

which slavery should not extend, the South would necessarily recover its old political power, and be able to help itself a little in the adjustment of commercial affairs. Every reasonable creature may know, if willing, that the North hates the Negro, and that until it was convenient to make a pretence that sympathy with him was the cause of the War, it hated the abolitionists and derided them up hill and down dale. For the rest, there is not a pin to choose between the two parties.

(Pilgrim X, 52–5)

It seems safe to assume that Collins would have found little to disagree with in this view, which indeed echoes the editorial line taken by *All the Year Round* in late 1861, when Collins was still a member of staff.[16] And it is perhaps significant that the author's personal writings provide no hint of any change of heart even after Lincoln's Emancipation Proclamation of 1 January 1863, which served generally to turn wavering British opinion firmly in favour of the Northern cause.

* * * * *

Collins's distaste for what he saw as America's aggressive, self-centred commercialism can be seen even more clearly in relation to the vexed question of international copyright. Here again we can see the impact on Collins's thinking of Dickens, who had launched a controversial attack on American piracy during his transatlantic tour of 1842. The dispute between the two nations over this issue indeed continued throughout the five decades of Collins's literary career, and was only resolved by Congress's passing of the Chace Act in 1891, two years after the author's death. Collins's uncompromising position on what he saw as American literary theft is explored in considerable detail in two journalistic pieces: 'A National Wrong' (1870),[17] and 'Considerations on the Copyright Question' (1880).[18] In both articles Collins's position is founded on a belief in the absolute, inalienable, and perpetual moral right of the author to control his own literary productions, whether at home or abroad. Such a simple ideal, it must be noted, was by no means compatible with the principle underlying both British and American copyright law throughout the author's lifetime. That is, that publication conferred on the author a proprietary right limited in duration, that could be freely assigned to another, and that was in practice typically leased or sold outright to a publishing house. At the same time, the growth of liberal-democratic ideals during the nineteenth century ensured that copyright protection would often be seen, like duty on paper, as both a restriction of free trade and a 'tax on knowledge', so that there were many calls for its curtailment or abolition. Without taking account of these tensions between the interests of authors as individuals, publishers as a class, and the people as reading public, with the varying concepts of right that they gave rise to, it is impossible to understand why the Anglo-American copyright conflict remained so intractable.[19]

As we saw in the previous chapter, the writing of 'A National Wrong' sprang from Collins's anger towards a small Dutch publishing house which, in the absence of any copyright treaty with Britain, tried to publish a translation of *Man and Wife* without permission or payment.[20] Branded in the London press as pickpockets, the publishers quickly capitulated and the author eventually received the tiny sum of 100 guilders as his share of the profits. However, exploiting the attendant publicity, Collins raised his sights from such petty theft in the little kingdom across the English Channel to grand larceny in the large republic across the Atlantic. Though 'A National Wrong' incorporates Collins's exchange with the Dutch publishers – figured as a triumphant encounter between a gallant English merchant ship and a rogue Dutch vessel hoisting the Black Flag – the main focus of the article is the dishonourable treatment of English authors in the United States. Despite the fact that American claims against the British government on account of assistance given to the Confederate cause during the Civil War (the so-called *Alabama* claims) were still outstanding, the accusation of piracy was levelled also at the Yankee congressman, stereotypically depicted as cloaking self-interest in the rhetoric of social justice and free trade, 'with his tongue in one cheek and his quid in the other'. The passage concludes resoundingly: 'so long as America stubbornly shuts her eyes to it [theft from British writers], her talk of Justice is but Cant, her clamour about the Rights of Civilisation, Bunkum'.[21]

In 'A National Wrong', though, there was no attempt to single out specific American publishers for criticism. Indeed, Collins rather naively assumed that, as a house recognizing 'the law of honor' in its dealings with English authors (BGLL II, 163–4), his own New York publishers would sympathize with his position and publicly support his campaign. In fact, the Harpers seem to have paid him less from a sense of moral obligation than out of economic self-interest: they had long fought against any bilateral copyright agreement, and were still widely recognized as 'redoubtable champions of literary piracy'.[22] They thus opposed the initiative to address the copyright issue following the settlement of the *Alabama* claims in 1871, continuing to hold that 'any measure of international copyright was objectionable because it would add to the price of books, and thus interfere with the education of the people'.[23] Precisely when Collins realized his American publishers' true position on this matter is unclear. [24] Like Dickens on his second North American visit of 1867–8, throughout his own reading tour Collins was careful not to speak in public on the copyright question, and his personal relations with the staff at Franklyn Square proved remarkably cordial. The British author got on very well with Joseph W. Harper Jr., a fellow sufferer from gout who now headed the firm, and established a lasting personal friendship with William A. Seaver, then a senior editor of *Harper's Magazine*. The most tangible result was the publication of Harper's *Illustrated Library Edition of Wilkie Collins's Novels*, which the author dedicated warmly 'to The American People' (Gasson, 74–5). But relations began to deteriorate not long after his return home, and before the end of the decade the New York house had ceased both to pay any royalty on sales of the collected edition and to publish the author's latest fiction. One ironic consequence was that Collins's warmest tribute to the virtues of the nation, *The Fallen Leaves*, failed to appear in an authorized edition in the United States and thus did not earn its author a single cent in the American marketplace.

The bitter indignation that Collins eventually came to feel towards Harper's is reflected in the tenor of 'Considerations on the Copyright Question', which takes the form of a protest letter 'to an American friend', initially published in New York in the *International Review*. The underlying argument is much the same as in 'A National Wrong' – that American law should grant a foreign author like Collins 'the same right of control over my property in my book ... which the law gives me in my own country'[25] – but this time it is driven by a far greater personal animus. Though the *International Review* supported the cause of international copyright, its editors were clearly uncomfortable with the strong language and belligerent tone of Collins's contribution, and appended a note to that effect. In the article itself Harper's is made to serve repeatedly as the most egregious example of a major American house putting its own trade interests before the cause of an honourable settlement. Just as significantly, Collins leaves plenty of circumstantial evidence to allow the curious reader to identify the American friend to whom the protest is addressed. The reference to Dutch ancestry, the military epithets, and other details all point unambiguously to Colonel Seaver. Though their friendship somehow survived this *contretemps*, Collins's decision to direct his protest to Seaver clearly indicates the intensity of his sense of betrayal by Harper and Brothers.

What is most disconcerting about Collins's 'sentiments on the copyright question'[26] is the way he refuses even to consider the compromise position that proved increasingly attractive to both American publishers and British authors from the 1870s and eventually paved the way for the Chace Act of 1891. The autumn of 1871 had seen a lengthy debate on the subject in the correspondence columns of *The Times*. A key contribution was that from Harper's New York rival William Appleton, setting out the case for American copyright protection for English authors on condition that their works be reprinted domestically. Grounding his argument in the rights of the people to cheap literature, Appleton emphasized that no reciprocal copyright agreement would be acceptable if the result were to allow the British publishing trade to impose its own restrictive practices across the Atlantic. In his own memorable words: 'every arrangement that England has hitherto offered is but a kind of legal saddle for the English publisher to ride his author into the American book market'.[27] Though Appleton's proposal was by no means an original one, there is no doubt that he had stoutly defended a position of which many *Times* readers were hitherto unaware. Many well-known English writers contributed to the *Times* debate, and a group of fifty afterwards signed a petition to the British Foreign Secretary in support of Appleton's proposal, including Carlyle, Ruskin, Mill, Spencer, and Darwin.[28] Though his old companions Edmund Yates and George Sala were among the novelists who signed, Collins seems to have felt no pressure to join them.

These calls for compromise were renewed in the summer of 1878 with the publication in London of the wide-ranging report of the Royal Commission on Copyright. Then even Harper and Brothers came round to supporting the Appleton proposal, though their pamphlet of early 1879 reflecting this change of heart was used by Collins in 'Considerations' merely as further evidence of the refusal of American tradesmen to abide by the 'law of honour'.[29] The most famous attempt to steer a liberal middle course, of course, was that of Matthew Arnold, in his March 1880 article 'Copyright'. There he traced the root of the problem to Britain's publishing industry, still dominated by the reactionary demands of the circulating libraries, which he contrasted unfavourably with the cheap book revolution effected in Paris by publishers like Michel Lévy. He thus concluded:

> The Americans ought not to submit to our absurd system of dear books; ... as a lover of civilisation, I should be sorry, though I am an author, if they did. I hope they will give us copyright; but I hope,

also, they will stick to Michel Lévy's excellent doctrine: 'Cheap books are a necessity, and a necessity which need bring, moreover, no loss to either authors or publishers.' [30]

Although, from early in his career, Collins had often raised his own voice against the 'extravagantly absurd prices charged for works of fiction' in Britain (BGLL I, 87), he seems to have remained unmoved by this challenging intervention which appeared several months before his own 'Considerations'.

With hindsight, it was doubly unfortunate that Collins missed this opportunity to support a compromise on the copyright question, and thus strike a rare balance between his distaste for self-interested American commercialism and his enthusiasm for the social openness encountered in the New World. If writers like Collins, with a popular following on both sides of the Atlantic, had lent their wholehearted support to the Appleton proposal, it is possible that compromise legislation might have been passed in the United States a generation earlier, and this might in turn have helped to advance the collapse in Britain of what Arnold had rightly denounced as 'our highly eccentric, artificial, and unsatisfactory system of book-trade'.[31]

* * * * *

At the least it should be clear that the representations in Collins's novels and short stories of foreign landscapes, characters, and themes, whether on the Continent or across the Atlantic, do not always tell the whole story. To understand more fully the complexities of the author's experience of and attitudes to things overseas, it is necessary to engage also with his journalistic and personal writings which can be surprisingly revealing of his hopes and fears. Though in this chapter we have concentrated on Collins's close encounters with Italy and America, similar lessons can be learnt by tracing in detail the author's engagement with imperial themes and his representations of more distant and alien others. As touched on Chapters 5–7, notable examples here would include the indigenous peoples of Central America in *The Woman in White*, the Hindu priests in *The Moonstone*, and the half-caste Caribbean slaves in *Black and White*.[32]

10
Collins and the Later Victorian Literary Marketplace

The early 1870s, when Collins was reinventing himself both as playwright and missionary novelist, was a period of considerable insecurity in the author's relations with both journal proprietors and book publishers. For around a decade and a half until his mentor's death in 1870, nearly all of Collins's fiction had appeared first in Dickens's weekly papers, where shared editorial responsibilities and collaboration on the special Christmas issues often imparted to the writing a spirit of camaraderie. Dickens had offered assistance with his own pen for *No Name*, when illness threatened Collins's 'advance on the press' (Pilgrim X, 142–3), and was happy to allow *The Moonstone* to stretch to thirty-two parts although only around twenty-six had been originally planned (BGLL II, 73–4). Thereafter, Collins was forced to sell his serials either to literary monthlies of lesser standing and lower remuneration like Bentley's *Temple Bar*, or to experiment with popular penny miscellanies like *Cassell's Magazine*, or illustrated middle-class family papers like the *Graphic*. The results were often uncomfortable as the proprietors tended to treat the products of his labours in a less than respectful manner. Cassell's wanted a 'damn it' deleted from *Man and Wife* (BGLL II, 152), while, in 1875, the *Graphic* peremptorily censored what it saw as 'an attempted violation of the heroine' of *The Law and the Lady* (B&C II, 391).

Collins's relationship with the book publishers had become even more unstable. As discussed in Chapter 3, ever since breaking with Bentley in the mid-1850s, the author had tended to auction his latest works to the highest bidder, and thus shifted restlessly between houses. Bradbury & Evans, Hurst & Blackett, Tinsley Brothers, and even the antiquarian bookseller F.S. Ellis had all issued single works. There were slightly longer stints in turn with Sampson Low and Smith, Elder, who were thus also granted the rights to reprint Collins's backlist in cheaper uniform editions. However, all the chopping and changing played havoc with the customer loyalty that such commodities were designed to encourage. When Collins returned briefly to the Bentley fold in the early 1870s, he was astounded to learn from the publisher by quite how far the sales of his reprinted novels were outstripped by those of his more conservative rival, Ellen Wood, who had stuck with the New Burlington Street firm since the success of *East Lynne* in 1861. This helps to explain Collins's decision to sign up with the progressive new publishing firm of Chatto and Windus in 1874, which thereafter issued virtually all the author's new fiction in volume and gradually acquired the rights to earlier work. Though this relationship lasted the author's lifetime, by then it was rather too late to catch up with the likes of Wood. Collins thus spent much of his energy during his declining years scrambling to increase the returns from his new literary enterprises.

Our main concern here, then, is with Collins's writings in the later 1870s and 1880s, whose strengths and weaknesses – the latter inevitably predominate – we intend to map both against developments in the fictional genres then in vogue, and against the changing print media through which they were made available to the reading public. The underlying argument is that, with his early high-cultural connections, Collins was increasingly uncertain of his status and his audience in the rapidly changing late Victorian literary marketplace. The fault lines in the later novels can thus be read as symptoms not only of the growing divide between 'gentlemanly' and 'commercial' modes of fiction production, but also of Collins's growing confusion as to which side of the divide he was on. We proceed by analysing the author's engagement with three key moments of change in narrative form and mode of publication in the later 1870s and 1880s: the newspaper novel and the decline of sensationalism (on *Jezebel's Daughter*), the challenge of naturalism to the circulating library edition (on *The Evil Genius*), and the emergence of the single-volume modern thriller (on *The Guilty River*).

* * * * *

In 1873 an original deal was struck between W.F. Tillotson, a Liberal newspaper proprietor in Lancashire, and John Maxwell, Mary Braddon's companion, publisher, and literary representative. For the sum of £450 Maxwell sold to Tillotson the serial rights to Braddon's latest novel *Taken at the Flood*, and the story appeared between August and April the following year simultaneously in a dozen local papers, including

Tillotson's own *Bolton Weekly Journal*. This was by no means the first appearance of fiction in the Victorian provincial press. Immediately after the repeal of the newspaper tax in 1855, serial novels had begun to appear with regularity in weekly news miscellanies, first in Scotland and soon in northern and western England and Wales. However, the deal between Maxwell and Tillotson was innovative in that it created the first systematic, nationwide syndicate of British newspapers for an original novel by an established author. It thus set a trend that would dominate the serial fiction market for the next twenty years or so. Rival fiction syndication agencies quickly sprang up both in the provinces and in the metropolis, but the market leader long remained Tillotson's 'Fiction Bureau'.[1]

The number of subscribers to the journals carrying Braddon's *Taken at the Flood* reached at least a quarter of a million, and by the mid-1880s well-constructed provincial syndicates for works by popular authors could approach double that. Such figures were well in advance of the sales of the most popular penny miscellanies, and the social range of the readership reached was rather broader. Tillotson's client authors were also of rather higher literary standing: the firm had quickly established a reputation in London literary circles and begun regularly to purchase fiction from a new group of upcoming metropolitan authors, many attached to the new house of Chatto and Windus. These clients gradually came to include not only masters of mystery and suspense such as James Payn and Charles Reade, but also more leisurely exponents of domestic and regional subjects, including Margaret Oliphant and Thomas Hardy. However, Braddon herself remained Tillotson's leading author until nearly the end of the 1880s, by which time she had sold a round dozen of her latest works to the Bolton firm. All the novels Braddon wrote for Tillotson rely to some extent on the sensation formula which had made her such a controversial figure in the 1860s, though her transgressive heroines by then tend to be rather more introspective than in the days of Lady Audley and Aurora Floyd. Being allowed more fully to enter the consciousness of such female protagonists must have encouraged in Braddon's readers a greater degree of empathy with their gestures of defiance and of understanding of the causes. Notable here would be not only *Taken at the Flood*, but also *An Open Verdict* which was running in the *Bolton Weekly Journal* when Collins signed his first contract with the Fiction Bureau on 11 July 1878.

Back in 1867, at the first signs of a downturn in his sales, Collins had considered reprinting his most successful sensation works in the penny miscellanies, or even of writing a new novel for them based on old stage pieces (Peters, 279), as well as discussing the idea of syndication in country papers with Captain Mayne Reid (1818–83), a popular author of adventure stories.[2] Though nothing came of these plans, *Jezebel's Daughter*, the first novel he sold to Tillotson, proved in fact to be a recycling of the plot of his 1858 play, *The Red Vial*. Collins was much the best known of the Chatto authors to sign up with Tillotson, and his contract was by far the longest: the agreements with Braddon were made through a simple exchange of letters between Maxwell and Tillotson.[3] Collins's contract specified payment of £500, the same sum received for *An Open Verdict*, though that novel was stipulated to be in thirty-three weekly instalments as opposed to the twenty of *Jezebel's Daughter*. The length of the instalments of Collins's contribution was specified as '10 manuscript pages equal to that contained in chapters 9 & 10 of "An Open Verdict" recently published in Bolton Weekly Journal'.[4] Since both narratives hinge on death by poisoning, there is a useful basis for comparing the respective generic affiliations of these two serials written for the Fiction Bureau.

As discussed in Chapter 7, *The Red Vial* is set in the house of a Frankfurt merchant, and the two leading roles are those of his housekeeper and male servant. The former is the widow of an eminent physician, who makes use of her husband's medicine chest to try to murder her employer because he opposes her daughter's marriage to the son of a partner. The latter doggedly tries to protect his master who has rescued him from a lunatic asylum, and fortuitously administers an antidote from the chest, which however brings on the appearance of death. The final act thus takes place in the Frankfurt 'dead-house', where the 'corpse' comes back to life and the villainess is accidentally poisoned. Written twenty years later, the Tillotson serial *Jezebel's Daughter* preserves both the outline and detail of this simple melodrama of murder and madness, but adds a further narrative layer through which Collins can vent his missionary impulses. The Frankfurt business is now merely the branch office of a larger English company and the narrator is a young Englishman whose aunt takes over the running of the firm on her husband's death. She uses her position to promote two causes – not only rescuing lunatics from the cruelties of the madhouse, but also saving young women from more disreputable occupations by introducing them as clerks into the family business. This sets up a potentially interesting clash between two powerful mature women, a devil driven by maternal instincts and an angel espousing feminist causes. Collins develops this theme only perfunctorily, however, and instead, as so often in the later novels, devotes most of his attention to evoking sympathy for the various 'friendless creatures' in need of salvation (Postscript IX). The narrative thus ends with the businesswoman taking on the role of second mother to the soft and yielding daughter of Jezebel as she marries the heir to the family firm.

In contrast, Braddon's *An Open Verdict* focuses most consistently on the contrasting characters and fortunes of two young women, and explores the dramatic interplay of their acts of transgression and submission. Beatrix Harefield is a wealthy heiress deprived of human warmth by her father, a strict and jealous man who drives his wife to desertion and an early death and forces his daughter into unwilling rebellion. Beatrix's sole friend from childhood has been the impetuous Bella Scratchell, whose poverty forces her to earn money as a morning governess and companion. Both are attracted by the hero, the grave young socialist clergyman Cyril, but when Beatrix's father dies of poisoning, Bella's jealous actions bring suspicion of murder on Beatrix. Beatrix recoils into saint-like self-sacrifice, and Bella into greed and sensuality. The latter's profligacy leads to her death in a riding accident, while the former's patient service is finally rewarded by reconciliation and marriage with Cyril. Despite their dichotomies, both women are presented as at once victims and victors, and fairly share authorial sympathy, in marked contrast to the noble hero who comes across as something of a prig. While Braddon is not averse to exploiting the mechanics of mystery and suspense, and a number of minor roles are familiar stereotypes from stage melodrama (notably Beatrix's rakish seducer complete with military moustache), the sensationalism of the narrative is counter-balanced by a strong impulse towards social and psychological realism. The main setting of *An Open Verdict* is in the north of England in the 1850s, and the novel attempts to imagine tension in the industrial city as well as among the village squirearchy. In its treatment of social and religious problems the narrative seems consciously to emulate Charles Kingsley's 'condition of England' novel, *Alton Locke* (1850), while the relationship emerging between the two small-town heroines, and the satire on provincial Grundyism, pay clear tribute to George Eliot's *Middlemarch* (1871).

The extremity of the contrast between the forms of these two novels is seen most clearly in their treatment of death by poisoning and their use of a Borgia motif. In *Jezebel's Daughter*, the housekeeper's physician husband has been left the formulae of a number of the infamous but supposedly lost Borgia poisons by a mysterious Hungarian master in chemical science. The husband has devoted his life to recomposing these with the aim of discovering effective antidotes which would allow their safe use in small doses in therapeutic medicine. The climax of the novel is then the description of 'the deliberate progress of the hellish Borgia poison, in undermining the forces of life' of the would-be murderess, and the 'nervous shudderings' which precede her remorseless death (Postscript VII). In *An Open Verdict*, the poison proves to be merely the commonplace painkiller laudanum, used as a narcotic by both wife and daughter to find relief from abuse by the tyrannical husband and father, and the fatal overdose self-administered when he is brought face to face with the consequences of his oppression. This information is immediately made available to the reader but is hidden both from the protagonists and from the coroner's inquiry. The community around is quick to point the finger of suspicion at the long-suffering daughter, but Braddon insists on more than one occasion that the true venom is in the slanderous tongues of the local gossips, their imaginations fed on a diet of popular melodrama. Clearly neither serial was considered a failure by the Bolton agency, as both Braddon and Collins continued to be in great demand among the proprietors of weekly news miscellanies all over the country and attracted increasingly higher rewards for their newspaper novels, but there is no doubt that Braddon pays more respect to, and makes more demands on, the intelligence of the provincial newspaper reader.

* * * * *

As we saw in Chapter 3, Wilkie Collins began to experience frustration at the conservatism of the library owners from close to the beginning of his career. Those feelings had hardened to disgust and anger by the early 1870s, when the poor sales of *Poor Miss Finch* were put down to 'the present insanely-absurd system of Circulating Library publication' (BGLL II, 335), or when there was an attempt to censor the title of *The New Magdalen* by that 'ignorant fanatic' Mudie (BGLL II, 387). In 1871 the author thus told George Smith that the monopolies wielded by the libraries were 'anomalies in a commercial country', predicting 'a revolution in the publishing trade' in the near future (B&C II, 349). The predicted transformation did not begin to take place, however, until the mid-1880s.

One of the catalysts was George Moore, whose first novel, *A Modern Lover*, was published in June 1883 in three volumes from Tinsley, the house that had made its name and fortune with Braddon's *Lady Audley's Secret* in 1862, and taken on *The Moonstone* in 1868, but was now facing hard times. Moore had spent much of the 1870s in Paris, where he had become an advocate of the latest theories in art and literature, whether Edouard Manet's impressionism or Émile Zola's naturalism.[5] Set between London and Paris and the bohemian and bourgeois worlds, *A Modern Lover* is the story of a handsome but impoverished artist who climbs the ladder of social success by casually betraying three women who sacrifice themselves for him. The *Spectator* was quick to suggest that Moore's purpose was to 'imitate the methods of Zola and his odious school'.[6] William Tinsley had published the novel with its provocative title and theme intact only on condition that the author reimburse his losses should the novel be refused by Charles Mudie and W.H. Smith, the major circulating library owners then still firmly in control of the form and content of new fiction. In the event, both purchased merely a handful of copies of the novel and kept it under the counter to be issued only if specifically requested. Fortuitously, a fire at a warehouse destroyed the many unwanted but insured copies and saved the author from having to write a cheque for £40 to honour his publishing contract.[7] Not content with this piece of luck, the quixotic Moore set about tilting against the system of library censorship itself.

His initial move was to join forces with the aging publisher Henry Vizetelly to issue his 1884 novel *A Mummer's Wife* in a single volume at six shillings. The novel describes the inner life of Kate Ede, the wife of a linen draper. She is seduced by her lodger, a travelling actor; deserts her husband and takes to the stage with her lover; divorces and remarries but gradually recoils from bohemian freedom; allows her child to die of neglect; descends into alcoholism and psychosis; and dies alone. This psychological drama unfolds against a background of relentless physical description – the grim streets, shops, and factories of the Potteries town of Hanley, the sordid lifestyle of the provincial theatre troupe, the draper's initial chronic attack of asthma, Kate's terminal bout of *delirium tremens*. As intended, this narrative was banned outright by both Smith and Mudie. Immediately Moore sent a lengthy letter to the London evening paper the *Pall Mall Gazette*, containing a blistering attack on the high-handedness of the circulating libraries.[8] In fact, *A Mummer's Wife* received a number of sympathetic reviews, and then achieved a *succès de scandale*, going into a fourth edition within the year of publication. At this point Moore issued a pamphlet with Vizetelly entitled *Literature at Nurse; or, Circulating Morals* (1885), which savagely mocked Mudie's policy of 'selection'. What was most at issue was the writer's freedom to choose the form of the narrative. Moore records Mudie, the personification of 'the British Matron', as stating that 'he did not keep naturalistic literature – that he did not consider it "proper"'.[9]

Thus the pamphlet attempted to show that many fashionable sensation novels actively promoted by Mudie were considerably more salacious that *A Mummer's Wife*, which had been judged 'an immoral publication which the library would not be justified in circulating'.[10]

Vizetelly was a well-read man who was well aware of the cultural issues involved. He had long acted as Paris correspondent of the *Illustrated London News*, where he had acquired a reputation as an authority on contemporary French literature. Moore's *A Mummer's Wife* was marketed as the third in the series of 'Vizetelly's One-Volume Novels', preceded by a translation of Alphonse Daudet's *Numa Roumestan* (1884); around the same time, Vizetelly had begun to issue a series of Zola's work in cheap single volumes, beginning with *L'Assomoir* and *Nana*.[11] With Matthew Arnold (see Chapter 9), Vizetelly understood that it was no coincidence that, in mid-century France, progressive publishers like Michel Lévy had been allowed to undermine the circulating libraries by slashing the price of new works of fiction, and had been rewarded with the flourishing of social and psychological realism. Meanwhile Britain had allowed Mudie to remain in control and was trapped in an endless cycle of sensation and sentiment.

Collins's response to these events is curious. Early in 1885 he wrote the opening of a new novel centring on adultery, desertion, and divorce which eventually appeared as *The Evil Genius*. The novel was once again syndicated by Tillotson's in the first instance. Given that *The Evil Genius* weighed in at little over 100,000 words, compared to not much less than 150,000 for *A Mummer's Wife*, it clearly required considerable generosity in the way of white space to stretch Collins's text out to fill three volumes. Moreover, Collins's publishers Chatto and Windus were among those beginning to issue new full-length novels by both major and minor authors in cheaper single-volume format, including Robert Louis Stevenson's *Prince Otto* (1885). In these circumstances, while Collins was still theoretically in favour of 'hastening the end of the dying system of the Circulating Libraries' (BGLL IV, 78–9), it seems pertinent to consider why the author did not follow the trail blazed by Moore and issue *The Evil Genius* in a format that could be purchased directly by readers.

As we saw in Chapter 1, though Collins held many volumes of French fiction in his library, and had admired the early explorations in realism of Honoré de Balzac even more than the melodramas of Eugene Sue or the romances of Alexandre Dumas *père*, he was almost wholly antipathetic to developments in France after the mid-century, especially the 'realistic rubbish' associated with the names of Daudet and Zola (B&C II, 409–10).

As reflected in a letter to his agent, Collins also expressed distaste regarding parallel developments in American realism: 'My idea is that these American magazines all stand committed to the new American school of fiction – and that my way of writing represents the abomination of desolation in their eyes' (BGLL IV, 256). Collins thus clearly felt no sympathy with the naturalist project and would have recoiled from any association with Moore.[12] Nevertheless the common themes of adultery, desertion, and divorce – by no means unusual ones at this period, as witness in George Meredith's *Diana of the Crossways* (1885) or Thomas Hardy's *The Mayor of Casterbridge* (1886) – provide a basis for comparison of *The Evil Genius* and *A Mummer's Wife*.

Before starting to write Collins had given an outline of the new story to a friend:

> The central notion is ... a divorced husband and wife, who (after a lapse of a few years) regret their separation. *He* finds that the woman who has seduced him is in no sense worth the sacrifice – and becomes a miserable man. She (passing in the world as a widow) has an offer from a sincerely religious man – hesitates (being a good woman) to marry him under false pretences – decides on telling him the truth – and is rejected with horror by her lover, who remembers his New Testament, and dare not marry a divorced woman. But these same religious principles urge him to bring the separated pair together, in the interests of their eternal welfare. He is innocently assisted by the child of the marriage ...
>
> (B&C II, 473–4)

In composing the novel itself, Collins made two significant departures from this plan. Firstly, he recast the worthless seducer as a vulnerable young governess more sinned against than sinning, and thus permitted a convincing account of the mutual affection and respect which survives the conflict of interest of the two women, who form an interesting variation on the old theme of the dark and fair sisters. At the same time he balanced pathos with comedy, not merely at the *dénouement* but throughout the narrative, in large part through the interventions of the stereotypical figure of the wife's mother. As we saw in Chapter 8, Collins's general inclination is to reject matrimony as a patriarchal device for the preservation of property and the male line, and approve the liberal view of marriage as equal partnership. However, the demands of comic closure place Collins in the anomalous position of overtly supporting the double standard of English divorce law, which then condoned 'sexual frailty' on the part of the husband but not the wife.[13]

In *A Mummer's Wife*, the divorce itself is treated in such a casual, inevitable fashion that it comes as something of a surprise to learn that '[d]ivorce was still largely out of the reach or even imagination of the poor' at this time, when the divorce rate was still only 0.007 per cent of all married couples.[14] Collins is much more concerned than Moore to explicate the intricacies of family law, to demonstrate the importance of social disapprobation in discouraging divorce proceedings, and to exploit the dramatic possibilities of differences between the English and Scottish legal systems, as he had done previously in *Man and Wife* (1870) and *The Law and the Lady* (1875). On the other hand, Collins's choice of setting in the remote Scottish highlands renders the social issues unnecessarily distant and blurred. Moore's naturalistic methods clearly offer a more profound understanding of the causes and consequences of infidelity, and we are left in little doubt that 'sexual frailty' is by no means an exclusive male prerogative.

The contrast between the forms of the two novels is seen most clearly in their respective references to their own narrative form. While at work on *A Mummer's Wife* in Dublin, Moore wrote to Zola that he was engaged in 'digging a dagger into the heart of the sentimental school'.[15] This he attempted not only by describing in stark detail the material circumstances determining Kate's subjection, but also by showing repeatedly that her very dreams of escape are shaped by the sentimental fiction which has fed her imagination since childhood. She is shown to have progressed from the fairy stories of the nursery, through the gothic romances in papers like the *Family Herald*, and finally to the sensational school of Braddon. The novels which Kate turns to at times of distress are not difficult to identify. One relates to 'the love of a young lady in the awkward predicament of not being able to care for anyone but her groom' and must be *Aurora Floyd* (1863), while Kate's favourite romance, which has as its heroine the wife of a country physician who 'used to read Byron and Shelley to her aristocratic lover' is clearly Braddon's *The Doctor's Wife* (1864).[16] This is curious because in his memoirs, Moore was to recall that Braddon's was the voice that awakened him in childhood to the call of literature, singling out *The Doctor's Wife* as the source of his love of Shelley and Byron.[17] Clearly the dagger needed also to be driven into the heart of the author's own romantic urges.

In *The Evil Genius*, by contrast, Collins's consciousness of narrative form is more simply reactionary. Through the mouth of the governess, who makes the money needed to advertise her services in the newspaper by selling a manuscript to an editor, Collins is able to express his old prejudice against the penny-novel-journals, dismissing more contemptuously than Moore the 'feeble and foolish' romances they offer, and the sensibility of their readers who are satisfied 'so long as the characters [a]re lords and ladies, and there [i]s plenty of love in it' (*EG*, 97). But at the same time, through the mouth of the wife's mother, he can poke fun at 'the new school of novel writing' – the realists who offer little in the way of story and no drama, but only a 'masterly anatomy of human motives' which is so dull as to be soporific (*EG*, 89). This sweeping rejection of both romance and realism leaves the novelist who has a social theme no option but the most conservative form of comedy. It is thus unsurprising that neither Mudie nor Smith found anything to object to in *The Evil Genius*.

* * * * *

The young Fred Fargus had joined the family auctioneering business in Bristol as a junior partner on his father's premature death in 1868, but decided to sell up in the summer of 1884. By then he was far more widely known as the author 'Hugh Conway'. By the early 1880s he had already published under that pseudonym a slim volume of verse, the lyrics to a number of romantic songs, and a handful of short tales of mystery and the supernatural. The stories had appeared not only in the *Bristol Times* and other local publications, but also in metropolitan magazines like *Chambers's Journal* and *Blackwood's Magazine*. Unexpectedly, though, it was a short novel which appeared at the price of sixpence in November 1883 as the third of the paperback Christmas Annuals issued by the Bristol house of J.W. Arrowsmith which became the publishing sensation of the year and brought him sudden national and international fame.

Only around half of the initial edition of 6000 of *Called Back*, as the novella was entitled, had sold by the end of the holiday season, but in the new year sales picked up, the story was reissued as a shilling volume in Arrowsmith's Bristol Library, and a total of thirty thousand copies were cleared by March 1884. At the same time, in collaboration with the critic and editor Joseph Comyns Carr, the author rapidly created a dramatic version which was to enjoy long runs in both provincial and metropolitan theatres. By summer 1887 over 350,000 copies of the book had been sold throughout the British Empire,[18] a much larger number were undoubtedly printed in various cheap and unauthorized editions in the United States, and the story was quickly translated into all the major European languages. Many contemporary commentators, like the enthusiastic reviewer in the widely read London society weekly *Truth*, tended to compare the story to Wilkie Collins's sensation novels of the 1860s,[19] but readers are now more likely to recognize Fargus's tale as a seminal example of the modern thriller.

Inundated with commissions, Fargus turned out a vast amount of new fiction in the year following the success of *Called Back*, selling material both to major provincial syndicates like Tillotson's and to prestigious metropolitan periodicals. Among these contributions was *A Family Affair*, which was serialized in Carr's monthly *English Illustrated Magazine* from October 1884, before appearing as a triple-decker from Macmillan the following year. It is generally considered the young Fargus's best work, and an indication of considerable literary potential. However, Fargus's most popular and remunerative efforts were undoubtedly two further thrillers for Arrowsmith, *Dark Days* and *Slings and Arrows*, which appeared as the Christmas Annuals for 1884 and 1885 respectively. However, many of these narratives appeared in volume form only posthumously. Perhaps the excess of literary labour led to physical exhaustion, for early in 1885 Fargus showed symptoms of tuberculosis and was advised to seek rest and recuperation in a warmer climate. While travelling on the Riviera, he was diagnosed as suffering from typhoid fever and died that spring at Monte Carlo.

Like almost everyone else in England, Collins was well aware of Hugh Conway's brief moment of glory. Around a month after the writer's death, he wrote to his agent A.P. Watt suggesting that, in order to copyright the title of his new story so that it could not be stolen by pirates if used in advance publicity, he should adopt the method pioneered by 'Poor Fargus' with *Dark Days* (BGLL IV, 100). This was to issue a 'bogus' story of a half-a-dozen pages or so under the same title, a practice that was in fact adopted with both *The Evil Genius* and *The Guilty River*. Indeed, it seems more than likely that *A Family Affair*, which combines sensationalism with delicate social comedy in treating the themes of adultery and illegitimacy was an influence on the form of Collins's *The Evil Genius*. It is then perhaps not surprising that when J.W. Arrowsmith approached Collins after Fargus's death to see if he would take over the Bristol author's role for the Arrowsmith's Christmas Annual for 1886, Collins was happy to agree to write a story 'equal in length to "Called Back"' (BGLL IV, 187). The result was *The Guilty River*, though it was far from achieving the popular and commercial success of Fargus's three efforts. When Watt wrote on Collins's death to settle the royalty account, Arrowsmith informed him that he still had 25,000 unwanted copies of the Bristol Library Edition of the story on his hands (Peters, 418–9). By then Fargus's mantle had already passed to Walter Besant, who supplied all the Arrowsmith's Annuals from 1887 to 1890, clearly with greater success. In the 1890s many of the Annuals were produced by the rising young stars of imperial mystery and suspense, including Arthur Conan Doyle with *The Great Shadow* in 1892 and H. Rider Haggard with *The Wizard* in 1896, both also reissued as short shilling romances in the Bristol Library.

The *Guilty River* and *Called Back* have rather more in common than the format in which they were published. Both centre on a love triangle, where one of the male rivals is suddenly handicapped by sensory deprivation, the rejected suitor attempts or commits murder, and the result is a transgressive but finally happy union. In *Called Back* the rich and independent Gilbert Vaughan hastily marries the pale willowy beauty Pauline March, the half-English daughter of an Italian patriot, only to discover at leisure that she is an amnesiac with the mental and emotional capacities of a child. Thus, before the union can be consummated, the husband needs to assume the role of detective in order to remove the veil from his wife's past. In doing so he simultaneously comes to understand a mysterious and melodramatic incident in his own youth, at a time when he was struck temporarily by blindness. The villain of the piece is the stiletto-wielding Macari whose desire for Pauline led him to murder her brother, in a traumatic scene strangely witnessed by both Gilbert and Pauline, then unknown to each other but finally happily united. In *The Guilty River*, the young landowner Gerard Roylake falls in love with Cristel Toller, the brown buxom daughter of the miller, his tenant. To achieve fulfilment, however, he has to counter not only the social disapproval of his step-mother and the neighbouring gentry, but also the extreme jealousy of the miller's mysterious and nameless lodger, a physician of great beauty and promise who has lost both his hearing and his sanity on discovering that homicide runs in the family.

Although we are told that Collins's hero has been educated on the Continent and the villain's mother was a New World slave, *The Guilty River* is set uniformly and claustrophobically in the gloomy woods crowding the banks of a murky river in middle England, one of those heavily symbolic landscapes familiar from the author's early sensation novels. At the same time the social issues raised are deeply embedded in the swamps of class prejudice. In contrast, *Called Back* is keener to exploit stereotypes of national and racial identity. Though revolutionary politics are not themselves a serious issue, political conspiracy in Italy and political exile in Siberia provide an exotic background, so that the narrative can switch from Turin to Moscow in jet-setting James Bond style, or indeed travel from London's West End to Old Town Edinburgh on a shrieking express train that looks forward to John Buchan. We can make a parallel contrast regarding narrative tone, as evidenced most notably in the respective climactic scenes. Though neither tale can bear great claims to enduring literary significance, there is little doubt that Fargus's use of language is crisper, more concise, more modern. In sum, though Collins attempts intermittently to reproduce the light romance of Fargus's thriller, he is constantly seduced by the attractions of heavy gothic.

The pacing of the two narratives is also very different. Fargus had written *Called Back* in less than six weeks,[20] but the aging and ailing Collins got into serious difficulties when he attempted to work to a similar schedule. Publication of *The Guilty River* was arranged for mid-November 1886, with a simultaneous appearance in New York in Harper's Handy Series. Collins had been late finishing *The Evil Genius* in March, only a month or so ahead of the newspaper serialization, and was seriously ill for some time afterwards, so that he only set to work on the Arrowsmith story in August and was still less than half way through in early October. He was forced into working twelve hours a day from the beginning of November to complete the story, and even then unrevised proofs had to be sent to New York to meet the publication deadline. Fargus's tale in fact gets off to a rather slow and laborious start, but, after the murder scene, increases the grip of suspense inexorably until the release of the dénouement. Collins, in contrast, gets in with a strong opening sequence underlining the *doppelgänger* relationship between hero and villain, but after the failed murder attempt, the narrative loses its way and ends in bathos and confusion. The tale 'was spoilt for want of room' as Collins put it in a letter to a friend (B&C II, 542).

Although *Called Back* represented a key intervention in the market, Arrowsmith of Bristol was by no means the only progressive house to explore the economic possibilities of publishing new shorter romances in single volumes at a fraction of the price of a triple-decker. The best-selling tales of adventure which established the reputations of both Stevenson and Haggard appeared as five-shilling volumes from Cassell's (*Treasure Island*, 1883, and *King Solomon's Mines*, 1885) or Longmans (*Doctor Jekyll and Mr Hyde*, 1886, and *She*, 1887), while Doyle's first Sherlock Holmes story *A Study in Scarlet* appeared from Ward, Lock at only a shilling as Beeton's Christmas Annual for 1887. In the long run, perhaps Mudie and the circulating library system were hit just as much by the economic threat of the cheap thriller as by the ideological challenge of naturalism.

* * * * *

The only new fiction which Collins seems to have read with enthusiasm during his last years were the adventure stories of Haggard and Stevenson. The former was also a client of A.P. Watt at this stage, and when his agent sent him copies of the Cassell editions of *King Solomon's Mines* or *Kidnapped* he responded with by then uncharacteristic animation (BGLL II, 220–1, 260–1). However, the failure of *The Guilty River* seems to have discouraged him from any further attempts at writing thrillers himself. *The Legacy of Cain* and *Blind Love*, Collins's last two novels, both exercises in old-fashioned sensationalism, thus duly appeared traditionally as three-deckers from Chatto and Windus. The works published late in Collins's life thus offer at best a half-hearted attempt to engage with new narrative forms and thus provide only a very occasional challenge to prevailing bourgeois values in the later Victorian decades.

11
Last Things

Wilkie Collins experienced his first major illness in his late twenties, when he was laid up for two months and reduced to walking with the aid of a stick, and for the rest of his life suffered increasingly severe bouts of what he typically referred to as 'rheumatic gout'. Though there may well have been underlying hereditary factors – according to the *Memoirs*, his father's symptoms also included '[v]iolent rheumatic pains' which 'attacked his right hand, arm, and shoulder, his left knee and ankle, and even his eyes' (Part III, ch. 1) – there can be little doubt that the author's condition was at least exacerbated by his addiction to rich food and fine wine. One of Collins's most enduring fictions – almost as elaborate and complex as *No Name* or *Armadale*, and sustained over many more instalments – was the denial of any causal connection between his atrocious diet and appalling health. (To celebrate the cheerful inventiveness of his self-deception, we offer you 'Wilkie Collins on Wine', an anthology of memorable remarks culled from his personal correspondence.) Those who met him for the first time commented on his semi-invalid status, pasty appearance, and clammy touch. The young novelist Hall Caine (whose reminiscences are not always to be trusted) remembered his eyes as 'large and protuberant' with 'the vague and dreamy look sometimes seen in the eyes of the blind, or those of a man to whom chloroform has just been administered' (cited in Robinson, 285–6). His old friend Edmund Yates recalled Collins in the 1880s as '[v]ery bent and gnarled and gnome-like, very much changed, indeed, from the dapper little man, I had met thirty years before' (B&G, 71), while Nathaniel Beard, son of his physician friend, remembered 'seeing him after an evening spent at our house ... walking up the street with the aid of a heavy stick, bowed nearly double, and looking like an old man of eighty, though he was but sixty-five'.[1] Given that many of the great names of

Victorian fiction – Charlotte Bronte, Thackeray, Gaskell, Dickens – did not live to celebrate their sixtieth birthdays, it is then perhaps something of a surprise to learn that Collins had attained a venerable age before he succumbed to bronchitis at Wimpole Street at 10 a.m. on 23 September 1889. Three months earlier he had suffered a paralytic stroke, effectively signalling the end of his career as a professional author.

* * * * *

The author's steadily deteriorating health made his world considerably smaller during the final decades of his life. His last overseas trip was in late 1877, and thereafter his longest journeys were to Ramsgate on the Kent coast, where he resided for lengthy stretches during the warmer months, using the local yacht club as a base for occasional sailing jaunts with Edward Pigott or Frank Beard, who was also his doctor. But the circle of old acquaintance was itself contracting alarmingly. His most intimate correspondents – his mother, his younger brother, and his mentor Dickens – were all gone by the early 1870s. A decade or so later it was the turn not only of his oldest friends, the Ward brothers, Ned and Charles, the former from suicide during a bout of depression, but also of his closest literary ally Charles Reade, who he hailed as 'one of the "last of the Romans"' (B&C II, 467). These losses were far from fully compensated by personal but rather intermittent relationships forged on the American trip, including Sebastian Schlesinger and William Seaver, or through the theatre, notably the actors, Frank Archer and Wybert Reeve. Indeed, a number of the younger literati who gathered around the author in his declining years, including Hall Caine and the critic Harry Quilter, seem to have been there mainly to serve their own interests.

Wilkie Collins on wine

The *parties* have knocked me up – I've made two *speeches* at supper and drunk so much of the juice of the grape that (to use the impassioned language of Elihu the Buzzite a comforter of Job) – 'My belly is as wine'.

> To Harriet Collins, 13 January 1844, B&C I, 16

How I shall be able to stand the tea & coffee breakfasts at home I don't know! ... I take to the déjéuner à la fourchette regularly – Oysters and Chablis – omlettes and radishes ... afraid I shall be as fat as a pig if I stay here much longer – do nothing but eat and drink – very wrong I know – shall repent upon leg of mutton and rice-pudding when I get home

> *To Harriet Collins, 21 September 1844*, B&C I, 24–5

What a night! What speeches! What songs! I carried away much claret and am rather a seedy barrister this morning. I think it must have been the *oaths* that disagreed with me!

> *To Edward Pigott, 22 November 1851*, B&C I, 76

I have begun the great reformation. Observe the hour above written [*10 minutes to 9*], and know that I am dressed, and *waiting* for the breakfast bell – a position I never remember to have been placed in before in the whole course of my life. ... I feel better already – I take no beer – and I stop short at my three glasses of wine.

> *To Harriet Collins, 7 July 1853*, BGLL I, 85

This is a rambling, scrambling, scrawling letter – but I can't write anything correct and regular, for I have not long done eating a very capital dinner, and washing down the same with copious draughts of Lachryma – and I am, as you know, one of that unhappy race who get particularly stupid after repletion.

> *To Edward Pigott, 4 November 1853*, BGLL I, 91–4

The doctor ... proposes no medicine. He is a jolly German with a huge pair of gold spectacles, and a face like an apple – and he smokes his cigar with me every morning after breakfast, like a man who thoroughly enjoys his tobacco. He allows of *all* wines, provided they are of the best vintages ... all cookery provided it is thoroughly good

> *To Charles Collins, 22 April 1863*, B&C I, 220–1

The hotel ... contains a cellar of the best Hock and Moselle wines I ever tasted – and possesses a Parisian cook who encourages my natural gluttony by a continuous succession of entrées which are to be eaten but not described.

> *To Nina Lehmann, 29 April 1863*, B&C I, 221–3

If I am alive, it is needless to say how gladly I shall take my place at your table. If I am *not* alive, be so good as to look towards the conservatory, when the butler comes round for the first time with the Champagne. You will perceive a Luminous Appearance – with an empty glass in one hand

> *To Lady Louisa Goldsmid, 15 May 1865 or 1866, B&C I, 247*

Dry champagne is good for your arm.

> *To William Tindell, 16 November 1871, BGLL II, 300*

The wedding was a triumph – and we were all the better for it. I look back on it with but two subjects for regret. First, the bridesmaids petticoats were too short. Secondly, I was medically forbidden to drink Champagne.

> *To Jane Ward, 6 January 1882, BGLL III, 320*

Come with the ducks, next time – receive my thanks in person – and let us drink one more bottle of Old Champagne, with 'gout staring us in the face', and you and I staring back again at the gout with defiant eyes and resolute stomachs.

> *To Sebastian Schlesinger, 27 January 1885, B&C II, 477–8*

The pints of champagne have disappeared. Will you send me six dozen more of the same 'Vin Brut' in half bottles? The sherry also is reported to be on its last legs. Please let me have a three-dozen case (as before) – and send another three-dozen case, addressed to | Mrs. Dawson | 10 Taunton Place | Park Road, Regents Park

> *To Beecheno, Yaxley and Co., 12 January 1886, BGLL IV, 141–2*

Due to his own immobility or on the doctor's orders, Collins was increasingly prevented from attending social gatherings, while his unconventional domestic arrangements in any case tended to exclude him from more fastidious households. However, he remained in steady contact with older female friends such as Nina Lehmann and Georgina Hogarth, who were well aware of the existence of what he preferred to call his 'morganatic family' (B&C II, 404). At the same time he embarked on faintly flirtatious correspondences with glamorous young actresses such as Kate Field and Mary Anderson, or married women such as Jane Bigelow, wife of the former American consul-general in Paris. As reflected in his portrayal of Zo in *Heart and Science*, or Kitty in *The Evil Genius*, he obviously enjoyed the vivacious company of young people, and always remembered to send birthday presents to his godchild Alice

Ward or Jane Bigelow's daughter Flora, for example. But, as we saw in Chapter 6, his elaborate marital role play with little Nannie Wynne is more troubling. With the full knowledge of her widowed mother, an acquaintance of both Pigott and Beard, this was doubtless a harmless game, but it is difficult not to think twice about jokes such as 'I shall be delighted to receive that conjugal embrace' (B&C II, 503). It is, of course, unlikely that the highly respectable Mrs Wynne was aware that, far from being the confirmed bachelor that he seemed, Collins was himself the father of two teenage girls.

Ironically then, given his youthful mockery of friends like Charles Ward for having 'a family and a respectable pot-belly, and a position in the country as a householder and ratepayer' (B&C I, 72), in his old age Collins was largely confined to the family circle in the role of *paterfamilias*. Perhaps the loss he felt most deeply during this period was that of his beloved dog Tommie (BGLL IV, 114). He then spent much of his leisure time, both in town and at the seaside, as 'William Dawson', with Martha, their two daughters Marian and Harriet, and younger son William Charles. In one of his last letters he wrote plaintively to Sebastian Schlesinger, who had known of the author's secret family since he had arranged insurance for their benefit in Boston in 1874, but was now resident in London: 'I want you to see my children – *why* you will easily guess ...' (B&C II, 56–7). His family circle was extended in 1878 when his stepdaughter Harriet Graves married a young solicitor named Harry Bartley. By 1884 they had three daughters, Dah (Doris), Bolly (Evelyn Beatrice), and Sissy (Cecile Marguerite), all of whom would later go on to the musical stage (Clarke, 194–9). Collins clearly also doted on this diminutive troupe of step-grandchildren, who often came over to Gloucester Place or down to Ramsgate. 'The Bartley's are within two doors of us, and the children are in and out a dozen times a day' (BGLL IV, 183–4), as he once wrote to Frank Beard from his seaside lodgings. In his final will drawn up by Harry Bartley in 1882, Collins recognized his responsibilities to both Martha Rudd and Caroline Graves and divided his wealth between the two families. He also seems to have recognized that, despite the substantial legacy received on the death of his mother in 1868, his estate was by no means that of a rich man. Indeed, his wealth at death fell just short of £11,000, far less than Ellen Wood's £36,000, never mind the £80,000 accumulated by Dickens, and this must in part have been down to his extravagant lifestyle. (As he conceded to Nina Lehmann when recommending himself in jest as a chef: 'My *style* is expensive. I look on meat simply as a material for *sauces*' (BGLL II, 125–6).) It was in large measure this felt obligation to enhance the value of the inheritance due to his children and grandchildren that forced him to undertake such a relentless schedule of literary labour over his declining years.

During his last decade Collins's annual output was typically a full-length novel and at least one shorter tale, all appearing initially in serial publications. With *The Woman in White*, Collins had experienced a sense of exhilaration in 'winning the battle against the infernal periodical system' (B&C I, 184), but towards the end he found the relentless pressure of the weekly deadline severely debilitating. His most punishing schedule was undoubtedly in 1886, when he had to complete the best part of *The Evil Genius* for Tillotson, plus the stage version, as well as to compose from scratch two final sketches in the 'Victims of Circumstances' series for the Boston *Youth's Companion*, *The Guilty River* for *Arrowsmith's Christmas Annual*, and 'An Old Maid's Husband' for the Christmas Number of *The Spirit of the Times* in New York. This he somehow managed, though it cost him a couple of breakdowns and made him realize that he was 'too old for writing against time at the rate of twelve hours a day', as he put it to Edward Pigott (BGLL IV, 213–14). But the situation was even worse by late 1888, after time was lost to an enforced move from Gloucester Place to Wimpole Street and yet another attack of rheumatic gout. This left Collins contracted to produce two full-length serial novels in less than a year, respectively for John Dicks, publisher of *Reynolds's News* and other penny weeklies, and for the up-market *Illustrated London News*. It is then agonizing to witness him trying to keep his nose to the grindstone, even after a serious traffic accident which lead to an attack of bronchitis. In the end, the task proved impossible: *Blind Love* had to be eked out with material previously laid aside and completed by another hand, while the second project never got off the drawing board.

Collins kept up his spirits with the illusion that his latest work was up to his best: with *Heart and Science* he had 'never written such a first number since "The Woman in White"' (BGLL III, 344), while the projected novel that was never started was going to be 'another "Moonstone"' (BGLL IV, 365). But, as suggested in Chapter 10, the reality was far different. The last novels tend not only to be formally unadventurous, but also to fall back too often on stereotypical representations of contentious issues – obvious examples are the retreat into sentimental Christianity in *Heart and Science*, the mockery of American feminism at the end of *The Legacy of Cain*, or the caricature of Irish nationalism in the Prologue to *Blind Love*. The increasingly reactionary nature of Collins's thinking concerning social and political matters towards the end of his life, reflected also in his private correspondence, can come as something of a surprise to those accustomed to the non-conformist attitudes of his early decades. At the same time, it is difficult not to be impressed by the meticulous professionalism that allowed the author to fulfil his literary commitments faithfully in the most trying circumstances and almost to the end. Even the task of completing *Blind Love*, assigned to Walter Besant of the Society of Authors, was rendered painless by the 'detailed scenario, in which every incident, however trivial, was carefully laid down' found in the author's little black book after his stroke.[2]

This sense of dedication to the writer's duty is also exemplified by the increasing centrality of professional relationships during the author's last years, when his literary agent A.P. Watt and his publisher Andrew Chatto come to number among his most faithful visitors and his closest friends. With both, Collins establishes elaborate ceremonies to contain the commercial contagion of contracts and commissions and maintain the relationship on a gentlemanly footing. With Watt, for example, he fabricates an almost Manichean conflict between the forces of light and darkness in the drama of the publishing world. The Lancashire fiction syndicator W.F. Tillotson takes the devil's part with some consistency – at one point Collins even suggests that he would like to board a train to Bolton and 'kick an unmentionable part of Tillotson's person' (BGLL IV, 177). Other combatants occasionally change sides. At the beginning of 1886 the owners of *Youth's Companion* are 'not publishers but angels' (BGLL IV, 143) yet have become *anathema* before the end of the year (BGLL IV, 215). But Watt himself is never permitted to fall from grace. Collins writes to him during an epic battle with a novel for the Bolton firm: 'When I have finished "The Evil Genius" it is plain to me that I shall write a Sequel called "The Good Genius", and that I shall request permission to put *you* in the foremost place in the character of my "Hero"' (BGLL IV, 139). The exaggerated quality of utterances such as these suggests that a more general anxiety and frustration about the way things are going in the literary sphere is being displaced on to professional relationships which thus become highly personalized.

* * * * *

Unsurprisingly, both Watt and Chatto were among the chief mourners when Collins's mortal remains were interred at Kensal Green Cemetery at mid-day on Friday, 27 September 1889. Alongside them were the author's executors (Harry Bartley, Frank Beard, and Sebastian Schlesinger), old companions such as Jane Ward, Holman Hunt, and Edward Pigott, and theatrical colleagues of long standing such as Squire Bancroft and Ada Cavendish. The ceremonies were of the simplest character while the inscription read only, 'In Memory of Wilkie Collins Author of The Woman in White and Other Works of Fiction' (Gasson, 67). This was in accordance with the author's wishes laid out in his will, which specified that the 'funeral expenses shall not exceed twenty five pounds'.[3] All the same, the author's passing gave rise to a good deal of controversy. There were soon two High Court writs on behalf of the executors against unauthorized productions of the author's plays by managers keen to cash in on the publicity.[4] Harry Quilter's ill-advised campaign for a national memorial in St Paul's Cathedral was attacked by the *Daily Telegraph* on literary grounds, and rejected by the Dean and Chapter due to 'other considerations', presumably moral or religious. The proceeds (in the end, little more than £300) were thus eventually used to create a secular 'Wilkie Collins Memorial Library of Fiction' at the People's Palace in the East End of London.[5]

Well before this, though, there had been whiffs of scandal in the press concerning the circumstances of the author's death, the attendants at his graveside, and the beneficiaries of his will. Prestigious dailies such as *The Times* – and respectable weeklies such as the *Illustrated London News* in which *Blind Love* was then being serialized – simply ignored Collins's domestic arrangements, discretely noting a floral tribute at the funeral from 'Mrs Dawson and family', and mentioning the value of the estate but not the beneficiaries when the will was offered to probate. Among the popular organs there were more colourful but less accurate accounts, most notably that in the London edition of the *New York Herald*, which was widely reprinted:

> He died alone, without a wife, a child, or a relative to soothe his last agonies with that love and sympathy that only comes from the ties of blood. ... By his side was only Dr. F. Carr-Beard, his life-long friend and physician, and the old housekeeper who for thirty years has looked after her master's comfort with the care and the devotion of a slave'.[6]

But it was in the weekly and evening metropolitan society papers that the real rumours were started, with Edmund Yates and Hall Caine, who both attended the funeral at Kensal Green, ironically among the first to start the ball of gossip rolling. Caine published an article of 'Personal Recollections' in the *Globe* of 4 October, including a wild anecdote about Collins knocking back laudanum by the wine-glass,[7] which intensely annoyed Harriet Bartley. 'Mr Hall Caine appears to be inclined to again advertise himself at our beloved Wilkie's expense. ... Small man and small mind but an *immense* SELF!', she wrote to Watt on the evening that the article appeared (BGLL IV, 392). Yates's obituary in the *World* of 25 September had told similar tales, but in his desire to lord it over less *au fait* sources, he went a step further in a follow-up article the next week. There he not only lambasted *The Times* for reporting the presence of Oscar Wilde at Kensal Green though he was 'not within miles of the place', but also mocked a rival society weekly for suggesting that the shabbiness of the writer's dwelling was due to 'the absence of womankind', hinting broadly that this was 'a startling statement to Mr Collins's intimates'.[8]

However, a much more honest and down-to-earth account of Collins's domestic arrangements was offered to the 350,000 subscribers of the jumbo Sunday edition of the New York *World*, then also running *Blind Love* as a serial. On 29 September, instead of the next instalment of the novel, readers were offered not only a two-column article of personal reminiscences by the actress Olive Logan Sikes,[9] but also a shorter unsigned report cabled from London on the day of the funeral. Since this striking article does not seem to have circulated in Britain, and is not cited by any of Collins's biographers, the paragraph concerning the author's will is worth quoting in full:

It will be some days before the will of Wilkie Collins will be offered to probate, but it is well known among his intimate friends that he provides liberally in it for the three children whom he acknowledges as his own. They were at the funeral to-day with their mother, and one of the numerous beautiful wreaths which surrounded the coffin was from them. But they were not among the chief mourners and kept out of view as much as possible. They never went near Wilkie Collins's house and few people here have heard of them. In his will Wilkie Collins refers to these children as his own and leaves one-half of his estate which, it is said, will not exceed $100,000, to be divided in their interest. The mother of these children was a housemaid in the employ of Wilkie Collins's mother and was very devoted to her while she lived. The other half of Wilkie Collins's fortune goes to his housekeeper, Mrs Graves, while she lives, and to the novelist's adopted daughter, Mrs Bartley, on her mother's death. This adopted daughter, the child of his housekeeper, had been a great pet of Collins for years, doing all his work as amanuensis.[10]

Like the information on Carrie Bartley, the details of the will are remarkably accurate and it seems unlikely at this stage that such knowledge would have been available to any but the beneficiaries and the executors. The most obvious source seems thus to be Sebastian Schlesinger, who might have been both less inclined than Victorian Englishmen to worry about what it was undesirable to publish, and more likely to chat freely to a reporter from a New York newspaper. Either way, the report at least casts a doubt on the assumption that the author's morganatic family did not attend his funeral (Clarke, 3; Peters, 432). It also offers an entirely plausible alternative to the hypotheses, for which there is no supporting evidence, that Wilkie Collins and Martha Rudd must have first met near her family home in Norfolk while he was preparing to write *Armadale* in 1864, and that he was responsible for her move to London (Clarke, 108–11; Peters, 293–4).

More generally, the way that Collins's death was treated in the press points to a sea change in the style of journalism in the later Victorian period – that triumph of signed, personalized, investigative, anecdotal reporting that was already becoming known as the New Journalism.[11] By no means everyone was happy with this erosion of the barrier between public and private matters. The phrase itself had been coined by Matthew Arnold, who preferred the classical, impersonal manner of the quarterly reviews or *The Times*, and described the new mode as 'feather-brained'.[12] Indeed, one of the key movers in its emergence was Edmund Yates himself, with his early apprenticeship in the anecdotal style as one of 'Dickens's young men', and his seminal role in the establishment of the gossip column in 'society' journals such as *Town Talk* (1858–9) and the *World* (1874–1922). Though Wilkie Collins would surely not have been overjoyed to see his own 'dirty linen' washed and hung out in public so soon after his demise, his own career as a writer often reveals a complicity with these developments. He too had learned the trade of journalism under Dickens and perfected the dramatic-idiosyncratic manner; as we saw in Chapter 2, he had supported Yates in his occasional brushes with the laws of defamation; he was usually happy to sit for interviews and encourage personal articles in the 'celebrities-at-home' style.[13] Indeed, on a number of occasions during his last years he had himself contributed to the trend, with autobiographical pieces in, for example, both the *Globe* and Harry Quilter's *Universal Review*.[14]

* * * * *

Wilkie Collins's career as an author spans more than four decades, covering all but the opening and closing stages of the reign of Queen Victoria. During that lengthy period Collins's writings offer a crucial witness – second in importance perhaps only to those of his mentor, collaborator, friend, and rival Charles Dickens – on the gradual and uneven emergence in Britain of a mass literary culture. In Collins's youth Walter Scott still dominates the fictional firmament, though Dickens is already the rising star. By Collins's declining years, his own ascendancy is eclipsed by the likes of Rider Haggard and Conan Doyle. But in between, Collins's explorations of sensation and suspense, his investigations into the uncanny and the unorthodox, are as important as any in shaping the modern popular genres of mystery and romance. The same period witnesses enormous changes in print culture, including the increasing legal codification of copyright which thus enhanced the concept, and raised the value, of literary property, and the growing professionalization of authorship, marked by the rise of the literary agent and the founding of organizations like the Society of Authors. These processes reflect the gradual emergence of print capitalism which leads also to the commodification not only of the literary text itself but also of the literary personality of the writer, so that both could be packaged and marketed in a similar way to new brand household goods such as Pear's Soap or Bird's Custard Powder. If Collins was not always certain where he stood with regard to these complex developments, his life in letters nevertheless constitutes a fascinating case study in the sociology of literature in the second half of the nineteenth century.

Notes

1 Collins's Education and Reading

1. See Baron Alfred-Auguste Ernouf, 'Romanciers Anglais Contemporains: Wilkie Collins', *La Revue Contemporaine* 28 (August 1862), 724–50.
2. The most detailed accounts of this period in the author's life are found in Clark, chs 3–6, and Peters, chs 2–5.
3. Except where noted, these brief lives rely on information from the *Oxford Dictionary of National Biography*.
4. For more recent research on Braddon's career in the theatre than that reflected in the *ODNB* entry, see Jennifer Carnell, *The Literary Lives of Mary Braddon* (Hastings, E. Sussex: Sensation Press, 2000), ch. 1.
5. See William Baker, *Wilkie Collins's Library: A Reconstruction* (Westport, CN: Greenwood Press, 2002).
6. The most intriguing of the tales is 'Ozias Hala' by one M.P. Dillon, which presumably planted a seed in the author's mind which came to fruition in Ozias Midwinter, the dark, enigmatic stranger with the uncouth name whose entrance on the scene precipitates the events of *Armadale*.
7. Cited in Edmund Yates, 'Men of Mark: W. Wilkie Collins', *The Train* (3 June 1857), 355.
8. See 'Portrait of an Author', *AYR* 1, 1859, 184–9.
9. See Émile-Daurand Forgues, 'Études sur le Roman Anglais: William Wilkie Collins', *La Revue des Deux Mondes* 12, 1855, 815–48, and P.D. Edwards, *Dickens's 'Young Men': George Augustus Sala, Edmund Yates, Edmund Yates, and the World of Victorian Journalism* (Aldershot, Hants: Ashgate, 1997), 75–7.
10. See 'Dramatic Grub Street', *HW* 17 (6 March 1858), 265–70.
11. See William Baker, *The George Eliot–George Henry Lewes Library: An Annotated Catalogue of their Books at Dr Williams's Library* (New York: Garland, 1977), and *Wilkie Collins's Library*.
12. In 1887, as six examples of favourite poetic pieces, Collins listed passages from Shakespeare's *King Lear*, Byron's *Childe Harold*, Scott's *Lord of the Isles*, Gray's *Elegy*, Dryden's 'Ode on St. Cecilia's Day', and Pope's 'Elegy to the Memory of an Unfortunate Lady'. See 'Fine Passages in Verse and Prose: Selected by Living Men of Letters', *Fortnightly Review* NS 42 (September 1887), 430–54.

2 Collins's Circles

1. William Holman Hunt, *Pre-Raphaelitism and the Pre-Raphaelites*, 2nd edn. (2 vols; London: Chapman & Hall, 1913), II, 143.
2. John Ruskin, *Modern Painters: Their Superiority in the Art of Landscape Painting to All the Ancient Masters* (London: Smith, Elder, 1843), 417.
3. Hunt, *Pre-Raphaelitism and the Pre-Raphaelites*, II, 183.

4. William Holman Hunt, 'The Pre-Raphaelite Brotherhood: A Fight for Art II', *Contemporary Review* 49:5 (May 1886), 744.
5. Charles Dickens, 'Old Lamps for New Ones', *HW* 12 (15 June 1850), 12–14.
6. John Ruskin, 'The Pre-Raffaelites', letter to the editor, *The Times* (13 May 1851), 8–9.
7. Ibid.
8. John Ruskin, 'The Pre-Raphaelite Artists', letter to the editor, *The Times* (30 May 1851), 8–9.
9. 'Our Literary Table', *Athenaeum* (10 January 1852), 50.
10. [Wilkie Collins], 'The Exhibition of the Royal Academy', *Bentley's Miscellany* 39:174 (June 1851), 623.
11. Ibid., 624.
12. Ibid., 620.
13. Ibid., 621.
14. Ibid., 624.
15. Aoife Leahy, 'Ruskin and the Evil of the Raphaelesque in *Hide and Seek*', *WCSJ* NS8 (2005), 19.
16. Charles Dickens to Miss Burdett Coutts, 12 April 1850, Pilgrim VI, 82–3.
17. P.D. Edwards, *Dickens Young Men: George Augustus Sala, Edmund Yates and the World of Victorian Journalism* (Aldershot, Hants: Ashgate, 1997), 1.
18. John Hollingshead, *Gaiety Chronicles* (London: Constable, 1898), 62.
19. G.A. Sala, *Things I Have Seen and People I Have Known* (2 vols; London: Cassell, 1894), I, 81–2.
20. John Hollingshead, *'Good Old Gaiety': An Historiette and Remembrance* (London: Gaiety Theatre Co., 1903), 1–2.
21. Sala, *Things I Have Seen and People I Have Known*, I, 114–5.
22. James Hain Friswell, *Modern Men of Letters Honestly Criticised* (London: Hodder & Stoughton, 1870), 160; see also the discussion in Edwards, *Dickens's 'Young Men'*, 129–30.
23. Edmund Yates, 'Men of Mark. No. 2. W. Wilkie Collins', *Train* 3:18 (June 1857), 354.
24. To W.H. Wills, 27 September 1851, Pilgrim VI, 497.
25. To W.H. Wills, 10 January 1856, Pilgrim VIII, 20.
26. [Charles Dickens] 'The Mortals in the House', *AYR* ('The Haunted House', Extra Christmas Number, 1859), 7.
27. Edmund Yates, 'Moi-Même: In Memoriam W.W.C., Obit September 23rd 1889', *World* (25 September 1889), 12–3. Reprinted in B&G, 70–1.
28. John Hollingshead, *My Lifetime* (2 vols; London: Sampson Low, Marston, 1895), I, 162.
29. The magazine was to be published by the house of Strahan, to whose *Good Words* Hollingshead was then a regular contributor. The project eventually materialized in 1865 in the form of the *Argosy*, with Isa Craig as its first editor.
30. See the illustration '"Tom Tiddler's Ground": The Committee of Concoction' in *Queen* (21 December 1861), 16.

3 Collins and the Earlier Victorian Literary Marketplace

1. See Benedict Anderson, *Imagined Communities: Reflections on the Origin and Spread of Nationalism*, Revised edn (London: Verso, 1991), 36.

2. Guinevere L. Griest, *Mudie's Circulating Library and the Victorian Novel* (Bloomington, IN: Indiana UP, 1970), 39.
3. After the mythical character in Thomas Morton's successful comedy *Speed the Plough* (1798), whose influence is enshrined in the often repeated phrase 'What will Mrs Grundy say?'.
4. William Baker et al., 'The Collected Letters of Wilkie Collins: Addenda and Corrigenda (2)', *WCSJ* NS9 (2006), 59–60.
5. William Baker et al., 'The Collected Letters of Wilkie Collins: Addenda and Corrigenda (3)', *WCSJ* NS10 (2007), 34–5.
6. See Royal A. Gettmann, *A Victorian Publisher: A Study of the Bentley Papers* (Cambridge: Cambridge UP, 1960), 143–4.
7. See Simon Eliot, *Some Patterns and Trends in British Publishing 1800–1919* (London: The Bibliographical Society, 1994), 147–8.
8. Linda K. Hughes and Michael Lund, *The Victorian Serial* (Charlottesville, VA: UP of Virginia, 1991), 4 and 14.
9. See Robert L. Patten, *Charles Dickens and His Publishers* (Oxford: Clarendon Press, 1978), chs 3–4.
10. R.M. Wiles, *Serial Publication in England before 1750* (Cambridge: Cambridge UP, 1957), 75.
11. John Sutherland, *Victorian Fiction: Writers, Publishers, Readers*, 2nd edn (Basingstoke: Palgrave Macmillan, 2006), 108.
12. Robert Donald Mayo, *The English Novel in the Magazines, 1740–1815* (Evanston, NJ: Northwestern UP, 1962), chs 2–3.
13. Louis James, *Fiction for the Working Man, 1830–1850* (London: Oxford UP, 1963), 29.
14. [E.S. Dallas], 'Great Expectations', *The Times* (17 October 1861), 6.
15. [Wilkie Collins], 'The Unknown Public', *HW* 18 (21 August 1858), 217.
16. Ibid., 222.
17. Ibid., 219.
18. See Dickens to W.H. Wills, 18 September 1856, Pilgrim VIII, 189.
19. See the unsigned notice in the *Saturday Review* (22 August 157), 188, for example: 'Our readers will easily recognise who is the Gamaliel at whose feet Mr Collins must have sat.' Reprinted in Page, 72.

4   Collins as Journalist

1. John Hollingshead, *My Lifetime*, I, 99–100.
2. Wilkie Collins, 'A Plea for Sunday Reform', *Leader* (27 September 1851), 926.
3. Wilkie Collins, 'Magnetic Evenings at Home: Letter I. To G.H. Lewes', *Leader* (17 January 1852), 63.
4. G.H. Lewes, 'The Fallacy of Clairvoyance', *Leader* (27 March 1852), 305.
5. See Keith Lawrence, 'The Religion of Wilkie Collins: Three Unpublished Documents', *Huntington Library Quarterly* 52:3 (Summer 1989), 389–402.
6. [Wilkie Collins], 'The Poisoned Meal', *Household Words* 18 (3 parts; 18 September–2 October 1858), 384.
7. [Wilkie Collins], 'The New Dragon of Wantley', *Leader* (20 December 1851), 1214.
8. [Wilkie Collins], 'Strike!', *Household Words* 17 (February 158), 169.
9. See Bliss Perry, 'The Short Story', *Atlantic Monthly* 90 (1902), 245–50.

10. John Plunkett, *Queen Victoria: First Media Monarch* (Oxford: Oxford UP, 2003), 1–12.
11. Simon Eliot, *Some Patterns and Trends in British Publishing, 1800–1919* (London: Bibliographical Society, 1994), 26–42.
12. Ibid., 32–3.
13. Graham Law, 'A Tale of Two Authors', *WCSJ* NS9 (2006), 43–51. This confusion arises despite the fact that the two authors differ so markedly – in generation, social background, gender identity, regional affiliation, religious faith, and literary style – perhaps sharing only their preference for strong heroines and supernatural themes.
14. To Anne Robson, [February 1859], *The Letters of Mrs Gaskell*, ed. J.A.V. Chapple and Arthur Pollard (Manchester: Manchester UP, 1966), 530–1.

5 Collins and London

1. Henry James, 'Miss Braddon', *Nation* (9 November 1865), 594.
2. Martin Hewitt, 'Prologue: Reassessing The Age of Equipoise', in Martin Hewitt, ed., *An Age of Equipoise: Reassessing Mid-Victorian Britain* (Aldershot, Hants: Ashgate, 2000), 13.
3. John Ruskin, *Modern Painters*; cited in Jerome Buckley, *Triumph of Time* (Harvard: Harvard UP, 1966), 58.
4. See William Greenslade, *Degeneration, Culture and the Novel, 1880–1940* (Cambridge: Cambridge UP, 1994), 20.
5. *The Times* (29 June 1861), 12.
6. K. Corbett, 'The Degeneration of the Race', *Lancet* 2 (August 1861), 170.
7. Unsigned article, 'Wilkie Collins about Charles Dickens', *Pall Mall Gazette* (20 January 1890), 3; cited in Sue Lonoff, *Wilkie Collins and His Victorian Readers: A Study in the Rhetoric of Authorship* (New York: AMS Press, 1982), 152.
8. David Glover, *Vampires, Mummies and Liberals: Bram Stoker and the Politics of Popular Fiction* (London: Duke UP, 1996), 93.
9. U.C. Knoepflmacher, 'The Counterworld of Victorian Fiction and *The Woman in White*', in *The Worlds of Victorian Fiction*, ed. Jerome H. Buckley (Cambridge: Harvard UP, 1975), 352.
10. Unsigned review, 'Esmond and Basil', *Bentley's Miscellany* 32 (December 1852), 576–86.
11. Tim Dolin and Lucy Dougan, 'Fatal Newness: *Basil*, Art, and the Origins of Sensation Fiction', in Maria Bachman and Don Richard Cox, eds, *Reality's Dark Light: The Sensational Wilkie Collins* (Knoxville, TN: University of Tennessee Press, 2003), 15.
12. Ibid., 18.
13. Frances Power Cobbe, 'Wife Torture in England', *Contemporary Review* 32 (April 1878), 55–87. J.S. Mill had of course made the general point much earlier that, contrary to received opinion, relations between the sexes have their basis in force; see 'The Subjection of Women', in *On Liberty and Other Essays*, ed. John Gray (Oxford: Oxford UP, 1991), 475–7.
14. Tamara Wagner, 'Sensationalizing Victorian Suburbia', in *Victorian Sensations: Essays on a Scandalous Genre*, ed. Kimberly Harrison and Richard Fantina (Columbus, OH: Ohio State UP, 2006), 208.

15. Unsigned review, 'Hide and Seek', *Morning Post* (13 July 1854), 3.
16. John Bowen, 'Collins's Shorter Fiction', in Taylor, 39.
17. See 'Hints for Scenes and Incidents', *Pall Mall Gazette* (20 January 1890).
18. Rosina wrote to Collins many years later to point out that Fosco was a very poor villain far eclipsed by her own husband, while Lytton himself described *The Woman in White* as 'great trash' (Gasson, 24).
19. See Gabrielle Ceraldi, 'The Crystal Palace, Imperialism and the "Struggle for Existence": Victorian Evolutionary Discourse in Collins's *The Woman in White*', in *Reality's Dark Light*, ed. Bachman and Cox, 185.
20. D.A. Miller, '*Cage aux folles*: Sensation and Gender in Wilkie Collins's *The Woman in White*' in his *The Novel and the Police* (Berkeley, CA: University of California Press, 1986).
21. Ibid., 173.
22. Richard Nemesvari, 'The Mark of the Brotherhood: Homosexual Panic and the Foreign Other in Wilkie Collins's *The Woman in White*', in Richard Fantina, ed., *Straight Writ Queer: Non-Normative Expressions of Heterosexuality in Literature* (Jefferson, NC: McFarland, 2006), 95–108.
23. Ibid., 102.
24. Ibid., 96.
25. Mansel, 'Sensation Novels', *Quarterly Review* 113 (April 1863), 481–514.
26. Collins's interest in class relations and disintegrating or shifting identities is apparent in *Basil*. It is also a focus of an influential article by Jonathan Loesberg, who situates the genre in the context of the contemporary debate over the 1867 Reform Bill; see 'The Ideology of Narrative Form in Sensation Fiction', *Representations* 13 (1986), 115–38.
27. Ronald R. Thomas, 'Detection in the Victorian Novel', in Deirdre David, ed., *The Cambridge Companion to the Victorian Novel* (Cambridge: Cambridge UP, 2001), 182.
28. Lillian Nayder, 'Agents of Empire in *The Woman in White*', *Victorian Newsletter* 83 (Spring 1993), 3. Nayder uses the terminology of Stephen Arata in 'The Occidental Tourist: Dracula and the Anxiety of Reverse Colonisation', *Victorian Studies* 33 (1990), 621–45.
29. K. Corbett, 'The Degeneration of the Race', *Lancet* 2 (August 1861), 170.
30. K. Corbett, 'The Degeneration of the Race', *Lancet* (23 February 1861), 203.
31. Maureen Moran, *Victorian Literature and Culture* (London: Continuum, 2006), 53.
32. Dallas Liddle, 'Anatomy of a "Nine Days' Wonder": Sensational Journalism in the Decade of the Sensation Novel', in Andrew Maunder and Grace Moore, eds, *Victorian Crime, Madness and Sensation* (Aldershot, Hants: Ashgate, 2004), 97.
33. Cannon Schmitt, 'Alien Nation: Gender, Genre and English Nationality in Wilkie Collins's *The Woman in White*', *Genre* 26 (1993), 300.

6 Collins and Women

1. Cited in Jan Marsh, 'Votes for Women and Chastity for Men: Gender, Health, Medicine and Sexuality' in *The Victorian Vision*, ed. John MacKenzie (London: V & A Publications, 2001), 98.
2. Unsigned, 'Recent Classical Romances', *Edinburgh Review* 92 (October 1850), 48.

3. [Wilkie Collins], 'Bold Words by a Bachelor', *HW* 14 (13 December 1856), 505–7.
4. [Wilkie Collins], 'A Shy Scheme', *HW* 17 (20 March 1858), 315.
5. Jane Gallop, *The Daughter's Seduction* (New York: Cornell UP, 1982), 77–8.
6. See Catherine Peters, 'Frances Dickinson: Friend of Wilkie Collins', *WCSJ* NS1 (November 1998), 20–8.
7. Mary Poovey, *Uneven Developments: The Ideological Work of Gender in Mid-Victorian England* (Chicago: University of Chicago Press, 1989); Nancy Armstrong, *Desire and Domestic Fiction* (Oxford: Oxford UP, 1990); Lyn Pykett, *The Improper Feminine: The Women's Sensation Novel and the New Woman Writing* (London: Routledge, 1992).
8. Lynda Nead, *Myths of Sexuality: Representations of Women in Victorian Britain* (Oxford; Blackwell, 1990), 91.
9. Lyn Pykett, *The Sensation Novel* (Plymouth: Northcote, 1994), 45.
10. Eliza Lynn Linton, 'The Epicene Sex', *Saturday Review* (24 August 1872), 243.
11. Cited in Monica Correa Fryckstedt, *On the Brink: Novels of 1866* (Uppsala: Acta University, 1986), 16.
12. Deborah Wynne, *The Sensation Novel and the Victorian Family Magazine* (London: Palgrave Macmillan, 2001), 24.
13. Christopher GoGwilt, *The Fiction of Geopolitics* (Stanford: Stanford UP, 2000), 64.
14. Barbara Gates, *Victorian Suicides: Mad Crimes and Sad Histories* (Princeton, NJ: Princeton UP, 1988), 32.
15. Jeffrey Weeks, *Sex Politics and Society: The Regulation of Sexuality Since 1800* (London: Longman, 1981), 25.
16. While this was more than the £3500 which Trollope obtained from Smith for *The Small House at Allington* (1862–4), it was far less than £10,000 which G.H. Lewes had negotiated for George Eliot's *Romola* (1862–3).
17. Pykett, *The Sensation Novel*, 27.
18. Lynda Hart, *Fatal Women: Lesbian Sexuality and the Mark of Aggression* (Princeton, NJ: Princeton UP, 1992), 29.
19. See Jenifer Glyn, *Prince of Publishers: A Biography of George Smith* (London: Allison & Busby, 1986), 143.
20. See Unsigned review, 'Armadale', *Reader* (2 June 1866), 538.
21. Unsigned review, 'Armadale', *Evening Standard* (15 June 1866), 4.
22. Cited in Amy Cruse, *The Victorians and their Books* (London: George Allen & Unwin, 1935), 323.
23. Unsigned review, 'Recent Novels: Their Moral and Religious Teaching', *London Quarterly Review* 27 (1866), 100.
24. See Jennifer Phegley, *Educating the Proper Woman Reader: Victorian Family Literary Magazines and the Cultural Health of the Nation* (Columbus, OH: Ohio State UP, 2004).
25. Kate Flint, *The Woman Reader 1837–1914* (Oxford: Clarendon Press, 1994), 277.
26. Alison Light, '"Young Bess": Historical Novels and Growing Up', *Feminist Review* 33 (1988), 66.
27. Ronald R. Thomas, 'The Moonstone, Detective fiction and Forensic Science', in Taylor, 66.
28. Steve Farmer, 'Introduction' to Wilkie Collins, *M*, 34.

29. Eric Sundquist, *Home As Found: Authority and Genealogy in Nineteenth Century American Literature* (Baltimore, MD: John Hopkins University Press, 1979), 91.
30. Lillian Nayder, 'Collins and Empire', in Taylor, 140.
31. Elizabeth Rose Gruner, 'Family Secrets: *The Moonstone*', in Lyn Pykett, ed., *Wilkie Collins* (London: Macmillan, 1998), 222.
32. Albert Hutter, 'Dreams, Transformations, and Literature: The Implications of Detective Fiction', *Victorian Studies* 19 (1975), 200.
33. Lonoff, *Wilkie Collins and his Victorian Readers*, 210.
34. Martin Priestman, *Crime Fiction* (Plymouth: Northcote House, 1998), 13.
35. Laura Claridge and Elisabeth Langland, eds, 'Introduction', *Out of Bounds: Male Writers and Gender* (Amherst, MA: Massachusetts UP, 1990), x.
36. Toril Moi, *Sexual Textual Politics: Feminist Literary Theory* (London: Methuen, 1985), 65, 58.
37. Michael Ryan, *Literary Theory* (Oxford: Blackwell, 1999), 105.
38. Cited in Alan Sinfield, *Literature, Politics and Culture in Post-war Britain* (Oxford: Blackwell, 1989), 25.

7   Collins and the Theatre

1. See 'Dramatic Grub Street', *HW* 17 (6 March 1858), 265–70; 'A Breach of British Privilege', *HW* 19 (19 March 1859), 361–4; and 'A Dramatic Author', *HW* 19 (28 May 1859), 609–10.
2. Wybert Reeve, 'Recollections of Wilkie Collins', *Chambers Journal* 6th Ser. 9 (June 1906), 459.
3. Richard W. Schoch, *Shakespeare's Victorian Stage* (Cambridge: Cambridge UP, 1998), 127.
4. Collins, 'A Breach of British Privilege', 361–4.
5. *Illustrated London* News (12 January 1849); cited in Raymond Mander and Joe Mitchenson, *The Lost Theatres of London* (London: Rupert Hart-Davis, 1968), 273.
6. *Illustrated London News* (29 December 1849); cited in Mander and Mitchenson, *The Lost Theatres of London*, 275.
7. Collins, 'Dramatic Grub Street', 265–70.
8. Ibid., 270.
9. Ibid., 269.
10. Henry Arthur Jones, 'The Theatre and the Mob', *The Renaissance of the English Drama* (London: Macmillan, 1895), 9.
11. Collins, 'Dramatic Grub Street', 269.
12. Michael Booth, *English Melodrama* (London: Herbert Jenkins, 1965).
13. David Mayer, 'Encountering Melodrama', in Kerry Powell, ed., *Cambridge Companion to Victorian and Edwardian Theatre* (Cambridge: Cambridge UP, 2004), 148.
14. Ibid., 146–7.
15. Queen Victoria, *Journal* (30 April 1852); cited in Schoch, *Shakespeare's Victorian Stage*, 134.
16. ['V.'], 'Anglicized French Melodramas', *Theatrical Journal* (19 May 1852), 153; cited in Schoch, 134.
17. Charles Kean to Sir William Stowe Harris, 17 June 1856; cited in Schoch, 136.

18. Kate Field, *Charles Albert Fechter* (New York: American Actor Series, 1882), 138.
19. Unsigned review, 'Olympic', *Daily Telegraph* (11 October 1871); reprinted in *The Woman in White: Opinions of the Press* (London: Privately Printed, 1877), 2.
20. Edward Dutton Cook, *Nights at the Play* (2 vols; London: Chatto & Windus, 1883) II, 117.
21. Henry Morley, *Diary of a London Playgoer* (Leicester: Leicester UP, 1974), 103.
22. Ibid., 162–3.
23. Edmund Yates, 'Moi-Même: In Memoriam W.W.C.', *The World* (25 September 1889), 13; reprinted in B&G, 70–1.
24. Unsigned review, 'Olympic Theatre', *The Times* (12 October 1858), 10.
25. Morley, *Diary of a London Playgoer*, 190–1.
26. *The Times* (23 October 1874), 7.
27. R.L. Brannan, *Under the Management of Mr Charles Dickens* (Ithaca, NY: Cornell UP, 1966), 87.
28. Charles Dickens to Mrs Richard Watson, 7 December 1857, Pilgrim VIII, 487–9; cited in Brannan 72.
29. Unsigned review, 'The Frozen Deep', *The Times* (13 July 1857), 12.
30. George Rowell, *Queen Victoria Goes to the Theatre* (London: Paul Elek, 1978), 73.
31. Unsigned review, 'The Frozen Deep', *London Review* (3 November 1866), 493.
32. See Lillian Nayder, *Unequal Partners: Charles Dickens, Wilkie Collins, and Victorian Authorship* (Ithaca, NY: Cornell UP, 2002), 60–99.
33. Cook, *Nights at the Play* I, 31.
34. Thomas Edgar Pemberton, *Charles Dickens and the Stage* (London: Redway, 1888), 92.
35. Unsigned review, 'No Thoroughfare', *Weekly Theatrical Reporter* (4 January 1868), 1.
36. Field, *Charles Albert Fechter*, 167.
37. Cook, *Nights at the Play* II, 107.
38. Unsigned review, 'Black and White', *Theatrical and Musical Review* (1 April 1869), 8.
39. Audrey Fisch, 'Collins, Race and Slavery', in Maria K. Bachman and Don Richard Cox, eds, *Reality's Dark Light: The Sensational Wilkie Collins* (Knoxville, TN: University of Tennessee Press, 2003), 315, 319.
40. Ibid., 316, 319.
41. Katharine Newey and Veronica Kelly, eds, *East Lynne: Dramatised by T.A. Palmer* (Queensland: Australasian Drama Studies Association, 1994), 46.
42. Edward Dutton Cook, *Nights at the Play* II, 106.
43. Unsigned review, 'Black and White', *Athenaeum* (3 April 1869), 477.
44. Kate Field, *Charles Albert Fechter*, 167.
45. Unsigned review, 'Surrey Theatre', *The Times* (8 November 1860), 6.
46. Willis Redshanks, 'British Drama', *Theatrical Journal* (12 August 1857), 252.
47. E. Willis Fletcher, 'Characters from the Drama of Life: No. IV. The Dramatic Adaptor', *Theatrical Journal* (26 October 1859), Part Two, 341.
48. From the judgement in the case of Reade v. Conquest of 1862; see John Russell Stephens, *The Profession of the Playwright: British Theatre 1800–1900* (Cambridge: Cambridge UP, 1992), 97–105.
49. Kerry Powell, *Women and Victorian Theatre* (Cambridge: Cambridge UP, 1997), 101.

50. See A.D. Hutter, 'Fosco Lives!', in Bachman and Cox, eds, *Reality's Dark Light*, 195–238.
51. Unsigned review, 'Olympic', *Era* (14 October 1871); reprinted in *The Woman in White: Opinions of the Press*, 6.
52. Unsigned review, 'The Globe Theatre', *The Times* (17 April 1876), 7.
53. Cook, *Nights at the Play* I, 250.
54. Unsigned review, 'The New Magdalen', *Athenaeum* (24 May 1873), 674.
55. Unsigned review, 'Rank and Riches', *Dramatic Notes* (London: Carson & Comerford, 1884), 28.
56. Yates, 'Moi-Même', 13.
57. In 'Collins and the Theatre', Jim Davis suggests that Collins was one of a number of people 'who wished to reform or improve the calibre of current provision ... to offer the theatre going public something more substantial than the popular burlesques and melodramas they appeared to favour' (Taylor, 171).
58. See 'The Well Made Play', in Dennis Kennedy, ed., *Oxford Encyclopaedia of Theatre and Performance* (Oxford: Oxford UP, 2003), 1442–3.

8   Collins as Missionary

1. Scottish marriages could at that time be constituted irregularly without a clergyman or registrar according to three different modes: by bare exchange of consent, by promise and subsequent intercourse, and by cohabitation and acquisition of the reputation of being married. See M.C. Meston, W.H.D. Sellar, and Lord Cooper, *The Scottish Legal Tradition* (Edinburgh: Saltire Society/Stair Society, 1991), 18–22.
2. On the connection between *Man and Wife* and Collins's earlier sketch for a play on irregular marriages, see Wilkie Collins, *The Widows*, ed. Andrew Gasson and Graham Law (London: Wilkie Collins Society, 2005), 1–3.
3. See Norman Page's Introduction to *M&W*, xv.
4. See James Payn and Wilkie Collins, *A National Wrong*, ed. Andrew Gasson, Graham Law, and Paul Lewis (London: Wilkie Collins Society, 2004), and the discussion of it in Chapter 9.
5. [Unsigned review], 'Literature and Home', *Putnam's Monthly Magazine* 6 (September 1870), 339.
6. See Graham Law, 'Reynolds's "Memoirs" series and "the literature of the kitchen"', in Louis James and Anne Humpherys, eds, *G.W.M. Reynolds and Nineteenth-Century British Society* (Aldershot, Hants: Ashgate, 2008).
7. [Unsigned article], 'Looks at Books: The Magazines', *Penny Illustrated Magazine* (17 May 1873), 14.
8. Unsigned review, 'Mr Wilkie Collins's New Novel', *Pall Mall Budget* (December 1883), 332–3.
9. Henry Norman, 'Theories and Practice of Modern Fiction', *Fortnightly Review* 34 (December 1883), 880.
10. Barbara Creed, 'Kristeva, Femininity, Abjection', in Ken Gelder, ed., *The Horror Reader* (London: Routledge, 2000), 64.
11. Unsigned review, 'The Evil Genius', *Saturday Review* (9 October 1886), 219.
12. For detailed discussion of the changes in English family law in the second half of the nineteenth century, see Allen Horstman, *Victorian Divorce*

(New York: St Martin's Press, 1985), and M.L. Shanley, *Feminism, Marriage, and the Law in Victorian England* (Princeton, NJ: Princeton UP, 1989).

13. See Lawrence Stone, *Road to Divorce: England 1530–1987* (Oxford: Oxford UP, 1990), 435–8.

14. Collins had been attacked for ignorance of the law on the guardianship of infants in an unsigned review of *Heart and Science* in the *Athenaeum* (28 April 1883), 538–9 (reprinted in Page, 214–5).

15. This crucial passage was a later addition to the manuscript, and was also revised significantly at the proof stage (see Peters, 417–8).

9 Collins Overseas

1. On the series of Bengali translations beginning with *The Woman in White*, see Collins's letter to A.P. Watt of 25 November 1883, BGLL III, 438; *The Moonstone* seems to have been the first Collins novels to be serialized in free translation in a Japanese popular newspaper, in the *Yubin Hochi* from late June 1889 – see Takagi Takeo, ed., *Shimbun shôsetsushi nenpyo* [History of Newspaper Novels: Annual Tables] (Tokyo: Kokusho Kankôkai, 1987), 149. It is, of course, highly unlikely that the author was ever aware of the appearance of the latter.

2. See Franco Moretti, *Atlas of the European Novel, 1800–1900* (London: Verso, 1998), ch. 3.

3. On a visit to the opera in Venice, for example, Collins is pictured 'with incipient moustache, spectacles, slender legs, and extremely dirty dress gloves' (to Catherine Dickens, 27 November 1853, Pilgrim VII, 215.)

4. The letter to Millais is lost but is attested in that to Harriet Collins of 25 November 1853, B&C I, 117–19.

5. See Collins's letter to George Bentley, 14 January 1854, BGLL I, 95–6. A few passages were later recycled for journalistic purposes in 'My Black Mirror' (*HW* 14, 6 September 1856, 169–75), where Collins offers an unflattering sketch of a visit to Austrian Italy.

6. The author's last word to his evangelical mother is 'my love to Charley (for whom I have bought a Roman Crucifix!!!!!!)' (25 November 53, B&C I, 117–9).

7. For an early example, see Collins's comments on the production of *The Frozen Deep* at the Olympic in late 1866: 'There isn't an atom of slang or vulgarity in the whole piece from beginning to end – no female legs are shown in it – Richard Wardour doesn't get up after dying and sing a comic song ... ' (to Nina Lehmann, 9 December 1866, BGLL II, 52–4).

8. See the letters to Frank Archer of 22 March 1877, to Georgina Hogarth of 12 July 1877, and to Augustin Daly of 25 September 1877, BGLL III, 157, 163, and 172.

9. See to Regnier, 18 November and 22 December 1870, BGLL II, 221–2 and 223–5, where it is suggested that not only the author but 'the whole English nation' support the French cause. We should note, however, that, in writing to a German friend a few months earlier Collins had stated: 'I am, like the rest of my countrymen, heartily on the German side in the war. ...' (to Emil Lehmann, 7 August 187, B&C II, 344). The opening scenes of *The New Magdalen* also bear witness to Collins's preoccupation with the outcome of the Franco-Prussian War.

10. For a general account of British attitudes to the American conflict, see E.D. Adams, *Great Britain and the American Civil War* (2 vols; London: Longmans, 1925).
11. See [Robert Cecil], 'Democracy on its Trial', *Quarterly Review* 110:1 (July 1861), 282.
12. The British government first issued a Proclamation of Neutrality on 13 May 1861 – see Adams, *Great Britain and the American Civil War*, 94–6.
13. See the report of the speech in *The Times* ('Mr Gladstone in the North', 9 October 1862, 7–8) and the accompanying editorial comment (8).
14. See, for example, Lillian Nayder, *Unequal Partners: Charles Dickens, Wilkie Collins, and Victorian Authorship* (Ithaca, NY: Cornell UP, 2002), 121–4.
15. See Arthur A. Adrian, 'Dickens on American Slavery', *PMLA* 67:4 (June 1952), 315–29.
16. See the companion articles, probably penned by Henry Morley, entitled 'American Disunion' and 'The Morrill Tariff', *AYR* 6 (21–8 December 1861), 295–300 and 328–31. The latter concludes: 'Union means so many millions a year lost to the South; secession means the loss of the same millions to the North. The love of money is the root of this ... the quarrel between North and South is, as it stands, solely a fiscal quarrel' (330).
17. The article was unsigned and written in collaboration with James Payn – see 'A National Wrong', *Chambers's Journal* 17 (12 February 1870), 107–10; reprinted in James Payn and Wilkie Collins, *A National Wrong*, ed. Andrew Gasson, Graham Law, and Paul Lewis, 13–18.
18. Wilkie Collins, 'Considerations on the Copyright Question', *International Review* 8 (June 1880), 609–18; reprinted as a pamphlet, London: Trübner, 1880, and London: Wilkie Collins Society, 1997.
19. For a fuller treatment of these issues, see Graham Law, 'Collins on International Copyright: From "A National Wrong" (1870) to "Considerations" (1880)', in *Wilkie Collins: Interdisciplinary Essays*, ed. Andrew Mangham (Newcastle: Cambridge Scholars Publishing, 2007), 178–95.
20. At this period, many mutual agreements were already in force between European states, including those between Britain and France (from 1852) and France and Holland (1855), though no such treaty existed between Britain and Holland. See W.A. Copinger, *The Law of Copyright in Works of Literature and Art*, ed. J.M. Easton, 4th edn (London: Stevens and Haynes, 1904).
21. Payn and Collins, 'A National Wrong', 107.
22. See James J. Barnes, *Authors, Publishers and Politicians: The Quest for an Anglo-American Copyright Agreement, 1815–54* (London: Routledge & Kegan Paul, 1974), 80.
23. See R.R. Bowker, *Copyright: Its History and Its Law* (Boston: Houghton Mifflin, 1912), 348–53.
24. In late 1872, on receiving a copy of an unauthorized American edition of *Poor Miss Finch* forwarded by his New York publishers, he still felt free to respond: 'How much longer will the great American nation lag behind Europe in the march of literary civilisation? *Turkey* concedes international copyright – and The United States refuses it! What an anomaly!!!' (B&C II, 358).
25. Collins, 'Considerations', 612.
26. Ibid., 609.

27. William Appleton, Letter on 'Piracy', *The Times*, (20 October 1871), 10.
28. See Bowker, *Copyright*, 350–1.
29. Collins, 'Considerations', 616.
30. Matthew Arnold, 'Copyright', *Fortnightly Review* 27 (March 1880), 334.
31. Ibid.
32. Lillian Nayder has analysed the author's treatment of colonial themes in depth in *Wilkie Collins*, ch. 5, and *Unequal Partners*, *passim*. An overview of Nayder's position can also be found in her 'Collins and Empire', in Taylor, 139–52.

10 Collins and the Later Victorian Literary Marketplace

1. Generally on the rise of fiction syndication in Britain, see Graham Law, *Serializing Fiction in the Victorian Press* (New York: Palgrave Macmillan, 2000).
2. J.E.P. Muddock, *Pages from an Adventurous Life* (London: T. Werner Laurie, 1907), 107–10.
3. See Graham Law, '"Engaged to Messrs. Tillotson and Son": Letters from John Maxwell, 1882–8' (Waseda University Law Society), *Humanitas* 37 (1999), 1–42.
4. 'Abstract of Agreements' (ZBEN/4/4), *Bolton Evening News* Archive, Bolton Central Library, Greater Manchester.
5. See Adrian Frazier, *George Moore: A Biography, 1852–1933* (New Haven, CT: Yale UP, 2000), ch. 2.
6. Unsigned review of George Moore, *A Modern Lover*, *Spectator* (18 August 1883), 1069.
7. Joseph Hone, *The Life of George Moore* (London: Victor Gollancz, 1936), 98.
8. George Moore, 'A New Censorship of Literature', *Pall Mall Gazette* (10 December 1884), 1–2.
9. George Moore, *Literature at Nurse, or Circulating Morals* (London: Vizetelly, 1885), 18.
10. Ibid., 5.
11. There were more than a dozen Zola titles in print by 1888, when, notoriously, Vizetelly was prosecuted and eventually imprisoned for publishing 'obscene libels'.
12. Collins was also antipathetic to parallel developments in American realism; see his late letter to A.P. Watt: 'My idea is that these American magazines all stand committed to the new American school of fiction – and that my way of writing represents the abomination of desolation in their eyes' (BGLL IV, 256).
13. See Graham Law, ed., Introduction, *The Evil Genius* by Wilkie Collins (Peterborough, ON: Broadview Press, 1994).
14. Lawrence Stone, *Road to Divorce: England 1530–1987* (Oxford: Oxford UP, 1990), 387 and Table 13.1.
15. Cited and translated in Hone, *The Life of George Moore*, 101.
16. George Moore, *A Mummer's Wife* (London: Vizetelly, 1884), ch. 8.
17. George Moore, *Confessions of a Young Man* (London: Swan Sonnenschein, 1888), ch. 1.
18. See J.W. Arrowsmith, Preface to *Called Back* by 'Hugh Conway' [F.J. Fargus] (Bristol: Arrowsmith, 1898), iii–iv.

19. 'Wilkie Collins never penned a more enthralling story' – see unsigned review of Wilkie Collins, *The Guilty River*, *Truth* (3 January 1884), 4.
20. See Arrowsmith, 'Preface to *Called Back*', iii.

11 Last Things

1. Nathaniel Beard, 'Some Recollections of Yesterday', *Temple Bar* 102 (1894), 315–39; reprinted in B&G, 141.
2. See Walter Besant's Preface to *Blind Love* (London: Chatto & Windus, 1890).
3. Transcribed by Paul Lewis and reprinted at: http://www.web40571.clarahost.co.uk/wilkie/will/willt.htm. Last visited: 1 September 2007.
4. See the report of the Chancery Division of the High Court of Justice, *The Times* (7 December 1889), 11.
5. See the letters by Harry Quilter, 'A Memorial to Wilkie Collins', *The Times* (3 October 1889), 8, and 'The Wilkie Collins Memorial', *The Times* (26 March 1890), 5; also the leader in the *Daily Telegraph* (5 October 1889), 9.
6. This was widely reprinted in the British weekly press on 28 September 1889, including in the *Liverpool Weekly Post*, *Newcastle Weekly Chronicle*, and *Weekly Scotsman*, all of which also carried *Blind Love* as a serial, having purchased secondary rights from the *Illustrated London News*.
7. Hall Caine, 'Wilkie Collins: Personal Recollections', *Globe* (4 October 1889), 4.
8. [Edmund Yates], 'One Who Knew Him', *World* (2 October 1889).
9. Olive Logan, 'Wilkie Collins's Charms' (New York) *World*, 29 September 1889, 16. Collins had met her with her husband William W. Sikes in 1879 (BGLL III, 238–9).
10. 'Wilkie Collins's Last Days' (New York) *World*, 29 September 1889, 16; reprinted in Graham Law, 'Different Worlds', *Wilkie Collins Society Newsletter* (Spring 1999), Supplement, 1–4.
11. Generally on these developments, see J.H. Wiener, ed., *Papers for the Millions: The New Journalism in Britain* (Westport, CN: Greenwood Press, 1988.
12. Matthew Arnold, 'Up to Easter', *Nineteenth Century* 21 (May 1887), 629–43.
13. Relevant examples include Edmund Yates, 'Men of Mark: W. Wilkie Collins', *Train* 3 (June 1857), 352–7; Unsigned, 'Celebrities at Home: Mr Wilkie Collins in Gloucester Place', *World* (26 December 1877); Unsigned, 'A Novelist on Novel Writing: An Interview with Mr Wilkie Collins', *Cassell's Saturday Journal* (5 March 1887), 355–6; and Harry Quilter, 'A Living Story-Teller: Mr Wilkie Collins', *Contemporary Review* 53 (April 1888), 572–93.
14. See Wilkie Collins, 'How I write my Books', *Globe* (26 November 1887), 511–14, and 'Reminiscences of a Story-Teller', *Universal Review* 1:2 (June 1888), 182–9.

Index

CPSIA information can be obtained
at www.ICGtesting.com
Printed in the USA
LVHW030444261119
638462LV00011B/919/P

9 781403 948960